RU EMERSON

NIGHT-THREADS

THE SCIENCE
OF POWER

DISCARDED

ACE BOOKS, NEW YORK

This book is an Ace original edition,
and has never been previously published.

THE SCIENCE OF POWER

An Ace Book / published by arrangement with
the author

PRINTING HISTORY
Ace edition / December 1995

ISBN: 0-441-00286-2

ACE®
Ace Books are published by The Berkley Publishing Group,
200 Madison Avenue, New York, NY 10016.
ACE and the "A" design are trademarks
belonging to Charter Communications, Inc.

PRINTED IN THE UNITED STATES OF AMERICA

10 9 8 7 6 5 4 3 2 1

For Doug
and in memory of
Bertie Wooster
(1982–1994)

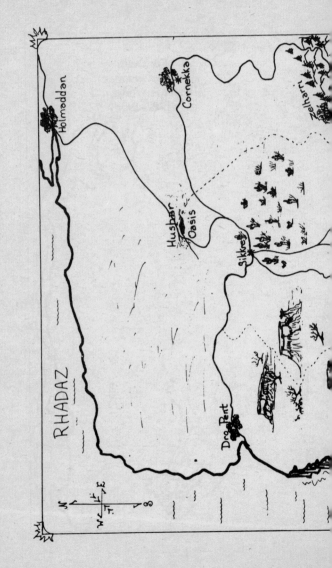

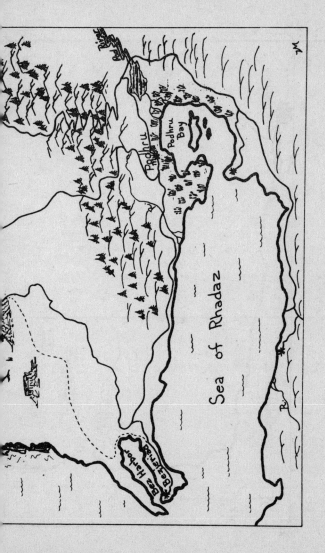

Prologue

BLACK storm clouds filled the sky over Bezjeriad, billowing across the low hills west of the harbor and turning the inland sea and inlet steel gray; wind blew steadily across the water, raising whitecaps.

No pleasant day to begin a sail from the most important Rhadazi port city, or try to negotiate the narrows to reach the harbor, and there were indeed no ships in sight. Lehzin, Duke of Bezjeriad, stared out the window of his highest tower, eyes moving restlessly from open water to the harbor, back again. Now and again he ran a narrow, long-fingered hand through thick, dark red hair, or picked nervously at a beard beginning to show silver. Rhadazi could sail in such weather, if needs must—so could many of the foreigners who had brought trade and prosperity to his city's docks over the past several years. Most of his own people liked the challenge: negotiate the bay and that narrow entry to the inland sea, fight the odd currents just outside the inlet and then the isthmus formed by Bezjeriad on the north and the French Gallic states on the south. . . . Lehzin considered the last time *he* had managed such a maneuver, in high seas and winter winds. Years ago, of course—Lariman, his father, had still been Duke, and properly furious with him for it. *I did no more than he'd have done, at that age, unwed and certain nothing could ever harm me.*

He felt along the hard wooden window seat for the little bottle the Healer had left him, drew the cork, and drank down a swallow. It tasted horrid, as always, and for a very brief, uncomfortable moment he wondered if it would stay where it belonged. "Bah," he mumbled aloud. "Seven days and my stomach still thinks it's aboard a very small boat in high seas." He set the bottle down, eyed it distastefully, and shoved it as far from him as possible.

Drugged wine. *I drank Zero to toast the Emperor? Someone is mad.* He and Eugenia both—but she'd taken only a tiny sip, because of Shesseran's birthday; Eugenia hadn't needed the Healer's wretched liquid since the first day. Every Duke in the kingdom had received drugged wine, if Afronsan had it right. Lehzin glanced at the handful of thin paper—the most recent telegrams from the Emperor's brother—and shook his head. Had someone seriously thought he might murder the Emperor, his Heir and all those who maintained the duchies, simply by sending each a special bottle of dosed liquor? "And if it went astray? Or some chose not to drink?" The Thukar and Thukara of Sikkre hadn't, because of prior bad experience; the Emperor didn't touch anything stronger than fruit juices these days—nor did young Aletto and his Duchess, up in Zelharri. Everyone knew that—locals and the foreigners who traded in Rhadaz alike.

It couldn't have been meant as a coup, then—but what? All the unknown enemy had really done was infuriate their aged and aesthetical Emperor, Lehzin decided gloomily. And push the angry old man into closing all Rhadazi ports and borders.

And so Bezanti sat in the harbor out there, Rhadazi ships not allowed to leave Rhadazi waters. The foreign ships had been gone for several days now.

The Emperor himself is mad, closing the land's borders, he thought flatly. *I can vouch for five points along my own coast where the yellow rope rings of Zero are brought in.*

Or where they were. Now, since Shesseran XIV had tossed out all foreigners and closed the borders to any imports, the foreigners who brought important, useful (and financially beneficial) goods into Bazjeriad Harbor were barred—but those who brought Zero might as well have been handed a free pass to land anywhere along the vast and largely un-populated seacoast.

He closed his eyes, turned away from the sight of so much commerce gone wrong, so much profit lost. It could make him ill. Or angry indeed. And anger directed against Shesseran was of no use at all; a man might as well shout at the wind to shift it into his sails instead of against them. The old man had always been stubborn and set in his ways, and he'd only grown worse in his age. Most of the credit for opening Rhadazi ports and the new trade would have to go to Shesseran's younger brother and heir, Afronsan.

It was a wonder Shesseran had left Afronsan as Heir, even more a wonder he hadn't insisted upon immediate re-moval of such things as the foreign telegraph.

Lehzin glanced at the uppermost paper, now three days old:

> MY PERSONAL THANKS FOR THE AID YOU GAVE THE YOUNG MERCHANT CRAY AND HIS PARTY IN ESCAPING RHADAZ. IT WILL NOT GO UNNOTED WHEN I AM ABLE TO REWARD. KEEP CLOSE WATCH ON THE ISTHMUS AND YOUR BORDERS FOR FOREIGN SHIPS, OR FOR THOSE OF MERCHANT CASIMAFFI, AFRONSAN.

Casimaffi. I trusted that man, even when proof seemed against him. Even after all the rumor that he'd been part of the plot with young Dahven's half brothers. Casimaffi had been so convincingly aghast, so appalled by the whole situ-ation. And, of course, his family company, his ships—they'd been useful to Bez, bringing in foreign goods, creating trade.

The same could be said for the merchant Cray, of course—and he was doing his best to track the foreign source of Zero. "Luck to him," Lehzin mumbled, and sorted through his pile of telegrams. They did little to improve his mood: More messages from Afronsan; word from the north that Jubelo was still very ill and Aletto hadn't yet wakened; nothing new from Sikkre, save that the men who'd attacked the Thukar's palace apparently didn't know who'd hired them. "Wondrous surprise." Another message, received early this morning, from Vuhlem up in Holmaddan, sent south to Cornekka via messenger and wired from Jubelo's palace, expressing fury for the insult of the liquor and worry for the Emperor's health.

"Of course Vuhlem wouldn't have taken brandy, even in toast," Lehzin told himself sourly. "At least, not openly." The old pig was the Emperor's contemporary and friend; they'd schooled together and Vuhlem supposedly shared his friend's aesthetical tendencies. Lehzin, who'd met the northern Duke only a few times when he was still Latimer's heir, thought otherwise—that high coloring, those red-rimmed eyes. That temper. His own father had carried the same sign, though Latimer drank heavily—and openly. Lehzin considered this briefly, shrugged it aside. Holmaddan's problems weren't anything to do with him, and besides, Vuhlem must be nearly seventy. Eventually, one of his furies or old age would do him in and he had only daughters to succeed him.

And at the moment, he must be angry indeed: Lehzin grinned. By now every Duke in Rhadaz knew about it: Vuhlem's expelling the caravans; the Red Hawk grandmothers' and Gray Fishers' imperious appeal to the Emperor, and Shesseran's angry defense of the caravans. *Had to take them back, did he? What a pity.*

One last, long sheet, this the message his man had brought him within the hour—from Afronsan, of course, and more the length he'd already become used to, in just the short while the lines had been in place. *What we did before this swift, simple communication—I scarcely recall.* He scanned down the page—it was mostly update. On Jubelo, who was eating once more, Aletto still down but his outlander Duchess and his guard captain efficiently managing for him. Personal thanks from Thukara Jennifer and Duchess Robyn for his aid to young Cray and his lady. And at the bottom—Lehzin stared at the paper, groped for the window seat and dropped onto it.

REPORT FROM DRO PENT SAYS VUHLEM HAS TAKEN PALACE, VERY LARGE ARMED FORCE HOLDING IT AND WU-DRON'S LADY PRISONER AGAINST WUDRON'S COOPERA-TION. THUKAR READYING A COMPANY IF IT BECOMES NECESSARY TO TAKE EAST GATES OF DRO PENT BY FORCE; ASK THAT YOU READY SHIPS AND MEN TO SAIL NORTH AND ATTACK FROM WEST. BE AWARE VUHLEM MAY HAVE SHIPS—WORD FROM SIN-DUCHESS LIALLA THAT VUHLEM COOPERATING WITH LASANACHI. KEEP LOW PROFILE, BUT BE READY AS QUICKLY AS POSSIBLE. LETTERS TO FOLLOW, AFRONSAN.

Lehzin dropped the page, buried his face in his hands, and groaned. "The whole world's gone mad," he mumbled. All the rest—and now this. Dukes attacking one another? Taking Duchies by force? What did Vuhlem want, all of Rhadaz? And if first Dro Pent—why, what would be next on his menu but Bezjeriad?

1

CHRIS came awake with a start as a hard hand gripped his elbow—Eddie's, he recalled after one heart-stopping moment. "Jeez, guy, don't *do* that!" He sank back into the plush cushions with a groan and clutched his temples. "God, my head."

"You have been stuck in that seat for most of the day," Edrith replied mildly. "And slept through three stops, including Liberté."

"Liberté—naw, I remember *that* one." Chris sat up cautiously, rubbed the back of his neck, and groaned again. Edrith's face loomed above him, all shifting shadows and odd lines from the low-burning gas lamp on the far wall and the rolling, jerking motion of train over rough track. "Oh, man? I have the headache from hell. Liberté—yeah. Some guy outside the window was bellowing that, and it sounded like they were beating the whole train with aluminum baseball bats."

"Alumi—never mind." Edrith dismissed the odd bit of unfamiliar English with no effort at all. "They divide the train there, remember?"

"*I* know that. Most on down to the big lake, rest out to the coast, and obviously on rock track that was new during the Stone Age." Chris edged up a little straighter, swore briefly as the car lurched, and edged the red velvet drape aside so he could look out. "It's *dark* out there."

6

"This surprises you? I said you slept all day, didn't I? This is the south, remember, there is no dusk to speak of. Besides, mix thick cloud cover, no moon, and you get what?"

"I just had to hook up with a comedian, didn't I? Where's my—ah. Bag." He pulled the thick case from under his feet and rummaged through the side pocket until he found a plain, flat tin box. "Remind me to buy Mom something nice this time out, I'd never have thought of getting any of these willow-bark thingies made up. There any water left?"

"Since no one drinks it but you, there should be." Edrith shoved to his feet and turned the lamp up a little, then crossed to the dry sink next to the curtain-draped door. He came back with a heavy clay jug, a two-handled cup. Chris fumbled one of the tiny teabag-like squares from the box and dropped it into the cup, poured a swallow's worth of water and swirled the contents, then drew a deep breath and drank it down. His nose wrinkled; he poured more water and drank, fast.

"Those have such a gross taste, I can't even believe it." He fished in the cup and drew out the now-empty gauze square. "Remind me, we get into New London this trip we just *gotta* track down a pharmacist who can do pills out of this stuff."

"Get the equipment and find a willing Rhadazi to work it," Edrith replied.

"Sure. Once Shesseran dies or comes to his senses. *Gaaa*. Gross." Chris wrinkled his nose, drank more water.

"If they taste that terrible, why you take them at all—"

"Yah. 'Cause it's basically the same stuff Jen used to suck down, pills from that big bottle, remember? Killed headaches? I take it 'cause I get 'em and the stuff works, that's why. *You* try Lialla's trick with Thread when your head aches, I can't swing it." Edrith grinned, shook his head; Chris rolled his eyes, then closed them. Eddie never

got headaches, probably wouldn't know what one was if it
landed on him with all four feet. "Gimme a few minutes,
okay?" He leaned back gingerly. The touch of prickly red
plush against his scalp set the whole thing pounding wildly
again. "God." He sensed rather than heard Edrith moving
around behind him; long, capable fingers worked the muscles on either side of his neck. A long, companionable silence, which Chris finally broke. "Hey. Thanks."

"Of course. Can you talk now?"

"I can listen, at least. What you got, you had to wake me
up? You get that wire sent to Fahlia?"

"Last stop," Edrith said. "Whether the Duke will be able
to send it on to the Heir, though, with the Emperor in such
a temper—"

Chris laughed, interrupting him midword. "Hey, don't
sweat that end of things, okay? We have enough problems,
and the last person I'm gonna worry about is Afronsan.
Wire was still in when we left, and I'll betcha it still is. Besides, anyone's gonna land on his feet once this mess is
cleared up—well, anyway, that can't be why you woke me
up?"

"Nev-ver," Edrith retorted. "But I thought you ought to
know the attendant will be here shortly to ready beds and
neaten the room. Also, since Liberté there are now only the
two private cars, ours and another, which is empty, one
standard-class sitting car with but seven passengers, the
baggage car, the attendants' car, and the dining."

"Okay—you can count. So?"

"So I have walked end to end several times and also
spoke with the attendant since our last stop. There is one
man who plays cards with him, which I thought suspicious,
but I have seen him since and I don't know him; there is no
one on all the train I recognize, no one who might be
Dupret's—at least, no one interested in me at all when I go
about, or walk the platforms whenever we stop." Faint
noises and women's voices from behind the screen, where

Ariadne and her maid Dija had a semi-private area; Edrith and Chris both glanced that way and Edrith lowered his voice. "I think the lady would be glad if you offered her perhaps a walk and a proper meal; she has not been outside this box on wheels in—how many days now?"

"Same as me, five of them," Chris mumbled. He was quiet for a moment, eyes focused on his fingers. He sighed then. "Yeah, you're right. I'm going nutty in here, she's probably half-goofy with nothing to do but read and sleep. And if someone sees us, well, so what? They'll probably spot us the minute we reach the coast and leave the train anyway." Chris considered this, eyes fixed absently on the far wall. Leave the train: He didn't want to think about it at the moment. Just the idea of leaving the safety of this car and walking the length of the train—*Get you in practice, dude. Get you warmed up to take on San Philippe.* Right. The train line ended in one of the busiest small ports along the coast; anyone might be watching for them. But in a town of that size, they stood a better chance of not being recognized; it wasn't as likely Dupret's agents would be there, anyone who knew him and Eddie by sight. *Our rotten luck, we'll run right into one of Dupret's boys.*

"A real meal, on a proper table, with servers," Edrith reminded him firmly. "There is fowl tonight, in a sauce of mushrooms and hot peppers."

"Which we'd get in here anyway," Chris said, still absently. He sat up straighter, shook himself. "But she's used to eating nice and all that, she probably *would* like that."

"Unlike either of us."

"Yeah. Especially you."

Edrith shrugged. "Such meals merely serve to remind me of the difference between a Dupret and myself: food which is not taken plain but covered in strange broths, and much too involved rituals for consuming them."

Chris leveled a finger at his nose. "Right. Don't give me that, you came in off the streets years ago and you can eat

pretty when you have to, Eddie, I've seen you. You know
how to do dinner deals at least as well as I can, and you're
like me, you eat anything that doesn't fight back." Edrith
laughed quietly; Chris laughed with him. "All the same,
guy, thanks for the nudge about dinner, I forget that stuff."

"I know you do. However"—he cast a swift glance toward the screen—"you should begin to remember. You are
wed to her and this lady will thank you for such considera-
tions. But I had a selfish reason as well. You and I need to
plan what to do once we reach end of line at San Philippe,
which is not very far at all now. You are sleeping too much
and thinking not at all. Some fresh air, food in a proper dining chamber—and the lady could use the time alone with
you, and you with her."

"Oh, yeah, sure," Chris mumbled. His eyes strayed toward the screen; he could hear Ariadne, her voice still
heavy with sleep. "Think about the *last* time the lady and I
were alone," he said, even more quietly.

Edrith laughed. "You mean when you were snatched off
the Podhru docks?" He kept his voice low, though it didn't
carry far at the best of times. "Well? Neither of you murdered the other." Chris glanced at him, startled. "Also, you
worked with each other so you could escape Casimaffi's
ship. I call that progress, you know?" *Murder. I never said
word one to anyone about Ariadne's little—ah—hobby.* If
Eddie had somehow learned—but his friend's face reassured him; Eddie was just pulling his chain, the way he always did. Not—hinting at anything. *Yah. Wonder how he'd
feel if he knew the lady had deliberately stalked and murdered five noble dudes in French Jamaica—followed 'em
down the kinds of back alleys he and I very carefully avoid,
then stabbed 'em dead? That the knife she wears next to
her knee isn't just her idea of costume jewelry?* Eddie knew
about the knife, of course; probably everyone in Rhadaz did
by now, the way gossip spread. But the rest—well, Eddie

wasn't going to find out about all those dead French Jamaicans. *Like I could talk about it anyway.*

He was still surprised that Ariadne had told *him* why she carried the knife that night aboard ship. It wasn't the kind of thing she'd spill to just anyone, and it wasn't the kind of information guaranteed to warm a new husband's heart. Then again, he hadn't given her any choice, he wouldn't have let her take his place out on that deck with that knife without a damned seriously good reason.

All in all, they'd needed each other that night; his skills and hers both got them out of a potentially deadly situation alive and unnoticed. She'd have drowned before ever reaching shore, without Chris. And Chris, who'd never killed anyone, let alone with a very sharp, long, ugly knife—*all right, so there was a chance I'd've got lucky and taken out the dude on deck in total silence; more likely I'd have made a mess of it and we'd both be dead by now.* His thoughts shied away from that ugly little moment: holding his breath while a totally and unnervingly silent Ariadne climbed up the ladder and vanished onto the deck, himself crawling onto the deck at her gesture a few, mere quiet moments later, and finding a dead man under his hands.

Great, he told himself. Think of something else, okay? Like who had wanted them badly enough to call for am ambush in Podhru, snagging both of them neatly off the Emperor's own docks, evading the guard and running for open ocean. The ship was easy enough, Casimaffi's *Windsong*, but old Chuffles wasn't the murdering kind. He didn't like CEE-Tech, Chris cut into his business, and unfortunately, he *was* the kind to sell out. As to who'd hired him, though, the list was entirely too long: Ari's father, Henri Dupret— the men trying to bring Zero into Rhadaz—Duke Vuhlem, who was actively involved according to Lialla. The Americans, the French, the English, any of whom might be behind the trade in Zero. Someone else? *Pick a card, any card,* he thought gloomily.

Poor Ariadne. They'd done nothing but run since she'd left her father's house with Chris; she probably hadn't had a good night's sleep the whole time. Probably hadn't had too many back home, of course: With Dupret for a father . . . And Dupret wasn't the only one like that. No wonder all those women in French Jamaica had formed their murderous secret society. *Hey. Whatever works. Women's Sewing Circle and Terrorist Society, you betcha. You can bend over backward until you fall on your face, like Mom did all those years she got pounded by the Arnies and Chucks, and it won't get you squat, except more bruises.* In a society like French Jamaica's, where there wasn't even a police force—well, it wasn't like Henri Dupret and his fellow noblemen hadn't created their own little hell, so it served 'em right.

He blinked; Edrith sat on the edge of the seat across from him, waiting. "Yeah, sorry, Eddie; I was thinking."

"Nothing pleasant, from your face. Don't tell me about it. Shall I get you a table?"

"Uh—table?" *Dinner, dummy,* he reminded himself. "Oh. Table. Sure. Make it an hour from now, I'm a mess and I bet the lady'll want to change."

"The lady will change what?" He jumped, and his heart thudded wildly in his ears. Ariadne had come from behind the screen and stood in the center of the room so Dija could flounce out wrinkled dark skirts. She pressed the back of one hand against her mouth, yawned neatly. Her hair hung loose, a wonderful blue-black mass of curl, a thick, cloudy frame for the narrow, honey-dark face and near black sleepy eyes. *God, I love that hair, and she almost cut it all off. Gotta remember to get Jen that curl-your-hair junk this trip out for stopping her.* One chance to run his hands through it . . .

"Change—ah. Thought you might like real dinner in the dining car," Chris managed, and held his breath.

She considered this briefly, smiled. "I would like real

dinner, thank you." A little stilted but friendly enough. The truce, or whatever it was that had started back on the Rhadazi south coast with both of them dripping wet and half-drowned, was apparently still holding. Chris smiled back, got to his feet. Edrith was already at the door, curtain pulled back and his hand on the heavy latch.

Chris pulled out his watch. "Okay, Eddie, make it an hour, if they can fit us in—or whatever. Give me time to comb my hair and all."

"Hair." Ariadne held out a long handful of her own and eyed it in disgust as Edrith nodded and slipped into the passageway. Dija caught hold of the fingers, pried them open, and deftly scooped the tress back over her mistress's shoulder.

"An hour, madam," she said. "That is barely time, if you wish more than a ribbon here, to hold it back." She gestured tying a bow at the back of her own neck; Ariadne cast up her eyes, shook her head, and allowed herself to be led back behind the screen.

Chris turned the gas lamp up another notch, shuddered at the ornate brasswork and the gruesome patterned velvet paper behind it, and set his bag on the plush bench. Somewhere in here, probably right at the bottom, there should be one last set of clean socks and a change of underwear. He scooped them up, pulled his good clothes off the hook behind the curtained inset in the wall that was his and Eddie's "closet," and went into the windowless little bathroom.

"Bathroom—right. Except no bath," he grumbled. Bath was possible, of course, but it meant a lot of hassle: a tub set up in the middle of the main room, buckets of water poured into it—and moving everyone else out of the private car until the bather was done. Even Ariadne had passed on it, and sponged down in the bathroom. There wasn't any such thing as a shower, of course. "Damn. Every time I think I'm adjusted, something like this hits home. I'd kill for a cool, hard shower and a bar of real soap." He poured

water into the basin, dumped a facecloth in it, and fished
the jar of washing powder from the curtained shelf beneath
the basin. "Ahhhh—forget that, all right?" At least there
was water, an indoor toilet, and a separate little room with a
door to enclose them and separate them from the main
room—which was more civilization than he'd found in a
lot of places, this end of the world. He scrubbed his face,
rubbed his beard, and decided it didn't need shaving yet.
"On a moving train? Like you would," he told his reflection
in the gilt-edged mirror. He splashed cool, fresh water on
the back of his neck and fought his way out of grubby linen
and into clean fresh socks and trousers.

The shirt was trouble; after banging his elbow twice on
the edge of the mirror, he swore and edged the door open a
fraction. No one in the main room. He cleared his throat.
"Um—I'm coming out of the bathroom to put my shirt on,
okay? So you know."

A silence. "*Ah-c'est bien.*" Ariadne's voice sounded
odd—like she was trying not to laugh, maybe. *More like
she's embarrassed,* he decided. He came into the room,
pulling the shirt on. Well—so maybe his own face was
pretty red at the moment, too. He sat on the edge of the seat
he'd occupied for most of the last five days, so the high
back was between him and the screen, and fumbled the
shirt together, swore, and rebuttoned it properly. A quick
glance toward the screen; trousers undone, shirt tucked in,
trousers fastened. He sighed faintly, pulled on the vest, and
sat down again to knot his tie.

"Decent again," he announced.

"*Merci.*" A moment later, Dija crossed the room and
went into the bathroom, emerging with the jar of soap,
pitcher, and the basin. She carried them back behind the
screen; Chris could hear soft voices, splashing, the rustle of
fabric and other, more obscure sounds.

"Ah—yeah. Think I'll step out into the corridor to wait
for Eddie, all right?" He didn't wait for an answer; the latch

clicked behind him and he leaned against the door, blotting his forehead with the back of his hand. "Right," he mumbled. "You're *married* to her, you know? So—how many days of riding around Bez, Sikkre, Zelharri, and Andar Perigha, camping out every night? All those nights in Khamal's house, one night in a smelly ship's cabin and washed up on the rocks, together, soaking wet—how many nights getting from Bez back over to Fahlia and how many on this damned train? Jeez, guy!" Well, but—He sighed and stared at the dimly lit ceiling. "Gilt trim and cherubs, ech. Yeah. Well, but. Camping's one thing; this is almost like sharing the same *bed* or something." Intimate. He could tell when she was simply changing her shirtwaist, when she was changing other—gods. His face felt very warm.

The latch moved under his hand; Dija leaned out as he turned and briskly announced, "She is ready."

"Wow—fast work," Chris said. Movement down the corridor—Eddie coming back in the next car. "Hang on," he added, "I'll be right in." Dija inclined her head and closed the door. "All set?"

Edrith nodded. "There's room to spare in the dining car; they said any time you wanted to come. Think they're glad to have someone to feed, actually."

"Okay. So if you and Dija want to—"

"You and Ariadne need the time," Edrith said firmly. "Dija and I will do fine here, thank you, and after all, the food is the same." He pulled the door open and stood aside to let Chris precede him.

Ariadne wore dark red, the one good dress she'd kept out of her baggage; another of those fancy things her father had ordered from France for her. *Yeah, what a jerk. But he has good taste, gotta admit*. The skirt was silky stuff that flared delightfully when she moved, and stopped just short of her ankles; the top was snug sleeved, edged at the throat in

darker red ribbon and at the elbows in deep rose-patterned
lace. Dija had somehow managed to get her hair into a coil
at the top of her head and fastened it with gold combs. It
made her look taller and elegant, but even younger than her
twenty years; the red complimented her honey-dark skin
and blue-black hair, her near-black eyes. Her cheeks were
flushed—skillfully applied cosmetic, perhaps, though Chris
couldn't remember her wearing that kind of thing. The sil-
ver-and-opal ring that he'd bought for her in Sikkre was on
the marriage finger, her mother's ring gleamed on her left
hand on the index finger. She held out the skirt with one
hand, eyed him sidelong. Chris nodded enthusiastically.

"Wow. You look great." She smiled and suddenly looked
much more relaxed. *Like it mattered what I thought, or
something?* "That's color's great on you, Ariadne."

"*Merci*—I mean, thank you, Chris." He held out his arm,
rather self-consciously; she took it and let him lead her into
the corridor.

They walked in silence; Chris kept her fingers tucked between his hand and vest, and she seemed content to leave
them there. The next car was the empty one, he recalled;
like their own, it had a narrow corridor down one side and a
private room on the other. The sole door was darkened, the
car utterly still. They went on, through the canvas-covered
doorway and onto a platform crossing the gap between
cars, into the common-class car he and Eddie would probably have taken if they'd been alone. Three middle-aged
men—French-Gallic mercantile class, by the looks of them,
Chris decided with relief: not the kind to worry about. Two
sat with their wives, and another, much older, snored resoundingly, his shaggy, bearded head tipped against the
window. One of the women eyed him in distaste, let her
gaze shift as Chris and Ariadne walked through the car. She
studied the younger woman's gown avidly. Ariadne smiled

faintly, but the other woman didn't notice; her attention was all for dark red silk and rose-patterned lace.

The other woman was arguing with her husband as she dug through a hamper, slapping napkin-covered dishes on the low table fixed to the wall and hissing at him in furious French while he studied a map, to all appearances oblivious save that his color was high.

Two people missing—*Eddie said seven*. Chris slowed and looked around. Ariadne gazed up at him, her eyes suddenly wide. *Hey, don't worry the lady, idiot.* He smiled, picked up the pace again. Probably in the bathroom or whatever coach class had. Or in the dining car. Whatever. Eddie'd seen them and passed them, that would have to do.

They reached the end of the car; Ariadne slipped under the canvas as Chris held it aside for her. She stopped on the platform and looked at the solid dining-car entry and her shoulders were tight, her eyes wary. Ariadne glanced back at him; he brought up a smile and nodded. "There are two other passengers, they're probably in there eating. But I swear Eddie checked the whole train thoroughly before I even suggested this. He says we're all right."

"I know you and he would do that." Her smile wasn't much better than his felt. "I only—"

"I know. Way things have gone for us lately, I don't blame you a bit for worrying." He squeezed her fingers. She brought her chin up and tightened her grip on his hand.

"It is just—one cannot see before going in there. But luck changes," she added defiantly. "Everyone says so."

"Well—yeah. Why not? And just about our time for that, I'd say." He led her across the platform, through the swinging door and into the dining car.

Wow. Chris blinked as they stopped just inside the car and waited for the attendant to come for them. This was ornate, at least as fancy as anything he'd seen anywhere, including Henri Dupret's study. There was one other passenger in the car, a man at the far end, facing them and deeply engrossed in his newspaper and the soup he was spooning rapidly into a heavily bearded face. Chris glanced at Ariadne, who eyed the man carefully, then shook her head. *No one I ever saw before, either. Good. One point for our side.*

He waited until they were seated, until the waiter had returned with a tray bearing shallow plates of soup and a wine bottle, two tall, brilliantly cobalt blue glasses. Ariadne tested the wine, shrugged. Chris cleared his throat. "Ah— any chance I could get juice instead?" The waiter shook his head; Ariadne spoke then, in low, rapid French. The man nodded, left, and returned moments later with a flask of orange.

Chris drew the thick napkin across his lap, poured orange into his glass, and sipped. "Mmmm. Great, no sugar. Thanks."

"Of course, Chris."

He waited for her to begin, as much to see which of the near dozen utensils she chose for eating soup as for mere politeness. Jennifer had beaten proper American table manners into him over the past couple of years, but he was willing to bet she'd have been taken aback herself by the array of dinner weaponry set out here.

The soup itself was cold, a very pale green—he assumed cream, tasted both melon and hot pepper, but the rest was too subtle to figure. *All good stuff, whatever it is.* Ariadne ate rapidly and he followed suit.

Several excellent courses later, he set aside an empty ice dish and blotted his moustache. Ariadne swallowed wine and sighed happily. "That was excellent. Thank you."

"Yeah. Definitely edible."

"I worried to leave that *chambre*. It was—not so bad as I feared, to venture outside."

"I know, first step's the hardest."

She let him refill her glass, glanced down the car. They had it to themselves, at the moment; the waiter had gone back into the kitchen at the far end, and the other passenger had finished his meal and left a while earlier. "How far—how long until we reach San Philippe?"

He drew out his watch, frowned at it, finally shrugged. "I think about half a day, not more than that."

"Half a day. To simply walk from this place into the open—"

"You and me both," Chris said. She frowned, shook her head. "I mean, I feel the same way. But Eddie and I are going to work on it tonight, figure out the safest way for us to get from the end of the train line to a ship."

"I know you will. Thank you."

"Well—sure." Silence; a friendly one, Chris decided. Ariadne finished her wine and patted her lips with the thick cloth napkin. "Ah—I sent that message up to Jennifer and Afronsan. About what you said, your father and his friend?"

"Sorionne," Ariadne said. "They—you think they can find who causes the trouble for Rhadaz by what I said?"

"Sure hope so. You don't remember anything else at all about that night? What they said, or any clue of who—?" She shook her head. "Well. You know, I thought maybe if I picked your brain, you know, asked some questions, you might remember something one of them said, anything at all—if you don't mind, I mean—"

"Mind? You know how I feel. But that night—I was not so close to my father and Sorionne, and Sorionne's nephew was at my near elbow, chattering the whole meal."

"So much for that," Chris said gloomily. "Still—Sorionne. What does he do for his money?"

"He has fields in sugar, like my father." Ariadne frowned, thought for some moments. "And mines—some new metal, I cannot recall the name, but my father had a little piece of it. It is pale and very light in weight; the French have not yet managed a way to work it though they have a supply of their own. But both the Mer Khani and the English have been at his door for it."

"Metal." Chris drove a hand through the hair at his temples and thought furiously. What metal in that end of the world? This wasn't exactly history and maps, not his field at all. Except . . . *Metal and pale and lightweight?* "Aluminum?" he asked. "Ah—right, wait, good old junior-year chemistry, bauxite?"

"Bauxite." Her pronounciation of the word was darker, he'd probably not have recognized it if she'd said the word first. "I think—yes. It is something in France also, a new thing and they only begin to work it but without any success to now. Or so I have heard. But Sorionne has control of nearly all the mines in French Jamaica."

"Aluminum." Chris ticked off fingers as he thought aloud. "Okay. Aluminum. Metals. Steel. Foundries? Rails. Engines? Wire . . ."

"Wire," Ariadne responded suddenly. "And rails."

"Yeah, but that's steel."

"Steel—yes, for the telegram and the trains, I remember now, Sorionne and Father arguing about the large firm which made wire and rails. There was a difficulty, because they wished control of Sorionne's bauxite supply for something else, not rails or wire for telegraph. . . ." She shook her head, visibly frustrated. Chris caught hold of her near hand.

"Hey, no big deal, it's a place to start." Something Jen had said: The guy who'd done the telegraph deal with her in Sikkre, also the denim deal—he'd been pushing trains? *I know I heard the guys' name, I'll bet I've even met with him.* Someone who'd pushed trains to Chris, who'd needed no push in that direction at all. "Great," he said finally. "It's a start, and I have this feeling—yeah. Let me think about it awhile, see what I can come up with. Probably have another wire to send north when we get off the train at San

Philippe." Another thought occurred to him. "Sorionne. That isn't the guy who—who wanted to marry you, is it?"

Her color was suddenly high; she nodded. "But that, at least, is no longer a possible thing, is it?"

"Ah—right. It's not. Like, no chance in this world, okay?" Her fingers were warm in his but he thought the rest of her had gone tense and wary. "Um, lookit. I—ah—you and I, we haven't talked about things, really. Ah—" He cleared his throat. "Jen said she told you that I wasn't—that I wouldn't—" His face was hot; hers was definitely red now. "Well, what she said—I won't."

"You—"

"Let me finish, God knows this is hard enough and I'll never be able to say it twice, okay?" She nodded again. "I know we're m-m-m-married, that priest did the whole thing and it took and—well, that's that. Like, forever, because it's your religion. I jus—I don't feel like it's real, if you know what I mean. It's more like—we got thrown together, kind of sudden-like, and we were strangers and now we're—we're friends, right?"

"Friends," Ariadne said faintly. She swallowed, managed a tight smile and the least little nod.

"Friends. That means—means we're getting to know each other, see how well we can like each other. I don't—I mean, I won't—well, I'm not gonna push you, okay?"

"Push—yes. I see." A long silence. It was Chris's turn to swallow; his throat was very dry. *Had to drink all that orange, didn't you, guy?* Ariadne's eyes had gone distant and she was still and quiet, long enough for him to wonder if he'd said the wrong thing somehow. "I see," she said again, finally. "I think I do. You—this is not because of—of the thing I said in my father's carriage about the knife. What I told you on that ship?"

He shook his head. "Hey. I'd be lying if I said I wasn't surprised. Told you I don't like knives, and okay, I was spooked at first, who wouldn't be? Then, crawling onto a

dead man. But it's—it's not because of that. I've just seen
too many kids, too many guys, who go for the—oh, hell,
who jump in bed with a girl first night out, and it messes up
everything. It can, anyway. I don't want to mess up any
chance we have, that's all."

"Yes. I see." Her forehead puckered. "I think I do. If it is
not the other thing—"

"It's not. I just wanted you to know, that's all." He stood,
held out his arm. "Walk you back to the private car, lady?"

Her smile was ironic once more; she inclined her head
and took hold of his arm. "*Merci,* sir."

Four people in the common car at the moment: the couple
who'd been arguing over the hamper, the older man who
now slept full length on his seat and no longer snored, the
woman who'd glared at him—she slept with her cheek
against the padded wing of her seat, whuffling softly. At
the end of the car, two curtained alcoves and the heavy,
regular breathing of a deep sleeper from one. They crossed
the platform, started into the empty private car. Chris was
vaguely aware of someone coming toward them, a narrow
man in a dark suit and broad-brimmed hat. Ariadne drew
him to a sudden halt and fumbled at her sleeve.

"Hey—you all right?"

"Ah, *merde*—there was dust in that opening—" She
brought up a lace-edged square and sneezed resoundingly.
And again. Chris looked at the man as he passed them; total
stranger, so far as he could tell in the near dark. The other
merely eyed them in mild curiosity and kept going. Ariadne
sneezed several times in rapid succession, swore, and
sneezed again, staggering into Chris, who drew her up by
her elbows. She rubbed her nose with the small cloth. "I *de-
spise* dust. Did I just see someone?"

"Here? Yeah. Went on by, though. No one I ever saw before. There's a car beyond us for the crew, Eddie said

there's a guy goes back and plays cards with them. No one he knows, either."

"Ah." She held the cloth to her nose a moment more.

"You all right?" She nodded. "Good. Let's get you away from that opening."

"Yes." She sneezed once more and swore angrily. "Now, please."

"You got it, lady." Moments later they passed through the canvas and into the next car.

The narrow man in the broad-brimmed hat pressed aside the canvas at the other end of the private car and stood with his back against it, rubbing his chin thoughtfully. There was no mistaking either of them—the man couldn't be anyone but M. Cray, and of course Ariadne Dupret would stand out anywhere. He consulted his watch in the faint light, thought for a moment, then strode back toward the common car and sought his sleeping alcove. Once inside, he turned up the small wall lamp and drew a thin leather memo book from an inner pocket. The message would have to go by wire from Marie Donne, only a short distance on. He'd have to be quick, get it ready, and find the attendant; the stop at Marie Donne was a matter of moments only. The message itself—at least that was simple, and very brief: MERCHANT CRAY, VISCOUNT DUPRET'S DAUGHTER ABOARD THE COASTAL, ARRIVE SAN PHILIPPE TOMORROW. He printed that out in large block letters, blotted the message, and folded it around a crisp new banknote. The car attendant would see it off the train and hand it over to the wire offices in Marie Donne. Thereafter . . .

Thereafter, a wise man who would live to collect his reward—why, such a man would depart the train at Emile, when there is a halt for fuel. It should be possible to hire a horse or a carriage from Emile to the coast. Much as he disliked either mode of transportation, it would scarcely do for the Viscount's half-breed daughter to get a good look at him. *I had luck tonight; she was distracted when I passed and the light was not good. I have changed this past year, but she might remember this particular among her maid's suitors.*

Best to let them think themselves unnoted. For the moment, at least. Once they reached San Philippe—he smiled grimly, turned down the lamp, and went in search of the attendant.

2

"JUST breathe normally, Thukara." The soft-voiced midwife laid both hands on Jennifer's stomach, pressed gently.

"I'm *trying*," Jennifer said, her own voice mildly accusing. "You're tickling me." Miysa looked at her sidelong. "I can't help it, I'm touchy."

"More than usual, even for you. Well, think of something else for the moment, if you can, and I'll be as quick as possible."

"Mmmmm." Think of something else, right. It was taking everything Jennifer had to stay on the large bed and under those cool, deft fingers. She looked toward the door, across the room, and into her dressing room, where Siohan was rinsing underthings and humming. She sighed, finally, folded her hands together across her ribs, and shifted into Thread. The midwife's twist of the silver cord and four red stones that lay on the low mound just below her fingers— another of Miysa's specialized charms, that silver thing, but the woman hadn't yet volunteered what it was supposed to do. Thread wasn't any use—midwife charms weren't simple market ones like those Dahven used to carry, but Jennifer couldn't sense any of them, specialized or no.

Miysa by Thread was a curious pattern: red, of course. That was the finding Thread, the first Jennifer had properly learned to wield. Under that, something as silvery as that

25

cord. Jennifer refolded her hands, hesitated only briefly, then refocused her attention to just south of her hands, and under Miysa's charm. No change in the pattern that was the baby, except size.

She looked up and shifted back as Miysa tugged her loose dress straight, wadded the silver cord in her other hand, and shoved it into a deep pocket. The midwife smiled. "I still cannot be completely certain, Thukara, but I think—yes, I'm nearly positive everything is all right."

"You think—?" Jennifer smoothed the gauzy red fabric across her knees and pushed up onto one elbow.

"Two things," Miysa said crisply, and turned down fingers. "The stones did not change color and they're extremely sensitive. Also, frankly, you still carry the child."

"I see." It stopped her breath for one moment. *The child is still alive, you've seen that much yourself.* She managed a smile and sat all the way up. "You think I'd have miscarried if the damage had been serious, is that it?" Miysa nodded. "Well—thanks for being honest with me."

"You've never wanted convenient truth from me, Thukara, and a lie would do you no good in the long run," the midwife said. She gathered up her other items, then fished a bottle from another of her several pockets. "Two drops in your tea, or whatever you drink on rising, each day until it's gone. Have it put into something strong flavored, so you won't taste this."

"Ah. Yes." Jennifer took the bottle and eyed it doubtfully. "What is it? How bad is the taste? And what kind of bad?"

"So your food stays put and does both of you the most good. As to the taste: well, you drink this in strong tea and you'll never need to know." Miysa leaned into the Thukara's dressing room and said, "Siohan, I'm done here. Send at any time, if you feel the need, Thukara." She inclined her head and left; Jennifer could hear her sandals clicking rapidly down the hall through the open doorway.

Siohan came into the bedroom a moment later, wiped her hands on her apron, and held one out for the bottle.

"You were listening." Jennifer rolled her eyes and surrendered it. "What—afraid I won't take it?"

Siohan laughed. "I could hardly help but hear, you know, not from here to the back of your dressing room. Let us say, I'm certain you'll find yourself too busy to ever remember."

"You're right, of course. Don't you dare put that stuff in my coffee, though."

"I wouldn't dream of tampering with your coffee. Why don't you stay here and rest a while if you can, Thukara? It's the heat of day, after all, and much too warm for the time of year."

"Well—"

"Think how warm it is in here, and how much worse it will be just under the roof, where your offices are," Siohan added persuasively.

"Well, I left enough paperwork on my desk that I shouldn't—"

"It will all be there for you, I promise. And the air should cool before much longer."

Jennifer laughed. "So it will. All right. An hour—no more, though."

"Good. I'll bring you a roll and some of your chilled coffee, shall I?" Jennifer nodded; Siohan patted the pocket where she'd dropped the midwife's little bottle, and went out. Jennifer fluffed pillows, tossed them toward the head of the bed, and fell back bonelessly.

"Ahhhh, yes, let's be lazy and worthless for once," she said aloud. She considered this and laughed.

"I am delighted one of us is cheerful." Dahven's voice. She looked up to see him slouched against the doorframe, the Heir's leather document pouch in one hand and a sheaf of telegraph messages in the other; his brows were drawn together in a single dark line. "I stopped at your office; they said you were here."

"Miysa came."

"There's—no problem?"

"Just a regular visit." No point in telling him what Miysa had said; he'd find a way to worry it, the way he had everything else the midwife had said thus far. "I'm giddy with the heat and playing hooky from my desk, that's all," Jennifer said. "That's an impressive glare. Why do I get a look like that? Did I do something wrong?"

"I—? Oh." He managed a grimace that was probably intended as a grin. "Sorry. I wasn't glaring at you, and you know it. No, Grelt and I have been snarling at each other over this armed company Afronsan wants at the ready."

"*Still* only at the ready? And still arguing? I thought it was all decided, at least as far as taking Dro Pent back."

"Jen—if the decision was only *Afronsan's*. You know the problem." She sighed. Dahven pried himself off the doorframe, dropped the dispatch case and the messages on the bed next to her, and threw himself into his chair. "What did the midwife say?"

"Not much. She left more horrid stuff for me to take, aren't you glad you aren't the one doing the hard work?" He laughed shortly, slouched even lower in the chair, and crossed his heels on the edge of the bed. "About Vuhlem— sorry, I wasn't thinking." Jennifer leafed through the top three messages, shook her head, and set them aside. "Afronsan has to first convince Shesseran there's a problem, that Vuhlem's behind it, that it's too serious to be ignored, and *then* convince the Emperor to go with force. . . ."

"Yes, well, enough," Dahven growled. "I got enough of that the past two hours or so." One hand drummed the polished wooden rest. "All that time wasted, same as it would be for anything else, with the additional problem that Shesseran and Vuhlem—"

"I know," Jennifer droned wearily. "They schooled together; I've heard." She sighed. "And, of course, Shesseran thinks the sun shines from an unnamable portion of Vuhlem's anatomy—" Dahven broke into an unwilling chuckle. She waited while he laughed, and watched some of the tension leave his shoulders; his hands lay flat on the wooden rests. "So, what's *your* problem?"

"Ahhhhh." Dahven tried to recapture his angry scowl but gave it up and rolled his eyes instead. "It's Grelt being difficult with me. He says I can have any say I like in the planning—and no part whatsoever in the execution."

Jennifer's eyebrows went up. "You mean, I'm not the only one in Sikkre with that much good sense?" He scowled, shook his head again. "Dahven, you know damned well you can't go to Dro Pent. You've got Sikkre, me, our—"

"I know that!" He sighed. "Sorry. I just—"

"Dahven. This is me, remember? I've helped you bust heads, this isn't the clinging-little-woman act, and Grelt isn't insulting you or babying you. You're not just Dahven, you're Thukar, you've got responsibilities, a wife, an heir on the way—"

"Ahhh, you're as bad as Grelt," Dahven broke in sourly. "I can take care of myself, I've been doing *that* since I was a mere babe. I'm not going off to get myself killed."

"No one means to do that, but things happen, remember? And the way things have been going the past year or so, it's not the best idea to leave Sikkre in the hands of an outlander female. Wouldn't Vuhlem like that? Can't you see him pulling a Jadek here? Poor little woman can't manage by herself, with an infant on the way, though that child might not be the Thukar's—"

"Jennifer!" Dahven waved his hands in her face and she grinned at him. "All right, all *right*. Sounds ridiculous until I remember everything Vuhlem's pulled lately—and gotten away with."

"So. Just in case, don't you think we ought to keep the

true heir—yourself, sir—in very good and *visible* health? And well away from the front lines?" Silence. "By all means, sit in with Grelt and help with the planning, we need all the edge we can get. Figure out a way for Grelt to bat Vuhlem over the head and dump the body a mile offshore, he quietly disappears, and Shesseran's no wiser."

"Jennifer!"

"I'm being practical," Jennifer replied flatly. "Keep in mind Vuhlem's pulled at least one fast one in Dro Pent and another with the brandy, he's playing for keeps. If he gets away with Dro Pent, think about what's next door and a very good catch. Hmmm?"

"Another reason I think I should go. You know I can take care of myself, and this way—"

She snorted rudely, silencing him. "Grelt can think on his feet, too. And you can take care of yourself, I know that. So can I. We've both proven it. Unfortunately, so has Vuhlem. And so have—I'm sorry—so have your father, your brothers, and the Lasanachi."

A long silence. Dahven finally nodded; he leaned forward and grabbed the leather dispatch case. "All right. No, don't look at me like that, I'm just grumbling. I was playing in Sikkre's lower market when I was five and running it for Father just a few years later; you can't expect me to like staying home while Grelt and others go to fight, can you?"

"Don't be silly. All the same, you haven't run the lower market by yourself for a few years, you delegate these days. What've you got there?" It was as good a change of worn-out subject as any; Dahven opened the case and drew out a small pile of loose sheets and two bundles of paper wrapped in red string. He swore as several note-sized sheets slipped from his grasp and drifted to the floor. Jennifer eyed the stack of telegrams sidelong, sighed, and pulled them toward her. "What's been decided, other than you can't go?"

"Thanks." Dahven cast her a wry grin and bent over to

gather up the loose bits. He leafed through the stack. "Has the Heir's wife even *seen* him since they wed? He must spend all his life at his desk. . . ."

"It's not quite so bad as that, she sees him. In fact, I hear she's using prophylactic until the Emperor dies, in addition to Afronsan's silver bracelet," Jennifer said blandly. Dahven blinked. "Well, wouldn't you?"

"With her husband Heir to an Emperor who can't beget an Heir of either sex on any of his wives and who's paranoid about everything in sight? I'm surprised Shesseran didn't make a provision of the Heirship that Afronsan stay single until he took the throne. Ah—was there a point to all this?"

"Took your mind off Vuhlem for a few moments, didn't it?" Dahven grinned, set most of the papers and the dispatch case on the floor, and broke the red string.

"Mmmm. It would be easier to go cross swords with Vuhlem than deal with all this mess. Roads. I'm so tired of roads." He turned a page, a second, turned one back, and sank a little lower in the chair.

"Consider the alternative." She scanned down the first narrow sheet, set it aside. "I wish they would finish that supply of paper the Mer Khani left, I hate the feel of the stuff."

"Mmmm." Dahven's attention was mostly on the document in his hands. "Way the Heir's using the wire, it won't be long."

Silence. Jennifer read through two more lengthy messages, shook her head. "No action yet; Afronsan's urging everyone to be ready but says he doesn't have a lever to use on his brother at this point. Shesseran's conceded the telegraph to be useful but he's flat refused any more new things; Afronsan's sent another wire to Fahlia for Chris to lay low and stay abroad for the time being. Poor Chris. He worked hard on those iceboxes."

"Shesseran isn't immortal; the work won't go to waste."

"I hope not. Mmmm. Lehzin's extremely cross from the sound of things, having trouble with some of his own people harassing the foreigners still stuck in port. But Shesseran won't let any ships come in to take them away, or let any of our ships carry them off, not even across the isthmus. Sounds like Chris and Ariadne got out just in time."

"Mmmm. Nice of Shesseran. Man's beyond rational thought."

"Obviously. Poor Lehzin. There's been no problem with our little pack of foreigners, is there?"

"No. I don't think our merchants feel the foreigners are responsible for the sudden drop in outside money, like the Bezanti do. Well—not yet. I daresay the Mer Khani would like to leave but not if they'll be stuck in Bez or Podhru."

"Don't blame them—ah. Cornekka's passed on a Red Hawk message from Lialla." Dahven looked up from his papers.

"Still not communicating with Zelharri directly, is she? I wish she'd quit using you as a go-between."

"Well, she hasn't asked me to pass anything on, so maybe she is. Communicating. And with Aletto in no condition to bully her into coming home, and Robyn not likely to bully anyone—"

"Damn Lialla. Does she even know about Aletto?"

"I think—yes, Red Hawk's grandmother passed word, I remember Robyn said."

"Well, damn Lialla anyway. What's she doing up there *now*?"

"Getting into trouble; of course. What else when it's Lialla? Actually—" Jennifer shook her head. "I shouldn't pick on Lialla like that, she's being more use than I'd have ever thought, up there."

"Really."

"Don't say it like that; she got that bottle out, didn't she? So we know for certain it's Vuhlem behind the drugged brandy? And she found out what Vuhlem was doing with his dirty money." Jennifer read down the message. "All right. She's still in the caravaner's house, and apparently the locals still think she's Red Hawk, like her friend Sil, so no one's bothering her at present. She's got more company, a woman from that village. Where that bottle came from, the one Rebbe analyzed for us?"

"Yah. Nothing on where it came from before that, though."

"Lasanachi ship. Nothing so far on where *they* got it, of course."

"Of course."

"She has more on Vuhlem's secret army from that wretched boy. He's lucky Lialla's dealing with him; I'd have popped him one days ago. We'll have to—no, I see, she had the grandmother send a message on to Podhru for the Heir, and a copy of this went down to Zelharri also. Nothing new about Zero. Here, you and Grelt will want this, troop stuff." Dahven took the long sheet, folded it, and set it atop his stack. Jennifer set aside a message, a second, picked up the third. "Oh, good, something from Chris. Wow—they're nearly all the way down the coast; says the train's fast, clean, and classy; feels like he should be hung by his bloated capitalist thumbs, way they've been living." Silence. "Says they're all fine, no problems since Podhru, just boredom. It's—" She ran a finger across the top of the sheet. "Well, all right, no problems up until three days ago."

"With Chris, that's certainly something."

"Right. He's—oh." She read rapidly down the rest of the sheet. It fell from her fingers and she gazed blankly in the direction of the door for some moments. Dahven set his document aside and waited. When she finally spoke, it was to herself. "Metals. Smelting, refining, steel—aluminum? Steel . . . Bearings, plates, cogs, and . . . right." She scooped up the sheet and turned to him. "All the Mer Khani are at that inn, aren't they?"

"All of them. Why?"

"The one who signed the deal for denim—little man, nearly bald. John Carrey—no, he was the telegraph foreman." She snapped her fingers. "Audren Henry, got it! The denim was a side deal, he works for the company that makes the telegraph wire, and he was in Sikkre to finalize the plans for connecting all the lines—"

"I remember him; also, I know he's still in Sikkre. So?"

"Yes, but he was also trying to sell me on trains, did you know that?" Dahven shook his head. "Trains—that was partly Chris, of course, so I didn't think anything of it when he started suggesting connecting lines between the Mer Khani and us, through the mountains. Especially since I knew Shesseran would never, ever go for it. Probably why I never mentioned it." Jennifer held out the wire. "Read this."

Dahven did, but he looked as perplexed when he finished as he did when he'd started. "Consortium I understand, at least the way Chris is suggesting: secret business partnership, right? But—the rest of it: Aluminum? Bauxite?"

"Lightweight metal, I don't know anything more than you about the manufacture of the stuff. Just that I think I remember Chris saying it was just coming into use in a very few places recently, and I know it's a hard one to make."

"All right: Chris thinks there may be companies out there—Mer Khani and involving these—these two names?" She nodded. "He thinks these might be the men who are trying to bring Zero into Rhadaz? And—wait. There was a tea company Chris told me about, your old world . . ."

"I—it's here, East India Company. Thanks, Chris, I'd've forgotten."

"Still—why? Let me see, it was—sell drugs to the natives to be certain they'd have a guaranteed good price for their tea. But Rhadaz hasn't anything like that tea, and the

Mer Khani haven't shown interest in any particular thing. Unless I'm missing some point."

Jennifer enumerated on her fingers. "We have land. Lots of it, not very many people occupying it. A vast seacoast. Wars have been fought for a lot less of either. We also have minable metals. Unless things are very different between this world and my old one, we have metals anyone in a burgeoning industrial nation would want."

"We have?"

"Ask Chris, if he ever gets back—or maybe we'll have the Heir do that by wire. Also—we have Mr. Henry right here where we can talk to him." She slid off the bed and shook her skirts down. "I'm going up to my office to track down a few particular contracts, and check some names. And then I think we send for Mr. Henry, and ask him some extremely pointed questions."

The Thukar's small hearings room was much less formal than the blue room—the walls were white, the floor dark tiled, the only furnishings two narrow benches flanking one deep window and near the opposite wall, a plain, polished oval table and half a dozen matched wooden chairs with padded arms. Dahven used the little room to wrestle out market problems, or deal with other matters where he wasn't likely to need to pull rank on the other participants. He and Jennifer settled at one end of the table, waited while one of the kitchen women arranged an enameled tray holding bowls of fruit and bread, plain cups, and a pitcher of cool wine, another pitcher of chilled herb tea. She set a thick clay jug and a tall cup of water at Jennifer's elbow, tweaked the bowls into line, and left. A moment later, the Mer Khani were shown into the room.

Audren Henry was indeed a small man, particularly next to the guardsman who escorted him and the two other traders who trailed behind him. *In with him on the cloth deal,* Jennifer thought. She could remember both faces, vaguely—not the names. Henry stopped short of the table, inclined his head, and indicated his companions as the guards drew back. "I—ah, I thought perhaps—ah—" He drew a large, dark kerchief from an inner pocket and blotted his forehead. "I thought, perhaps the Thukar and Thukara would not object if—"

He never before had stuttered so. Terrified, Jennifer realized. Odd, there was nothing in her note that should have frightened him so. She set that aside for later; likely she'd be terrified, trapped as this man was in a foreign country and an increasingly hostile climate. *From the look of him, you'd think Dahven had the headman and the block all ready for him.* Not funny. She set that aside with an effort. But it would certainly explain the two men: witnesses. She settled her elbows on the edge of the table; glanced at Dahven, who shook his head minutely, then gestured for the guards to leave them. *My show. Thanks, my sweet,* she thought dryly. "You have nothing to worry about from us. I had some questions on one or two of the recent contracts, and thought you could help me."

"Um—questions. I—yes, of course." He glanced at his companions; all three took seats at the end of the table.

Jennifer took a sip of water. "There's tea and wine, help yourselves. I'm not going to bite anyone, Mr. Henry." He managed a weak smile and sat back a little further in his chair. The other two men took a little wine and filled their companion's cup. Jennifer fingered the small pile of contracts under her left elbow. "You work for several different companies, if I recall."

"Um—well, yes. And myself, of course. It's—it's easier to send one man into Rhadaz, with instructions from several different interests.

"And—there was—there was no reason not to close a contract of some kind for myself." He swallowed. "If the opportunity presented itself. I didn't think it was—that there would be a difficulty—"

"No difficulty there, Mr. Henry, and I understand how hard it must have seemed to your people to get someone into Rhadaz to conduct trade bargains. Even with the Heir's willing assistance."

"Ma'am—well, yes, it wasn't anything simple."

"So while you were finalizing the telegraph setup, you made a deal in the Sikkreni market for cloth, along with one or two others." Momentary silence. Henry watched warily as she flipped pages and ran her finger down one sheet. She looked up and said sharply, "Who told you to suggest steam trains to me?"

"Who—I—trains?" He shook his head; thinning hair clung to his temples. His face had gone very pale.

"Let me rephrase that," Jennifer broke in crisply. "How important was it to the head of New Holland Mining that you get the Rhadazi to agree to at least one rail line between your side of the continent and ours?"

"I—it wasn't—the merchant Cray—!"

"Yes, I'm aware of Chris's fascination with trains. Let me rephrase once more. The head of New Holland Mining: Is he also involved in our current problem with Zero?"

"I—Zero?" The little man paled so suddenly, she thought he might faint; one of his companions eyed him nervously and would have spoken, but Henry gripped the man's forearm and gave him a wide-eyed, urgent look she couldn't begin to translate. "Thukara—ma'am, I *know* about the stuff, everyone does, but—but that I'd have anything to do with it! Why, ma'am, that's dirty trade, no man with a conscience would touch it!" Silence; Jennifer waited. "The trains—why, my bosses at the foundry in West New Holland only suggested I put in a word for them where it might do the most good, and, ma'am, we all know you're outlander and used to faster transport than what's here."

"How?" Jennifer asked sharply.

"How? Well, I mean—ma'am, we've our own outlanders, one or two of 'em who've taken up with men in the

foundry trade and who know about things like the large airships, fast vehicles of one sort or another and the special
roads for them. But—" He was silent for a moment, lips
moving and eyes closed. "But that—that wasn't so much
the matter, it's only what the merchant Cray's said often
enough. Well, when he showed interest and then said to
talk to you about 'em—about the steam engines and the
new width tracks, well, I was only doing what seemed like
good business for all of us, you see that, don't you?" He
blotted his chin on his sleeve and watched her anxiously.

"It's logical," Jennifer admitted. She let her fingers drum
on the pile of contracts. "I just wonder why it upsets you
so."

"Well—I—"

"Ma'am," one of the other two put in quietly, "after all
that's gone down here, man can't get back to a ship of his
own, let alone back home. And after all the killings the past
moon-season or so, on the streets and—well, and here in
the Thukar's palace yards—you can't much blame a man
for being fearful of his skin. Or his neck. Besides, it's not
like a man in Audren's boots here could tell his bosses no,
if they told him to do something for them."

"That's so." Henry nodded emphatically. "Some, like the
owner of the cloth mill down south who's supplying cotton
for the denim cloth—he'll listen when a man like me tells
him how things are in foreign places, and what I can press
for in Rhadaz, and what not. And why. Some, like the
foundrymen—well, the men I work for came up poor and
the hard way, and now they're rich and own half of West
New Holland and all the mines, and there's no telling them
a single thing. They don't listen, they talk. Ma'am, if they
don't like what I do for them, they'll discharge me flat."

"I understand. I had to work for others before I came
here." Another little silence; she glanced at Dahven, who
slumped in his chair, eyes moving from one to another of
the men opposite, but without much visible interest, and he

was pulling apart a thick piece of seed bread, making little balls of it. "About the Zero," she prompted. "You don't know anything about it, and your employers don't, either, is that it?"

Henry swallowed. "Ma'am, I told you, everyone knows about it back home—anyone who's gone to sea or south from our borders for certain, most of the raw stuff comes from the Incan states, and it's thick in the south islands—New Portugal and all. You've probably heard it's in all big cities along the east slope, New Amsterdam and New London, right down to the Da Gama Isles off the southern tip. But it's confined to the slums, pretty much. There was talk a while back to make it illegal, but the Parliament decided not. After all, it's only the dirt poor who use it; they'd likely be dying of drink or filthy living conditions otherwise." Jennifer could feel her face heating and Henry must have seen something; he stopped talking abruptly and cautiously edged back in his chair.

"I'm not unfamiliar with the attitude," she said crisply. "I think we prefer to keep our social dregs alive, and maybe even see they get some kind of chance."

Dahven dropped his bread. "You should be aware by now that in Sikkre we at least try to treat our dirt poor as people. It isn't always easy or simple. All the same—" He turned a hand over, looked at Jennifer, who nodded.

"The Zero isn't wanted or welcome here," she said. "You are all aware of that by now, I'm certain."

A chill little silence. The third trader set his cup aside and shifted uncomfortably. "Ah, Thukara? You won't recall me, it's Oliver Stewart. Beg your pardon, but I don't understand why you needed to send for Audren, to give him such a warning. If we'd any part in that kind of trade, I doubt we'd've been fool enough to even enter Rhadaz, let alone get caught here after that fiasco on the Emperor's birthday. It would be—well, as bad as carrying guns, or bringing in alcohol, wouldn't it?"

"Perhaps. Possibly not. And that wasn't the reason you were sent for, Mr. Henry, if you recall." She held up the top contract. "I've been doing a little research, comparing documents, checking names, companies—and there's a pattern, a name or two that crops up whenever metals are involved. The telegraph wire, some of the workings for the new cloth mill, the three-horse harvesters that were dealt for this past spring. Steel carriage springs and joints." Silence. "Geoffrey Bellingham and John Perry, Mr. Henry. New Holland Mining. Tell me about them, please."

Audren Henry shook his head violently. "Ma'am, I can't!"

"You can," Jennifer said evenly. "I suggest also that you had better."

"They're—they're partners in the largest steel mill in the country—our country, New Holland Mining. Those men also own the new bauxite foundry; there's one or two other ventures, possibly, I don't know about."

"And?"

"And—I don't know what you want, ma'am, honestly!" Henry drew out his kerchief, blotted his forehead, and wadded it hard in one white-knuckled fist. Jennifer waited. "They're hard men, ma'am, I can tell you that. Hard and ungiving, and if either even *thought* you had something from me about them, why, that'd be the end of me, I'd lose my position and never get another!"

"They won't learn from me—and none of you men are likely to tell them, are you? Are they involved in the Zero that's reaching Rhadaz?" Henry stared at her. The silence stretched. "All right, you don't know or you won't say."

"If I thought—" The little trader shook his head and fell silent.

"No good offering you a place here, and safety, in exchange for whatever you know or suspect?" Jennifer asked after a moment. He shook his head again.

"I know nothing, suspect nothing. And I've a life back there, and family."

"Well, the offer stands, keep it in mind." Jennifer got to her feet and the three foreigners rose; Henry needed both hands on the table to keep from falling. "Think about it, if you will." *Not likely,* she decided sourly as the three inclined their heads and hurried from the room. "Wasn't *that* a useful little exercise?" she demanded as the door closed behind the men.

"Eat something," Dahven suggested, and set the bowl of bread between them. "You didn't really expect him to say anything, did you?"

"Not—all right, probably not. I'd say he knows something, though."

"Maybe. More likely he's simply afraid *you* think he does."

"Thank you so much," Jennifer retorted sourly. She fished out a plain, dark roll and bit into it. "Bauxite foundry, huh? I think Chris does have something, this could be the connection between French Jamaica and the Mer Khani, unless they're getting their raw ore from someplace else." She finished the roll, washed it down with water, and sorted through the contracts for a blank piece of paper. Dahven watched idly, still playing with his seed bread as she thought a moment, then began printing out a message.

"Afronsan?"

"I want a little more input before I send any of this to him. No, this is for Duke's Fort and Cornekka, so someone can check though the paperwork there."

THUKARA JENNIFER TO DUCHESS ROBYN: SUGGEST SOMEONE READ THROUGH ALL CONTRACTS, ESPECIALLY FOR ANY MER KHANI METAL PRODUCTS, AND RELAY SIGNATURE NAMES AND ANY OTHER NAMES TO ME. EVERYTHING OK IN FORT? LOVE, JEN.

DUCHESS ROBYN TO THUKARA JENNIFER: DAMNIT, YOU SEND SOMEONE YOU WANT THAT ANY TIME SOON,

EVERYONE HERE TOO HASSLED TO MANAGE, ESPECIALLY
ME. NEED YOU TO SEND ME DECENT HEALER; ALETTO
CONSCIOUS BUT NOT HIMSELF, WORRYING. ROBYN.

The room Aletto and Robyn shared was brightly lit with
late-afternoon sun, warm from a fire that had burned to a
deep ruddy glow. Wind battered against heavy glass windows, and in one or two places where the seal was imper-
fect, billowed thick drapes flanking the glass. Robyn sat on
the bed, a pile of pillows at her aching back and Aletto's
hand in hers. His fingers moved slightly and she turned her
head to look at him; his eyes opened briefly and closed
again. Robyn sighed very faintly: *Nothing yet. Drat that old
woman and her powders, they're about as useful as sugar
water.*

If only Jennifer could find someone willing to come to
Duke's Fort . . . Maybe, Robyn thought, someone who'd do
better around children than the old local woman. Who
would no doubt be terribly offended. *Well, let her be. I'm
not chancing Aletto or my babies, just to keep an aging and
hidebound healer happy.*

She looked across the room. Iana sat cross-legged on a
fat blue cushion, not far from the hearth, and blew bubbles
for her brother, who watched them gravely. They looked
normal enough—a little quiet, of course. But in all the days
since she'd brought them home, neither child would let her
out of their sight, not even for a moment. At night, they
slept on the small beds Robyn had moved from the nursery,
at the foot of their parents' bed.

Well, she could scarcely blame them. *I won't go back in
the nursery myself.* Her own feeling was that time would
mend matters, particularly if she was there for them, ready
to talk if either one brought it up. *Not pushing, though; I
hated that when I was a kid, parents and other people pry-
ing, trying to find out how you felt about something so
awful you couldn't even think about it.* Like her mother

abandoning her, divorcing their dad back when such things weren't done, then going off to hawk Watchtowers.

Iana brought up the wire wand her mother had made, blew iridescent soapy liquid, and watched as a steady stream of bubbles sailed toward the fire, veered in the opposite direction as hot air moved them, then slowly floated toward the floor. Amarni put out his hand and gravely broke one. Robyn worked her shoulders back and forth to settle the cushions a little more comfortably. At least these two *had* a mother to talk to, when they were ready. More than she'd had when things went sideways.

She glanced toward the large windows flanking the fireplace. The sun had just dipped below the outer wall, which would make it—nearly time to eat. *Wonder what they'll come up with tonight.* She hadn't been particularly hungry in days; too much to worry and too many of Aletto's duties had dropped squarely onto her shoulders, even with Gyrdan willing to help, delegating his own usual part in the border-guard patrols to others. If Vuhlem's men were still bringing Zero in via the Cornekka road, they must have it plenty easy, she decided gloomily. Some of the guards going out right now were younger than Chris and had little experience. Gyrdan must be half-mad, waiting for Aletto to snap out of it so he could get back to what *he* needed to do.

A tentative tap on the door: probably the kitchen. Iana jumped and clutched her bubble wand; Amarni turned to gaze wide-eyed at his mother, who smiled and nodded. "It's all right, son. It may be dinner. I'm hungry, aren't you?" She raised her voice. "Come in!" But it was Lizelle, who cautiously peered around the edge of the door, who hesitated there, both hands on the latch. Cool air from the hallway came with her. "Come in," Robyn repeated. "You're getting it cold in here."

Lizelle edged around the door, back to it, pressed it closed, and stayed there, one hand gripping the latch. "How—how is he?"

Robyn shrugged. "No different. No worse, anyway."

"I—I just heard, Catra says you sent her away, that you're having a healer brought from Sikkre."

"That's right."

Lizelle's chin came up and she took two steps into the room. "That's hardly fair to Catra, do you think?"

"It's less fair to Aletto," Robyn said evenly. "Catra has plenty of other business in the market, and whatever good she's done others, she hasn't put my husband back on his feet." Lizelle continued to stare at her, that stiff, down-the-nose look Robyn disliked so. "It's no reflection on her if she doesn't know how to deal with something like this; she seems to be fine for setting bones and curing fevers."

"I've heard about Jubelo, in Cornekka." Lizelle took two more steps and stopped; her hands were twisting at belt level, white knuckled. "He drank less than Aletto did, and he's still ill. And—and Jubelo's older but he's whole bodied. . . ." Her voice trailed away; Robyn set Aletto's hand aside and got to her feet. A quick glance at the children; they'd seen Lizelle and gone back to play.

"Your son isn't as crippled as you try to make him out to be, Lizelle. Or as helpless."

"Yes, well, *you* have a son nearly die like Aletto did, and you'll understand what it means to worry about a child." Her eyes fell on the small beds pushed against the end of the Ducal bed; her lips twisted. "*I* at least never spoiled either of mine the way you—"

"Keep your voice low," Robyn hissed angrily. Lizelle stared at her, slack mouthed. "They've been through a lot recently, I won't have you making them feel guilty on top of everything else. And another thing: I heard you out in the hall yesterday morning trying to push past Aletto's man. I absolutely will not have you talking around those two children about how ill their father is, and what that stuff might have done to him. They have enough to deal with, without being afraid Daddy's going to die."

"You're indulging them," Lizelle snapped, though she kept her voice prudently low. "It's been—it's been days, they should have forgotten all that by now. If you'd let them."

No wonder Lialla came out so weird; this woman hasn't got the least idea what goes on in a kid's head. She sighed. "Lizelle, think about it, will you? Think about walking into your nice, safe bedroom and having someone grab you. Their whole world was turned upside down, they get back to find nothing the same around here except the walls, their father's in a coma, grandmother's nice little maids are gone away, and grandmother's tearing her hair and wailing about how daddy's gonna die. It's hard enough on *me,* and I'm old enough to realize bad shit happens that it isn't somehow my fault, and that it probably won't ever happen again." Silence. Lizelle would no longer meet her eyes; her own gaze was fixed on her son. Robyn drove a hand through her hair. "Look, I realize your own world isn't exactly on keel these days. I'm willing to give you a lot of slack because of the drug thing, your girls, your health—yes, your son, too. You want to blow fits, scream, yell, tear your hair, cuss me out—fine. Do it in your own rooms, with the doors closed, will you? Want to yell at me, send for me, I hate it but I can deal with that better than worrying about the additional load on those kids."

Another tap at the door; Lizelle jumped and Iana got to her knees, bubble wand hanging forgotten from her fingers. "Come in!" Robyn said loudly; she went across the room to kneel beside Amarni, who sat so very still he didn't seem to even breathe. "It's okay, kiddo, just some soup for you. Bet you're hungry, huh?"

"I'm hungry," Iana announced. She dropped the wand in the dish of soap and water, scrubbed her hands down her loose britches and got to her feet.

Robyn stood, drawing Amarni up with her. "Lizelle, if

you want to stay and eat with us," she began, but when she turned, Lizelle was gone.

"Duchess?" Avran from the kitchens stood just inside the door, a small, high-piled tray in her hands. "She just—ran out." She brought the tray in, set it on Robyn's desk. "I could—if you want me to—go after her. . . ."

"No, it's all right." Robyn swung Amarni onto his chair and watched Iana scramble onto hers. "We'll just—we'll make a small picnic of it, all right, kids? Just the three of us." Wrong thing to say, perhaps; but Iana picked up her cup and Amarni got onto his knees so he could dip bread into his. Neither looked toward the door or the bed. Robyn sighed, then filled a mug for herself. At least their appetites were still good. *Chicken again. Well, at least it's not that awful thing they used to do with dried fish and cream, and it's not red meat.* She sipped. Chicken broth was boring, the way the kitchen did it when she wasn't there to spice it up herself—but right now she didn't have time to add that to all her other tasks. *Eat the nice, boring soup, girlfriend. You're gonna need all your strength before the week's out, guaranteed.*

3

𐤑

K EPRON swore and slammed both hands against the heavy stones of the fireplace, then swore again and shook them gingerly. "You simply do not listen to me! Like all—!"

"If you say 'all women' once again, I'll remove your ears," Ryselle hissed. He glared at her, sucked a bleeding fingertip. "If you're looking for sympathy, look elsewhere," she added flatly. "It's your own fault if you're bleeding."

Lialla fed two small sticks to the fire, glanced at Sil, who rolled her eyes and minutely shook her head, then rose to her feet between the two glaring Holmaddi and held up a hand. *My four-footed, donkey-brained problem, isn't it? And I asked for it myself. Still—how nice of you, Sil.* "This bores me," she said crisply. "No," she added as both strove to speak at once, "not a word. Ryselle, help Sil with the fire, will you? Kepron—you haven't shown me anything new in two days, go down to the far hearth and practice access and exit."

He glowered at her, shook out his bruised and scraped hand. "*I* cannot do such a thing during the day, however *you* manage—"

"Then learn how," Lialla ordered. The exchange sounded unfortunately all too familiar. *Bah. Thanks to you, too, Jen.* She fished in her pocket, drew out a wad of red string. "If you aren't going to bother trying, take this and work the

47

seventh pattern until you can do it with your eyes closed. And calm yourself; I want to talk with you when I come down there, I don't want to be yelled at while I try to offer you some sense." He hesitated, snatched the string, and stalked the length of the room. Lialla watched him go, then folded her arms and turned what she hoped was a mildly inquiring look in Ryselle's direction.

Ryselle glowered back. "I'm *sorry,*" she growled.

"Oh, no, you're not," Lialla said. "But I doubt I would be, in your shoes. All the same, you can't let the boy push you to anger: It's hard on everyone around you, and it keeps you from being able to Shape."

"I can—"

Lialla shook her head. "No. I know from my own experience how much temper gets in the way of magic—Light and Thread both. And when was the last time you were able to hold Light, let alone Shape it?" Ryselle sighed, shook her own head. "Three days ago."

"I know when it was. And why! Because that young whelp wasn't—"

"Wasn't here." Lialla sat cross-legged on the hearth, palms to the low fire. "Ryselle, listen to me, I'm not telling you anything I haven't learned the hard way. You have reason to be rough tempered: your brothers, your mother, the boy saying something stupid about women every time he opens his mouth. I understand that. You can't let it matter. You have to set it aside—all of it."

"Oh. Just like that—"

"Yes," Lialla said evenly. "Just—like—that." Silence. Ryselle angrily shoved sticks into the heart of the fire. "Think of it as part of your training. In a sense it is; when Aletto and I fled Duke's Fort, every single time I had to Wield was an emergency of some kind. If I hadn't eventually learned how to block infuriating or frightening things out, I wouldn't be here to teach *you*." Another little silence. "Think of it this way, if you prefer: any time you let Kepron upset you with his stupid, cutting little remarks, he's won something, and you've lost. Are you going to let a mere boy do that to you? He's only parroting words he learned from the men around him."

Ryselle's shoulders sagged. "I *know* he is," she said. "It's simply that—"

"Irritating. You think I don't know? But you don't believe any of that nonsense, do you? All women this, every woman that, how stupid and typical of women—" She paused; Ryselle's cheeks were very red and her eyes hot.

"I—well, of course I don't!"

"Then why pay heed to it?" Sil asked. She got to her feet and dusted ash from her knees. "We need vegetables for that broth, if it's to be soup tonight. Why don't you come with me, Ryselle, and help me decide what to purchase?"

"Fine idea," Lialla said, before Ryselle could object. "Take a little time, calm yourself. Think about what I said. Get a loaf of that rye bread from Emios, if you go that way."

"If he has any left at such a late hour," Sil said. "Come on, Ryselle." The village woman sighed heavily, but got up and went with her, down the narrow stairs that led to the back gate. Lialla waited until she heard the muted thump of the lower door closing, then turned and went down the enormous, temporarily empty room. Her hands made hard little fists. *This time I swear I will put such a fright into that boy*—*! One more snotty remark and I'll*—*I will send word to his captain where to find him!* She wouldn't do that, of course. Not really. But at that moment, it made a very satisfying picture, and it ought to make a good threat. *If I need threats, after I shake him until his teeth rattle.* He was as tall as she, but all long bones and, boylike, no real muscle; yelling at him hadn't gotten her anywhere, maybe he'd understand a good, hard thump. *He'd understand that; it's all he's ever known.* Blows and abuse—Lialla forced that aside hastily.

She tugged the lightweight red wool scarves around her shoulders and shivered down into them. They'd had the compound to themselves for three chilly fall days, herself, Sil, the boy, and Ryselle; the air was cool at this end and damp, since they hadn't bothered to keep a fire burning in the far hearth. Lialla's nose wrinkled; large and open as the chamber was, she could still smell mildew. It reminded her of the lower halls of Duke's Fort during the neglect of Jadek's years and for one brief moment, her stomach tightened painfully. *That's past, years past, like Jadek's slap; leave it,* she ordered herself angrily. Easier said than done, of course. She was as much proof of that as Ryselle—or this wretched boy.

She paused, glared at the back of the boy's head, but the anger was already gone. No, she wasn't going to murder him, or even smack him one; she understood all too well what his problem was. *Like that helps anyone, including Kepron,* she thought gloomily, but the Chris-like twist to the words brought up a brief, mood-lightening grin.

Kepron stood with his back to her, eyes fixed on something outside the tall window nearest the stairs down to the stable; a half-finished pattern hung between his fingers. To all appearances, he was concentrating on something so hard, he hadn't even heard or sensed her presence. She folded her arms, studied what she could see of his profile, his hands. He had good fingers, she decided—long and tapering, and ordinarily very deft at string maneuvers she had to fight to accomplish. His face—well, at the moment, it was almost attractive, a boy's unfinished, vulnerable face. Something glittered on his lashes, or so she thought; but a blink and it was gone. *If I didn't know better, I would say he'd been weeping.* Had she ever seen him so much as smile? Like Aletto, those last long years under Jadek . . .

She bit her lip. It wasn't the same thing at all! She didn't have the same ties to this boy as to her only brother, and Kepron hadn't been through even a portion of what Aletto had endured. Still, the boy'd saved her life. *Yes. And you saved his in return; you're matched. Don't you dare coddle this wretched brat because of your brother and all he's been through.* Still, she owed him. He'd learned things she wouldn't ever have, in Vuhlem's provinces: She'd overheard Vuhlem's men talking about shipments of Zero to Dro Pent but the boy had found the bottles of Zero-drugged liquor in crates marked for Vuhlem and risked his skin to bring her one. He'd told her about the secret companies Vuhlem had, outside the city—all right, she decided in exasperation, most of what he knew came because he was a Holmaddi male, attached to a soldier's company, because he could go places no woman could. But he'd put his life on the line more than once. Male ego, most likely, what Chris would call a "bullet-proof" attitude—still, Lialla thought, dead's dead, however you come by it. And it still incurred the debt.

Part of her still wanted to kick his arrogant backside from here to Bezjeriad; she knew she wasn't going to. *Funny: I really meant what I said to Ryselle simply to silence her. But only a fool would hold an immature and cloistered boy responsible for what those in control taught him. Holmaddi men—and a mother who was too short-sighted to do other than parrot their words. Only someone as arrogant and one-sided as the boy could see why he's the way he is and still give up on him, young and sequestered as he is. One final chance—all right, Lialla, you can give him that much.*

Her foot scraped on the floor; he blinked rapidly, glanced at her sidelong and brought his string figure up, fingers once again busy at the complex seventh pattern. His shoulders were stiff once more, his whole posture unyielding, that lower lip beginning to edge out well past his teeth. "How many of those have you done, so far?" Lialla asked quietly. He eyed her sidelong, shook his head. "That's it— part of one?"

"I was—I was thinking," he mumbled.

"Were you? I am glad to hear it." That earned her another quick look, but he wouldn't properly meet her eyes and the fire seemed to have gone out of him for the moment. "Kepron, listen to me." A long silence. He finally nodded once, sharply. "There isn't a Wielder in all Rhadaz who'd blame me for dropping you as a novice and kicking you out of the compound for good—"

"Well? Why don't you, then?" Still a mumble.

"Because I don't want to. *If* I can help it." She watched as he hooked a loop with his littlest fingers, slipped it over another loop, and pulled it through with his thumb. "I told you I was willing to help you, and I meant that. But you've got to help *me*. You aren't a child any longer, you're old enough to think for yourself—not just what you want, but what's there, and why, and what that all means to you."

"Huh."

"You want Thread—you told me so. You openly wanted it back in that village, where it could have earned you a nasty beating, or a one-way trip out to sea in a large sack."

Silence. He swallowed. "I didn't really want Thread then; just—magic of some sort. Something that wasn't the thing chosen for me, because I was the boy, the male. Something that could free me of Holmaddi, and my father's company, and his path." Another silence. Lialla waited. "Thread. I've—I still want it."

"Good. I still want to teach you. And I will, if we can agree on a few things."

Another sidelong look, this one notably wary. "What things?"

"You're messing up: Loop under with the middle finger—no, not that way, under. Good. Keep the pattern going. You say you don't want to become another hidebound Holmaddi male; what you're doing right this moment with your hands shows me you meant it. But you sound exactly like one of those village men." His lips twisted, his hands jerked, bringing a loop down, letting another slip from his index fingers, forming a completely new pattern. He glared at it and swore under his breath. "Relax; take a deep breath and start it again. Remind yourself—before you begin—that you are not your father, not Ryselle's father, not the villager who will marry your mother; you are neither Vuhlem nor any of his captains."

"*I* know that."

"Of course. At least, your lips and your mind know it; your gut hasn't caught up yet. You can't be blamed for being born Holmaddi, or for growing up Holmaddi. But the rest is up to you; you can leave the Duchy, learn another way. You don't like Holmaddi men? Be different."

He laughed sourly. "You make it sound so simple."

Lialla shook her head. "It's not simple, I know better than you think. I was once as set in my own ways as you are in yours. I'm proof it isn't impossible. It's like Thread, like anything else. You have to want it badly enough." Silence. Kepron gazed down at the wad of red string; what she could see of his face gave no clue to his thoughts.

Finally he turned and looked at her. "They say—everyone says it's blood, breeding. Who you are. You've met my mother, and if you recall the village elder—"

"Ryselle's father—"

"Then you know what my father was like, except he was also army. Two such as that, their blood—"

"That's not true, Kepron. Oh, it may hold partly true, perhaps, but blood isn't everything. If it were, then all men would be like the Holmaddi—like your father. They aren't. You'll see when you leave this Duchy and go south."

"Oh?"

"If blood and breeding were everything, my uncle Jadek would have been a good man, like his brother—my father. He—he wasn't; he chose another way. It's what you want, your choice, not just what your blood brought you." He'd gone back to his red string. "One thing I can tell you for certain: That temper will cost you dearly. You can't afford to be eccentric, arrogant, and crotchety until you're old, at least a Pale Yellow Sash, preferably wealthy, and well known for your skills. At that point your clients and your students will forgive you plenty, if you're good enough. Though I still think it's no decent way to be. I've dealt with too many aged, crotchety Wielders; they're too hidebound to be good, and too overbearing to be proper instructors. But no one puts up with an arrogant and temperamental novice. Including me, before you ask. Because it bores me, and because I know, from my own experience, that you'll never even attain a Dark Blue Sash unless you learn to control the anger or redirect it." She shook her head, sighed faintly. "I can see it in your eyes, I make it sound so simple." She consciously mimicked him; the least, embarrassed grin twisted his lips for one moment. "You can do that, learn that kind of control. I did—and, after all, I'm merely a female."

He let the wad of string slip from hand to hand, finally began picking the snarls from the long loop. "You laugh at me."

"No. If anything, I'd still like to strangle you for wasting all this time. You notice I'm controlling the urge, though." That brought another of those brief, abashed grins. "I'm going back to make certain the soup is all right; you practice that, do one without pause, bring me the finished pattern—and I'll show you how to braid a three-part Thread rope after we eat."

The broth was bubbling, perhaps a little too thick; Lialla added a dipper of water, sat cross-legged on the hearth, and soaked up what heat she could. *Fall in Holmaddan City— brrr. Vuhlem's welcome to this.* There might be snow in Zelharri already, in the higher passes; there might be fog and rain. It couldn't possibly be this foggy, rainy, and *cold* all at once. "And if it isn't foggy, rainy, and cold here, that's only because it's *windy,* rainy, and cold. Wretched northern coast." Her hands and feet were a little warmer; now her back was chilled, despite the layers of wool. She sighed, shifted around, and warmed her back.

Kepron still stood close to the window, his back to her, but he was hard at work, building a complex cradle of red string and working it back out to a simple loop. She let her eyes move past him, glanced out the long window across the chamber from him. Gray sky, of course; she could just see the tops of two of the compound's trees, red and yellow leaves swaying back and forth. A thin drift of fog partly obscured them for a moment, was gone. An even thinner line of washed blue sky and light; cloud muffled it at once, and the vast room seemed even darker than it had before.

She could hear noise out there, beyond the caravaners' compound: men shouting, cheering, a few high women's voices. Too distant to make out what was going on. She got to her feet; walked toward the nearest window, but the outer walls on the boulevard side of the compound were too high for her to make out anything other than the bright red and yellow awnings on the dyer's across the way. She shrugged, wrapped her arms around herself, and went back to the fire.

The lower door slammed against the wall and back into its frame, resoundingly; footsteps clattered up the narrow stairs. Sil and Ryselle burst into the room moments later, both carrying several small bundles, both out of breath. Sil knelt to set her things by the fire; she set Ryselle's bags down and rubbed her hands together briskly. "Oh, it's not at all *nice* out there just now, horribly chill, windy, and raining once again. But you'll never think what we just saw!" She looked up; Lialla shook her head. "Vuhlem! The man himself, actually taking a ride along the main street with a dozen of his household men at his back. Waving at people and smiling—I think it was meant to be a smile," she added doubtfully.

Ryselle crouched on the other side of the hearth and tested the broth. "It looked like no smile I ever saw, not even my father's," she put in. "This needs salt," she added briefly.

"I added a little water, nothing else," Lialla said. "Vuhlem? What was *he* doing out this far from his palace, and in such weather?"

"No idea," Sil replied. "Unless—the rumor Green Arrow's grandmother sent back via Silver Fishers?"

"That wasn't wholly rumor, that was a message from Sikkre. Vuhlem's said to be in Dro Pent, with an army, and in full control of the Duke's palace *and* his lady. But the message was from the Thukara, and I know Jen, she'd never pass mere gossip on such an important matter."

"It sounds like wildest rumor to me," Sil said. "Except that it involves Vuhlem, who has too many soldiers, too much money, and access to the wrong kinds of friends."

Lialla snorted. "Friends—you mean the Lasanachi. But why would he—wait. You think Vuhlem's making certain he's seen in Holmaddan City?"

"I don't know why else he'd be out in the public streets; you aren't familiar with the city the way I am, either of you, and I can tell you this is the first time I've ever seen the man about like this, or heard of him doing such a thing. It's well known among the caravaners that he despises his commoners, and won't mix with them at any price. But there's rumor in the market because of all the problems down south on the Emperor's birthday, and Shesseran's expelling the foreigners' ships. Not that it matters greatly to most of the local men that the borders and the harbors are blocked, of course; not here." Sil's brow wrinkled, and she was silent for some moments. "Mmmm. Confusing: I can't think why Vuhlem would be out in the streets just to prove he's in his own Duchy, either. There's no local rumor about him being gone, and why would he care about Podhru gossip, so far north as he is?"

"There aren't any Emperor's men in the city at present?"

"Mmmm—well, you know, Lialla, that's just possible; even though Shesseran has total faith in his boyhood friend. Better yet, even a man like the baker knows Shesseran's Heir wouldn't trust Vuhlem to empty his chamber pots. If I were Vuhlem, I'd assume Afronsan has men in the city, to pick up loose rumor and send it south."

"*I* assumed that much," Lialla said mildly. "With no telegraph in Holmaddi, and the messenger service strictly a Vuhlem to Shesseran link, which is highly prejudiced in Vuhlem's favor— Of course, Afronsan can always get information from the caravans—"

"Well, yes," Sil replied. "But no one's said anything to *me* about gathering information for the Heir—or to you, since you'd tell me. And we're the ones who're here all the time; we're the ones who'd be asked. No, I'd wager Afronsan has his own outside means of learning what passes throughout Rhadaz." Sil grinned suddenly. "Tell you what, though: I would give my share of this soup *and* a year's worth of silver to have seen the look on Vuhlem's face when the Emperor ordered him to give the caravaners back this building and leave us alone."

"No, you wouldn't," Lialla said vigorously. She rummaged through Ryselle's bags, pounced on the dark brown loaf, and tore an edge off it. "I've seen Vuhlem angry; it's a daunting sight." She set the loaf down, ripped the smaller piece into bites, and popped one in her mouth. "Mmm. That's wonderful. How long until there's soup to go with it?"

Ryselle laughed; Vuhlem and all, the outside trip had taken some of the tension from her. "Even *you* must know how long it takes to cook a carrot! Long enough for you to show me something new? Perhaps?"

"Well—all right." Lialla glanced down the long room. Kepron sat with his back to the wall, eyes closed, fingers working the string—her eyebrows went up. *Eighth pat-*

tern—is it really? She turned back to Ryselle, who was on her feet, brushing at her skirts, glanced down at Sil, who sat cross-legged among the bags, rapidly paring vegetables and tossing them into the pot whole. "Sil, if this won't bother you, I'd as soon stay warm."

"No bother," the caravaner replied cheerfully. "Hold close to the fire, I don't blame you at all. And, who knows, I might even learn something useful."

"You," Lialla informed her, mock severe, "couldn't turn that stuff to stew, if you needed magic to do it."

Sil sighed, very heavily. "Oh, well, but I can do *that,* no magic needed. Still, no talent whatever—but no time to dabble in it, alas." She laughed. "You won't bother me, do what you like so long as it doesn't smother the fire."

The sky cleared off at sunset, bringing a last gleam of light to the compound windows and a sash-rattling wind. "Of course," Lialla said gloomily, as Ryselle passed bread, "the sky clears late, so it can get colder tonight."

Sil swallowed a mouthful of soup and laughed. "We have the fire, you have your choice of the private rooms, and you don't have any reason to go outside."

"Outside." Kepron sounded even gloomier than Lialla. He picked up his soup bowl and drank hot broth from the side before poking through the vegetables with his fingers. *Not precisely manners that would pass in Duke's Fort or the Thukar's palace,* Lialla thought judiciously. *But at least he's neat about it.* She set that aside and drank some of her own soup. Eating manners were something he could learn elsewhere, *not* from her.

Ryselle tucked a bite of bread in her cheek and blew on her soup. "How odd; I just realized, Lialla. He *can't* go outside, can he?" Kepron stirred and his eyes narrowed; Lialla hastily swallowed and prepared to separate them, but after a moment the boy glanced at her, at Ryselle, then shook his head and went back to his soup in silence. "I'd hate that myself," Ryselle added mildly, and tore off more bread.

Not much of a truce—it would do as a start; Lialla cut a carrot with the side of her spoon and ate. A long, reasonably companionable silence, broken only by the crackling of the fire and the occasional rattle of windows as wind struck them.

Kepron set his bowl aside, got to his feet, and stretched. Lialla looked up at him. "If you'd like something to do besides sit and use your fingers and your mind, I have a suggestion." She indicated the six-foot ash staff resting against the wall, next to the fireplace; the wood was a pale yellow, a replacement for the staff she'd left perforce in Village North Bay when Vuhlem's soldiers hauled her in. "You asked about my bo; interested in learning how to use it? Any of you?"

Kepron looked at her, at the staff. "It's an outlander thing, isn't it? But I thought the outlanders used those metal things—guns?"

"No, that's the foreigners—the Mer Khani and others. I learned that"—she indicated the bo with her chin—"from a genuine outlander. I'm not so good with it, but it's still decent protection when the magic won't respond for some reason. That does happen, even to the best, so it can't hurt to have backup. But it's also a good way to get your blood moving."

Ryselle cleared her throat tentatively. "Um—I could use that also."

"The weapon or the work?" Sil demanded.

Ryselle shrugged. "Well—both. I'm used to hard work, and I fear I'll grow soft here, without my goats and my chores. But—to learn some kind of weapon, to learn how to guard myself. Yes, I would like that." She took the empty bowls from Sil and stacked them close to the fire, then tested the pot of water with one finger and eased bowls and spoons into it before resettling it in hot ashes.

Kepron picked up the staff, turned it over in his hands and eyed it doubtfully. "It's simply—it's only a stick!"

"Just so," Lialla said. "It's not a sword, but it can work against swords. I know; I've done it myself." The boy gave her an even more doubtful look, ran his hands over the staff, and set it against the wall again.

"Swords. My father knew nothing of them. Save when there was a ceremony, he wore one with his dress breeks. Dull blade, shining hilt, like all the other men in his class. My company—if I had stayed there, another year or so, they would have taught me pike maneuvers, perhaps given me a bow and arrows, and such a sword to wear in parades or ceremonies. Only certain men learn sword, and never young ones, or sons of common soldiers."

"Duke's sons don't always learn, either," Lialla said. "My brother may be Duke of Zelharri, but he still can't do more with a sword than wear it with his dress breeks. And he prefers a dull blade; a sharp one might cut him at the wrong place and time. Still—he's good with one of these. Good enough."

Sil laughed and got to her feet. "This is less my kind of activity than your magic, sin-Duchess. I believe I'll take a walk, maybe see if Emios will want any of the new shipment of flour when it comes."

"What—another two days?" Lialla demanded.

"No, that's the five-wagon Blue Quail company from Cornekka. They'll be here long enough to reshoe horses and get fresh meal for themselves. Red Hawk comes up from Sikkre in four days, if I reckon properly, and they should have rice flour this time."

"Four days—what's the hurry?" Lialla stood and shook out her wide-legged britches. "Especially since you don't know if they'll even have the stuff? You can't *like* walking around in the dark and in this sort of weather?"

"It doesn't chill me the way it does you. And, besides, it can't hurt to get the gossip about Vuhlem while it's fresh."

"Oh." Lialla considered this. "Well—I suppose it can't. Be careful—" She shook her head, laughed. Sil was grinning widely. "Yes, well, of all the people I don't have to tell *that*. All the same, don't step on the wrong toes out there."

"Trust me," Sil replied gravely. "I behave out there as though the Duchy were in the power of a hot-tempered old bear of a Duke—will that serve?" She looked at Ryselle. "Don't wash those, you've taken that task the past five days, and we said we'd share the messy jobs. I'll take care of them when I return." She drew the folded, beaded scarf from her hair, bundled it into a deep pocket, fished the heavier and more practical brown wool out of another. "I'll be back before the market closes for the night."

"You'd better," Lialla said mildly. "If I have to come rescue you—" Sil laughed, waved a hand, drew her dark, heavy shawl from its hook, wrapped it around her shoulders, and clattered down the steps.

At the bottom, she drew the door closed behind her, glanced toward the windows above, and hurried across the barren courtyard, settling the brown woolen head scarf across her ears and firmly tucking the ends about her throat. *Brrr. Not remotely nice out here tonight. If Lialla had sorted out what I really had in mind for tonight—well, fortunately she was distracted enough by her two novices that I doubt she had the least suspicion of the gap between what I told her and what I meant.* Sil cast a practiced glance at the sky as she slipped into the narrow, deserted street. The moon was half-full, high and blue-white enough to cast strong shadows when visible, but thick clouds had begun to roll in since sunset, and when the moon slid behind them, it was black indeed. *My night vision is better than even the grandmother's, and a night like this makes the perfect moment to overlook Vuhlem's palace and his docks.*

Later, on the way back to the compound, she could gather gossip from the market and talk to some of the women whose men spent the night hours in the local alehouses. *If there's nothing to see out on the shore, Lialla won't even need to know where I went.* She drew the shawl more snugly against her arms as a chill breeze swept down the street, rattling dry leaves.

The upper market was still going strong, despite the early dark, the wind, the threat of rain; the lower market would be mostly men at this hour. Sil evaded the lower by cutting through alleys and two quiet residential streets, eventually coming out near the northern edge of town and the narrow road that connected the city to the Duke's palace.

Like the upper market, despite the hour and the chill there was traffic along the road: Vuhlem preferred to have his provisions brought in late, when he wouldn't be bothered by the sight of so many carts and wagons. Sil took up a position behind a cart piled high with fresh hay, cast a cautious look around her as the sky lightened: Three women came down the road heading back toward the city, one with an empty two-handled basket resting against her hip. Not far ahead of the hay cart, two boys trudged along with a cage full of dark-feathered birds. *I don't stand out at all,* she decided. The long shawl covered all but the lower edges of the wide-legged caravaner britches, and her head scarf, the shawl itself, were Holmaddi. *Daresay some would find it a matter for interest, a female caravaner going to the palace.* Vuhlem surely one of them. Well, but she wasn't going to bring herself to the Duke's attention, was she?

The moon went behind cloud once more; the driver behind her cursed roundly, and when one of the city-bound women laughed, he cursed her as well.

Twenty or so paces from the heavy gates that blocked entry to the palace grounds: Sil slowed, dropping back behind one wagon and then another, her eye on the sky; the moon vanished under thick, black clouds. *No one coming this way, and the ledge is just there.* She moved quickly,

crossed the road, and slid down the sandy bank, fetching up
against prickly brush. *Around this, quietly and quickly—
there.* She'd be invisible from the road, even if the clouds
suddenly moved off; from the water's edge or offshore, she
shouldn't be seen at all, if she stayed in the shadow of the
wind-stunted trees that edged the high ground.

Fortunately, her night vision really was good: The narrow bit of open ground was uneven, rocky in places and
wet where water had pooled after the recent rains. There
were supposed to be ravines along here. *Walk carefully.
You want to get back to the compound in one piece.* A broken leg could prove highly embarrassing—at best.

She nearly fell anyway, when the ground dropped
steeply and unexpectedly away. Sil cursed under her breath
and clung to chill, damp rock, waiting for the moon to reap-
pear. "Not even that deep or long," she grumbled when it
did, and she could see around her once more. She crossed
uneven ground quickly, scrambled up the opposite bank,
and moved on. Ten paces further along the ledge, another
sharp dropoff, but this one seemed more useful. *Trees
along the east side and it's both deep and broad at the far
end.* It was steeper than the last one, the dirt and rock unpleasantly crumbly; she clung to exposed roots and brush to
let herself down as the moon went under cover once again.
Wind soughed through the branches above her. Sil felt her
way with a cautiously extended foot, worked slowly down
to the end of the cut and crouched down to catch her breath;
one hand clung firmly to one of the thick, slightly prickly
bushes. *I think I remember this seemed a good idea when I
first had it,* she thought dryly.

At first, there wasn't much to see, even with the sky
clearing just a little, and with the water to reflect the dif-
fused moonlight. Still—the ledge wasn't as high at this
point as it had been, and the beach was fairly shallow; there
were two long Lasanachi ships rocking gently on either
side of the long stone mole, their sails stowed, their decks

deserted. Docks: to her right, built into the base of the cliff that held Vuhlem's palace; a stack of unremarkable crates away from the water, mostly under the cliff shadow. Sil narrowed her eyes and stared hard: Caravaner rumor had it that there were passages inside, so goods could be brought across the docks, inside and up to the palace without need of the broad path she could see leading in the direction of the outer gates. All she could see was the partly lit dock and a black cliff, and she finally gave that up.

The mole, then, and the two long ships. *Not the galleys one used to see; maybe the rumor's true, after all.* There had been recent outcry over slave rowers—not just in Rhadaz after Thukar Dahven's escape but, it was said, in foreign places as well. The Lasanachi were said to be refitting their sleek ships with brightly patterned African sails— which were, of course, faster and cheaper anyway than slave labor.

As she watched, two men came from under cliff shadow and strode across the sand, onto the mole. The muted thunk of footsteps on hard wooden decks; one remained on the nearest deck while the other went below, only to emerge moments later with a bundle. *That's a child,* Sil realized. *What are they doing with—with a pale-haired lad?* Moonlight flooded the mole and the ship's deck, reflecting bluewhite off a thatch of short-cut hair. She swore under her breath; the moon was gone again, and she couldn't make out anything else, except by sound; a child's fretful cry, a man's growled, threatening response—retreating footsteps. The faint *sploosh* of low tide slapping against the beach.

I'd better go, she decided. *It's growing late, and I don't want to face an empty road when I reach it.* Also, Lialla would begin to worry before much longer. As to what she'd seen—well, it might be useful; Lialla could help her decide. She edged around cautiously, stood with care, wincing as chill, stiff muscles protested. She began working her way up to level ground by feel.

Above her, sudden light; a branch snapped. Sil froze; pale yellow lantern light raked the ground just in front of her feet; "I know you're down there! Show yourself!" *Ah, wonderful.* Sil drew the shawl around her shoulders, hugging herself close with trembling hands, and took two wary steps forward, blinking in the sudden light. "Female? What is a woman doing out here, alone at such an hour? This place is Duke's land!"

Sil swallowed. "Um—yes, sir. I know that, sir."

"Then what are you doing here? Do your men know where you are?"

Men. It wasn't much of an idea, but nothing else suggested itself. She fumbled the beaded scarf from its deep pocket, let it slide from her grasp and shoved it away with her foot. A nervous giggle escaped her. "Um—well, sir, it's—you see, Bertril and I came here, three days ago, and—" She froze as the guard slid down the bank; the lantern was suddenly almost in her face and what she could see of the man behind it wasn't reassuring. *Nearly as black-a-vized as Vuhlem himself.*

"This is no place for a tryst," he snapped.

"Well, no, sir—I know it's not, but there wasn't anyplace else for us, and—well, sir, I lost my scarf and tried everywhere else it might be and this was all that was left. . . ."

"A scarf!"

"Well, sir, but it's—you see, my husband gave it to me, and he'll be furious if it's gone when he returns, and—"

"This—wait. This Bertril isn't your husband?"

He was taking it, Sil thought.

"Uh—no, sir." She bit her lip as the lantern moved, taking in her face and then her shawl; a hard hand yanked at the heavy brown wool. Sil let the shawl go. Her caravaner shirt and the silver clan token were plainly visible.

"Ah, seven hells, you're a *caravaner*!" His disgust was plain.

"Well—yes, sir."

"Well, just you listen to *me*! You get yourself back to that compound of yours, and don't let yourself be seen out here again, or even the Emperor won't be of any use to you! It's a long way down to that beach; take the wrong step and you might just break your neck, d'you understand me?"

Sil swallowed, nodded. "Yes, sir. Ah—my scarf?"

"Scarf," he muttered. "All right, you can have a moment to look for it." He held the lantern high; Sil made a show of beating the near bushes for it, then snatched it up with a little cry. "That's it? All you lost here?" She nodded again. The guard took her by the arm and half dragged her back to level ground. "All right. There's the path and that way's the road. I'll be right behind you with the light."

He still sounded suspicious, Sil thought warily. But not much short of the road, she could hear shouting up by the gates; the guard came up beside her, listened a moment, then pointed. "I'm needed up there; I'll be back along this way, though, and I'd best not find *you* anywhere near. Understood?" Sil nodded meekly. "Then be gone!" She nodded again, and moved as quickly as she could toward the road. Without the lantern, it was suddenly very dark out here indeed.

4

CHRIS locked his personal bag and booted it across the luggage-crowded car to join the rest of the bags. Ariadne stood near the door, fingers drumming nervously and impatiently against her skirts while Dija adjusted the new broad-brimmed straw hat and pinned it firmly to the tight braids coiled at the back of her head. Edrith slouched over the back of the seat Chris had used for most of the long journey, chin on crossed arms and eyes fixed on the wide, tree-lined boulevard that led to the San Philippe station. "Too early to see anything, guy," Chris said. He blotted his forehead with a dark cotton handkerchief, tugged his sleeves straight, and shoved the handkerchief into his trouser pocket. The air had become increasingly muggy as the train came down out of the high country.

"It can't hurt if I keep a watch," Edrith replied absently. "You know?"

Chris joined him at the window, arms resting on the seat. "Yah. All I can see out there is, it's hot. Lookit the color of that sky, and there's no one out in the open." He eyed his shirt's long sleeves with distaste. "I *had* to come up with this idea. I'm gonna be really pissed it if all turns out to be for nothing."

Edrith glanced at him, went back to his study of the boulevard. "I can see water out there; we're very close." He glanced back toward Ariadne and Dija; the maid gave Ari's

hat a final tug and went to gather her own things. Ariadne
gave the hat a tentative pull and winced, then slid a small,
tassled bag onto her arm. "It's a good idea, Chris," he went
on after a moment. "I still think so, or I wouldn't have
agreed to it, you know? People in this end of the world who
know the two of us expect to see us together, dressed for
the climate and not like the fashionably rich. If we are di-
vided into two couples"—he lowered his voice so Ariadne
and Dija couldn't hear him over the racket of the train—
"and if there *is* trouble—"

"Yeah. Better safe than sorry, I've always said so. And if
there's a better idea, I sure's hell can't think of it. Hey.
Maybe we'll finally get lucky and there won't be anyone
hanging around San Philippe station *or* the docks who
knows us. Or, if there *is* someone—"

"Then they should not know us, separated and looking
like this," Edrith said as Chris hesitated. "Particularly you
and the lady, since you both are so very recognizable, ordinarily. And if the worst comes to pass, then at least there is
a decent chance two of us will know where the other two
have gone."

"Have been taken," Chris corrected him. "I don't
know—it sounded fine last night. Practical, all like that.
This morning, it seems to have more holes than a Swiss—
never mind."

"Since you and the lady would not remain in Sikkre behind locked and guarded doors, any notion has as many
holes as a Swiss," Edrith said.

"Like it's safe in Sikkre anyway," Chris said gloomily.
"How many times has someone nearly done Jen and Dahven?"

"Who counts? Any is too often."

"Yeah. Sure. But they got brutes with broadswords all
around 'em, and so far that's worked."

"For Jen and Dahven. Remember what you tell me,

Chris: You can hide until they get you anyway, or you can do—"

"I guess so." Chris sighed. "No, you're right, I'm where I gotta be. And so are you. And Ari—well, she's been a lot of use so far. I'd never have picked up on a bunch of important stuff, if I'd talked her into staying with Jen or Mom." Chris lowered his voice even more; Edrith leaned toward him to catch the words. "I'm just—well, I'm not gonna be happy if she gets hurt because of me, you know?"

Edrith nodded. "Remember the lady was not precisely safe at home. And that she knew the risks when she chose to come with you."

"I know. Doesn't make me any happier about the whole—hell, it's all a mess. Listen, though. You swear to me you'll keep close to Dija, I'm nervous. Anything *does* happen to me and the lady, Dija's as good as dead this far from home and on her own."

"And then I am dead, because Vey will murder me." Edrith sighed very faintly, then turned his attention back to the window. "I swear to you—we are slowing. No—you move away from the glass, in case." Chris swore under his breath, backed away from the window, and hauled the broad-brimmed dress hat from its shelf. He'd bought it a year before, on impulse, because it went with the look of the white shirt and the vest. But he'd worn it only once: he'd felt ridiculous and the inner band made his forehead itch. *Me in a hat, rully. Well, a ball cap, of course* . . . He felt sillier than ever now, playing Bogart or something. But a year of living in his luggage had flattened it often enough to take the stiffness out of it. Dija had managed to mostly uncrumple it with the steam kettle and the ornate cast iron she used on Ariadne's clothes, so it didn't look totally disreputable, just—used. Still not entirely comfortable, and the band still itched. But it did the job: covered his all too obvious hair and shaded the upper part of his face. He pulled it down, low on his forehead; Ariadne took hold of the brim and resettled it, back a little and slightly offside, then stepped back and studied him for a moment. "Where you had it looks—wrong. Suspicious. I still would not know this is you from a little distance."

"Good. I wouldn't know you from any other classy lady, with all that hair hidden. Let's hope no one in San Philippe has better eyes than either of us."

The train slowed further, then came to a halt with a hideous screech of metal wheels on track. Edrith winced, studied the platform intently, finally shrugged. "There is no one on the platform, save the two men for baggage and the master of station. Another—wait—" He moved a little to one side and was quiet for some moments. "A family, in shade just there by the station sign. Six of them, I think: man and woman, and several very young." Ariadne came up behind him and looked where he pointed. The man stepped into the open and pointed at something, spoke to someone behind him; two of the children came out to gaze wide-eyed down the length of the train.

Ariadne shook her head. "I do not know them."

"Me, either," Chris said. "Besides, they're going the other way, and they've got all those kids—no one we have to worry about." He stepped back from the window. "All right, I guess we're ready as we're gonna get. Remember, Eddie, Ari and I go first, you and Dija keep us in sight if you can, but if not, get a carriage and go down to the passenger docks, we'll be there. And we'll hang around if we have to until you show."

"Remember I have to deal with the luggage."

"I remember. The big pile with my leather bag on top, we store; get those four cases held here for me, I'll have 'em sent for when we find out what ship we're taking. You can bring the others with you or—you decide, okay? I don't think there's gonna be more than one ship heading to New Lisbon from a small port like San Philippe, and there might not be anything today. Remember which hotel—?"

"The Coq d'Or," Edrith said readily.

Chris glanced at him; his friend's face was blandly expressionless. "Yeah, I know, you could tell me all this in your sleep. Indulge me, okay? If there's more than one ship, I'll wait until I see you somewhere close by and point out the right one to Ari; you won't need to find a reason to talk to me that way."

Dija handed Edrith a length of muted red silk; he made a face but dutifully looped it around his neck and tucked the ends into his shirt. "I know."

"You don't know us, right?"

"Don't know you," Edrith agreed. He let Dija fiddle with the scarf, rolled his eyes when she handed him his battered hat, now cleaned, steamed, and fitted with a band and feather Chris suspected came from Ariadne's clothing.

Edrith settled the hat, offside like Chris's; Chris grinned at him and touched the edge of his own. "Great costume, guy. Once we get on ship, use your own judgment; if you don't think things feel right, go with that, and stay in your cabin. Chances are, we'll stay out of sight the whole trip, anyway."

"Right."

"It's a short crossing, after all. And I don't think anyone's gonna hassle us. New Lisbon—that's where there'll be trouble, if there is any."

"Because my father still does business there," Ariadne said; her voice showed no expression. She came away from the window.

"Well—your old man and any of the dudes who might've hired *Windsong;* there's a lot of business in the main port, and not all of it clean. But we should be okay, really: The local governor doesn't put up with too much dirty stuff, and he's got real low tolerance for violence—there's armed watchmen everywhere, especially along the wharves and around the harbor. We won't be there long, anyhow: Once we land, Eddie and I know guys—couple,

three we truly trust; we'll get one of them to hire a small
boat or a carriage, take us north to Havana—sorry, Mondego. After that, we'll be ok."

"We will be fine," Ariadne said. She *looked* calm, Chris
thought; sounded it, too. He knew she could act, of course.
At the moment, he was pretty strung up, and when someone
tapped at the door, he jumped. Dija spoke against it; Chris
couldn't make out the muffled response. Dija glanced at
him inquiringly. "It is the man for our bags."

"Fine, let him in." Chris pulled his personal satchel from
the pile of luggage and held out his free arm for Ariadne.

The sky over San Philippe bore than brassy tint that
warned of a high storm to come; the air was thick, sultry,
and oppressive. The open part of the platform was empty
when they stepped down from the car, except for the boy
holding the wooden step in place for them. Chris could see
the white-uniformed *chef de tren* escorting the richly clad
family of six and two enormous wagons of luggage toward
the other private car. "Jeez, I thought *we* had a lot of stuff,"
he muttered, but when Ariadne glanced at him curiously, he
shook his head. *Keep the mouth shut unless you're thinking
first, dude,* he reminded himself. Even after so many years
away from L.A., his English was noticeably different from
anyone else's: uniquely Chris.

So was the walk; he remembered just in time to slow
down, match his pace to Ariadne's. Besides, Eddie would
need time to take care of the luggage; even though they
could find each other on San Philippe's small waterfront,
he'd prefer to keep the other two in sight as much as possible. *In case someone spots us right away; my lousy luck,
they'd do just that. Besides, I know what Eddie's like—
walking trouble magnet.* Well, Eddie was responsible for
Dija; that should settle him for the time being.

Ariadne's fingers clung to his sleeve; what little he could
see of her mouth and jaw under that broad, face-shading hat
was set and very tense. "We'll go in a minute or so," he

said quietly, then raised his voice a little; the accent, he decided, wasn't notably outland at all. "Walk a little here, stretch your legs." They wandered slowly down the platform, turned, and walked back in the other direction. "That was a nice way to travel," he said casually. "Much better than ship this time of year."

"Very nice," Ariadne agreed. "It rocks, but not nearly so much as a ship, and the food was much better. And it was pleasant to have room to walk about." She was gazing back along the train, one hand holding the hat brim against a sudden warm puff of wind. "I see them," she added in a very low voice.

Chris looked up; Eddie—truly unrecognizable from this distance—had just stepped aside to let Dija precede him. Dija looked odd in one of Ariadne's hats and her loose, silky frock coat. Not Rhadazi at all, Chris thought with relief. He turned then and started toward the street. "Good. There should be a carriage for hire out here."

There were four, one already occupied by the man and woman they'd seen arguing and eating in the common-class car. They were arguing once more—or still—when the open cart pulled into the street and turned west, toward the mountains. Chris's eyes went up, following the sharp-edged peaks; he touched Ariadne's hand and pointed. "Look, near the tops, the white stuff? Way up. That's snow."

"Snow? But you said it came with cold!"

"It's cold up there, I'll bet you. Too bad some of the cool air hasn't dropped down to where we are."

She nodded. "Storm weather; this could bring the bad winds."

"Swell. All we need is a hurricane." Chris picked out the only closed carriage. "None of those open carriages for me, I think we could use the shade. Driver—you take up to the port? Um—*à la havre, por favor?*" Ariadne winced and closed her eyes.

*   *   *

If anything, it was hotter down by the piers; brassy sunlight
reflected blindingly off the water, and there was no wind
whatsoever. Chris's nose wrinkled as they passed a line of
small, open fishing boats, where dark, barely clad men
cleaned baskets of fish and tossed the orts to a shrieking
flock of gulls: The smell hit him like a blow. Ariadne
gasped and fumbled for her handkerchief; the carriage sped
up a little, and with one last turn, pulled to a halt next to a
tall stone building. The driver handed Ariadne out, took
Chris's silver, and drove away. Chris glanced back the way
they'd come, long enough to assure himself that Eddie and
Dija were in sight, then went inside.

Not quite an hour later, Chris handed another silver coin to
the boy who'd packed their bags and a laden hamper out to
the African *Maborre,* closed the thin plank door, and set the
bar across it. Ariadne dropped her purse on the tiny cabin's
only surface—other than the low, wide bed that took up
most of the room—a table that swayed when she touched it.
An ornate silver oil lamp hung from one of the cross beams
in the low ceiling. Chris indicated the door, set thumb and
forefinger a tiny distance apart, then touched his finger to
his lips. Ariadne nodded.
    "We're fortunate," Chris said after a moment, and kept
his voice low. He shoved bags against the curved outer
bulkhead and pressed aside the brightly patterned cloth that
covered the cabin's only window; the glass was ancient,
handblown, and he couldn't see a thing through it, but at
least it let in some light. It didn't open, but even if it had,
there wouldn't have been room for anyone larger than his
three-year-old half sister to crawl through. *Up the side of
the ship, in the middle of the ocean? Reality check, Cray.* A
little fresh air would have been nice—but there wasn't any
that qualified as *fresh* around here, not in his books. "It's
plain but clean enough. And sailing tonight on the tide.

Two years ago, we would have been here for days, waiting for transport."

Ariadne shrugged, sat on the edge of the bed. "It is larger than some," she admitted. "And the food—that was a good idea, to bring our own."

"Got it from those folks on the train. Besides, no offense to the guys running this ship, but a lot of what they eat even *I* can't handle." He held up a hand, crossed quietly to the door, and listened intently for a moment, then nodded once and came back over to the bed. "It's okay," he murmured. "That was Eddie going by just now. And I heard Dija's voice; they're both here."

"Good." Ariadne was quiet for a while; one hand played restlessly with the fringe on her bag. She fingered the pins at the crown of her hat, hesitated, and drew them out, and set the hat on the wobbly little table. She hesitated, glanced briefly at Chris."There is room enough for two here on this bed. I think I shall nap." She drew her feet up, lay on her side facing away from him, and closed her eyes. After a moment, she murmured, "The straw even is fresh, there is no bad smell."

"Good." *Well, what else is there to do for the next few hours?* Chris thought. He couldn't go out on deck until they left port, just in case; there wasn't anything to read, and he'd planned and replanned the next few days as well as he possibly could. The *Maborre* rocked gently on its anchor, small waves slapped against the brightly painted hull. *Lie down,* he told himself. *She said you could. You don't, she's gonna think—well, who knows what? God, how does she sleep in all those clothes?* And how were they going to get that hat back on her head, without Dija? He tossed his own hat atop the baggage, vigorously rubbed his forehead where the band had been, and lay back. *Pillow'd be nice.* Maybe one of his bags . . . he decided to stay where he was, let his eyes close.

The ship itself was African, and so was the captain, the

crew a real mix, like so many were in this end of the world: everything from WASPy-looking types to a flat-faced South American, to the blue-black elegant-looking fellow who'd shown them below decks and pointed out the cabin. Everything in between. No one even vaguely familiar to him. *Lots of people down here that aren't involved in Zero, or working for Dupret,* he reminded himself. The French spoken up there bothered him—a little. But so many of the crews, especially the mixed ones like this, used French as a base language. Nearly everyone spoke or understood a little of it, this end of the world.

There might still be passengers coming aboard—men or even families who paid small coin and stayed on the rear deck throughout the voyage. No, he wouldn't be going up top until they reached New Lisbon, and then only after Eddie cleared it for him. *Jeez, Cray, you getting old and spooked, or something? Think of something else.*

New Lisbon: They'd make the southern port in something under twenty hours, even if the winds stayed light; the trip north to Mondego would take another—call it half a day, Chris decided. He bit back a yawn. Beside him, Ariadne shifted a little; her breathing deepened. *Mmmm. Half a day. Maybe all of one; have to find someone I really do trust, then there's getting the boat, getting all of us onto it, we'll be hugging the coast all the way around, that takes time. . . .*

He crossed his legs, bit back another yawn. *Get into Mondego, anyway; they've got cable laid back to the Peninsula and up to the Mainland. I can send wires to let Jen and the Heir know we're okay, see if one of my contacts up in New Amsterdam can't do some record searching for me.* Funny: having to get someone else to do that for him. *Yah. But I'm not an American anymore, am I? And like I'd know how to do a search like what we need, anyway.* Get—yeah, there were a couple guys he'd worked with in the capitol, they'd made good money off his deals and so far as he knew neither had any connection with steel. Maybe wait for an answer from Jen or Afronsan—or both—before he wired north. *If the old dude hasn't cut the wires, that is.* Well, this wasn't the place to worry about *that*. He yawned widely, folded his arms across his chest, and fell asleep.

He woke some time later, too warm, disoriented, a little queasy from the motion of the ship, which was rocking a little more forcefully, and what felt like three directions at once. Ariadne sat cross-legged on the end of the bed, rummaging through the hamper. "I heard someone, just now," she said quietly. A brief smile. "In French worse than yours. The anchor comes up shortly—a little early because they think there may be wind, and this is no place for a ship to face it. They anchor again in deep water, and wait for daylight. Will you have bread, fruit?"

"Mmmm." He yawned, sat up, and stretched. "Better eat while I can, I suppose. Gets too rough, I won't want to. Let's see—bread and some of that stuff in the pot." She handed him a napkin, followed by two flat, large rolls, a knife, a black-glazed clay pot, and an orange. "You're eating?"

"I did, already. Just now." She drew out the wine flask, poured a little into one of the clay cups, sniffed warily, shrugged, and drank. "Not so bad. A little tart, you would not care for it."

"No. The orange'll do fine, thanks." He broke one roll in half, pried the top from the pot, slathered his bread thickly, and bit into it. "Mmm, gotta get this stuff into Rhadaz, even if no one wants it but me."

Ariadne took the knife from him, scraped a little onto her finger, and tried it. "It tastes of nuts."

"It is. Had something like it back home; boy, do I miss peanut butter." This didn't taste like peanuts, of course; the texture was the same, though, the stuff as filling—and the

green feeling subsided as he ate. He finished the second
roll, cut the orange into quarters, and bit into it. Water
would've been nice—but not San Philippe water, Chris
thought. Nothing along this end of the coast, actually; the
orange would have to do. He took the damp cloth Ariadne
held out, wiped his hands and mouth; his moustache was
sticky with nut butter. "Think I'll live now." He jumped as
men strode up the passage, and someone shouted down the
hatch. French—he couldn't make out what. Ariadne was
right; someone's accent was atrocious.

"They raise the anchor," Ariadne said. A moment later,
chain rattled against the hull; the ship turned and began to
gather speed. Deep orange sunlight slid across the bed, was
gone. Chris got unsteadily to his feet as Ariadne repacked
the hamper. "Better make a light while we can still see to
find the lantern."

Across the passageway and two doors down, Edrith pressed
his ear against the door, then came back and sat on the edge
of the bed. "That was crew; we are on the way." He spoke
Rhadazi, his voice very low. Dija gazed at the door; her
hands were trembling. "They are all right down there. Once
we clear the harbor and halt again, I will go up top and look
about."

"If the wrong person sees you—"

She has reason to be nervous, Edrith reminded himself.
*This far from home for the first time, I was nervous and so
was Chris. And we've probably frightened her badly, all
that's happened and now these precautions. Don't be impatient with her for this.* "It's all right, no one came aboard
after us, and I saw no one who is trouble. Besides, it is dark
up there and no one ever recognizes me. Why don't you get
some sleep? Better to be fresh when we reach New Lisbon,
don't you think?"

She sighed, then nodded and set Ariadne's hat atop their
luggage so she could lay down. Her eyes closed. Edrith got

up to lower the flame on the little lamp and sat, back against the outer bulkhead. *She won't sleep. Well, I doubt I will either, even if I am certain the ship is clean; nothing about this whole last trip has gone right.* He twisted partway around so he could look up at the narrow little window; it was getting dark out there. By the motion, they were moving into deep water. He'd be able to go up top, maybe pick up on some gossip—if no one was in the passage, let Chris know they were all right so far.

All right. Hah. It didn't *feel* right, hiding in the belly of a train and then a ship, not having his finger on the local pulse. *And that is why you feel discomfort now,* he told himself firmly. The only reason, surely; there hadn't been the slightest hint of trouble since Podhru, many long days behind them now. *No one could have expected us to take a train down to here, and then a ship back up to New Lisbon. Dupret has only so many men, and same for those who bring him the drug, or take it to Rhadaz. For all those who know Chris, they still aren't so many set against the entire population.*

Dija breathing softly and evenly. She wasn't really sleeping, he was fairly certain. *I couldn't sleep myself—not the nerves but the water.* They were running with a strong current, all at once, outside the harbor for certain. The ship came about suddenly; he heard men running across the deck and the chain rattled down the hull. *Anchored already. And the ship is wallowing. I hope Chris manages this better than he normally might.* With luck, his friend would be asleep. Edrith eased himself from the bed; Dija sat up at once. He smiled, he hoped reassuringly, and said in soft Rhadazi, "I will go see what happens up there, and come back at once to let you know. Stay here, do you promise me?" She hesitated, finally nodded. "Remember your promise to her as well, Dija," he added. "Do nothing, call no attention to her or to Chris. It could be dangerous."

"I will not."

"Bar the entry behind me. I will knock three, a pause, then two."

"Three, a pause, two." She got off the bed, brushed down her skirts, and followed him to the door. He waited until he heard the bar fall, then started up the passage. It wasn't entirely dark here, thanks to a lantern at each end. No one else in sight, and only one other private cabin down here, so far as he could tell. *That door was closed earlier, it is closed now, it must be theirs.* He let his fingers trail across the thin wood, drummed them lightly as he passed, then clung to the carved rail as he climbed the steep stairway. A gust of wind hit him as his head broke into the open; he edged cautiously onto the deck.

There was something of a westering moon: bright enough, but sailing in and out of thick cloud. Two enormously tall, thin black men leaned against the rail, gesturing extravagantly, talking in their own language. Farther along the rail, two sailors worked to secure a heavy rope, while a third waved his arms wildly and jabbered in rapid, nearly indecipherable French.

There were, as he'd suspected, no other passengers—not on deck, at least. The ship rolled, lurched into a trough; Edrith clutched the rail and, moving slowly and hand over hand, found himself a place near the stern that was largely out of everyone's way.

The air was much cooler out here, the breeze stiff but refreshing. The water looked ugly: all white-capped waves. Still, not as bad as the last time he'd taken ship, with a furious Ariadne and a very ill Chris. *I dislike rough water, and this ocean altogether. I wonder if I would like Chris's airships any better, though?* At least they didn't travel through *water*. He gripped the rail hard, stared into the distance until he found land—not as distant as he'd have thought, but much farther than he could ever hope to swim. Farther along to the south, a few lights—San Philippe, and a nearer light that must be the marker for the end of the harbor. He felt very vulnerable out here all of a sudden. *Ernie is right; I must learn how properly to swim. I think Chris could reach land from here, and possibly so could Ariadne. Dija and I would drown. And Vey would haunt me forever.*

One of the crew behind him ran down the deck toward the prow, shouting urgently in bad French, then in his own language. Edrith frowned. Ship? Boat? He stared across open water, shading his eyes against the harbor lamp and the distant shore lights. Gloom was suddenly broken by moonlight: he could see it now, too, a nobleman's shallow-water pleasure-boat, its brilliantly patterned sails bellied to their fullest. Light flickered from the bow; one of the sailors aboard the *Maborre* ran barefoot across the deck with a shielded lantern and flashed an answer. A gabble of voices behind him, French, English, and the little brown sand gods knew what else all together; he picked some sense from it all with four years' ease of practice, and some of the tension went from his shoulders. *A passenger who expected them to sail at the posted hour and was surprised by the storm and early departure. No doubt angry for having to chase Maborre down.*

He debated going below at once, decided against it. With the scarf, the hat, all the rest, no one would recognize him ashore at midday; here, with the moon playing crazy tricks on a man's eyes, and the deck playing worse, he'd stay where he was, check out the newcomer. Someone who could afford such a boat wasn't likely to be anyone he would know, but Dupret—well, he'd make sure, then tap reassurance on Chris's door before going to let Dija know all was well. *At least the sea is no stronger than an hour ago; I doubt there is any danger we will swamp.* He swallowed hard. Best not to think about such a possibility.

The small pleasure craft was suddenly on them; a voice shouted something in what sounded to Edrith like Portuguese. One of the crew shouted back in the same language, then bellowed at his companions in rough French. A rush of men to the far rail, and someone tossed rope down; moments later, a tall, lean man climbed up, eased his leg over, and stepped onto the planks. The captain came onto the deck and hurried across.

"Albione, *ici*. You left too soon," the newcomer said stiffly. "I have business in New Lisbon tomorrow, and expected to board at the usual hour. You have obliged me to pursue the ship."

"Sir, M. Albione, my apologies." The captain doffed his cap and bowed. "The weather—"

"Yes, yes, well, never mind, such things occur. My luggage—"

His French, Edrith suddenly realized, had gone from as bad as any crewman's to excellent, frigidly accentless. He felt for the rail behind him with one hand, began to edge back toward the hatch. Two steps, three: He froze as half a dozen men swarmed onto the deck. Albione suddenly held a long-barreled pistol. "Captain M'baddah, unless you wish the *Maborre* to continue this voyage without you—*or* to begin a new one to the bottom of the sea—you will cooperate."

"Sir—but, sir! I don't know what you wish!"

"Two passengers came aboard early today, man and woman, richly dressed, she in a very large hat and dark silk gown, four large bags for their luggage—don't deny it!" he added sharply. "They were seen and identified. I want them."

"Sir, I cannot—"

"You can! Your ship and your life, against two who mean nothing to you except the cost of their passage!"

"Sir, my repute, that of my people, of my ship!"

"Gone to the bottom before the moon reaches its height," Albione said flatly. "The price of passage will be guaranteed to you either way. They are no one, to you or to anyone save the man I serve. And Henri Dupret is son of the Duc d'Orlean. Choose, and quickly!"

"First cabin, left side at the base of the stairs—"

Edrith took a wary step toward the hatch but froze as one of the men who'd just gained the deck sprinted across the planks and drew a thick-muzzled pistol from his belt. *Splatter-shot;* one of those nasty things that was good only at close range—like this—but fired a wide band of metal shards and could, they said, maim or kill half a dozen men at once. "No one here moves!" the newcomer shouted; his French was at least as atrocious as that of anyone on deck. *Like I would, faced with that thing.* Edrith slowly and carefully spread his arms wide to indicate he held no weapon. The crewmen on both sides of him backed toward the rail, and he backed with them. Two of the other newcomers ran light-footed for the hatch.

"What's that?" Chris sat up, rubbed the pockmarked glass, and swore. Ariadne shushed him vigorously, listened, then stood on the bed, head cocked toward the upper deck.

"I cannot be certain, I think a boat—"

"I see a light out there—I think."

"Ah. A passenger, angry the ship left early."

"Oh." *Rich one,* Chris thought. *Who else would get a boat out here in this kinda weather?* Who else would be in such a hurry? He turned away from the window and let the curtains drop into place; Ariadne stepped down from the bed and started toward the door. Footsteps hurrying overhead, down the passage. "Hey, I don't like the sound of—" Sudden silence; something crashed into their door, shattering bar and door both. Two men jammed into the already-overcrowded cabin. Chris jumped forward, putting himself between the door and Ariadne. "Hey! Do you mind? This is a private cabin, get out!"

One of the two held a broad-barreled pistol, the other a long knife. He shoved hard; Chris lost his balance and fell across the bed. He rolled, threw himself back to his feet, only to find the pistol pressed hard against his chest. "M.

Cray. There is a man who would speak with you. And the lady." He glanced over Chris's shoulder. "Miss Ariadne, you left the island before your father could bid you proper farewell."

"My father! Frenault, you will pay for this with your blood, you and this *canaille* both." Ariadne spat; the man with the knife scrubbed his cheek and swore.

"Ari," Chris said quietly. "Don't. Bad idea, all right?" He moved cautiously toward the side of the cabin when the first man pressed the pistol harder against his breastbone and indicated direction with his head. The knife wielder backed up, Ariadne's arm in a hard grip.

"Do you care for him?" Frenault asked flatly. "Or at least for the state of your dress and your luggage?"

Chris winced as the barrel dug into his skin. "I think he means it, Ari. This thing—makes a mess, okay? Blood and stuff everywhere."

The knife wielder looked around the small cabin. "There were two others—his man and a servant?"

Chris shrugged cautiously. "She's Rhadazi, couldn't handle all the foreign stuff, we sent her back north on the train." Frenault gave him a look; Chris shrugged again. "Hey, you got contacts, you can check it. Eddie had to go with her, 'cause she only speaks Rhadazi."

"Armann, you ask Tomaso, when we get up top. He had the message that was wired from Marie Donne, he was watching the port when these two came to buy passage. He can wire to the train." Ariadne glanced at Chris; her lips twisted. "Thought yourselves unnoticed, did you? There has been one man or another keeping an eye on that private car most of your journey south. M. Dupret knows how to manage these things, and he has many allies."

"Yeah," Chris said flatly. "I notice."

"Tell her about the pistol, and what it does when fools challenge the holder of such a weapon," Frenault said. He stepped back, held it so it covered both of them.

Ariadne brought her chin up. "I know of such coward's weapons."

"Stay still, and *this* coward will not need to use it upon you. Armann, bind them."

It wouldn't work, he knew it wouldn't; he had to try. "Hey," Chris said softly. "Leave the lady, all right? I'm the one causing Dupret trouble, and she's only—" He fell prudently silent as the pistol barrel tapped lightly against his throat. Ariadne closed her eyes.

"M. Dupret would not hear of such a thing, to let his daughter travel in such a ship alone. But he wishes to see her once more."

"He will be sorry that he ever wished it," Ariadne said.

Back on deck, Edrith kept his hands carefully in sight and held his breath. Noise down there—plenty of it, but unfortunately nothing that made sense above the racket up top and the whine of wind through the rigging. *Dija, I swear if you break your word I will throttle you myself, and let Vey* . . . If Dija left the cabin, Vey wouldn't matter because none of them would see him again. Albione was arguing with one of his own men; the captain shouting at both impartially; he couldn't make out much until the aristocratic Frenchman bellowed, *"Silence!"* Silence he got. "Erionis says there were other passengers, two of them?"

"An Englishman, a trader and his lady—"

"Ah, to hell with the English," Albione snapped. Edrith bit the corners of his mouth. *Yes, you don't dare fence with the English, even so far from their own waters, do you?* Apparently his ear for accent was as good as he thought it—that, or the captain's was tin. *Good choice, in any event. I hope.* They were far from safe yet—Albione might decide to sink the ship and hope the weather would get the blame.

Someone shouting down the hatchway; he bit his lip again. *Dija, you swore to me* . . . But a scant moment later, Albione's men came back into sight, dragging Chris and

Ariadne with them. Both were heavily bound. Albione gestured; the two were brought over to him. "Captain. You have the money they paid for passage, and I leave you their baggage and other goods, that should go far to settling the cost of your ship's 'honor.' And your own. If you are wise, you will forget the entire incident."

"Incident," M'baddah snarled, but he spoke to the Frenchman's back; Albione gestured imperiously. Chris met Edrith's eyes without any sign of recognition, was bustled after Ariadne, and moments later both were gone, lowered to the small sailing ship. The man guarding crew and Edrith held his pistol at the ready, backed slowly away. Moments later, he too was gone, the nobleman's fancy yacht turned and on its way south. Edrith ran to the rail, peered anxiously after it. If they went back inland, he'd have to find a way, bribe the captain to set him and Dija ashore once more . . .

But the small vessel continued south, avoiding San Philippe and its harbor entirely. Another ship, then? The way Albione talked—that surely meant there *was* a ship out there, ready to weigh anchor and head for French Jamaica. But he couldn't see anything. Behind him, pandemonium. Edrith weighed several options, finally shook his head and pushed his way through to the captain. *Poor Chris. Thought we'd all be safe until we reached New Lisbon. Poor Dija; she must be half-frantic, wondering what was going on. Little brown sand gods, I wish I were a wealthy English trader.* Such a man could calmly take charge in such a situation. For a young Rhadazi who had not so many years earlier been a very low-class market thief . . . He drew a deep breath, folded his arms across his chest. "Captain M'baddah." His English accent probably wasn't as good as it had been earlier; the captain didn't seem in any condition to notice, though. "The man Dupret—the local authority isn't any match for him. I think it best if you leave for New Lisbon as quickly as possible and report this matter."

"Report. Of what use to report? They are gone!"

"The French consul, of course. Dupret is an important man, but not the only in French Jamaica; he must answer to others who may not wish scandal over such an incident." His voice gained strength, the accent felt right, all at once. "Also, my own government will lodge protest with the French; my lady and I might have been murdered in our tracks, it is intolerable."

The captain touched his forehead. "My good sir—"

"Scarcely your fault, my good captain. Ordinarily one doesn't encounter such villains aboard a good ship like your own." Edrith glanced around; the small ship was nowhere in sight. "I had better go below, reassure my lady there's no cause for alarm. I'll vouch for you once we reach New Lisbon, of course. Nothing you could have done but get yourself murdered. Filthy cutthroats," he added in a low, arrogant voice as he turned and stalked down the deck.

His knees wanted to tremble; aware of the captain and crew watching him, he managed to maintain the persona he'd put on as they left the train—*gods, was it only this morning? I don't know if I can hold on to this*. Well, he didn't have any choice, did he? Captain M'baddah and his crew had enough problems at the moment. Worse still: Dija would be dreadfully worried; it wouldn't get any better when he actually told her what had happened.

5

C HRIS'S head ached. Midday sun slammed down on the open deck and the air was even worse than that of the day before: thick, sullen, unbearably hot. The sail above him hung limp, as it had for most of the morning, but the deck pulsed rhythmically; his lips twisted. *Sure, Dupret, you don't know from steam ships. Me, too.* The *Amiable* churned steadily through flat seas, angling south and a little east, sending a trail of steam/smoke behind her.

He glanced at Ariadne; she must be at least as miserable as he was, trussed both to him and to the mast. And she had all those skirts, all that extra material. The skirts were wrapped around her legs; she probably couldn't have moved them even if their guards would have let her. She raised her head briefly, froze as one of the two men on guard snarled gutter French at her, let it fall to his shoulder once more. Chris shifted warily, stretched his stiff, un-manacled legs out, very slowly indeed, and crossed them. Didn't help his backside, which had gone to sleep hours earlier—like the arm Ariadne was using for a pillow. *No testing the shackles on the hands and arms and no talking.*

He didn't really need to remind himself; Albione had put four hulking guards on them from the moment they were hauled onto *Maborre*'s deck, and they'd made the rules clear immediately—and painfully. Nearly an hour of tack-ing and wallowing in disgustingly rough waters on that little yacht had brought them here, where they'd been chained to each other and to the main mast, ropes and all. Two of the guards had stayed with them; there were always two, sometimes three, all visibly armed and watching them very closely indeed. *So I'm about thirty pounds heavier for all the chain, I can't move an inch, and all I do is ask one of them, "Now what?" and he almost kicks my teeth in. Like, what, we're supposed to be able to cook up a getaway out here, like this?* It would be funny or flattering—maybe both—if it weren't so damned uncomfortable.

He was very thirsty; Albione had ordered them given water every other hour, but it wasn't nearly enough. *Well, hey, everything's got a bright side, at least I'm not gonna have to ask for the toilet. Bet they'd love that. But the water's probably right out of that swamp they call a lake in San Philippe. Watch me die of dysentery before Dupret ever gets his hands on me, swear I'll haunt him forever.* His stomach hurt, but that, logic applied, was nerves mixed with lack of food—nothing since bread and nut butter from the hamper aboard the *Maborre*, nearly a day earlier. And that orange. He ordered himself to forget about the orange—the wonderfully juicy, sweet orange. . . .

Wonder where Eddie and Dija are now. He sighed, very faintly. If Eddie'd done the right thing, if the *Maborre* hadn't gone back to San Philippe, they'd be docked in New Lisbon by now—and Eddie and Dija would be on their way to Mondego. *Keep that wire office in mind, guy, get your butt up there, fast. That captain could spend the rest of his life in San Philippe trying to get someone to even listen to him bitch. Mondego's our best chance—if we got a chance at all.* At least Eddie would know where they went, when they weren't seen alive again. *Where the bodies are. Sorry, Mom, Jen. Sorry, Ariadne. But, hey, I got no idea how we're gonna get out of this one.*

Someone in the bow shouted excitedly; he couldn't make out what for the steam engine noises under him and the two

guards arguing. *What now?* He couldn't understand most of
what they said, best of times. *Si-lahns!* came across just
fine, of course; probably as well he didn't know the rest of
what followed French for *shaddup! Kinds of words Mom
doesn't like me to use in any language, betcha. Nasty impu-
tations about my parentage and all. If only they knew.* Ariadne shifted a little and murmured, "Land—" against his
ear. One of the guards closed the distance between them
and slapped her, hard; she yelped in surprise and pain, then
spat and swore viciously at the guard. He raised his hand
again; she closed her mouth and glared at him instead.
Chris gritted his teeth and prudently kept his fury behind
them; last time he'd tried to defend her, he'd nearly eaten
one of those long, ugly daggers. Not that he was any good
to her just now, but he'd be of even less use dead.

Remember that, he ordered himself. *You might just be
able to pull something off, down the line; you won't if
you're Purina Shark Chow.*

Of course, if this whole charade was leading where he
knew it must eventually lead, Dupret would meet them at
the wharf in Philippe-sur-Mer and shoot them or run them
both through on the spot. Messy but effective. *It's only in
comic books and movies that the bad guy gives the good
guy a chance to get loose and run. Besides, who's gonna
tell him he can't spill blood all over the docks, or arrest
him if he does?*

Albione stuck his head up through the hatch and gestured; one of the men ran over from the bow, squatted
down, and spoke to him in a low, rapid voice. Albione gestured sharply, the man shook his head, then ran back to the
bow. Albione came up onto deck, ran a hand over already
smooth hair, and stretched. *Yah, lookit him,* Chris thought
in disgust. *He's been sleeping, probably had a nice, cool
drink and a snack—one chance at this jerk, just one.* The
crewman came back; Albione listened to him for some moments, his eyes absently studying whatever he could see be-

yond the ship's rail that cut off Chris's view. He nodded,
gestured dismissal, and came over to the main mast. For
some moments, he stood, hands on his hips, looking down
at his prisoners. Ariadne tilted her head back so she could
gaze down her nose at him; her eyes were chill. Chris knew
his color was high. *So I'm pissed, I'm supposed to care if
he knows it?* Silence. Albione laughed shortly.

"I see you both are capable of learning how to follow
rules. *Quelle surprise,* I did not think either of you had so
much intelligence. Miss Ariadne, your father sends word he
looks forward to seeing you once again." Silence. The least
of smiles moved the corners of his mouth, was gone. "You
have both caused M. Dupret quite enough trouble." He
glanced at the guards. "Get them water," he ordered in
French, then added in English, "We remain out here until
dark; there will be another signal when the carriage is on its
way to the docks. I tell you this now so you will understand
clearly: You will not speak to anyone, either of you—not to
my men or to each other—or these men will beat you
senseless. You will make no attempt to escape, either of
you, or both are dead. Do you understand?" Chris eyed him
narrowly, finally nodded once. "Miss Ariadne?" She inclined her head, then turned away from him. Albione spun
on one heel and walked back to the hatch.

Chris drank tepid water from a metal cup one of the
guards held for him, then glanced up at the sun; hours to go
before dark. But in another hour, this part of the deck
should be in shadow. His face felt burned, probably was. A
puff of hot air billowed the cloth above them, creating
shade for one blessed moment. His eyes closed. There wasn't
anything else he could do; he might as well try to sleep.

Dija was crying again, trying to be quiet about it and almost
succeeding. Edrith, who had been napping fitfully as their
carriage jolted north over a rough road, kept his eyes
closed. *She wouldn't thank me for saying anything, and—*

there isn't anything else I can say for comfort, anyway.
Dija knew the odds at least as well as he did—by now
Dupret's men might have tossed the two overboard, or
Dupret himself might have murdered them, if he were
aboard that ship.

Maborre's captain had been utterly shaking with fury
once Albione's men cast off; he had been all for chasing
them down, or fighting the tide and storm winds to return to
San Philippe and lodge a formal protest. Edrith was still astonished he'd managed to persuade the man to a sensible
course: chase Albione and the man would send them to the
bottom; he would probably also kill his prisoners. *And San
Philippe—they haven't even a militia, only a soldier or so
spread from the garrison at Marie Donne. Hell, they
haven't an embassy of any kind—French, Gallic, any at all.
But why would they side with an African captain of a single
ship, with no wealth or station, against someone like
Dupret—or even Albione?*

Albione: Edrith couldn't exactly remember where he'd
come up against the man, what circumstance, there'd been
so many foreign names and faces these past few years. He
hadn't gotten a clear glimpse of the man aboard *Maborre,*
only the sense of height and elegant thinness. But somewhere he'd run across the man, or heard mention of him;
he'd remember eventually. Obviously, another of those sec-
ond-son-to-near-royalty types, possessed of enormous
wealth, a towering pride, and the certainty of Dupret and all
his class that they were above any law save their own.

So *Maborre* had kept on course and brought them to
New Lisbon, where Captain M'Baddah had stalked off to
find port authorities and lodge his protest there and then
with the French and Gallic embassies. Edrith had been left
on the docks with a pile of luggage and a very distraught
Dija. *Maybe she is right; maybe I did wrong convincing
M'Baddah. Maybe Albione would have been caught off
guard, not expecting a ship like* Maborre *to chase him*

down; we might have taken them back. Maybe anything. Chris himself would warn his friend and business partner against second-guessing the past.

Incredibly bad fortune all around, he decided gloomily. *But I have done it this way; I continue the way Ernie would, reach Mondego, send wires to everyone and anyone who might resolve this lawfully.*

And word back to Rhadaz, to tell Chris's family. Well, he wouldn't think about that until he had to. Beside him, Dija coughed quietly and blew her nose. Edrith sat up; she blinked red-rimmed eyes and turned away from him to blot her face on a corner of her kerchief. "Dija, you'll make yourself ill. Remember that they got away before."

She nodded. "I know."

"Remember Chris is clever, and so is she; Dupret's men might not be able to hold them—"

"I know." She nodded again. He patted her arm awkwardly; those two words were her only response, as they had been since he broke the news to her. He didn't know what else *he* could say to help her.

The sun had set a bare hour before; with tropical suddenness, it was black night—nearly too dark to catch sight of the four-horse enclosed carriage just pulling onto the broad docks of Philippe-sur-Mer. The moon would not be up for two more hours and there were enough clouds to obscure all but the occasional flash of whitecaps, out past the placid harbor. The coachman climbed down and flashed a lantern toward open water; a flash in reply from almost no distance at all, followed by the faint sploosh of oars. "Albione, *ici,*" came from the water.

"Maurice, *ici,*" from shore. The coachman fully bared his lamp; a long boat came quietly in, three men in rough sailors' cotton caps holding their oars high while a fourth stood in the bow, reaching for the nearest rail. In the very middle of the boat, Albione himself, immaculate in white

linen jacket and trousers, and at his feet two bound prisoners. "You have them, sir," Maurice said quietly. His under-
lit face bore a sudden, unpleasant smile.

"Yes—not here. You brought the enclosed coach? Good.
You and you—bring them, quickly, and keep things quiet
here!" Albione moved forward and was handed from boat
to dock. "Shield that lamp," he added curtly. "There may
be someone here to see—"

"There is no one," Maurice said flatly. "His Grace ordered the docks cleared this evening, after your first message came. There is rumor everywhere, among the
dockworkers and the laborers."

"Yes, well." Albione waved a dismissive hand. "Your
master said they are not to be seen; we chance nothing." He
permitted himself a cold little smile as Chris and Ariadne
were bundled past him and into the coach, inclined his head
as Maurice handed him in after the two, closed the door,
and climbed onto the driver's box.

Ugh, Chris thought sourly. *I hate that big, nasty dude
and I truly hate this coach.* Bad memories of both. It was
utterly dark inside the carriage, with Albione on the seat
facing forward, the two of them facing back.

Any thought he'd had of making a break for it had vanished when the crewman had hauled him to his feet at sundown. His legs were so stiff and cramped he couldn't have
stood on that dock without help, and he'd barely been able
to keep his feet under him when they'd rushed him across
the docks. *Besides, I don't doubt for a minute Albione
would kill her on the spot, if he even thought I was thinking
about running.* Save Dupret the trouble.

Ariadne leaned against him cautiously; when Albione
gave no sign, her fingers sought Chris's and gripped them,
hard. His grasp tightened in reply. *They haven't searched
either of us—maybe if no one does, and she still has that
dagger . . .* Well, it was a thought, at least. One dagger
against a bunch of thugs armed with pistols, right. Still, it

was something, and just now he'd welcome anything at all on their side. *Don't forget Eddie.* Ariadne's fingers moved again, and she pressed something into the palm of his hand—small, metal, and very warm, feathered somehow by the feel of it. *Hide it.* She might have spoken aloud, so strong did he sense what she wanted. *Right. Hide something—with the original Mr. Bloated Thumbs sitting over there waiting for me to pull anything at all, and Godzilla on the bench out there in charge of the horses . . .* He bit the corners of his mouth; a sudden vision of Robyn and himself, out camping, Robyn frantic about bears and then Bigfoot and possibly aliens. Like aliens were going to abduct an aging hippie and her bastard kid from the middle of a Sequoia campground—or any of these guys were gonna search someone who looked cowed and didn't have a way off the island anyway? *Chill, Cray. You laugh, the dude'll probably run you through.* Not funny. He gripped Ariadne's curious little offering between thumb and index finger and shoved it into his sleeve. *Seems to me the stitching was coming apart about here, and I was too damned lazy to find someone to fix it—hey. Proves there's a reward for procrastinators.* He slid the whatever-it-was between the inner and outer layers of shirt cuff on his left arm, gripped her fingers once more, and hoped she'd understand. *Yeah. Like, understand what?* He wasn't certain he had any idea what *she* wanted, handing him her fiendish thingie, as his mom would've called it. *Maybe she thinks I'll toss it at Albione or her dad; maybe it's a voodoo thingie and I'll start sprouting long nose hairs, fangs, scare 'em all to death.* Almost funny—except for the circumstances.

And he wasn't all that certain she *wouldn't* use him like that. Her mother'd had the magic, didn't she say that? And of course charms—if it was a charm—anyone could buy and use those. *So what is it, what's it for, what's it do—and why do I have it?* What use was it? The down spiral of increasingly gloomy thoughts was broken when the carriage drew to a sharp halt and the door was flung open. Dupret's darkened town-house door only steps away and, holding the carriage door and another half-shuttered lamp, his man Peronne.

Albione jumped down and stood with folded arms, waiting for Peronne to unfold the carriage steps; Chris could see lamplight gleaming on the barrel of the nobleman's pistol against the man's immaculate white coat. He gestured with it, the least amount, and spoke in a low, flat voice: "Bring them from there, you and Maurice. You two, remember what I told you." He waited until the bulky Maurice came down from the driver's box, turned on his heel, and strode inside. Ariadne gave Chris a resigned look, sighed faintly, and went unresisting with Peronne. Chris edged himself out of the carriage as well as he could for bound arms and dead legs; Dupret's enormous bodyguard grabbed his near shoulder and hauled him out. When it became clear Chris couldn't walk, the man swore under his breath, wrapped an arm around his shoulders, and hauled him off his feet. Three long strides; the door closed behind them with a very solid thud and Chris heard the bolt snap into place.

Momentary dead silence. Then Albione's arrogant, impatient voice: "Light, so please you." A heavy thump; Ariadne swore furiously. Peronne slid the lantern cover aside to bathe the narrow, high-ceilinged hall in light. He set it on a small table and went to open the door to Dupret's study. More light, all at once, pouring from the study and from the hallway above. Chris blinked rapidly but it was some moments before he could see.

Ariadne sat in a pool of spread, badly wrinkled skirts, glaring up at Albione, who stared down his nose at her. Peronne was gone, but there were voices in the study, beyond the open door. Up the broad staircase, on the landing, a dark woman was lighting the last candle in a hideous, visibly expensive chandelier. Dupret stood very still in the hallway just above her, hands in his pockets and his face expressionless.

Behind him: someone. Chris squinted as the chandelier was shifted into position—he couldn't tell. Ariadne hissed something under her breath, got her knees under her and rose unsteadily as Dupret started down the stairs.

"My dear child, how pleasant to see you once again," he murmured, and as he reached the last step, added, "Peronne, take M. Albione into my study, give him brandy. I will join you in a moment, my friend." Albione nodded curtly and followed the servant; the door closed behind them. "Maurice, unbind them." He waited until the servant was done. Chris's arms fell heavily to his side. His fingers were numb, his wrists ached and burned. "Thank you. Now, go tell Marie my guests have arrived, see that the room is ready." The servant bowed deeply and strode down the long hall, through a narrow door set under the staircase. Dupret drew a small knife from his vest pocket and began cleaning already immaculate nails. "You left the island much too soon, Ariadne; it was not my intention that you go so far."

Ariadne laughed sourly; one long-fingered hand clung to the newel at the base of the stairs and Chris thought she'd have fallen without its support. There was nothing wrong with her voice, though. "Yes! You would have kept us atop the hill, next to my mother and under as many *mètres* of dirt!" Dupret's head snapped up; his eyes were black. Ariadne glared back at him. "You think I do not know what you had done to him, to bring him here, what you had put in his champagne? Do you think I am not aware what you mean now, despite this pretense?"

"You know more than is sensible. Both of you."

Chris cleared his throat. He wanted to put Ariadne behind him, but his legs were working full-time just to hold him up, and his arms weren't cooperating just yet, either. "Hey. Inquiring minds and all that. I'm just trying to figure out why we're here, and not at the bottom of the San Philippe harbor."

Dupret offered him a cold little smile. "But such an end for a noble child and her husband! Besides, we did not talk much, you and I, when you were last here."

"Yah. Like that's *my* fault."

"Besides," Dupret went on, "according to the man I had aboard the trans-Gallic express, there were four in that compartment: you and she, a woman servant and a man who might be your servant or your usual companion. But when you were discovered upon the docks in San Philippe and later aboard the black ship, there were only two."

"I told your fancy thug," Chris growled, "she got home-sick and Eddie had to take her back north."

"Tell another one," Dupret said flatly. "A businessman to break from his business and pay two train fares, merely to accompany a *servant*?"

"Yeah, well, you'd what? Have clonked her over the head and dumped her in the bay? Eddie and I don't operate that way, and neither does Ari, okay?"

"There were none leaving on that train from San Philippe, save a local merchant and his family, all known to the *chef de tren*. There were no such persons in the two ho-tels, no horses or carriages sold or rented. For the servant, I care nothing, but your companion—"

Chris laughed. "Sure, I'll *bet* you'd like to get your hands on him. Does the phrase 'Fat chance' give you any ideas?"

Dupret raised one eyebrow, finished cleaning his left thumbnail and stepped down onto the tiled hall floor. He was smiling, but his cheeks were splotchily red, his eyes all pupil. *Yow,* Chris thought. *Forgot what a nut basket this dude is.* His throat was suddenly very dry. Dupret's right hand seemed to have taken on a life of its own; his fingers were dextrously weaving the little knife over and under, back and forth. Chris forced his eyes away from it.

Ariadne shoved herself away from the banister and stepped between them. Dupret stopped. A very long, tense silence. The Frenchman finally nodded once. He looked at the nail knife, smiled faintly, closed it, and put it away. "I see." He turned away, shouted up the stairs, "Lucette!" A muffled response from somewhere above. Dupret stood aside, gesturing toward the stairs. "After you, so please you."

Chris managed one step but he groaned faintly as his foot came down. Ariadne glanced at him, then wrapped a strong arm around his waist. Using her for balance, he managed to get his legs moving; after the fourth step it was a little easier, but the stairs were purest agony. On the landing, he glanced at her; her face was drawn and her lips set in a hard line. "I can manage," he murmured.

"Yes," Ariadne said, but she didn't let go of him. Chris was very conscious of Dupret, two stairs below them. His back felt extremely vulnerable. His knees wanted to sag with relief when they reached the top of the stairs and Dupret walked around them, but the man merely indicated direction with a wave of his arm and bowed them on.

Ariadne stopped short, dragging Chris to a halt. "Lucette?" A young woman came out of the nearest doorway. *Lucette's the maid, right?* Chris asked himself. *She looks more like the kept woman to me.* "This is *my* rose silk!" Ariadne's voice vibrated with outrage.

"It *was* your rose silk," Lucette replied shortly. She ran a fondly possessive hand across the spread of skirt. A deep red stone in a heavy gold setting nearly overpowered her long, narrow hand. Dupret came around them and stroked her shoulder.

"Certain things have changed around here," he said softly.

Ariadne brought her chin up. "I see this for myself." The other woman smiled coldly, raised one hand to cover Dupret's. The other toyed with a small pendant, set on a long silver chain. Dupret disengaged his hand, patted hers, and indicated the open doorway she had just come through. Dim light touched the hallway.

"You will stay in here, for now," Dupret said. "And be grateful I do not kill you both on the moment. You and I"—he looked at Chris—"we will talk, tomorrow. You will consider the way of sense, and tell me where your partner is, or it will go hard on both of you."

"Sure," Chris said. "Like you won't kill us anyway, right?"

Dupret smiled; it wasn't a nice smile. "There are ways to die, and ways. Some take longer than others. Remember that." He turned to Ariadne. "You will remember how great the drop from these windows is, and what is below them. Also, there are men inside and others watching the house. You cannot get any distance, and an attempt to escape will only anger me. You do not wish me angry. Also, if either of you dares try an escape, you will both pay for it. You understand this?"

"Right," Chris said flatly.

"There is nowhere you can go—no one of this island would dare aid either of you against me; no one of the foreigners will, either. My sweet, there is food for them, and water?"

Lucette nodded. "Marie brought it, just now."

"Then—there is nothing else for us to say to each other tonight. Unless you—?"

Chris sighed heavily and said, with exaggerated patience, "He's on his way north with Ari's Rhadazi maid."

"You lie no better than you play at cards, M. Cray." Dupret shoved him inside and pulled the door to. Chris heard Lucette's high, giggly laughter, Dupret murmuring something too low for him to catch, then retreating footsteps.

The room was large, with high ceilings; one small lamp on the far wall was lit, two candles in a plain silver sconce on the table set against one wall, between two many-paned windows. A large bed, hung with white gauzy drapes, stood in the corner; there was a door opposite, an enormous, ugly cabinet next to that. Carpets littered the smooth, shiny dark wood floor. It spoke money, of course, but not as outrageously as Dupret's study or his dining room.

Ariadne stood with her back to him, hands clutching the nearest chair, all her attention seemingly fixed on the table, the ornate tray and the linen napkin partly covering it. Chris gritted his teeth and crossed the room. His thighs ached ferociously and something in his left knee stabbed sharply whenever he put weight on it: *Just from sitting too long,* he told himself. Painful, anyway. Her shoulders were tense.

He suddenly felt sick. *All that futzing around, and what'd I do? Only walked her right back into Daddy's loving arms. Great job, Cray. How's it feel, being about that far from dead?* He shoved that aside, as best he could. "Hey, lady," he said softly. "Thanks for getting between me and the nasty little knife. You shouldn't have, though."

She nodded. "I know. Now he will think to use me against you, you against me—"

"Not how I meant it; he could've cut you instead."

"No." She shook her head, hair which had long since come loose from Dija's fancy plaiting tickled his nose. "He resembles more a cat that way; it would give him no true pleasure to simply do murder, he plays with us first. He is mad."

"I agree with you, guy's nuts." Taking her maid as a mistress and giving the girl Ari's clothes—*that* was cold. "Wonder how his card-club friends feel about his new girlfriend."

"Lucette did not go to him of *her* choice, not even for the clothes and jewels."

"You think not?"

"I know it."

"Well, I guess. After all, somebody hits on a servant around *here,* she'd be a total fool to say no, wouldn't she?"

"A fool, and then dead. Even so, she is not as much his as he appears to think of her." Ariadne turned to face him; her hands clung to the chair behind her for support. "The chain at her neck—that is also mine. My mother's before that. There are forty of them in Philippe-sur-Mer, and each of the women—"

"Your society, right?" Ariadne nodded. "She knows what it is?"

"I took her there, a year ago—she has taken the oath also, it was the only way I could be certain of her when my father first brought her as servant to me. She wore the gem tonight so I might see it, the way she moved her fingers upon the stone—by that, she told me she will get word to Aleyza, who is chief among us. If there is to be outside help for us—" Her face fell. "*Merde.* Of what use?" She shrugged broadly; her hands fell to her sides, slapping dust from the wrinkled skirts.

She's even more depressed than I am—that's not useful. "If we can get out of this house somehow, we'll be okay," Chris said. "You know the streets, and I know people on the docks. And what he said about the foreigners? That's crap. He can't *order* them not to give us passage, if they want."

"You think?"

"Sure. The English and the Mer Khani might make nice with guys like Dupret, he's a Duke's son and has rich friends, but he doesn't run the world, remember? Just a very small corner of it, and some of them might not mind an incident that would let them come take over this island. I know a lot of people, too. Besides, if Eddie gets to Mondego—"

"If. A big if. My father is the certainty." She sighed, very faintly. "I knew he would take us; all along, I knew it." Chris opened his mouth, shut it again without saying anything. "If we stayed north, came on ship, that train—any." Silence. She looked up at him. "I say this not to tell you to give up, know that. I say it so you know I do not blame you."

"Oh. Well—thanks. We've done all right so far, the two of us. We'll manage. Main thing is, we could've been dead by now, half a dozen times over. Albione could've dumped us overboard instead of dragging us with him; your old man could've shot us dead the minute we got in the house." He turned away, studied the room. *Fly casual, Cray.* "And you know, maybe it's better this way, 'cause if he had grabbed us in Rhadaz, way things are right now, who'd have made noises to the outside world about us? We've got Eddie, and you said Lucette's on our side, you've got those women here—" She shook her head. "Okay, it isn't much. But every minute we're still alive, I say it shifts the odds in our favor, just a little."

"If—if you say. But what he said to you—"

"Ah, hey. Got an idea, let's not talk about what he's gonna do when I don't tell him where Eddie is, okay?" He stepped around her, drew the cloth off the tray. "All right, there's bread, water, fruit—orange juice? Really cute, Dupret. Like I'd even think about drinking any of *your* orange juice."

"The thing I put in your hand, in the carriage," Ariadne said. "You have it still?" He fiddled with his cuff, worked it free and held it out. "A small thing my mother's cousin creates; you cannot buy one on the market." She held it low over the glass mug, shook her head as the fluffy little feathers trembled. "Leave the juice, there is something—not Zero, I think."

"You're kidding. That thing detects poison?" She nodded, passed it over the rest of the tray. The feathers quivered once more only. "C'mon!"

"It finds things which are not right—and it does another useful thing or two as well. If Lucette had been against us, she would have warned him of that—and the knife. The juice and the butter; leave them."

"Like my bread plain anyway. What about the water?" For answer, Ariadne poured herself a cup and drank it down. Chris followed suit, and bit into a chunk of bread. "Hope you don't mind if I eat standing up; think I'd die if I had to sit down right now."

"You see I do not sit." Ariadne's reply was muffled by bread. She poured more water for them both and began peeling an orange. She swallowed bread, washed it down with a sip of water. "These were my rooms. My father did not lie about the drop. You would break both legs, or your head; it is all stone out there."

"I was afraid of that."

"If the door were not locked—"

"Guarded, too, I'll bet."

She nodded, set her bread down. "The washing *chambre* is there. If there is water to wash—your pardon." She crossed the room and closed the narrow door firmly behind her. Chris picked up the second orange and walked over to the nearest window.

The room wasn't well lit; even so, he couldn't see anything outside but a faint light down below and off to his right. Kitchen or servants' quarters, maybe. It was a *long* way down to where that light was, though—and as he looked, he could see a dark, bulky figure pacing toward this end of the house. He pulled back from the window, let the curtain drop into place.

Now that he had a little food and liquid in his stomach, he was uncomfortably aware of other things: a shirt that was stiff with sweat; boots too tight over swollen feet. His hands and wrists ached and his face and neck felt burned. He popped another chunk of orange into his mouth, took a steadying breath, and pulled one shirt cuff back: His wrists were rubbed but not nearly as badly as when the Cholani took him four years ago. *Hey, that's something. Yeah,* he thought gloomily. *And won't that be a comfort when Dupret starts pulling your fingernails?*

A faint whisper of skirts; he turned as Ariadne came up behind him, a dripping cloth in one hand. "Here," she said. "For your face. It is very soft."

"I look that bad?" He buried his face in cool, damp fabric and sighed.

"You are too red," Ariadne said. "There is more water in the washing, Marie left the basin full and a pitcher besides."

Chris sighed again. "Bless you, my good woman, that is purely wonderful." He blotted his face and throat, draped the cloth around his neck. "What's that?" Ariadne held up a bit of yellowish paper, folded several times.

"Here—away from the window, those curtains are not entirely a block to the outside. It was between the washing cloths." She began unfolding it, turned it over, back to front, then top to bottom. "Lucette's hand." Chris peered over her shoulder; the lettering was shaky, in tiny print, and in French. "Ahhhh. I understand a little. My *grand-père* is very ill, my father had word from Uncle Philippe, who is in charge of all the estates and moves to take the old man's place at court. Father is furious because my uncle says he knows of the drugs." She scanned down the page, shook her head. "Her spelling does *not* improve with use. My uncle says my father is no longer family, that he may keep the estates here and all the profits, and in turn to expect nothing from France." She was quiet for some moments, her eyes fixed on the sheet.

"That's it?"

"Nothing else, except Lucette says we will talk if there is any chance—and he is certain *I* wrote to France, against him."

Great. Just terrific. Does it get any better than this? He drew a steadying breath; took hold of her shoulders. "What'll he—?" He stopped; there wasn't much point in asking what he'd do to her. Ariadne concentrated on refolding the small note. "I will put this down the drain, he would murder that poor girl on the moment if he even suspected—"

"Ariadne—I wish I could say something besides I'm sorry. Like that's any help."

She reached up to cover his right hand with hers. "I am sorry, too; you did not ask for this, or for me."

"Sure, I did. I could've grabbed Eddie and taken the next ship out when your old man asked me to play cards that afternoon. You know?" She glanced up at him, away at once. "I'd've been dead a couple times, if you hadn't been there. But—" He swallowed; his mouth was suddenly very dry. "I think I'd have been a lot poorer, in a lot of ways, without you."

"Poorer?" She turned to look at him.

"I mean—I'm glad we met, got together, however it happened. I'd hate it if I never got a chance to say that—I mean—"

"Oh." She wrapped her arms around his waist and buried her face in his shirt. Chris gathered her close and brushed her hair with his lips.

6

ROBYN straightened up with a faint groan and rubbed the back of her neck. It ached. So did her lower back. She gazed down at the still form under her and mumbled, "You better come out of this soon, babe, I'll have to trade you in on a model that works. Hell; me, too." That brought a faint grin to her face; it turned to a grimace as she dug her fists into the small of her back and twisted back and forth to get the kinks out.

Aletto lay flat on his stomach, arms at his sides, naked except for a cloth over his backside. She gazed at him thoughtfully, measuringly. Even after so long down, he still *looked* good. Just enough visible muscle—not bulky, which she didn't care for. His skin was pale cream, even paler than hers. *Gotta get this boy out in the sun a little more,* she decided. Just a little; she didn't like the beach-boy look but he'd been such a gorgeous shade of gold that first year. *If there's ever sun again. When was the last time we saw sun here?* This time of year in Zelharri, it was cloudy or foggy—or raining. She surely envied Chris and his new wife about now, down in the Carib, all that sun and warm air. Lovely, clear blue water for swimming, too. *Can't remember the last time I swam. Used to like it, too, even if I wasn't much good at it. Mere thought of splashing in a cold creek these days—brrr.*

Chris married; she still couldn't believe it. Ariadne was

wonderfully, exotically beautiful, too: all that black mass of
hair, those cheekbones, that black coffee with a little cream
complexion. She'd thawed nicely, after the first day or so,
too—shy, Robyn thought. Maybe worried how Chris's
mother would take having a bride sprung on her, or maybe
because of her skin. There wasn't much of *that* kind of
prejudice in this world—still more than she'd like to see.
Ariadne'd be sensitive about that, if there was prejudice
where she came from. "Like I'd care, so long as my kid's
happy. Wonder how I'll like being Grandma Birdy. Lordy,
what a thought. Bet they'll be pretty kids, though." Chris a
daddy; *there* was a thought for sure.

She glanced over her shoulder, toward the brightly burning fire. Iana and her brother were almost in their nurse's
lap, listening raptly as Frisa told them a story, her face ani-
mated, her hands constantly moving, bringing it all to life.
Robyn couldn't hear anything but an occasional word, the
woman was keeping her voice purposely low, the story a
secret delight for the three of them. "Thank all the local
gods at once I found a way to get that young woman back
here," Robyn murmured. She gave her back one last hard
dig with her knuckles, rubbed more cream into her hands,
and went back to working her way down Aletto's spine. So
simple, really, once she'd had a little time to think about
it—all she'd had to do was send word for Frisa to bring her
mother, let the old woman have one of the small rooms
near the kitchens for herself and her few things, and everyone was happy—including, Robyn thought, Frisa's mother,
who was much too old and frail to run a small goat holding
by herself.

The benefit already showed on the kids: Iana had relaxed
noticeably the past day or so, and Amarni—he was still too
quiet, even for a normally reserved child, but he wasn't
clinging so much. Robyn had even managed an hour to herself, out in the courtyard, the afternoon before, and Amarni

hadn't been panicked when she returned. Small-step progress, but any counted.

She wrinkled her nose. The steam pot on the little table by Aletto's head was really putting out at the moment. Whatever the healer had in there—she recognized the pungency of pennyroyal, actually liked it (if in smaller doses than this), but there was something else that made her eyes water. "If it works, though."

The healer had been emphatic it would—this particular potion, she'd said flatly, was over a third spell, strong in that and the herbal blend: it would awaken anyone not already dead. Robyn liked Jennifer's healer; she was years younger than Catra, easier to talk to or ask questions without feeling foolish and untutored, the way Catra'd made her feel. Iana liked the woman; that counted for a lot, too.

And Aletto *had* been nearer awake, late the last night, after the steamer began seriously bubbling; when Robyn had spoken against his ear, he'd grunted something in response, she hadn't been certain what, and she hadn't gotten anything else out of him. Yet. She shook her head firmly. *Yet.* The stuff *would* work, was working already, he was going to be fine. "Has to be," she whispered. She moved her thumbs slowly up both sides of his backbone, then leaned forward to use her palms against his shoulder blades. "Won't have anything else, you hear me, babe?"

"Sure." Whispery, harsh, nothing like Aletto's regular voice. It caught her by surprise, set her back on her heels; for one heart-stopping moment, she thought she'd imagined it. She slung her leg off his back and leaned down so her face was close to his, pressed hair away from his face with the back of her heavily lotioned hand. Aletto blinked rapidly, licked his lips.

"Aletto? Babe?" Her voice sounded no better than his.

He coughed, tried to clear his throat. "Birdy. Oh, Robyn, gods, I feel awful, how long did I sleep?"

"*Shhh*. Don't try to talk, sounds like it hurts you. I'll get you some water, hang on."

"Mmmm." She helped him roll over, pulled the bed-clothes up, and tucked them under his arms, high on his chest; caught her breath as his eyelids closed. But a moment later, they fluttered open again. "Wobbly," he managed. "Feel—like a leftover drunk. Except—except I don't . . . " He frowned, shook his head faintly.

She managed something like a smile. "*Shhh*. We'll talk later. Kids are concerned about you." She went over to the fire and knelt.

"Hey, you two, your dad just woke up. Wanna come say hi?" Iana scrambled to her feet, her eyes enormous; Amarni let Robyn help him up, then clutched his sister's hand. "It's okay, honest. He's still kind of sick, but I bet anything he'd like to see you." She got back up; her knees creaked. "Frisa, would you mind getting me the jug of drinking water, over by the door? And then see if you can't get someone to go find Zepiko."

"Of course, madam." The nurse smoothed Amarni's hair. "It's all right, young master, your father's awake, just like your mother promised." Amarni caught at her skirts. She smiled, knelt, and eased his hand free. "Your mother's here, Amarni, you're all right. I won't go very far, if you don't want me to, and we'll finish the story in a little while."

Aletto's eyes were open again. He smiled and held out a hand as Robyn brought two very hesitant children across the room; the hand trembled. Iana clutched his fingers with both hands. "Hello, *principessa*," he whispered. "And there's my boy. Come here, Amarni." Robyn scooped him up and deposited him on the edge of the bed. Iana rolled herself into Aletto's arm; Amarni buried his face in his father's shoulder, hard. Aletto patted the boy's back; he looked confused. *Doesn't remember yet*, Robyn decided. But his basic reactions were still good. Upset kids: soothe

the kids. "It's all right, son," he whispered. "Everything's all right, don't cry, it's all right."

Robyn poured him water, then set the cup down so she could help him sit up; Amarni came with him, his face still hard against Aletto's shoulder. "Here," she said, "you hang on to the brats, babe, I'll get the water down you." Aletto drained the cup she held to his mouth, then sighed faintly.

"Hurts—to swallow."

"It should," Robyn said. "You haven't done much of it for the past few days."

"Days?" He shook his head. "Was I sick? I—there's a hole, I can't remember—" He looked up at her blankly. "I'm sorry, Birdy, I just—can't—I don't know."

It caught up with her, all at once; without the bed to lean against, she would have fallen, and for one terrifying moment, she thought she might be physically ill. She patted Aletto's hand. "Everything's fine, honestly, babe. Don't worry about it, we'll talk about things later. Tonight, after they're asleep, maybe." She swallowed, tasted bile. "Hey—ah. Hug with your kids for a little bit, I'll be right back." She crossed the room on trembling legs, closed the door of her dressing room behind her and leaned against it. Tears spilled over and rolled down her face. "Oh, God." She hadn't really believed he'd ever come out of it; she hadn't dared cry with Amarni and Iana so panicked, white-faced and terrified servants depending on her, Lizelle in a state of hysteria, with the Fort to run—all of it.

She didn't dare be sick; didn't dare cry now, either; her eyes got puffy and red, they'd see. She didn't want Aletto to know how close he'd come, not yet. Maybe not ever, she still couldn't decide about that. She groped across the little room, found the basin and clay jug of wash water, splashed some on her cheeks, and held the cool cloth against her eyes for a moment, then swallowed hard, and went back into the main room.

* * *

Zepiko was there, just coming through the door with Frisa right behind him. She held up a hand to get his attention and cast the manservant a telling glance; she'd already warned him not to say anything to Aletto if—*when*—he regained consciousness. Not until she'd had a chance to tell him herself. Zepiko primmed his lips; he hadn't been happy about being cut out, Robyn thought, but he'd survive it—and more important, he'd do what she said. Aletto was smiling as the man came to the end of the bed.

"I'm glad to see you. I need the—mmm—the necessary, and I feel too weak to walk it myself." Despite herself, Robyn smiled. That silly euphemism Lizelle and his nurses had used—Aletto still used it, and blushed whenever Robyn spoke in more forthright, earthy terms.

Frisa came around Zepiko and whispered something into Amarni's ear. The boy listened, finally nodded, and let himself be plucked from the bed. Iana scrambled down and went after her brother, but after two steps, she turned and gravely blew her father a kiss, using her whole arm to send it. Aletto blew one back, more restrained and fairly shaky, but he smiled as he puffed it toward her. Iana turned away and ran over to join her nurse and her brother; Aletto bit his lip and closed his eyes as Zepiko got an arm around him and hauled him to his feet.

Robyn watched anxiously as they went into the washing and the servant pulled the door closed; Aletto was scarcely able to move his legs. *He hasn't used them in days; don't fret something until you have to,* she reminded herself flatly. She turned away to pull the bed back together; Aletto would be hellishly embarrassed if he came out to find her staring at that door.

So would Zepiko, who was at least as prudish as his master.

The weather had finally turned cool in Sikkre—cool and crisp enough that when Jennifer had gone out to run early, she'd felt like an extra lap around the inside walls of the palace. At the time, it had felt great. Now, after several hours sitting in her office, her left knee was complaining sharply, and her ankles ached, something she'd have to keep totally to herself. "One word," she mumbled under her breath, "and Dahven, Siohan, and the midwife will pull my poor old cross trainers and make me put my feet up. Right." The left knee had always given her trouble, anything over four miles, and the ankles—well, there was the small matter of all that extra weight. "Thank God it ain't all me."

She sipped a little water, turned one contract over and reached for another. Some of them, the cloth deal and the like, had been signed locally by Mer Khani—Alliance—representatives. Auden Henry's scrawl seemed to be everywhere. "Forgot he was in on the paper deal." Big, complex matters, like the telegraph, had been carried back to the east slope, and signed personally by the parties involved. Telegraph—the metal pulleys and the gears for the paper mill—the woolen mill down on the Bez coastline, with its mechanized looms, all those complicated bits of wire and levers, the sawmills in Zelharri—every one of those contracts had been signed in New Holland by Geoffrey Bellingham, countersigned by John Perry. Maybe Chris really *was* onto something, this time.

A note from Robyn, clipped to the sawmill contract, written in Robyn's neat, looping Palmer: "Thanks for new healer; think things will be OK. Had one of the bean counters go through the contracts, this was all he could find, hope it helps. Sorry I snarled at you, R." Jennifer grinned, set the note aside; maybe she'd even find time to write a proper letter in reply. Maybe poor Birdy would even have time to read one: between running the fort, taking care of Aletto, and trying to make life normal for those two poor traumatized kids, she must be about half-nuts. "Get Chris to find us a Xerox machine, she and I can both run copies of ourselves, give them all the hard work."

She took another sip of water, sighed, and drew the third pile of contracts over. This and one more to go—maybe she'd have some real answers by the time she was done.

"Ah—ah, Madam?"

Lizelle caught her breath in a ragged little cry; one of the newer kitchen girls stood in the open doorway, pleating her apron between nervous hands.

Nothing. Nothing to fret. "Yes?" She couldn't remember the child's name; not that it mattered.

"Duchess Robyn sent me to tell you, His Grace is awake, she said, if the par-Duchess wishes to come greet her son—"

Lizelle waved an impatient hand. "Yes, yes, thank you. All right!" she added sharply, as the girl dithered in the doorway; she twisted the apron and fled. Lizelle turned away and drove her hands through her hair. *Control,* she reminded herself. *Merrida taught you how to control your emotions; you did so, all those years with Jadek.*

And for what? So she might survive him, with Merrida's aid, care for her children—properly weep for her poor Amarni and emerge from the box she'd put herself in the day Amarni died. "Yes. Amarni's dead. And Jadek. But Merrida is gone, too; Aletto has Robyn, the children, his duties, and his palace; Lialla has—whatever Lialla has that is not me, not here, not any of us. Changeling daughter. And I? After all this time, what does Lizelle have?" Why ask? She knew the answer.

Her head ached dreadfully; so bad the pain, she couldn't find Thread to deal with it. But she'd never been much good with healing Threads, anyway.

They didn't need her, down there. Still—Robyn had bothered to send her word. Robyn wasn't what she'd have chosen for Aletto—if she'd chosen him any woman. *I know how badly his body was weakened by marsh sickness—and then to bear the rigors of not only the Ducal seat but a wife, children!* Somehow, she'd always seen the future differ-

ently: Aletto in his father's chair, of course, after Jadek
stepped aside for him. But Lialla should have wed and born
the children who would succeed him—with Lizelle to care
for him, advise him, Merrida to aid her. Robyn and the children took all his attention; she pushed him to *doing* things.
Robyn was an outsider, she didn't *know* marsh sickness!
Couldn't or wouldn't listen when Lizelle tried to tell her. If
he died young because of Robyn and her bullying . . .

Her hands were twisting together like things with a life
of their own. She gripped the fingers together, hard, and
walked from her rooms, through the door that kitchen girl
had left open. *(Jadek would have known how to deal with
such slovenly manners toward a noblewoman, particularly
a par-Duchess. He'd be appalled by how slack things have
become in Duke's Fort, without him!)*

Robyn hadn't meant her to respond to the message, of
course. If she had, there would have been proper invitation,
not just word conveyed by a clumsy, green servant, but the
right paper, an invitation Robyn wrote herself, using the
proper forms—something Robyn said she couldn't be bothered to learn. But even simply, "Come down and see him,
talk with him." That would have meant something. Not this
formal, snotty "If the par-Duchess wishes to come greet her
son . . . " *Talk with him. The last time you talked to Aletto*—
Lizelle bit her lip, shook her head slightly. It pounded; her
vision blurred briefly. No! She wouldn't think about that
night! Maybe Aletto wouldn't remember what she'd said to
him, she could only hope so. She'd never meant for him to
know about his father, his blood. Amarni would have been
appalled to have the boy learn of his shapeshifter blood, in
any fashion, let alone such a clumsy revelation by the boy's
mother.

She put that aside; not as difficult as it would once have
been. Amarni—she couldn't recall much of him, these
days; only Jadek. All those years of Jadek—what could
Robyn or Aletto know of *real* pain, compared to her years

with Jadek? "Go," she urged herself. "Surprise them all, surprise Robyn, walk into that apartment you shared with Amarni and then with Jadek and smile at them, go kiss your son."

She was out the door, halfway down the hall, moving rapidly, long scarves fluttering behind her. But her feet slowed as she neared the Ducal suite. She could hear laughter through the slightly open door—Aletto's, Robyn's higher giggle. Iana, shouting something in a delighted, shrill voice that drilled into her nerves, Robyn shushing the child, but not sounding at all stern. For a long moment, Lizelle stood quite still, listening to the giddy, happy babble of conversation in the Ducal suite. She spun on her heel, then, and walked back to her rooms, barring the door behind her.

"They don't need *me*," she whispered. Tears blurred her vision; she dashed them angrily away with the back of one hand. "They take my maids, my—my help—everything, and then they—then they *laugh*!" Little sparks of light just at the edge of her vision threatened nausea, part of an even worse headache to come. "Ah, gods!" she whispered furiously. "One of *those,* and nothing to counter it, because they *took* everything from me!" An ailing woman, whose every breath brought pain—and how had her wedded daughter responded? Not with love, understanding, oh, no!

"She just took everything from me—*everything*! My son, my girls, my—my medication—" She'd helped Aletto and the others remove Jadek from the Fort, though no one remembered *that* these days—well, she hadn't thwarted them at the time, though as a Wielder, she could have. "I could have," she whispered. "I was powerful enough, even then, I know I was. I could have—" But she hadn't. And they'd attacked Jadek, stood there and watched him fade and die. Lizelle rubbed her temples, swallowed. Jadek had mostly been kind to her; it wasn't his fault things provoked him to anger so often. She'd learned how to live with his temper, his moods, it hadn't been all bad . . . .

The future lay before her, nothing good to it: More pain, these rooms, ill-trained servants and even the food wasn't worth eating these days: Robyn supervised the kitchens.

"The window," she whispered. A long, quick drop—then nothing. Everything done. She crossed the chamber, had her hands on the latch, the glass parted, and a cool wind ruffling her hair.

It *was* a long drop. Lizelle hesitated on the window seat, her eyes on the courtyard below. It wouldn't hurt, there'd barely be time for fear. But something that felt like guilt held her back: *What if no one discovered me at once, and the first who did were Iana and young Amarni? Or that stupid, raw kitchen girl?* She'd thought often of hurling herself to the pavement; never before considered what might follow, except her own end. Aletto—if somehow he was there first, if he saw her shattered body, he'd have nightmares forever. He'd done nothing to deserve such a thing. And—be honest, Lizelle ordered herself as she closed the window and slid onto the seat to stare into the gloom and fog beyond it. Robyn had shown her how to think that way—a sense of others, how one's actions made ripples to affect others.

"One thing you were good for, wedded daughter. Conscience. That kind of conscience." She sighed, let her head rest briefly against cold glass. "All right. The—the other way." A quiet end atop her bed. She moved to her small writing desk, drew the materials toward her and wrote, blotted the paper, and folded it before she could change her mind, then crossed quickly to the hearth, shoved logs aside, and felt for the corner of the brick that would engage the spring beneath it. The brick out, her fingers searched the deep little hole; her heart sank. It couldn't be gone! But the jug was farther back than she'd realized, under the lip, out of sight or feel of even someone who knew about the

cubby; they'd think it empty, they wouldn't find the jug.
Whether anyone had known about the brick, or searched
the hole—but the jug was still there, nothing else mattered.
Trembling fingers wrapped around the neck, drew it carefully out. Thin clay. If it shattered—disaster. She clutched
it close; an emptied and well-rinsed, enameled cosmetic jar,
it held all that remained of her share of the birthday
liquor—all but a single sip on the Emperor's birthday,
whatever Aletto might have thought—and the rest she hadn't
mentioned to Aletto that night: a separate bottle, meant for
Robyn. She glanced warily toward the door; no one there.
The bar was in place. She walked steadily across the room,
drew the bar aside so no one would need to force the door,
or force it too soon, then turned and took the five steady
steps necessary to reach her bed.

Inside the pillow that had been the former Duke's, and
then Jadek's—her fingers found the small opening she had
cut in the stitching years ago, edged inside, and drew out a
tiny paper packet, much folded, the edges of the paper
frayed and darkened with age. A powder: she'd nearly
taken it the night her Amarni died. "But there was Aletto.
And Lialla. And Merrida, to convince me I must be there
for them. Curse you to every black hell there may be, old
woman, I wasn't strong enough to bear Jadek, and you
knew it!" She prised the cap off the bottle, poured the powder into it, and drank it down. It tasted dreadful. She licked
her lips, closed her eyes, concentrated on breathing. *You
dare not be ill. Become ill now, and there will be no way
out for you, except the window.* She lay down on the bed,
smoothed her skirts, folded her arms across her breast and
closed her eyes.

It would be hours before anyone came with dinner; *they*
would never come, Robyn and Aletto and the children, they
were too happy among themselves. She bit her lip. It wasn't
their fault they'd found something that made them happy,
even if it excluded her. *Stay that happy. Once I thought my*

life would be so good as yours is. A single tear edged from under her lashes. She blotted it on the back of one hand, then set her jaw, drew a deep breath, and concentrated on a complex red string pattern: twelfth pattern. Even Merrida had been unable to work anything above seventh.

" . . . and he yelled at me, rude creature, and told me to leave," Sil finished. She shrugged broadly, let her arms slap against her sides. "And—here I am." She looked up. Lialla was staring at her, wide-eyed, and even Kepron looked alarmed.

"You're utterly mad," Lialla said finally.

"I thought *you* were the sensible one," Ryselle muttered. She looked, if anything, angry; Sil couldn't decide why.

"I am," she replied calmly. "We needed to learn what Vuhlem's up to—"

"Not like *that*," Lialla protested. "And *you* said you were going to gather gossip in the market. I suppose that was only so I wouldn't have Kepron sit on you?"

"I don't think Vuhlem's personal guard is much for gossip," Sil said. "Not about anything important, and certainly not in the market. Did you really believe I was going after more unfounded rumor? We have enough of that to fill books." She waited. Lialla cast up her eyes and sighed. "And they don't let the tradespeople who deliver supplies to the palace out where they can overlook Vehlem's docks, they keep them on the road, and watch them closely."

"You might have warned us, at least," Ryselle growled. She sounded angry, too. "So we'd know where to look for your body."

Sil laughed. "I'm a caravaner. Vuhlem doesn't mess about with us, remember? The Emperor—'"

"Would not do much," Lialla broke in, "if there was a dead body on the sand, neck broken, just below a nasty drop. Even caravaners can have accidents, you know. But *you* said the guard didn't realize what you were at first;

what if he'd run you through and only *then* discovered what he had?"

"They'd have taken you out to sea and dumped the body," Kepron said flatly. "He might have done that anyway, people disappear in Holmaddan all the time, you know. Vuhlem uses that to keep people in line. Friends of my father's, in his company—I know four, personally, who still have no idea where their women and children went, but they suspect just that: a small boat, and a one-way ride to sea."

Sil shook her head. "Not caravaners," she said flatly. "Disappear is something even Shesseran would understand, especially up here—you think he doesn't know about how Vuhlem keeps order? Even if he doesn't act on that knowledge. But a caravaner—we're sacred to Shesseran, thank all the gods at once; Vuhlem knows it and he wouldn't like the fuss. And if you'd listen, and quit yelling at me, all three of you." Her voice echoed in the enormous room.

"Who is yelling?" Ryselle demanded flatly. In spite of herself, Sil grinned.

"All right. Yes, I might have warned you, but I know you, Lialla: you'd have never let me go. And I might have gathered gossip like I said I would, but I wouldn't have gotten what I did; same thing if I'd waited until daylight and gone along the regular footpath from the city, so I could look back the half league or so along the shoreline to Vuhlem's docks. You can't see much from out there, the public path is too far from the Duke's palace, and besides, there's always a guard or two somewhere around, making certain no one loiters. I thought the chances were better no one would expect a loiterer where I was—and I was mostly right, wasn't I?"

"Mostly," Ryselle muttered under her breath.

"I wouldn't have seen what I did see, and I think it could be important: There was a boy, a pale-haired babe of about four years or so, bundled in blankets. He was being carried from a Lasanachi ship late at night and in very, *very* quiet circumstances."

"Purest luck you saw that much," Kepron mumbled. "And we don't really know that it's important." *He* looked put out; angry he hadn't been asked along, or thought of it himself, Sil decided.

"That's true. Still, I had the luck; now, we need to decide what it means, and who the boy is."

Lialla fished red string from her pocket and threaded it over and under her fingers. Sil leaned against the fire-warmed stones of the hearth and closed her eyes; Lialla's fast-moving fingers and the ever-changing string patterns made her dizzy. "Who he is—I have a good idea," the sin-Duchess said. "I—drat, wait—all right." She mumbled as she caught the dropped loop, slid it back into place over her index fingers. Sil bit back a sigh. "If what you say about the surreptitious nature of things is so, there's only one possi-bility, the Dro Penti heir. Vuhlem has Dro Pent, he takes hostages for good behavior—that's known. And Wudron's the only fair Duke in all Rhadaz, his lady's the palest crea-ture I ever saw, even her lashes are very light gold, almost invisible. I've never seen the boy, he was born since I was last in Dro Pent, but Wudron's daughters all have that same pale skin, that nearly white-gold hair."

"It needn't be a noble," Kepron began, but Lialla was al-ready shaking her head.

"Most Lasanachi are fair haired but they don't travel with family, certainly not with babes."

"So. All right. But—it could be anyone's babe, couldn't it?"

Sil shook her head this time. "But why? Why have a child aboard a Lasanachi ship at all? Vuhlem hasn't sons, and his daughters are too young to wed or make him grand-sons. There's no honest reason for a lad that young to be brought to Vuhlem's palace by sea, and carried in se-cretly—those Lasanachi ships were certainly docked well before sundown, so a babe arriving honestly would have been carried inside at once. This child was smuggled into the palace at the dead hour."

"You're right about the ships," Ryselle put in. She still sounded angry; her words were clipped. "The tide was wrong for landing in a north harbor past midday."

"So the boy—well, it looked furtive to me, and I think you're right, Lialla. Vuhlem has no reason to kidnap any other child and smuggle him into the palace. Especially if he has Dro Pent—the heir would make a perfect guarantee that Wudron wouldn't run to the Emperor crying invasion and foul."

Ryselle swallowed. "Perhaps not. The Duke did take children once, that I know of; the village just inland from us. Took all the eldest boys and held them in his dungeons under the palace, until the village paid the taxes."

Sil waved a dismissive hand. "He does that so often, though. There'd be gossip if it were merely a Holmaddi child and taxes. But again, why would he ever slip a single, bundled local child into the castle by stealth, and by night? I remember some years ago, one of the villages just down the coast toward Cornekka: He had the boys bound and marched right through the streets of the city and out to the palace. So everyone would know it wasn't wise to withhold coin from the Duke."

"Mmmm." Lialla was quietly busy with her pattern; Sil glanced at her rapidly moving fingers, looked hastily away. Ryselle tugged at her skirts.

"You look cold and exhausted. Sit, I'll fix you tea."

"That sounds good." Sil eased her way down, kept her back against the warm stones, watched Ryselle build the fire back up, and edge the water pot into the hot coals. "You washed up," she said, and shook a finger as Ryselle glanced at her. "That was supposed to be my task tonight."

"I was worried," Ryselle mumbled; she fixed her eyes on the little square of cloth, began powdering several different kinds of leaves onto it. Her lashes were damp. "It gave me something to do."

"No, it's Wudron's heir," Lialla said finally. "Has to be. Remember what Jen said in her last message, Vuhlem had Wudron's lady? Maybe she wasn't a proper hostage. Vuhlem wouldn't think a mere wife worth bothering with, after all, even if Wudron might think so. But a son, an heir—especially since he hasn't any himself. You couldn't make out anything else, Sil?"

Sil shrugged. "Not enough light. Just—small, maybe four years, pale hair and skin, and he was whimpering. That could have been fear or simply the hour, but the man carrying him wasn't being kindly."

"Lasanachi wouldn't know what the word meant," Lialla said. "No sign of—of Vuhlem's Triad?"

"Nothing I could see. But I wasn't there long, and I probably could've tripped over them and not known any better."

"Maybe," Lialla replied. "I wish I knew where it is, and what it's up to. Under, up." She muttered to herself for a moment, manipulated string between her thumbs and index fingers. Kepron sat cross-legged, his mouth a little open as he watched what she did, his own string limp across his knees. "We'd better send word south to Sikkre as soon as we can. Remind me to ask Jen if she's heard anything about that Triad. But she'll know what to do about the boy—the Thukara will, I mean."

Sil laughed. "I know she's Thukara. Told *me* to call her Jen, too—and that even after I risked my neck to tell her you'd come bach north. The old Thukar would have murdered the messenger; I'd never have made it back here."

Lialla grinned. "If it *had* been old Dahmec, why would I have sent you there? Ah, hah!" she added triumphantly, and held out her hands. "Seventeenth pattern!"

Kepron groaned. "Seventeenth? Gods of the chill deeps, how many *are* there?"

"Lots," Lialla replied promptly. She looked at his face

and laughed. "I'm not going to insist you get that far: Most Wielders don't make it beyond ten; it isn't really necessary for Wielding, anyway. I just—I like doing them."

"Then why—?"

"Why you?" Lialla finished for him. "Because it's an excellent way to clear your mind so you can work Thread, and it's good discipline, which most novice Wielders need anyway. In my case, my mentor set me to them, and I found I liked the puzzles, better than she ever did. Sil—who's coming in, when—what clan, I mean? We need to get a message sent south, soon as possible."

Sil sipped tea, considered this. "Blue Heron, I think—a day or so, small group. Silver Star, for sure. I have a suggestion, though," she added. "Since Vuhlem's man got a fairly good look at me in the light of his wretched lantern, and just to keep Ducal questions at bay." She glanced at Kepron, grinned. "How'd you like to get outside tomorrow? Walk the market with your caravaner wife?"

He stared at her, finally shook his head. "I can't go out there, you know I can't!"

"*I* think," Sil put in mildly, "that if you're clad as a caravaner, and with a caravaner, no one will look too closely at you. I'm supposed to have gone desperately in search of a beaded scarf my jealous husband gave me; I think it wouldn't be a bad idea for said husband to take a short walk with me in the morning. We all know you can glower convincingly," she added, and grinned as Kepron glared at her.

"You think that's necessary?" Ryselle was watching her, nibbling an already-too-short thumbnail.

Sil shrugged. "Probably no more necessary than Vuhlem's ride through the streets today. What did you call it, Lialla? Window dressing? Probably that guard's already forgotten about me. Just in case, though. It can't hurt, can it?"

Lialla considered this as she wadded up her red string

and shoved it into her pocket. "I guess not. You'd better find a scarf to cover his hair, though."

"Of course. Plenty of things down in storage; there's always a few bundles of spare clothing around." She set down her cup, got back to her feet. "I'd probably better go search out a Gray Fisher's scarf—maybe the rest of the kit. Do it now—unless you don't mind a damp and musty shirt?" she asked.

Kepron wrinkled his nose, folded his red string, and said, "Wait. I'll get a lantern and help you."

Lialla was quiet until the two had crossed the long room and gone down the steps to the stable area; she then slewed around to look at Ryselle. "I think he's growing manners— are you all right?" she added sharply.

Ryselle blotted her eyes carefully on the edge of her scarf and nodded. "Of course," she said. Her voice was tight and trembly. "I just—" She broke off, shook her head angrily.

Lialla touched her shoulder. "I know. She scared me, too."

"If Vuhlem had—" Ryselle blotted her eyes again, this time against her sleeve.

"*Shhh.* I know. As Sil herself would say, he didn't."

"Mmmm."

"Here, is there any tea left? No, not for me, drink a little yourself," Lialla urged. "I can hear them coming back already."

"Thanks," Ryselle mumbled. She turned toward the fire, lowered her face to the steaming mug and let her eyes close briefly. *How many days have I known her? I've never had such—such a friend. She's caravaner, of course, and so she's like all the young caravaner women that men like my father don't want us to know: competent, strong. They're all like that, and yet, Sil is—* She swallowed tea. Better not to even complete such a blasphemous thought; not even to herself.

* * *

It was quiet and dark in Duke's Fort; down in the kitchens, an apprentice fed the fire, and outside, men and horses stood in the foggy courtyard, ready to ride out on border patrol as soon as the second company came in.

Robyn and Aletto had the Ducal apartments to themselves for the moment; Frisa had persuaded Iana and Amarni to share her room for the evening. The old nursery stood vacant and cold; Robyn was already deep in plans to turn it into part of the Duke's apartments, to give Frisa and the children the spacious and sunny rooms Jennifer and Dahven had used that first summer.

Aletto lay flat on his stomach once more, while Robyn rubbed ointment into his back and shoulders. "That all right?" she asked softly.

"Good," he said. "I don't feel anywhere near as stiff."

She worked her fingers down his right arm, back to the shoulder. "Have to get you out and walking tomorrow."

Aletto laughed briefly. "Sounds awful, at the moment. No, I know you're right. I do feel better, most times, when we walk. But I can hardly believe it's been that long—"

"Let the guards and the servants see you," she said, and lightly slapped his shoulders. "They've been pretty worried. There. Want me to work your leg muscles?"

"Not right now." He maneuvered rather awkwardly onto his elbows, rolled over, and fell flat on the pillow. "Sit, talk to me some more." His fingers found hers.

"I'm sticky—"

"I don't care. I just—I thought you were gone forever, all those awful things I said. Then to find out you hadn't left me—on purpose—"

"I know." She gripped his fingers. "I'm just sorry you had such a scare. But I wouldn't leave you, and I'd never take your—*our* children and desert you. Ever. You should know that."

"I wasn't thinking—"

"I know you weren't," Robyn broke in tartly. She kissed his fingers. "Hey, if I haven't split by now, I never will, okay?" He nodded, kissed her fingers in turn; his nose wrinkled. "I warned you my hand was camphor-flavored from that muscle goo the healer left me. Besides, if your mother hasn't driven me away by now, with all her hysterical fits, that isn't gonna happen, either. Though I'm about ready to flatten her, I swear. She could have *told* you about your father, before this!"

Aletto sighed, scrubbed his lips on the covers. "No, she couldn't. She doesn't think that way—and I probably would never have accepted it before—before you."

"I suppose," Robyn said dubiously. "Anyway, now we know. So—no big deal, right? We deal with it, that's all."

"I've probably ruined Amarni for life. And Iana; thinking she doesn't count, that only the heir—"

"*Shhh.* Don't remind me. Aletto, your kids love you. Time'll come, you can say something to both of them about it, you know. I mean, you were upset and surprised and said something dumb; people do. But you can explain things to kids."

He sighed faintly. "You make it sound easy."

"No. It isn't. But kids tend to trust their parents; I know you can't push that too far, but still, a good father like you can explain things and they understand you meant well, even if you did screw up. These two kids will." Aletto shook his head. "C'mon. Raising kids isn't ever easy. Especially if you want to do it right, like we're trying to do."

"And not like my mother did," Aletto said. He sighed, very faintly. Smiled at her. "You helped me see that. She has reasons for being the way she is; Jadek—hurt her, I couldn't understand it until I had you, Birdy. But even before Father died, I could never talk to her, not really tell her anything."

Robyn hesitated. *Go with care.* "She tried. I think she truly did. She loves you and Lialla. But she's just not—she doesn't understand how kids think, what's important to them."

"Or grown children, either," Aletto replied gloomily.

"Mmmm?"

"Headache," he reminded her. "She has one, won't come see me."

"Oh. Right. Well, if you want my opinion, she's embarrassed, doesn't know what to say to you, after telling you your dad could shift; and by the way, here's some drugged wine to take the pain away. So she's putting off having to deal with the whole mess. That's typical Lizelle. But I'd be pretty embarrassed, myself: even though she didn't know what that bottle of stuff would do to you, she knew better than to give you booze."

"She kept telling me I could handle it—"

"I know. I pried all the messy details out of her, after I got back with the kids—didn't I tell you? I tried explaining how it's like her damned Zero, you start and you can't stop, but I didn't get through."

"She doesn't realize about the Zero, that it's got her," Aletto said. He sighed. "If she won't come here, I should be able to walk down to her rooms tomorrow."

"Good idea. If you can't walk that far alone, I'll hold you up most of the way, let you go see her alone. She'll think you really *are* pissed off, otherwise."

"Thanks."

"Sure." Robyn frowned. "You know—that Vuhlem booze. For Shesseran's birthday. How much was there?"

"Don't know—wait." He was quiet for a moment or so. "She said a basket came, a bottle for her and one for me—"

"For you, or one for us, like you and me?"

"Don't know. Why?"

Robyn shrugged. "I just wondered. We located the bottle she kept back, it was just about empty. I just—" She shrugged again. "Remind me, will you? Ask her about that tomorrow." She snapped her fingers. "Oh, right. We got a wire earlier today from Cornekka; Jubelo's captain is pretty certain he can locate the twins' family and get them free; we may be able to let your mother have her girls back again."

"Only pretty certain?"

"Cornekka's a big Duchy, remember?"

Aletto shifted his weight cautiously; sighed as Robyn tugged his pillow straight. "And as easy to comb as Zelharri—I know. That might help a lot. Give Mother the comfort of her girls, give her a chance to get herself together. We'd better not say anything to her until we're certain, though."

"Of course not." Robyn slid off the bed. "I'm going to have the fire banked for the night and get them to bring a jug of mulled cider, that sound good to you?"

"It sounds wonderful." Aletto watched her cross the room to the bell rope. "Birdy?"

She turned to look at him. "What?"

"I'm—I—"

She smiled and blew him a kiss, Iana-style, using her whole arm. "Yeah, babe. Me, too."

Down the hall, the par-Duchess's fire had been banked hours earlier, and the woman who had tended her rooms since the twins left tiptoed over to the elaborately curtained bed to turn down the lamp. The par-Duchess had apparently taken headache powders hours earlier and, still fully clad, slept heavily. The woman listened for a moment; her brow furrowed. The par-Duchess must be catching cold, the way she breathed. Well, sleep would surely help with that, as well as the headache. It wouldn't be wise to bother her simply for the change of clothing, either; Lizelle's tempers were renowned, particularly over a small matter like that.

The woman left the lamp burning very low, then went in search of her own bed.

The room was quiet, except for the occasional crackle of a dying fire, and Lizelle's harsh, labored breathing.

7

CHRIS woke disoriented and aching in a dozen or more places; his face hurt. For a long moment, he stayed flat and very, very still, unable to remember why it seemed desperately important he not move, where he was, why he ached so—why the bedding under his cheek was silky against scratchy beard, why it smelled very faintly of Ariadne. *Her bed. Oh, God. We fell onto it late last night, clothes and all. In—ah, jeez, in Dupret's house, in French Jamaica. Wonderful. Can anything else go wrong?* He couldn't recall anything else at the moment, nothing of Ari's rooms except forcing his swollen feet from miserably snug boots and letting the nasty, salt-ruined chunks of hardened leather drop to the floor. The gut-wrenching fear— Dupret. "Oh, *man?*" he muttered. His face was red with sunburn; that thanks to Albione and his damned open-deck sail to French Jamaica. At least for the moment, there wasn't a brute looming over him, waiting to knock him silly if he twitched. *Sure. Then again, Maurice might be—ah, hell and damn, forget that!*

"Shhh." Ariadne spoke very quietly against his ear; her breath ruffled his hair and her fingers lay against his lips. "There was talking outside the door, just now." He must be getting used to her utterly silent approaches; for once, he hardly jumped at all. Ariadne moved away from him; Chris clenched his jaw and tried to push himself up, but his arms

131

didn't want to cooperate. The counterpane slid from his shoulders.

He tried again, finally managed to ease himself up on trembling arms, then forced himself upright and swung his legs down. *Did she really pull the covers over me, last night—after I passed out? Nice.* Unexpected. Ariadne cast him a scowl that he couldn't begin to interpret: Was she angry? Worried about him? Or something else—who knew what? She turned and moved on swift and utterly silent, little booted feet to the door, where she stood for a long moment with her ear against the panel. She shrugged finally and came back to join him.

"They must have gone on." She kept her voice very low. "I can hear breathing outside, though; the door is guarded."

"Yeah," Chris said gloomily. "Real surprise, huh?" He gingerly dug fingers into his biceps, bit back a cry as his muscles howled in protest. He forced himself to keep on massaging gruesomely stiff arms, then looked up at her.

She was fully clad, light boots and all; he seemed to remember that she'd shed the boots and stockings almost at once the night before, once they'd been locked in, that she'd unbuttoned her shirtwaist so she could unlace the stays. *Yeah. If I had an old man like Dupret, who'd tried to sell me to his fat, old buddy, and I was back locked under his roof, maybe I'd want everything covered, too.* God, what a thought. Still, he himself felt vulnerable in a way he hadn't ever before, not even when the Cholani had nabbed him and pounded his feet to a jelly. *At least they didn't threaten my—right. Forget that, it won't help anything.* He tried a smile. "Hey, lady. How long did you let me sleep in?" She shook her head. "Did you sleep at all? Honestly, Ariadne, okay?"

Her smile didn't reach haggard, dark eyes. "A—well, a little. But I woke late, in the cool hour, and there was no sleep in me. I had enough rest on that boat. I—" She shrugged, would-be casually, though her eyes remained haunted. "I thought instead."

"Ah." He gripped the fingers of one hand with the other, alternating squeezing uncomfortable digits until they began to feel less like overstuffed sausages and more like part of his hands. "Good woman." She managed a brief smile. "So—you come up with anything?"

Silence. She came over and sat next to him on the edge of the bed. "No." Her mouth drooped. *His own kid. Damn Dupret, anyway,* Chris thought angrily. "Chris, I am sorry."

"Well, hey." Part of him wondered how long he could keep up the light tone, not show how scared spitless he really was. Probably until Dupret knocked the spit out of him. Like she didn't know how scared he was, anyway. *Chill, Cray,* he ordered himself flatly. "I haven't done any better so far with the thinking bit, have I? I mean, if we'd stayed in Rhadaz, instead of coming back south—" He caught his breath in a sharp gasp; Ariadne gripped his forearm and muscles protested wildly as her fingers dug in hard. Out in the hall, someone with heavy, booted feet was running. Maurice's sharply angry voice, just outside the door, too muffled to make out what he said. Then silence. Chris swallowed past a very dry throat. "Um, listen. Please. I think—you're probably ahead of me all the way, working things out, this whole ugly mess, but I gotta say something, all right?" He hesitated; it wasn't going to be easy—not just telling her what he had in mind, but saying it out loud, where he could get it himself. God knew he didn't want to get it. Ariadne eyed him sidelong, then caught hold of her lower lip with very even white teeth and nodded. Her glance strayed from him to the door, back again in sharp, nervous jolts. "Ah, Yeah. Your old man and his buddies are gonna come back sooner or later, want to know where Eddie and Dija went." He half expected protest; she merely nodded again, gestured for him to go on. He swallowed.

"They didn't give us last night off on account of we looked tired, and they cared."

"No." She got to her feet, wandered over to the small table next to the window, picked up a small pewter vase, and turned it in her hands.

"All right. You *know* I'm not really going to tell them what they want to know, unless I got no choice, or—ah—or I can't help myself." Her eyes closed; her fingers seemed to have a life of their own, tracing the uneven lip of the vase over and over again. "And—um, they're gonna do their best to push me to the point of 'can't help it,' but not so far that I can't still talk."

Ariadne slammed the vase onto the table; the sound echoed in the high-ceilinged, near empty room. "I know this! They—they hurt you, until you tell them what they want to know." She spun around, crossed the room, and gripped his hands; her eyes were brilliant with unshed tears.

Chris freed one hand, blotted her lashes with a gentle fingertip. "Ariadne, honestly, I'm sorry. If there was any way I could—"

"No." She clutched at him. "We said all that last night. There is no point to say it again. I am sorry, too, if it makes this easier somehow for you. Spend better the time, you and I both, to get us alive from this house."

Chris swallowed. "Thing is, sooner or later I'll have to tell them *something,* you know? Guys like your old man don't give up because they made a bruise somewhere and you whimpered."

"I know," she whispered. Her color was high; her voice cracked.

"Yeah—right. So—I don't know much about this question and no-answer stuff, who'd want to? I do know that I have to decide the best time to slip them the lie." She shook her head; frowned. "I can't just tell Dupret some wild story about where Eddie is the minute his brutes waltz in here with the baseball bats, he'll know it's a lie. He's gonna have to feel like—" Chris swallowed. His throat was suddenly very dry, and his stomach hurt. "Like he beat it out of me."

She swallowed; she'd gone pale under honey brown skin. "I—I see."

"Why I'm telling you all this—please, Ariadne, look at me, will you? I swear I'm not gonna make myself into a martyr and leave you all alone, not if I can help it. I've had the get-pounded-on bit, couple times; I do not like being hit. I am not going to let your old man and Maurice half kill me before I give them some kind of information. Way I understand these things, anything I ever read about them, people with brains figure either they're totally tough and they'll die before they squawk, or they're gonna give up a lie at the right moment. I'm not ready to die, Ari, I swear that. Not if I have to leave you here alone to deal with your old man. I won't do that to you."

"Yes." Ariadne blotted her eyes and swore under her breath. "I—thank you."

She didn't believe it, he thought gloomily. *Knows Dupret too well.* "But—you'll have to help me with this."

"Help?"

"What I tell him—eventually, you remember what we worked out back on the train? In case he keeps us apart and asks you to see if our stories match?" She nodded. "You'll have to back me up, keep cool, and don't tell him anything different. But, um—" His mouth had gone dry. "He might keep us together, maybe think you'll get upset enough to tell him what I won't—"

"Ah—ah, *merde*." Ariadne tried to turn from him; he gripped her hands, pulled her close, and wrapped his arms around her.

"I'm sorry. But—it's what he'd do, isn't it?" Silence. She finally nodded. "Yeah. My luck. Yours, too. Ariadne, you're gonna have to let me just handle this, don't let him even begin to think you care what happens to me."

"Chris, I can't—"

"You can. You have to. They *have* to punch on me first to learn what they want to know. Eddie and I've been a team for a long time, anyone in this end of the world knows I'd never say where he is without pressure."

"Yes—all right, I know this." She freed a hand, blotted her eyes against her sleeve. "You want me to swear—what? That I will not draw the knife? Or tell them where Dija and Eddie went when we separated at the train depot?"

"I know you wouldn't do that. Not to save your own skin. I want you to swear you won't say any of that, do that, to save *mine*. Because, they get their hands on Dija and Eddie, and all four of us are dead. They got no reason to keep us alive, do they? Once they have all of us?" She paled even more, shook her head. Chris laid a hand against her cheek; she flinched, then laid her fingers on his. "Ariadne. What you did last night, downstairs, letting your old man know he had to go through you to get at me—I appreciate the thought, don't get me wrong. But it's dangerous, and not just for you. Dangerous, because—well, it gives your father a two-edged weapon against both of us. If he told Maurice to beat on you so's I'd cooperate, I'd have to do just that."

"Oh." She was quiet for some moments. "You don't dare—"

"Lady, I couldn't do anything else," he said flatly as she drew a harsh, shuddering breath. "Ariadne. The very first time I met you, Dupret's handprint on your face and all, I swear I never saw anything so beautiful in my life. I wanted to kill him right then for daring to hit you. And I didn't even have a clue there was so much terrific person behind that face, that"—he freed one hand, drew a salt-stiffened strand from across her shoulder, and let it trail through his fingers—"that gorgeous hair."

"Ah, *merde,*" she whispered, her face suddenly pale and

stricken. "And what I saw was merely a companion of my father, fresh from a night of gambling and—"

"Jeez," he muttered, "don't remind me, all right? I know what I looked like."

Ariadne shook her head. "No. Later, when I saw you properly, the eyes—such a color of blue, and then I remembered the look you had when you first saw my face—the shock in your eyes there, that any man would strike hard enough to show the mark." She hesitated, gingerly laid a hand on his arm. "And—such very good shoulders, the muscle there, a woman could see that even through shirt." She bit her lip. "I did not realize this at once, but I began to see it, a little here, more there: A man of physical strength, who did not think it weakness to side in any fashion with a woman whose father beat her and forced her to wed. It was—I never before knew there was such a thing." She looked up at him. "I—I do what you ask in this. I swear it, my Chris."

"Good." He swallowed sudden dread, kissed her hair. "So you don't know a thing, all right? Not one single thing about what I planned for this trip. I didn't tell you—because I didn't trust you or I decided you're a girl, why should you have to know anything? Decide what will work best for you, then stick to it. Whatever they say or do to me. Swear. You can't do *anything* your old man's gonna interpret as, he'll get more information out of me if he pounds on *you* instead."

"I—I see." Ariadne's voice was a little too high.

"We both know he'd pound on you, all right?" Chris paused; Ariadne, her cheekbones very red, nodded sharply. "Enough said. I would purely hate that. He pounds on you, I try to kill him, and we're both dead. And if I have to talk before your old man kills me, Eddie and Dija are dead, too. That isn't useful, to any of us. We don't do it that way."

"No," Ariadne replied faintly. Her grip on his fingers

was momentarily crushing. He freed his hand, kissed her knuckles.

"Now, you said you thought your women's group, your society, or whatever, that they could get us out of here. I know Eddie's out there, somewhere, doing everything he can to rescue us." Fat chance; Chris doubted there was any leverage, however magic-skilled women in French Jamaica or a Rhadazi ex-thief outside of it were. No point in telling Ariadne that, though. "So, all I plan on doing is giving your old man a reasonable-sounding lie, at the right moment when he's likely to believe me, because I look like they've hurt me enough or I'm so wuss, I can't take being pounded. Coward enough," he added, as Ariadne's brow creased. "I think what I came up with is something he'll have to check on before he kills us. If I do this right, I can buy us some time. It's—hell, it's not much, but at least it's something. All we have, unless you got a better idea."

Ariadne shook her head; she sought his fingers once more and gripped them hard. "I—I do not—" She shook her head again, and swore under her breath. "All right. All those hours, while you slept, and I tried to find a plan—you are right, there is so little here, and all depends on Lucette and the *Anlu*—the women. I—maintain, you said. I try to do that, to give them no purchase, one of us against the other. I do understand what you say, you make us time. And I know him; he is that sort of cautious. He will not dare—dare to murder us, unless he is certain all is as he wants it, that he has you and me, and Eddie as well, and even Dija. So, I—will try."

He wrapped an arm around her shoulders and drew her close. "Best I can ask. But honest, I won't let things get too rough." *Jeez. I hope I won't.* Probably the French resistance fighters who got mangled by the Gestapo thought the same thing. *Terrific. Had to get hooked on history, huh? Chill, Cray!*

"Please—please, do not." She didn't believe it, either, he

thought. Wisely, she didn't say as much. He was quiet for a moment, watching the top of her head. She nodded finally. "Yes, all right. You buy us the time. And then we somehow get out of this, my Chris."

"We will." She sounded so calm, he thought, and wondered at that. But then, so did he.

Ariadne started violently and swore under her breath; more conversation out in the hall, this too low-voiced for her to understand. A moment later, they heard the locks clatter, and the door was thrown open. Chris caught his breath, pulled himself to his feet, and tried to press an extremely reluctant Ariadne behind him.

Marie stood in the opening, a tray in her hands, Maurice blocking the whole doorway behind her. *Jeez,* Chris thought disgustedly. *Only breakfast, delivered hot to your doorway; toast and anticlimax, anyone?* The servant cast a furtive glance at Ariadne, eyed Chris warily, then carried the tray over to the table, set it down, picked up the dinner tray, and left. Ariadne stood very still, her chin up and hard, challenging eyes on Maurice as the bodyguard backed out to let Marie pass; he cast her a teeth-only grin, then pulled the door shut behind Marie, but before the door could fully close, it slammed into the wall once more. Lucette swore at Maurice as she strode impatiently into the room. She wore lavender silk; her long blonde hair was pulled back into a plain plait tied in purple ribbons; no ornament, save Ariadne's rose. She stopped only when another step would have taken her right into a rigidly furious Ariadne.

"There was a small silver box in this room," Lucette said crisply; she brought her chin up. Her hands were clasped at her breast, Ariadne's token between them; her eyes flicked toward the massive, motionless Maurice, back again; her index fingers crossed briefly. The bit of silver flashed brilliant blue, faded once more to a mere silver rose. Her voice remained haughty, and she seemed unaware of anything save Ariadne. "Silver, with fleur-de-lis upon the lid."

"I know that box," Ariadne said flatly. She had to tip her head back to meet her former servant's eyes. "So?"

"I want it."

"I do not have it."

"Liar," Lucette snapped.

Ariadne managed a tight laugh. *"Salope!* Whore! That box was my mother's, a gift of my *beloved* father, and so it is mine! Do you think it becomes yours, merely for sleeping with Henri Dupret?"

"It is not yours! That last morning, Henri told me what things to send to the Parrot, what others to retain here, that box was never to have left this house!"

"It did not," Ariadne snarled.

"Liar! You took it! And you had no right to that box, or the gems within it; Henri has promised them to *me!*" Ariadne shrugged broadly and laughed; Lucette swore under her breath and brought up a hand as if to slap her, but when Chris stepped between the two women, she said quietly and forcefully, "Hold, I do not harm her, *m'sieu.* Madame, Aleyza comes for tea today, once *he* and Maurice are gone. Later I tell you more. A—apologies." Her open palm cracked across Ariadne's face; Ariadne gasped and swore in furious French. "Swear all you want, *petite garce!* You hid that box, before this man could wed you and take you away! You will tell me where, now!"

"Find it yourself, filthy strumpet!" Ariadne hissed. Out in the hallway, Maurice chuckled.

"Miss Lucette—this amuses me but there is otherwise no point, you and I know that Miss Ariadne will not willingly tell you anything. Let them eat now. Later, she will gladly say whatever you wish to know—after *I* have had the opportunity to persuade her." Lucette snarled something Chris couldn't translate, spun on one heel, and strode from the room. Maurice was still laughing unpleasantly as he closed the door and locked it.

"What was *that* all about?" Chris asked. Ariadne drew

him over to the table, pulled the cover from the tray. Her face was very pale all of a sudden.

"Sit, eat."

"Yeah, right." The food was plain—servant stuff for the nobleman's daughter and in her father's house, he thought angrily: like this room, barren of ornament or anything but the basics, however it might once have looked. The tray held nothing but dark, coarse bread and some sugary, dark red jam to spoon onto it—no knife of any kind, or course—and a steaming teapot. Two thick pottery mugs. "Think this is all right? Never mind," he added gloomily as he tore off a corner of the bread and ate it. "What's the point?"

"It *should* be all right," Ariadne said cautiously. She pulled the teapot toward her, removed the lid and sniffed, drew out her feather charm. "Safe," she said, then leaned toward him. "The box; that was a trick of Lucette, to come in here and to show Maurice she is no friend of mine."

"Sure about that?" he mumbled around his bread.

"Her hands about the rose and how she moved them, each movement of hands means something. What the rose did when she spoke, did you not see that?" Chris nodded. "Maurice has never trusted anyone, save my father; my father trusts few, save Maurice and—a little—Lucette. She needs this much trust from stupid Maurice—a little only. Access to this door, late today."

"I—you say so," Chris said dubiously.

"Truly. What she said when Maurice could not hear—you understood her?" He nodded, tore off a bit of bread, and chewed. The sugary stuff was almost too sweet, even for him. He couldn't begin to guess what kind of fruit it was made from. "She used the box as excuse to give me the message. She knows my father would never have allowed that box removed from this house, or permitted it to be packed, even if he had thought that day he would retrieve all my things from the Parrot, once you and I were—were dead."

"Right."

"No, listen: The box holds a bracelet of antique silver and Incan emeralds; it is worth nearly as much as all his holdings in French Jamaica. He would never dare chance it out of his front door." Chris swallowed bread, washed it down with tea, eyed her in patent disbelief. "I swear it."

"You know that. But does she?"

Ariadne laughed grimly, and poured tea for herself. "Lucette knows that I did not secret the box in this house; when she packed the satchel I took with me the morning the papa said the words over us, she slipped a note inside the silver box, and the box itself into the pocket of my green *faiscance* dress. I found it when I chose what garment to wear when I greeted your aunt Jen." She poured more tea for them both, shoved his cup across the table. "Eat, drink."

"Right." His stomach hurt, and his throat was almost too tight to let him swallow. "Uh—how's your face?"

She shrugged, drank tea. "Lucette could never hit anyone hard enough to hurt, even if she wished; she created noise enough to convince Maurice, which is all that matters." She looked at him over the rim of the cup. "I wish—" she shook her head, didn't finish. Chris picked up his cup, sipped gingerly. Herbs, something that tasted a little like pineapple. *You should be so lucky, Dupret put arsenic in the tea.* Dupret would never kill him so easily; the man wanted information, and he was the kind of guy who'd want someone like Chris to know what was coming—and to feel it when it did.

"Hell," he mumbled into his cup, "I wish they'd get in here, get it over with." Ariadne reached across the little table and gripped his fingers. Her eyes were very dark.

"This is—how he did always with me, to make worse the punishment. The extra hours to think."

Chris finished his tea, grimaced. The stuff had an odd aftertaste. "Yeah, well, he's doing a great job."

* * *

It was nearly midday before the door opened again; Chris, who had been pacing the floor for more than an hour, stopped in the middle of the room; dread sent his pulse pounding. Ariadne looked up from the book she had been pretending to read—Chris hadn't seen her turn a page yet. Her face was expressionless; Chris hoped his was. Maurice stepped aside to let Dupret and Lucette enter, then closed the door behind him.

Dupret held a small pistol where they could see it and understand the threat it represented, then let the arm fall casually to his side. He touched Lucette's shoulder, gestured with his head; Lucette carried another pistol, rather as though she feared it might bite her, then crossed the room and stood, arms folded, at Ariadne's side. Ariadne ignored her, closed the book, and let it drop to her lap. Silence; no one moved. Maurice broke the moment by fetching one of the straight-backed chairs and setting it with a clatter in the middle of the room. "You might save us a small amount of trouble," Dupret remarked, "by telling me where your friend and the woman are." Chris shook his head; he didn't trust his voice at the moment. Maurice gripped his arm and shoved him onto the chair. "Your friend and the woman," Dupret said again, very softly. There was tension in the words.

"Like I'd tell *you* anything," Chris said flatly. He didn't sound anywhere as scared as he felt at the moment. *Swell. Small blessing,* he thought sourly.

Dupret laughed. "Oh? I should say, you will eventually. Whether you wish it or not." Chris shook his head once again. Maurice smacked him across the face with an enormous, open hand, knocking him from the chair; lights exploded behind his eyes. The bodyguard picked him up with no effort at all and shoved him back onto the chair; this time one hard hand held him there. Dupret's breath ruffled the hair against his ear. "Your friend. And the woman."

Chris didn't even bother to shake his head this time. Maurice hit him again, several swift, open-handed blows. His lip was swelling rapidly; there was blood on his tongue and he couldn't see clearly.

Question, silence, more hard slaps; his ears rang. "Your friend," Maurice said flatly. His voice was low, gravelly, his French so oddly accented that Chris didn't realize at first what he'd said. "And the woman. Where?"

He drew a deep breath, shook his head. Maurice let go of his shoulder, took a short step back, and slammed an enormous fist into his body, brought another up under his jaw when the first blow doubled him over. His neck snapped; everything went blue-white.

"Wait a little, Maurice." Dupret's voice reached him from what seemed a very great, echoing distance. "Until he can talk again—if he chooses, of course. But, if not—"

He couldn't breathe, he couldn't think: *Not yet. Nothing yet. Just—stall him.* Maurice hauled him upright; his lower ribs protested sharply and he let out a shrill squawk, nothing like his own voice. A rapid exchange of French, much too fast for him to follow in the best of circumstances— Lucette and Dupret, and then something from Ariadne. *"Si-lence!"* Lucette snarled at her.

He forced his eyes to open; everything swam. Dupret leaned over him. "The woman, your friend. Tell me now."

Chris swallowed. "You—go to Hell." Dupret backhanded him; not hard at all, compared to what Maurice had done. The Frenchman smiled then; his eyes were all pupil and very bright.

"No doubt I shall go there, but in my own time, not yours. Do you wish to be there first to await me? You and she both? Ariadne," he said evenly. "You might save him a little discomfort—"

"Gimme a break," Chris growled. "You think I'd've trusted *her* with anything important?"

"Ariadne?" Dupret asked. Silence. "You will answer

your father when he speaks to you, Ariadne!" he snapped furiously.

"*Canaille!*" she spat at him. "What would you? You put me in his lap, part of his baggage, and you think that now I am his wife and now he adores me? I am the child of Henri Dupret! Stupid Papa! The entire journey, he tells me nothing, but that we go here, then we go there, finally we go to New Lisbon. We leave the train and suddenly there are only we two, him and I, but when I ask where is my maid, where my baggage—he swears filthy words in my face, then says to me, 'Be still, you fool of a woman!' "

Dupret laughed very quietly. "Ah. M. Cray, do you not like my daughter? She is young and beauteous, like her mama, have you no taste? Or—is it that you truly do not trust her? You think—what? That I set her to spy upon you, for me?" He laughed. "My poor, misunderstood Ariadne. What a pity you will never have the opportunity to straighten that matter; I weep for you." Silence, a long one. Dupret finally stepped back, motioned Maurice forward. Chris set his teeth together and closed his eyes as Maurice smiled and brought his fist up.

He lost track of time, of how many times and where the huge bodyguard struck him. Somehow, he was flat on the floor again, with no recollection of landing there. His ears whined shrilly; his whole body hurt. Maurice grabbed his collar and threw him back into the chair; ribs, his stomach—half a dozen things shrieked protest. Dupret pinched his ear. "Where?" he whispered.

"Not—no." He couldn't manage anything else.

"Where? Wait, Maurice—your hands are clearly of no more use, he plans you beat him until he has no more wit to respond, or you kill him. Besides, I grow bored with this." He grabbed the long tail of hair and yanked Chris's head back, slamming the back of his skull against the chair. His eyes flew open. Two of Dupret, hovering over him; two of

Maurice, looming behind the nobleman. "One—final—
time."

"Can't—"

"You can. Maurice." Dupret kept his grip on Chris's
hair, stepped to the side; Ariadne's voice spiraled as the
bodyguard brought up a long-bladed dagger. Maurice was
laughing; he drew the blade down Chris's arm, pulled it
away with a flourish. A line of blood followed.

Chris stared at the slash that ran from elbow to wrist, at
the blood-tipped dagger Maurice held, ready to cut him
again. It slashed down, hard, across his knuckles. The room
spun; he caught at his bleeding arm with his right hand, but
Maurice slapped the fingers aside with no effort at all. He
was smiling, intent clear in his eyes. *Oh, God; he's gonna
cut me to ribbons. He wants to cut me to ribbons.* Chris
suddenly couldn't even breathe; if he'd been able to speak,
he was no longer sure what words might come out. *New
Lisbon, then went north from there, Madrone, the Camroon
Inn Spider, they're waiting to hear from me—* He didn't
dare say that, couldn't, they'd all die! He couldn't; he
caught his breath harshly as the dagger came up, hilt
wrapped in Maurice's steady, capable, huge hand; the
bloodied point neared his face. *My—blood. I'm gonna
bleed to death, right—right, oh, God, right here.* Ariadne
was screaming at her father; Lucette shouting furiously at
her to shut up. Blood ran the length of his arm, across his
hand; his knuckles throbbed and burned but he couldn't
feel his fingers at all. Blood soaking into his pants leg . . .

Ariadne was still shrieking, swearing furiously; Dupret
turned and shouted back at her, and one hand clutched
Maurice's dagger arm. Momentary respite—all that hysteria on Ariadne's part, just enough time for him to remember what was important. What he'd planned, what he *must*
say. Word—for—word. He swallowed bile, licked puffy,
bleeding lips. "Oh, God, all—all right. Tell you, don't—

don't cut me again." He caught his breath harshly; his whole body sagged.

Dupret couldn't have understood the words, even if he'd been able to hear over the two women. He surely knew defeat when he saw it, though. "Ariadne!" he bellowed. "Be still or I shall let Maurice make a study of *your* face with that blade, so this man will never again look upon you with anything but horror! If I allow him to live beyond this hour! *Or* you!" Sudden, blessed silence. Dupret let it spin out for some moments, then demanded, very softly, "Where?"

"They—stayed behind. San Philippe."

"No. A lie; they were not at any hotel, my man checked."

He could barely understand his own words, his mouth was so swollen. "No—no, swear, no hotel. Stayed—with a man, we do business with his brother. Outside of—of town."

"Outside of town?" Chris nodded carefully. "Explain this to me—why?"

"We do—that. Travel separately, most times. 'Specially this last year. So—if my ship was—stopped or"—he swallowed—"or wrecked, or if *you*—well, anyway, one of us would be all right. Could report where the—the other was." He shivered back into the chair as Maurice fingered the edge of his knife.

Dupret chuckled softly, maliciously. "It did not work so well, did it? This—this plan. The man Edrith has made report about you and her to no one; surely he has run, and still runs, to be away from me, and my agents. Perhaps all the way back to his native Rhadaz. He has sense for his own skin, though clearly none for yours. All the same, we will find him. Even in Rhadaz, if we must." Silence. Dupret's fingers dug into his shoulder. "Where—what place in San Philippe?"

Chris shook his head cautiously, but as Maurice loomed over him once more, he swallowed and said hastily, "Wait, no! P-please. All—right. After—after we left on the

Maborre, they came into town, to—to the Coq d'Or.
They're—ah, *hell.*" His voice cracked, tears blurred his vision; he was breaking down totally and sickened by the
whimpering wreck that was himself. *I broke. I couldn't
take it.* "They're—they were going to take the next ship to
New Lisbon, after ours, from San Philippe. Meet us there."

"Where in New Lisbon?" Dupret prodded.

Chris sagged; he shook his head. His voice trembled.
"The—I can't remember—the name of the inn—"

"You remember it. *Where?*" Dupret's voice slammed
into him, the man's fingers dug into his shoulder. Chris
caught his breath painfully, nodded.

"That, there's a British inn, just up—the main road
from—from the docks."

"The Lion?"

"I—yeah," Chris mumbled. "That's it." He opened his
eyes. Dupret's face, uncomfortably close to his own face,
was blurred by the tears in his eyes. The man's breath—
garlic and brandy scented—threatened to make him ill.

"You might have said all this before and saved yourself
some discomfort." Dupret smiled, a most unpleasant smile.
His eyes were dangerously black. "How strange, M. Cray: a
man of your size and strength, and yet you turn pale as a
woman and weep at the sight of so little of your own
blood." The smile broadened; he patted Chris's cheek in a
travesty of compassion. "I will remember this; if you have
told me anything not the truth, I will know before very
long, and you will pay for the waste of time and the lie. I
can see a man spin his life out, a drop of his own blood at a
time; it takes a very long time to die so." He waited. Chris
stared back at him, finally shook his head. "There is nothing you would alter about your story? Remembering Maurice has the knife, and does not like it at all if he must wait
a day or so between the second cut and the third?"

"Yeah," Chris mumbled; his face felt flushed. "I'd keep
my mouth shut."

"I doubt that, M. Cray. Very much, I doubt it." Chris doubted it, too. Dupret straightened, leveled a long arm at Ariadne, and his eyes held that flat, half-crazy black stare. "You, Ariadne! Remember what has passed here this morning; remember particularly that Maurice does not like you, and why this is! What he does to injure those he does not like. And then, consider if you can perhaps recall two so small things for your beloved papa: where is the silver box with the Incan emeralds, and what particular lies did you write to your Uncle Philippe in France, to cause trouble for me?" He didn't wait for an answer, merely snapped his fingers imperiously as he let go of Chris's arm, turned, and strode away. Maurice was already at the door, holding it open; a pale Lucette went out rather quickly, followed by Dupret. Somehow, Chris braced his feet against the small carpet, kept himself in the chair until the door closed and the outside bar fell into place. He sagged then, his eyes closed. He was blessedly unconscious before he hit the floor.

He was awake in what could only have been a few moments later; Ariadne had dragged his body around so that his head was in her lap and she was both weeping and cursing as she tried to tie one of her handkerchiefs around his fingers. He hissed sharply; pressure made the cut almost unbearable. His ribs hurt, sharp stabbing pain when he tried to take a breath; his stomach suddenly lurched, and the room was much too warm. "Don't—Ari, don't, wait a minute, let me—" He swallowed hard; there was an awful taste in his mouth and he was sweating freely now. "Gotta—oh, hell."

"Wait." She couldn't have understood much of what he was trying to say, but his intent was clear. "Not here, the balcony." She got to her feet, hooked her arms under his, and pulled urgently; the small rug slid with him but in jolts as whatever normally held the rug in place tried to grip the slick floor. Chris briefly scrabbled with his feet but it

wouldn't move. *No time*. He desperately tapped her arm
and shook his head. She let go of his arms at once but
quickly bent down to help him onto his hands and knees as
he fought himself up that way, then steadied him as best
she could so he could crawl the last few feet to the small
balcony. He barely made it into open air before everything
came up. Someone down in the courtyard shouted, a man's
wordless yelp of disgust and surprise; Ariadne snarled
something back at Dupret's guard, then steadied Chris's
shoulders as he tried to get his heaving stomach under control. Without any success.

Silence. Chris concentrated on breathing for some long
moments. Ariadne finally scrambled to her feet, touched his
jaw very lightly. "Wait, do not move, I bring you a little
water."

Never gonna move again, Chris thought dazedly; the reaction had him trembling so hard he didn't dare try to
move. His stomach was threatening to let go yet again. The
cut on his arm—it was nearly the length of his forearm, and
sweat made it sting worse than ever, but it wasn't bleeding
quite as much, or so he hoped. Not like the slice across his
upper knuckles: Ariadne's handkerchief had soaked
through. *Dizzy. How much blood have I actually lost, I
wonder?* Ariadne was back at his side, one arm around his
shoulders, a cool, wet cloth blotting his bruised lips; she
dropped it, held a cup for him. "Only a swallow," she
warned softly against his ear. He nodded very cautiously,
rolled liquid around his mouth, then spit it out. He averted
his eyes at once; it came out very red.

Someone below them in the courtyard was grumbling in
furious gutter French. "Ah, *die* of it, you bastard!" Ariadne
snarled. Chris leaned gratefully against her, cradled the cup
between shaking hands, then took another mouthful, swallowed it, and let his eyes close. "Think—it's gonna stay
put. But—sit here," he whispered. "Just—a minute, okay?"

"I will gut him for this!" Ariadne sounded very near tears

all at once. He held up a hand, she fell silent. After a few moments, the world around him settled a little; his stomach churned and his lower ribs hurt in sharp, nasty little bursts. But the nausea had eased—enough.

"Okay," he whispered. "Let's—get back inside. No," he added as she tried to help him up. "I got—no pride left, sweetheart, I'll stay down here, just don't—let me fall over, huh? I think my—my ribs are shot."

It took what felt like forever to get as far as her bed, and then he simply couldn't pull himself onto it. Ariadne stripped the lightweight down coverlet off, dropped a pillow on the small carpet and eased him onto it, then drew the coverlet to his shoulders, covering him as completely as possible. She sat down next to him, cloth in hand. "I—I do not know what to do to help you," she said desperately.

"I—yeah." He freed a hand, gripped her fingers. "Look, it's okay, everything's gonna be fine. I—I wasn't yelling at you, just now, honestly—"

"If that mattered—"

"So's—you know. I'm just—" He couldn't get any more words out; he was chilled, his body was wracked with shudders of cold despite both the thick, silky thing she'd wrapped around him and the warmth of the afternoon. *That's shock,* he realized dully. Hard to care. *You have to, though. You don't dare sleep. If they come back, if Ariadne's alone, and you out cold*— Whatever. Impossible to get excited about any of it; he just wanted to be warm, to sleep—his eyes sagged closed; his whole body ached like he'd just come down with a flu.

Her lips brushed his forehead. "Sleep, my Chris," she whispered against his ear. "I will watch. They won't come again today, it is—is all right. Sleep, and I watch over you." She repeated the words; meaningless, soothing words. He nodded and, between one word and another, fell asleep.

It was quiet, and moistly warm in the large room when he

woke; Ariadne had fallen asleep on the floor next to him.
He lay very still for a long moment, eyes half-open, watching her sleep. It wasn't fair: Dupret was probably going to
kill him as soon as he found no Eddie in San Philippe, and
he'd either kill Ariadne, too, or sell her to one of his rich-
pig buddies. Which was infinitely worse. He swallowed
past a suddenly tight throat. *Some way to get her out of this.*

He must have been speaking aloud, unaware he was. Ariadne's eyelashes fluttered. She gazed at him, eyes searching his face; her mouth, which had been full and soft in
sleep, hardened. "No. Both of us away from this place, or
neither. I do not leave without you." He opened his mouth;
she laid soft fingers against bruised lips. "No. Has anything
you said so far to send me away, proven of use? And that
was—was before—" She kissed her fingertips, touched his
lips again, glanced at the window, then sat up in one fluid
movement. "Can you move at all, get from the floor to the
chair, or my bed?" she asked.

Chris gritted his teeth. "Gotta. Your old man finds me
down here, shivering like a—"

"He will not come back this day," Ariadne said flatly. "I
told you, did you think I lied to make easy for you? But I
know his ways; he likes causing pain but only if there is
purpose to it. Just now, he has no more cause to tell Maurice to hit you."

"Oh, yeah? I can think of a few causes."

"He sees only this of Eddie and Dija," she broke in hur-
riedly. She'd gone pale; Chris clamped down on his lip
cautiously and said nothing else. "He has difficulties of his
own; with his plans for France and my uncle Philippe, he
will be busy for some time, to find a way to make all that
come right."

"Good." He wasn't sure he could believe that; if she did,
he wouldn't dissuade her, though.

"Yes. The chair—I only thought, it might be better if you
were in it, the soft one, if—when Aleyza comes."

"Ah—right." The old woman who'd organized the—the Anlu? she'd called it? Those like Ari, who'd had enough of macho violence, anyway. Well, terrific. He'd had enough of macho violence himself.

He was suddenly reminded of the women in his mother's Wicca, back in L.A. all those years earlier. As if women already made antagonistic by the macho types would really care what *he* felt; anything with testosterone was the ipso facto enemy. Still, maybe not. Not everything was black and white, and Ariadne had an in with those women.

She was waiting for an answer, he reminded himself. "Good—idea." He shook his head as she held out her arms to help him. "Let me. See if I can make it up. If—they can get us out of here—*ouch!* damn!—I swear there's something broken in there! If they can, I'd better be able to move out on my own feet."

She nodded sharply. "You think once more; good. It is"—she drew the small, plain silver English watch he'd bought her out of her breast pocket, glanced at the window once more—"it is nearly the hour for tea."

"I hope—" Chris set his teeth, dragged himself up on the side of the bed and swayed there for a moment, then drew himself upright and managed the five steps that brought him to her overstuffed reading chair. She got both arms under his good elbow, helped him ease himself down into it. He sat there for a long moment, eyes closed, breathing in fast, shallow pants so as not to aggravate his ribs any more than they already were, to get the room back in focus when he did look at it once more. Not to puke again. "God," he said feelingly. "I hope something really does come of this. Your women. I—don't think I can take another dose of Maurice." He remembered something. "What—was that, at the end? What your father said to you?" She shook her head; she wouldn't meet his eyes. "Tell me," he insisted. "What he meant, about Maurice doesn't like you."

"Just that"—She shrugged, would-be casual, but her face

and the set of her shoulders were tense—"that I tried to kick him once, just before *you* came, in a bad place. Because he took advantage of my other maid, Honorine, and made her—with child. I wanted to kill him, but I knew—not enough then about men—and so, I did not properly hurt him, I bruised only his pride. And he—he has not forgotten. What pain I caused, or what I intended." She shook her head; salt-stiffened hair flew around her face. "We forget Maurice, ourselves—all that!—for now."

"Everything? Don't think so. What your father said, after the bit about Maurice?"

"I told you last night; you heard him as well. And Lucette, earlier. My uncle in France has learned of the Zero, and he is truly angry. Uncle Philippe has the honor my father does not, or their father. And so, my *beloved* papa thinks, which of the people around me wishes my doom? And he sees the tale as my doing, that I wrote to Uncle Philippe and exposed his dealings in that drug."

"Oh, jeez," Chris breathed. Dupret, letting Maurice pound on Ariadne—"We *gotta* get you out of here!"

"Not," Ariadne said flatly, "without you, my Chris. Ever in my life. Wait." She stepped back, listened a moment, then shook her head. "I thought there were voices below. Those cuts; I had better clean them." He shook his head; she held up a hand. "You know what a cut becomes in a climate like this."

"Like it's gonna have time to get gross and kill me—"

She shook her head again. "No. Say nothing like that. I clean the cuts and cover them both. Is it not better if you cannot look upon that?"

"Got—" He glanced at his arm, swallowed. The line of dried blood on his forearm was starting to throb unpleasantly. His fingers were swollen, the handkerchief stiff. "Got a point, lady. Mmm. Go for it." He could hear her rustling around in the washing; two men conversing outside the window in low voices and someone laughing derisively.

Yeah. Big, tough Rhadazi, poke him with a knife and he pukes. Great. Knew I didn't like blood, 'specially my own. That, though— That he'd turn white and stutter, practically whine and crawl— Well, his reaction had definitely served the purpose: convinced Dupret he was telling the truth, bought them some time, like he'd planned, even if he hadn't planned on getting—cut. Or acting like a total chicken-shit. If he could get the pair of them out of here before the Frenchman learned otherwise—get Ari out, anyway—*I literally cannot take another dose of Maurice. I almost talked before. This time—jeez, I don't know if I could stop myself. What was Mom's old line, I'd tell secrets, make up secrets, just don't hit me.* He hissed as a cool, wet cloth touched his bare forearm.

"Shhh," Ariadne soothed. "I am careful." She eased his fingers, cloth and all, into a bowl of cool water.

"Do—what you gotta." He set his jaw, kept his eyes closed, and let her work. Surprisingly, she was extremely gentle. Once she'd finished, he opened his eyes and managed what must be a pretty mangled-looking smile. "Thanks. Feels better."

Again to his surprise, she laughed, very quietly. "Ah, you lie. But such a *polite* lie."

"Still. Your old man comes in, sees this, he's gonna think—"

"He knows already." Her cheekbones were notably red, and she wouldn't meet his eyes. "When Maurice cut you, what I said to him—never mind. He knows."

"Yeah. Know what? We got lousy timing, both of us."

"Timing?" She frowned, shook her head, but held up a hand when he would have spoken again; this time she was visibly blushing well into the throat of her shirtwaist. "Yes. Well. I see. We mend this of timing, once we are from French Jamaica." She crossed to the small balcony and closed the doors. "It is too warm, I know, but quieter if Lucette—" She caught her breath sharply as the door latch clicked sharply; Lucette came in, followed by a stooped, elderly woman in black taffeta that made a high-pitched, irritating, swishing noise with her every slow step. She was supported by a woman with white hair and blue-black skin who wore a loose dress of red, yellow, and blue cotton and an enormous high-piled head scarf of all three colors together. Her dark feet were bare. Ariadne bowed to the older woman, then smiled and stepped forward to clasp the black woman around the neck. "*Tante* Emilie," she murmured, and kissed her cheeks in turn. "Madame Aleyza," she added more formally to the elderly Frenchwoman.

Aleyza let Emilie assist her into a chair at the table, waited until she was made comfortable, a cushion under her feet, a glass of peach-colored liquid at her elbow. "Mademoiselle Ariadne," she said in reply; her French was precise, her voice high and shaky with age. She cast a black glance in Chris's direction; he considered attempting to get to his feet—manners, he reminded himself warily, stuff like that counted among her class, and this woman might be all the hope they had at the moment—but he doubted his legs would hold him. Ariadne cast him a sidelong glance, made a discreet chopping motion with her hand; *stay where you are,* both clearly said.

Lucette stepped forward. "Miss—" She held out the magic-tinged rose and curtseyed deeply. "Madame Ariadne, this is yours, of course. I—your pardon for the blow—"

Ariadne gripped her hand, closed her fingers over the rose, and drew her back to her feet. "No. Time, as you say, is short, and I know why you struck me, what my father has done with you, after I left this house. How much chance you had to tell him *non*. Not your fault. This of my father, first; tell me quickly what there is in France."

Lucette nodded sharply. "Yes. Two days ago, *Le Chat* came to port, with all the brandy still aboard her, and a message; he was there to take it and he returned to the house in a full fury. These rages—"

"I know the rages," Ariadne said. She glanced at Chris; Lucette paled, bit her lip. "Go on."

"The rages worsen, you do *not* know how much of late—"

Chris frowned; Lucette's French was rapid, oddly accented, and his ears rang, anyway. This last was easier to understand for some reason. "Dupret has the Moorish disease," he said. Aleyza glanced in his direction; her lip curled, and she looked away at once, dismissing him as male and so, beneath count. He'd expected it, really; it still rankled. "Ask Peronne," he added as Lucette stared at him.

"Ah, *Dieu*!" Lucette paled, her skin muddy under the bright cosmetic as she suddenly understood. Ariadne gripped her fingers, hard.

"Yes, I am sorry you learn it so, but the disease can be dealt with, remember that." *Oh, jeez,* Chris realized bleakly. *Way to go, big mouth. She's only sleeping with the dude, which means—*

"Sorry," he mumbled. Ariadne cast him a quick glance, shook her head the least bit.

"Yes," she said. "It seems likely Henri Dupret has the Moorish disease. The rages, if nothing else. But that aside for now, if you can, *petite*."

Despite suddenly haggard eyes, Lucette managed a weak smile. "You always call me that, as if I were half your size, instead of the other way about."

"Not nearly so small. Pay heed, Lucette." Ariadne patted her cheek. "Aleyza or another of the women will help you, there are powders my mother's kin create with the aid of the old gods, swear you will obtain the powders and faithfully take them, *petite*," Ariadne urged. "In the chance it is truth, the disease." Silence. Lucette finally nodded; her mouth drooped. "This of the message, though—from France?"

"Yes." Lucette nodded, seemed to gather scattered

thoughts, and nodded again, sharply. "I waste time . . . The old Duc has had a fit; he is unable to speak and his entire left side does not move. Your Uncle Philippe, he says the old man does not know him two days of three, and there is a *crise* in the east, the King impatient for victory in the war there—"

"As always," Ariadne put in. "And so?"

"Philippe, he takes the charge, and sits in your *grand-père*'s seat on the King's council, and somehow he learns that this southern drug has been spread among the eastern armies, and that it has come because his *papa* the Duc d'Orléans ordered it, and his *frère* Henri was willing to send the drug to France. Philippe, he is in a fury, and in the letter, he says to Henri, 'You have vast holding in Jamaica Française, you have wealth and power there, and from this day on, it is *all* yours: I take no percentage, levy no tax— and you, in turn, make no claim upon me, or the house of Dupret, or anything in France you may have once thought to hold.' So, your uncle. And Henri—I have seen him in a black rage, but never so strong as this." She caught hold of Ariadne's fingers. "He said perhaps this man, or that, or this captain or another—but finally and so certain he had it that it was you, miss, who wrote to your uncle once Henri could not censure your letters, that it was you who brought this calamity upon him."

"I did not—" Ariadne had been shaking her head for some moments. She, too, was very pale, though not the ashen white Lucette had turned. "Had I thought of it—but I did not. So unfortunate, if I had, I could have created so much more hell for him than what he now sees. No matter. If he thinks I did as much, he will kill me, simply because the rumor might be true. No—he will have Maurice do murder. Henri Dupret kills only those against whom he duels, not those who could not meet him in gentleman's style, and I, after all, am only female."

She kept her hold on Lucette's fingers, turned to Aleyza,

who had been watching the two with great interest. "The gods know that I have suffered for true, Aleyza," she said flatly. She caught hold of Lucette's rose, held it out; her words took on a definite chantlike rhythm. The rose pulsed deep red. "Anlu, the power and the strength upon me; Anlu, the will and the way through me; Anlu the aid of my own and the light against the dark." Silence. "Look at this, Aleyza," Ariadne said finally. She flung one arm wide to include Chris. "Look at him! See what my father has caused done, what Maurice did, all to protect Dupret's fortune that comes from Zero! And when he learns Chris lied to purchase for him and me time to get away from French Jamaica, he will kill us in such a fashion that—" She stopped, stared. Aleyza was laughing, a high-pitched, old woman's cackle. Ariadne's aunt took one nervous step back, and appeared to be trying to vanish against the white-washed wall.

"Ah, yes," Aleyza said finally. Her eyes were bright with tears of laughter, and she still chuckled wheezingly. "Oh, yes! By Anlu! You dare! Only *you* would have such arrogance!"

"I do swear!"

"Swear by our society, by the rose—swear by the very male God of the French Catholics, what does it matter? You ask my aid—our aid, and my presence in this house, old and ill as I am, and all for—you wretched girl!" Ariadne still stared at her. Aleyza laughed again. "It has often occurred to me, Miss Ariadne—or shall I say, instead, Madame Cray?—to wonder how it would be when one such as yourself found herself possessed by a man? Not simply given to a man but—well, yes! One so passionate against is so often passionate *for,* especially among women!"

Ariadne pulled herself together, let go of Lucette's hands altogether, and took two steps to stand over the old woman. "Among women? What do you dare say of me, madame? I had no choice in the marriage! You know as much! But if you think Chris is like all men—"

"All men," Aleyza said flatly. "*All. Men.* Once you would have said exactly as much, young woman. And now—you've set aside your oaths and bargained maidenry for the marriage bed of this 'Chris,' have you?"

"How *dare* you?" Ariadne whispered.

Aleyza laughed once more. "You think I don't know about men and marriage beds? I was wed once, I had a man take me on that bed, not once, but many times! And I swore—never mind what I swore. You would never understand, would you? Because you accepted, where I rejected! You've bowed down, taken *his* coin, *his* name, his clothing for your back! You've turned squarely against us and all you swore to uphold. And now, because a whim of fate blew you into the grasp of a man not as—as amenable as this—this 'Chris,' you beg for my aid—not for yourself, oh, no!—but for this 'us'? My own dishonor cries against such a thing, and against you, Ariadne!"

8

℥

ARIADNE stared at the old woman, her mouth open and her eyes wide with shock. Chris shifted slightly but kept his own mouth prudently closed; this Aleyza patently wanted nothing from *him,* and anything he tried to say could only make matters worse. From behind the older woman's chair, the dark woman Ariadne had called *tante* sent her eyes his way and shook her head very slightly; her index fingers were crossed over her breast and he could suddenly see the silver rose hanging there. It glowed briefly as he watched, a deep, warm, and possibly warning red, then faded to plain silver once more. Emilie's eyes flickered toward her elderly companion; she compressed her lips.

Ariadne shook herself; Aleyza brought her chin up, and waited. "That you *dare* say such a thing to me," Ariadne finally managed. She spoke very softly but anger edged the words. "After all the years I have endured in this house, under that fiend who is my father; after what I did for the women of French Jamaica, and for you in particular!"

"The past is dead," Aleyza countered flatly. She primmed her lips. "Like my husband. Whatever you did for any here, or any of us—you turned that to nothing when you put yourself and that"—she cast Chris a withering glance—"that *man* together as 'us.' " She held out her arm, turned her head slightly. "There is nothing for me to do here, Emilie, Lucette." She was panting slightly as the two women hauled her to her feet. Ariadne gazed at her, arms still folded. "I pity you, you foolish young woman," she said.

An unpleasant, short silence. Ariadne's lip curled. "Not half so much as I pity you. Tomorrow, there is the small chance I will grow less foolish, but you will remain old and stupid."

Aleyza stood very still; her skin flushed a muddy, mottled red and she turned to let Emilie aid her from the room. Lucette dithered, then murmured, "There may be another way, trust me and do nothing yet." Aleyza snarled at her from the hallway; Lucette hurried out, pulled the door to, and slammed the bar into place.

Ariadne stood very still, eyes fixed on the door. She sighed finally, very faintly, turned, and knelt at Chris's side. "I did not mean to put you to such a test."

"I know."

"She—does not like men. I just—never thought she so hated all men. Not beyond sense."

"Well—she's got her reasons obviously."

"Oh. Yes, well. She has. Or had; she has been a widow nearly two years." The corners of her mouth quirked briefly. "Robbed and stabbed in an alley, or so everyone said."

"Ah." He coughed painfully, swore under his breath as his lip began bleeding again. Ariadne got back to her feet, went into the washing, and came back at once with a squat mug of water and a wet cloth. "Listen—you don't think *she'll* want to kill you now, do you? Have you killed, because you know so much about them, because you're one of the enemy now?"

Ariadne shook her head. "There is not one of the Anlu who would dare come against *me*."

"Ah—oh. All right." *Great.* "Um. Another thing. Your ex—um, Lucette. She said your old man and the brute were gone, but I'll wager anything the servants know she brought that old woman in here—"

"Of course. By now, all the house servants know. But what of them in his proper mind, or hers, would carry the tale to my father? Why be loyal to *that*?" Ariadne blotted his face with the cloth. Chris shook his head faintly. She shrugged, answered her own question. "Oh, Peronne might have, once; he had a small loyalty to my father because he was young. That is years since gone, though he will never like or trust me because of the bargain I made him: silence about the stolen wine for sword lessons. Even so, he cares for my father even less. The women are one and all terrified of Maurice and my father both, and Elonzo—he still carries the marks on his back Maurice put there with a whip."

"Ah, nice. But—these are servants, not slaves. They could just leave—"

"Of course. But then Henri Dupret says, 'That servant is worthless,' and no household would ever hire him. My *tante* Emilie, who was just here, she went from this house to the sugar fields, no one would pay her for anything else save the—one of the houses—until two years ago, when Aleyza was able to choose her own household."

"Houses?" She shook her head; her color was high. "Oh. Sorry." *Those* houses. "I guess—" He jerked convulsively, dropped the cup as the bar rattled away from the door and it began to open; water splashed the floor, his pants, Ariadne's skirts. Lucette, her face very pale, slipped through the narrow opening, shut the door at once, and leaned against it; she was clearly out of breath.

Chris reached for the cup, caught his breath in a near-silent hiss; Ariadne touched his shoulder. "Leave that, please, I get it," she said quietly as she stood; Lucette hurried across the room. Ariadne gripped her fingers.

Chris cradled his ribs with a cautious hand, and slowly leaned back in the chair. "Mmmm—you get it."

"Miss—I am sorry, madame, I never thought she would—"

"My fault, not yours, *petite,*" Ariadne assured her quickly. "I did not think when I spoke. But she would never have found aid for Chris, only for me; it is not good enough."

"I know. I see this, you and he. Your aunt Emilie put a word in my ear, privately, just now; she will find her brothers, help for you. Somehow, we get you from here tonight. Henri—he has a meeting tonight, at his club, with Lord Sorionne; Maurice goes with him, as always, for protection. Sorionne will not come here; he has no trust in Henri anymore and Maurice frightens him." Her fingers gripped the silver rose.

"He sent word to San Philippe already?" Chris asked. Lucette shook her head, then nodded when Ariadne repeated the question in rapid French.

"Apologies. I could not understand—yes. Albione has gone there with the steamer; *he* does not expect it back until two days, or four if they must also go north. He speaks of having the English lay wire in the sea, to the mainland at least, to end such delays. He is very angry."

"I noticed," Chris mumbled. Ariadne blotted his brow carefully, then handed him the damp cloth; he held it against his lip. "Why, though? I mean—" It was hard to think. "Why is this Sorionne afraid?"

"Because he aided Henri in the making of brandies, but now he says, 'We have been found out by your brother Philippe, who will tell the King and my own family, I do this no more.' Henri says he is coward." She glanced at Chris, then quickly away. Her hands gripped the silver rose so tightly her knuckles were white. "You—think, *m'sieu,* you believe he has"—she swallowed—"has the—?" She was trembling visibly. Ariadne caught hold of her shoulders and pulled her close.

"Ask Peronne, or Marie; Peronne told it to me. Lucette,

it is not the end of everything, you must go to Emilie, or another like her, someone with the old gifts. Get the powders and take them. And if you came with us, when we leave here—"

"Go where?" Lucette asked dully. "After what he has made of me, what am I anywhere?"

"My true friend," Ariadne began; Lucette shook her head.

"No. Whatever life I have is here; what family, all I know. And"—she drew a harsh breath, scrubbed a hand across her eyes—"and if I could be of some use, perhaps; he says things when I am around that he would not ever say around you, I am still a servant in that way; he pays no more heed to me than to the chairs. I can pass word to Emilie, or to my brother, who works on the docks, who can tell the English or who you choose, to tell you what he does."

"I will not have it." Ariadne scowled at her. Lucette drew a plain square of cloth from her sleeve and blew her nose on it. "If he catches you, you are dead."

"Perhaps I am, anyway. And if I go, and he takes another young girl? That would be against my soul—"

"It—"

"It would. It does not matter, however; I will not go." She started, glanced at the window; someone in the courtyard below was bellowing for Marie. "Time is short, listen and do not argue. My brother knows many of the foreigners who dock in Philippe-sur-Mer, and he says many of the foreign captains do not like Henri Dupret, who gives himself airs and tries even more now to order what they may and may not do here. He will find a safe ship to give you passage; I will free you from the room after Maurice goes to drive the coach, and watch *his* back. Emilie will send someone to help you get away." She looked beyond Ariadne to Chris. "Can you walk, do you think?"

"God—I have to, don't I?"

"Emilie saw you; she will know to have transport or one

strong man at least, to help." She pulled the rose and its chain over her head. Ariadne shook her head, took the chain from her hands, and set it back into place.

"Keep that. You will need it more than I—I am done with Aleyza and hers, by her own choice. And *he* might become suspicious if he saw later it was not there." Lucette nodded, kissed Ariadne's fingers, then came around her to bend down and touch her lips lightly against Chris's cheek.

"You must take very good care of her," she whispered.

He touched her fingers. "Get us out of this room, and I swear I will." Lucette blotted her face with a trembling hand, turned, and hurried from the room. Ariadne waited until the bar clapped into place, then sank to the floor and buried her face against his knee. Her shoulders shook. Chris patted her hair.

"He will suspect her, it will take nothing else but suspicion," she whispered finally. Her voice was thick with tears. "He will suspect she spies on him, and he will kill her."

"I think she's going to do her best to not make him suspicious," Chris said after a moment. "I bet anyone who lives in this house gets good at that, same as you did. And maybe we can do something to help her once we get out of here." She looked up; her eyes were red rimmed, disbelieving; her cheeks wet. "Besides," he said flatly, "if we get out of here, I swear to you right now, he is never going to have a second chance at either of us. And maybe he won't live long enough to hurt her, either." She merely sighed, very faintly, let her head back down onto his knee, and closed her eyes.

If I live that long, Chris thought gloomily. Chances were, neither of them would see another sunrise; there were enough holes in Lucette's would-be plan—well, more holes than he cared to think about. *Bad as one of Eddie's.* If Dupret caught them sneaking out of this house or anywhere on the island, he'd likely be pissed enough to shoot them both, only later cuss himself out for not having kept Chris around for another question-and-answer session. Alternatives, though: Wait for Maurice? He shivered; his ribs protested. Ariadne stirred.

"That," she said, and set a light hand atop his. "You must let me look, feel a little; if there is bone broken, at least wrap something around so you can breathe with more ease."

He considered this, sighed. "Much as I'd rather not—but I'd never make it to that door tonight if it hurts like this. Be careful, though, okay?" She merely nodded, got to her feet, and went back into the washing, emerging a moment later with the washbasin, which she set on the floor by his feet. She pulled the long cloth from the little table, glanced cautiously toward the door and then the open French windows, drew the knife from under her skirts, and cut the cloth into hand-width strips. Chris set his jaw and tried to unbutton his shirt, but the hand with the long cut was clumsy and he swore. Ariadne shoved the knife back into its sheath, smoothed her skirts and came over to undo the buttons for him, gently eased the shirt from his britches and stared at his stomach, stricken. He managed a sick-feeling smile. "Hey—don't scare me, either, all right? Ah—I'm not gonna even try to look. How bad is it?"

"It is bruised," she said softly. He closed his eyes as she set cool fingers against his chest, slowly slid them down to his floating ribs. He gasped; set his jaw again as she jerked her hand away.

"Go on; I'll stay quiet, I swear."

"I cannot tell—Emilie's brother has my mother's gift, but he is not here . . . ah, *merde,* broken or no, what matter if it hurts so?" She was quiet for some moments, her fingers moving lightly across his stomach. He kept his teeth together, somehow remained quiet; pain ran sharply all the way around his ribs and vibrated through his belly. *God, if he broke something like my kidneys, maybe I'm dead anyway.* Ariadne freed the back of his shirt; her hair brushed against his chest. She worked quickly then, wrapping strips of cloth around his lower ribs. "Is that too tight?"

"Snug," he managed through clenched teeth. "Not too snug."

"Good." She still sounded worried. "Hold this," she ordered, and set his hand against the cloth. She rummaged for a few moments in the narrow cupboard just beyond the table, came back with a threaded needle, which Chris eyed warily. "I am careful," she said softly, and set his hand aside to stitch the ends in place. "Can you manage food?"

His teeth wanted to chatter; blood pulsed angrily under her bandage, set his head to thumping. "I don't—think I can. Maybe if—if I could lie down a little. Some—water, first?" She held the cup for him, got under his other arm and let him use her for balance as he struggled to his feet, held him upright while he caught his breath and let the dizziness ease, then kept him upright as he moved cautiously toward the bed. It seemed to take forever, and once she got him seated, he caught his breath in a ragged sob. "Oh, God. That hurts." She shifted her weight, got both hands clasped together behind his neck and eased him slowly onto his back, scooped up the coverlet, and draped it over him. "Thanks," he whispered, and let his eyes close. Ariadne brushed damp hair from his forehead and eased it behind his ears.

He couldn't sleep; his stomach ached, the muscles shivered deep down. And though Ariadne's wrapping helped a little, the lower ribs gave him a sharp reminder of their presence every time he drew breath. The tip of his tongue stung where he'd bitten it early on; exploring with it cautiously, he found several other raw places inside both cheeks. No loose teeth, at least. *This time.*

The constant dread was even worse than the physical discomfort: he could tell Maurice was out there, somewhere, ready to come back and eager to pound on him some more.

Or cut. He drifted in and out of a dazed doze, too exhausted to even open his eyes when he heard Ariadne move away quietly, then something scraping across the floor; it stopped next to the bed. She leaned over him; her hair brushed the back of his hand. *Worried,* he knew. *Tell her it's all*— He dozed off instead, and woke with a start from ugly dreams that pulled a faint cry from him.

"Chris?" Ariadne spoke, low-voiced, very near his ear.

"Mmmm. I'm—all—ri . . . " He couldn't make real words; his lips hurt too much to move.

She blotted his forehead, pulled the coverlet over his hands once more. "You are all right, sleep if you can." Silence for a moment; he forced his eyes partway open, blinking furiously against the bright afternoon sunlight. Ariadne had pulled the low-armed overstuffed chair across the room and sat close to his pillows; she had the book in her hands once more and was frowning at it. Chris let his eyes close and drifted off once again.

Dupret's face, Maurice's—they faded in and out, first one, then the other; the voices echoed as if they were in an enormous, high-ceilinged cavern: *Where is Eddie? The woman, where?* Ariadne's face, too: frightened, and then furious, and then taking first Dupret's place, then Maurice's, the long heavy knife she wore under her skirts in her hand, the blade between his teeth—Dupret behind her, laughing. *You do not trust her, do you?* The knife cut the tip of his tongue. He cried out and, with a convulsive gasp, woke.

Ariadne was at his side, fingers against her own lips in warning, one hand on his cheek. The room was gloomy, the sun gone. *"Shhh,"* she whispered. "Wait, it is all right." She ran barefoot across the room, pressed her ear against the door. But even Chris could hear them out there now, even over the constant ringing in his ears. Maurice arguing with Dupret and at least one other person; he couldn't make out the words. Dupret shouted them all down finally.

"*Merde!* I must listen to such noises, even here?" Maurice said something; Dupret overrode him. "To what point, if he is not aware enough to pay heed to what you do, and make answers? But we shall be late, and Sorionne will use the excuse to—bah, enough! We go! Lucette, you will wait until tomorrow to persuade the girl; the box has kept so long, it keeps a few hours more." Sullen response; Chris caught the tone, not the words. Maurice rumbled something and Lucette snarled at him. Retreating footsteps and in the distance, a door slammed.

Ariadne came back to him; she seemed to be fighting laughter, but when she reached the bed, her face was grave. "You look—"

"Mmm. Don't tell me." The words were mushy; he couldn't manage fricatives at all.

She shook her head. "No, I think—better. More bruised but not so pale and shaking. Water?" He nodded cautiously, freed a hand so he could grasp the cup. "No, wait, I help." She clambered onto the far side of the bed, knelt next to him, and pulled him partway up, stuffing pillows under his shoulders and head. The ribs protested wildly.

"Um—can't— Help me—all the way up." He sent his eyes toward the washing. She nodded, got off the bed, and came around to pull the coverlet aside and help him ease his legs down. The room faded briefly, came back as he braced his weight against his good hand and concentrated on getting a little air to his brain. She waited until he nodded, eased herself under his arm and lifted, stayed with him until he nodded again. He let the arm slip from around her but kept his hand on her shoulder. "Um—need you for—balance. I—ought to try to walk, though. And I need the—the washing—"

"All right. I stay—like this. If you need me." His legs were all right, fortunately, but he was unnervingly weak. Halfway across the room, he let go of her shoulder and managed the rest of the way on his own, though she stayed right next to him, in case he wobbled, stopping only as he reached the washing door. "I wait here." Her color was high. "In case."

His own face felt flushed. "Thanks." He kept a hand on the wall as the door closed behind him and eased into the room very carefully indeed; it would be the utter rock bottom if he fell in here and she had to come rescue him. Everything took time, his right hand didn't work very well—as much Ariadne's bandaging job as the actual cut— and both hands jerked, beyond his control at odd moments. The worst was turning to the sink and catching sight of himself in her mirror. "God." His lip was split and badly swollen, liberally marked with dried blood; one eye was black underneath, the other purplish and so puffy it was a mere slit. Everything else looked—"God," he said again. "Ugly. Ugly man." He dipped a fresh cloth in the water basin, blotted his face cautiously, and dabbed at his lips. He swore silently as one of the cuts reopened. "Leave it," he mumbled. Ariadne would be starting to worry, he was taking so long. He caught sight of himself in the mirror again as he turned away, shuddered, and groped his way to the door. She was pacing the room, but stopped and came over at once as he emerged from the washing. He caught his breath, let go of the door, and nodded. *Like that reassured her; no wonder she looked so scared. If I had a face like this to look at—*

"The bed?" she asked. She stayed where he could reach her, but didn't offer to help.

"Um. Maybe, if I could eat a little something."

"Yes. Here, there is still bread. Perhaps now Maurice is gone, Lucette or Marie will bring soup."

"Bread's fine. Bland." It stood half a chance of staying put, anyway. He set his teeth as they reached the table, lowered himself into the chair.

Bread helped; at least, it eased some of the internal ache and the dull gnaw of hunger. Ariadne tore bread in half and then into smaller and smaller bits. Nothing left in her hands; she stared at them, then at the table, made a face at the resulting mess, but scooped up some of it and ate. "The tea is cold," she said.

"Water's better, I think." Still hurt to talk; he was managing better, making more sense. Ariadne fetched his cup, poured whatever was left in the clay jar for him, watched him drink. Tepid now; and it had an odd, metallic aftertaste. *You decided he wouldn't poison you, it's just pipe taste,* he told himself firmly. "What was all that out there?" His voice came out a little too high.

"That? Oh. Lucette wanted to come in, but Maurice was there. She made an argument with him about the box; she tells him, I go in now, make her tell where is it? Maurice laughs and says no, if anyone asks Miss Ariadne of the box, it is the master, and if anyone beats upon—upon Miss Ariadne it is he, Maurice. So she curses him and he laughs even more—and then *he* comes and shouts at them both for wasting the time and for arguing in his house like so many spoilt children. And Lucette sulks and Maurice—he is angry, too, that my father puts him with Lucette in such a way, and they leave for his meeting with Sorionne."

"They're gone. You're sure?"

She looked a little drawn; Chris didn't think she was nearly as calm as she sounded. Of course, with Maurice threatening to start pounding on *her*—"*He* said so," she said. "But I heard them go down the stairs, and there was hurry because of Sorionne."

"I think I got that part. The old fat dude's getting scared just like Lucette said, isn't he?"

"Sorionne was never the man to take chances, not of any sort. So if he heard already of my *grand-père* and the letter from France, he would wish to distance himself as far as he could from my father's disasters. My father—will not like that."

Chris ate more bread; sniffed his cup and finally drank. "So that was the front door I heard slam."

"No, that was Lucette. There was someone left in the hall, perhaps Peronne, to watch the door. But I went to listen while you were in the washing; he does not sit with his ear to the door, as Maurice does. He paces and grumbles to himself, and I think he is very bored." She drew out her watch, glanced at the windows. "There begin to be clouds; it will be very dark in an hour. Peronne or Elonzo, no matter which on the door; they will not be challenge to any who come for us."

"I hope not. Hour." Chris pushed to his feet; it was the least bit easier this time. At least the room didn't fade on him, and he managed to keep his balance on his own. But ten steps were exhausting. As for walking anywhere farther than that bed, or taking out someone guarding the door, Chris thought, *Forget it. Hope that aunt of hers brings some muscle.* Ariadne went around him, pulled the coverlet back, and pushed the spare pillows out of the way; he sighed faintly as she helped him back flat. "Thanks. Really."

"Better, I get you from this house, and from French Jamaica entirely, and *then* you thank me."

"Lady," he murmured, "you got it." He let his eyes close.

He woke sometime later to utter chaos: it was quiet and dark in the room, but beyond Ariadne's French windows, he could see the ruddy light of distant fire reflected on the low clouds, hear the shouts and curses of a mob. He levered himself onto his elbows, gasped as the ribs bit hard, and rolled, very cautiously, onto his other side. Ariadne was a dark, still shadow on the narrow balcony, but she must have heard him move; she came back into the room at once.

"It is the dockworkers, they make riot in the streets because of the restriction on the foreign ships, and there is no work for four days. But, perhaps it is my *tante* Emilie and the brother of Lucette, creating a diversion so, and using the four days for excuse."

He pressed himself onto hands and knees, groaning. "Jeez. Glad to hear someone's having fun." She lifted the hair from his forehead, waited as he eased himself slowly around, sat, and edged his feet to the floor. He sat still for a moment, catching his breath. "Wait. Diversion—you really think so?"

She shrugged. "I think—I hope so. Can you walk, a little?" Before he could even decide, she held up a hand, said, "Hold, and be silent!" urgently and glided toward the door. A moment later, she came running back. "Peronne just left this door to guard the front entry, I heard him run down the steps. So, there is no one—" She caught hold of the door handle, then jumped back. "The bar," she murmured, and chopped a hand in his direction for him to stay put.

The door opened and an extremely tall man filled the opening—not Maurice, Chris realized after that first heart-stopping moment, but a much thinner man whose skin shone blue-black in the light of the hall chandelier. He wore only pale britches that fell just below his knees, a short bit of vest. Ariadne wrapped her arms around his waist and hugged him, hard. The man hugged her back, then whispered something Chris couldn't catch; Ariadne caught hold of his arm and pulled him across the room. Ariadne's aunt Emilie appeared as a bright-edged shadow in the doorway behind them; the door closed.

"Oncle Frère!" Ariadne exclaimed softly. "I did not know you were in Philippe-sur-Mer." Chris frowned. *Uncle—Brother?* "Chris," she added softly, "this is my oncle Frère—my uncle Patrice."

"Patrice?" Chris held out his hands; the tall man gripped them carefully.

"My brother was also named Patrice, and so I was called Brother, to tell us apart. And so, Uncle Brother."

Chris managed a faint grin. "Like it. Hey, we're getting out of here?"

"But yes, and as soon as Emilie makes certain of the hall and the back way," Patrice assured him. He leaned closer, eyed Chris curiously. Then chuckled. His voice was *very* low, but held nothing of the gravelly *basso* threat of Maurice. "But I know this man," he said, still chuckling. "He gave me good coin not so long ago, to carry one satchel from his ship to the Parrot. So few milk-skinned men do this, one remembers those who do." The laughter faded. "Dupret does not wish you well, my friend; we get you from here tonight."

"Good," Ariadne said. She sounded calm once more, but she was plaiting her fingers together. Patrice freed a hand, patted her shoulder, and held up a cord from which depended a wire cage enclosing a pale stone. "Hold this; you know how it works. Stay by the door." And as she hesitated, he flapped the hand at her. "Go, go, child, I watch over your man, get him to his feet. Emilie said the so-nice Maurice—"

"Yeah," Chris said. "So nice. Really. I'm all right, Ari, go watch the door." She gave him a doubtful look, wrapped the cord around her fingers, and crossed the room.

Patrice eyed Chris for a long moment, and when he spoke, his voice was a non-carrying near whisper. "How badly you are hurt?"

"I can walk—I think," Chris added honestly. "Mostly I think it's just bruises, except maybe my ribs."

"Yes. Well." The roar of the mob outside the French windows increased dramatically all of a sudden. "We can manage, I think." Ariadne hissed at him, held out the wire-and-stone charm; it was glowing faintly. "We go now." He hauled Chris to his feet, half carried him to the door.

Just short of it, he stopped suddenly; Ariadne caught her breath and bit down on the side of her hand. Mob noises came from the front of the house all at once, but the echo-

ing slam of the lower hall door muffled them once more.
Heavy footsteps, men running up the staircase. Patrice held
up a hand, wrapped one of Chris's hands around a bit of
twigs and cord, closed his own enormous paws over the
younger man's. Chris could all at once hear very well.

"Was that *utterly* necessary?" Dupret's voice, icy with
barely contained fury.

"*M'sieu,* I did what I had to." Maurice sounded nearly as
angry. "I brought us safely from your club, *on* foot, *through*
the streets—and we both still breathe. What more would
you?" Momentary silence. "Was it utterly of necessity that
you create as you did?"

Another silence, broken by a loud, cracking blow.
"That," Dupret snapped, "for anyone—including yourself,
Maurice!—who would dare question what I do, and why!"
Another silence. Chris was vaguely aware of Ariadne, a
still form outlined against the door by the reflection of
flames from the far street, via the open French doors.
Dupret's suddenly, unnervingly warm voice followed a
nasty silence. "Ah, my friend, forgive, I beg you! That so
many matters demand my attention! My brother, my
daughter, my wretched brother! And now Sorionne!"

Another silence. When the man next spoke, Chris would
have sworn he heard tears in Maurice's voice: "My good
sir, no. There is nothing to forgive. That—that you—*non.
N'importe pas*. But what you did this night—I did all I
could to protect you, my good sir. Know that."

"But—of course," Dupret murmured. "And I know that
no one else in all French Jamaica could protect me so well
as you. Still. Sorionne."

"May he rot," Maurice said flatly.

Dupret giggled—the most unnerving thing Chris had
heard thus far; he shivered, and Patrice's arm tightened
around his shoulders. "He assuredly does already, my
friend, consider the climate! But—*non*. We must consider
the damage caused tonight."

"You struck Sorionne," Maurice said flatly, "and he fell from the window. Dead as he landed."

"I know this!" The wall shook as one of them slammed a fist into it. "Still—what was needed is done, now we need decide what to do about his sons, who may well take outrage and demand satisfaction of honor. Come, the study, you and I; bring Peronne from the door, there is no need for him here."

"The front door, sir—"

"What mob would *dare* come here to make damage?" Dupret giggled again. "We drink, you and I, to greater profit without Sorionne, and we decide how best to settle this—and to settle the matter of my brother Philippe, now that neither Sorionne nor my daughter can tell him anything."

How come they didn't see the door unbarred? Chris wondered dazedly as the nobleman and his servant clomped down the main stairs. But the answer came right away: the bar slid quietly from its place, and Ariadne's aunt opened the door to beckon urgently. "The way is clear, but there are men everywhere, *his* men, watching. Frère, you make all the changes of cart and horse we planned, swear it!"

"Of course, Emilie."

" 'Of course, Emilie,' " she mocked him sharply. "Don't you sound so cool to me, this is a bad time, we need to hurry!"

"We hurry. Boy, you able to walk, or should I carry you?"

"I—yeah," Chris said breathily. "I can walk."

"Good," Emilie said, then hissed, "Go, go, go!" Before anyone could move, heavy boots came up the main staircase. "Maurice," Emilie breathed. Patrice swore breathily, hauled Chris behind the door. Emilie simply vanished from his line of sight as the door quietly eased shut. It creaked open almost at once; Maurice shoved it open and cursed angrily.

"Allo! Peronne, what are you doing in here? The master wants you!" Silence. "Where are you?"

"Peronne." An alto voice sent shivers up Chris's back. Ariadne stepped into the light. "There is no Peronne here. *Bâtarde.*" Maurice smiled; his teeth gleamed as he brought up an enormous fist. Ariadne's knife was a shining blur that came underhand in a full arc and vanished. Maurice swore faintly, coughed, and sagged into the doorframe, then slid to the floor. Ariadne stood over him, her face grim.

"Guard of my *beloved* father," she whispered. "Meet him in Hell, and tell him how sorry Ariadne was that she could not cause you more pain at the end." She stooped, tugged hard; brought the knife up with her as she stood. Chris closed his eyes, bit his lip; the blade was dark, sticky. He gasped as Patrice hauled him off his feet once again, hurried him out the door and down the hall. The light was bright against his eyelids, gone; they plunged down a steep flight of stairs.

"Sorry, my friend," Patrice said softly against his ear as they reached ground level. "I see this hurts but there is no time to waste." Chris forced his eyes open as warm, scented air blew past him. Ariadne vanished through an open door into darkness. Patrice followed, paused on the threshold.

"Whatever are you doing still here, go, go, go!" Emilie materialized at his elbow, snapping her fingers softly; she sounded very nervous all at once.

"The men on guard outside."

"Three—no more," Emilie said, and drew her hand meaningfully across her throat. "Remember, every change! If any of *his* men see you, Patrice—"

"Hush, woman, we make it so they don't see us." He hauled Chris through the door, across the brick courtyard, and into total darkness. "Stable," Patrice whispered.

"Mmmm," Chris replied. He couldn't have managed real words at the moment. The smell of horse and polished leather was all around him. They were through the stable, then out the far side and into a narrow alley between high, solid walls. Merchants' entry, Chris remembered. A covered cart waited for them, and Ariadne, her face anxious, stood by the canvas flap at the back.

"Go, shoo, in," Patrice murmured. Ariadne scrambled into the cart, turned to hold out her hands. Chris fell onto a pile of rough, dusty sacks as the flap came down. He used his elbows to drag himself a little farther in, and collapsed again. The sacks smelled like grain; the cart itself had a fusty odor he couldn't place. The pain in his side was grindingly sharp, nearly unbearable; he gasped as the cart jolted forward. Ariadne eased down next to him, felt for his hand. Her fingers were cool and damp, her pulse very fast.

Say something, he told himself. *She just killed—she'll think—* "Good job," he managed. Her fingers tightened on his briefly.

The cart jostled down the alleyway, turned onto the street, and began to move more quickly. Chris held his breath, listened; he couldn't hear anything but the clink of harness, hooves against brick or stone, and the very distant sound of that mob. From the front of the cart, then, Patrice's low, non-carrying voice: "Two hours, perhaps three. The English *Hawk* will send a boat for you, we meet it this side of Point-Azur. But we cannot go straight there. Dupret's men are everywhere these days, and they watch for anything—"

"Two, three hours," Chris said hastily. He didn't want to think about Dupret's men standing in shadows, watching and waiting . . . "Still be dark in three hours, good."

"Boat will not come until sunrise," Patrice corrected him. "The tide and the reef; the ships are not permitted to leave port anyway before then—so no one can sneak from Philippe-sur-Mer, as you and your man did the one time, Ariadne. Your aunt Emilie says good-bye."

*   *   *

It was quiet for some time. Chris had no idea where they might be, except by the occasional lights they were still inside the city. He lost track of the times Patrice helped him from one cart in a darkened alley or stableyard, and into another. He itched from straw; one cart had no sides or roof, so Patrice had thrown straw over them both, and a filthy, fishy blanket over that.

He spoke to them, now and again, a word or two— mostly warning. "There is a man—three doors down, stay still. A man on horse, coming from behind us. Two men with pistols—" He had broken into a ragged cough at that point, using cough as an excuse to avert his face, Chris thought. His own stomach was painfully tight, his mouth dry. Ariadne clung to his hand. The sounds of the rampaging mob faded, dwindled, was gone entirely. The air was cooler, dryer—less wharf-scented.

The current cart was pulled by an aging donkey and had carried chickens; there were feathers, chicken fluff, and the odor of chickens everywhere. Ariadne had fortunately retained enough wit to pull an armful of clean straw from the previous cart before she and Patrice got him in; even so, he continually fought not to sneeze as down floated across his upper lip or tried to go up his nose.

"Quiet here," Patrice said very softly. "And no one in sight."

"Do not trust to that," Ariadne warned as quietly.

"I do not."

Silence then; the donkey's hooves were muffled by the dirt road. Chris eased down a little flatter; Ariadne's fingers tightened on his and she leaned close to him. "I'm all right," he whispered. "Just—really tired."

"Sleep, if you can," she whispered back.

"Can't." But the slow-moving cart creaked rhythmically back and forth; somehow, he lost track of time and even movement. When he next opened his eyes, the cart wasn't moving and he could smell sea.

It wasn't entirely dark anymore; he could see Ariadne kneeling down by his feet, the canvas flap in her hand. She let it fall as he moved slightly. "*Shhh*. Everything is all right. Patrice goes to wait for the ship."

"Oh. Good."

Her hand pressed damp hair from his brow, rested there a moment. He let his eyes close. "You feel warm." She sounded worried.

" 'S all right. I always sleep warm." He didn't. No point in both of them worrying. *Hawk* was English, some of them carried healers or at least someone to dispense powders. New Lisbon wasn't that far, either. Once they got off this island. *If*.

The wagon springs creaked. Chris's skin prickled but it was only Patrice. "I see it," he said. "We go now, reach the water as the boat arrives, get you both gone."

"I like it," Chris said. Getting him out of the cart wasn't any fun at all; he was sweating freely by the time Patrice had hold of his shoulders and his feet on dry sand.

"We two manage from here," Ariadne said. "You go; all those men of my beloved papa's last night, if one of them worked it out, somehow—"

Patrice shrugged. "Perhaps; still, no one followed us from the city, and there has been no traffic on that road since we stopped here."

"There may be no need to follow," Ariadne said flatly. "At the wharfs, if someone there overheard—" She glanced over her shoulder. "Please, go. If he suspects you—"

"He suspects any who are his servants or the kin of your mother; we give him no cause to suspect us of helping *you*."

"He needs no cause." Patrice merely shook his head. Ariadne sighed. "At least hide the cart better."

He glanced back toward the road. "Well—yes, all right, there is time, and to make you happy. Wait here."

Chris leaned against a tree and ran a cautious hand across

his eyes; they felt gritty. It wouldn't be a bright morning; too many clouds. Beyond the narrow belt of trees and scrub lay sand, a litter of branches and logs, and steel gray water past that.

Ariadne kept one hand on his arm; she pointed suddenly. "Look, there—a ship."

"Ours?"

"I—I think yes," she added suddenly. "Look, to this side of it."

A long wooden boat had separated from the ship and was moving steadily toward the shore. Patrice was suddenly and very quietly back with them, his hand under Chris's elbow once more, but they waited where they were, still in shadow, just beyond the sand. The boat slid down the front of a low wave; someone jumped into hip-deep water and dragged the bow onto shore.

Patrice gave Ariadne a nudge. "Go, girl, we follow." She caught her lip between her teeth, broke cover, and ran, skirts wrapped high around one hand. Her feet made deep holes, squeaking in the coarse, dry sand. Chris eyed it with misgivings, but Patrice lifted him with ease and started forward. "You don't want to walk this, my friend." He covered the distance to the boat in half a dozen long-legged strides, delivered Chris into the hands of two seamen standing on shore.

Ariadne was already in the boat, waiting, the knife in her hands. "Please, Oncle Frère, you've done all you dare, go at once!" Patrice blew her a kiss, then turned and walked quickly away; a moment later he vanished between the trees. Ariadne let her breath out in a gusty sigh, then held out a hand for Chris.

"Have care," Ariadne said quietly, "he is injured." Chris closed his eyes as two men scrambled to the bow to scoop him up and settle him on the nearest seat; Chris clawed for something to hold on to as the boat began to ease back into the water. One of the men still in the water threw himself in, then the other. The boat rocked alarmingly.

"Ready?" One of the English asked.

"I—ah, *hells*!" Ariadne swore. Chris stared across her shoulder. Dupret slid from his horse and crossed the sand; he held a long-barreled pistol in one hand and another was shoved through his belt.

"Stop!" he shouted. "That man killed my servant!" The sailors glanced at each other, and one of them eyed Chris warily.

"Liar!" Ariadne shouted back at him. She held up the knife where he could clearly see it. "*I* killed him! And I am glad!"

"Murderess," Dupret hissed. "I knew this morning, when I found you and him gone, and they came to tell me a ship had left harbor, that you planned this escape! Murderess! You English *dare* not remove them from Philippe-sur-Mer, you have been already warned! That man has committed serious crimes, and by her own words she convicts herself!"

"Look at my husband, look at his face, you English, see what the man Maurice did!"

"Maurice?" one of the sailors asked. "I know that one, big nasty-tempered brute of a man. He did that to you, mister?"

"Mmmm," Chris managed.

"Cast off, boys," the sailor said sharply. "Lady did us all a favor, so far's I can see."

Dupret spat and drew his second pistol. "I shoot!"

"We have guns also, Dupret!" one of the others shouted back. "Four shots to your two."

"I have other men and more guns, not far behind!" Dupret topped him.

Ariadne laughed. "But there is a shipful of witnesses out there! Will you kill them all?" Dupret looked beyond her, hesitated. She rose to full height, balancing against the sway of the boat, reversed the knife and threw it, hard. One of the sailors gasped; the hilt quivered in the sand, between Dupret's feet. He paled suddenly; his eyes were wide.

"Keep that," she said flatly. "I will get another, with *your* name upon it if you dare ever seek us out again. I swear that by my mother."

"You—" He couldn't seem to manage anything else, except to stare from her to the knife. The boat was backing through the water; Ariadne dropped down to one knee and gripped the gunnels as it rode up a wave, down the back side. Dupret stared after them, pistol hanging loose and apparently forgotten at his side.

9

JENNIFER rounded the corner of the large fish pool at an easy lope, slowed still more as she emerged from the trees. It was windy on the ancient parade ground; dust whirled upward in narrow spirals and branches skittered along the hard-packed dirt. Wind whipped the knee-length, very baggy breeks she wore as a compromise since her old running shorts had gotten too tight. The extra fabric twisted around her legs; the slightly damp shirt billowed. "Inhale, two, three, ex—hale—oh, drat!" The slow run became a fast walk; another gust wrapped her knees together; she caught hold of fabric, yanked it loose, and kept going, the shirtfront firmly in both hands. "Steps, turn around, go back," she panted. It had been hard enough getting up the energy to run this morning: the air was late-fall chilly and the wind made it downright cold; low clouds scudded across the sky. Fighting her clothes was the last straw. Jennifer cast the upper towers a sour glance, brought her head down so she could watch the ground before her feet. She liked this kind of weather—so long as she could watch it from behind secure windows, from a warm room. "Yah," she mumbled as she neared the steps. "You *sat* all day yesterday, *and* the day before. You want to look like your mother, after a couple kids?" Not that her mother had been obese, exactly; just—*just soft. And heavier than I want to ever be in my life.*

The endorphins weren't kicking in today, like they usually did by this point in a run. "Maybe it's just as well
Dahven and Sretha won't let me run in the streets anymore.
Get—exhausted out past the city gates, have—have to walk
back? *Bo*-ring!" Of course, that was part of the problem:
She did get bored running the same route within the walls
every single time—particularly a double or triple loop like
she had to do in here to get any decent mileage. She
slapped the low wall next to the steps—where she and
Chris had sat and watched Ariadne duel with Dahven—
turned, and shuffled off toward the woods. "Pick—up the—
pace," she told herself.

A short while later, she emerged from the trees at a walk.
"Yah. Fun—when you quit," she told herself. The wind
slackened suddenly, just long enough for her to hear her
name being shouted from the steps. She looked up; Dahven
stood in the entry, a bundle of paper clutched in his hand.
She sighed faintly, blotted her forehead against her sleeve,
and walked a little faster. Dahven stepped aside, closed the
door behind them. She sighed. "Oh, does that feel good."

"What—the run? Even on a day like this?"

She laughed breathily. "No, silly, don't look so horrified!
I meant, the lack of wind. And quitting, today." She led the
way into the family dining room, dropped into her chair. He
hitched up a leg, sat on the table next to her. Jennifer eyed
the bundle of telegraph paper with distaste. "That much
since last night?" He dropped the pile. "You read them?"

"Just the top one," Dahven said. "Eniss brought the rest
while I was reading it; thought you'd want to see at least
this one right away." He snagged the top sheet of paper,
handed it to her. "Want water?"

"Mmmm, please." Jennifer scanned down the first few
lines, let out a gusty sigh of relief. "Oh, thank goodness.
Eddie says they've got Chris and Ariadne back. When did
he send—? Four days ago! My God, that's awful!"

Dahven ticked off the fingers of his left hand. "Mondego

to the mainland to the northeasternmost town in the Gallic
States, by horse to Fahlia, by ship across the isthmus—I
hope Adreban really *does* go ahead and have line run south
to the States."

"Shesseran wouldn't like that," Jennifer said absently.
She set a finger on the sheet to mark her place, glanced up.
Dahven shrugged.

"He doesn't pay much heed to Fahlia and Derra Vos;
Adreban's used to doing what he likes, whatever the Emperor says. And after all, with his sister married to Shesseran's heir—"

"I suppose. At least we heard something. With shipping
shut down, we might not have found out for—oh." She
stared at the sheet. "Black eyes, a fat lip, two cracked ribs.
Nice. Hope Eddie got a good healer for him, ribs can be
painful."

"I know." Dahven shoved her cup next to her elbow, settled on the edge of the table again. "Food should be here in
a moment."

"Food. Food? Dahven!"

"You're supposed to eat a proper breakfast, remember?
Not just coffee."

"I had bread." Jennifer drained the cup.

"Sretha and the midwife both sent instructions to the
kitchen." Dahven picked up another message. "Ah, finally,
it's from Dro Pent, Wudron's own writing." Jennifer set
Edrith's message aside, picked up the next in the stack, but
let it drop to her lap as Dahven whistled thoughtfully. "Not
good." He handed her a sheet of heavy cream-colored stuff.

"This is worse than the last Dro Pent message," Jennifer
grumbled. She tossed it on the table. "Can't make out a
word of it."

"He's in full panic." Dahven picked it up, turned it right
side up. "Wudron, that is. Says, 'Rumor is rife in city that
Vuhlem holds Dro Pent, and Emperor means to take Duchy
back by force. By all the gods at once, pay no heed to the

rumor, and tell the Emperor he must not! Dahven, your pledge of utter silence, Vuhlem took my son, he says he will kill the boy if I do anything to give him away. I know he would use such an attack as Shesseran's upon my city as excuse and do murder upon my heir.' " He let the sheet fall, folded his hands together; his eyes were black. "How very like Vuhlem."

Jennifer slammed the long table with her fist. "Damn the man! Dahven! We can't let him get away with this, the boy's barely five, isn't he?"

"Just five."

"Wonderful. If Vuhlem gets away with *that,* what's next?"

"Another attack on Shesseran? I don't know; probably Vuhlem doesn't, either. Taking the boy was stupid. Still." Dahven's voice trailed off. He considered this in silence for some moments; his fingers drummed the table. "If he has the boy in Holmaddan, I don't see what we *can* do. His palace is enormous, probably the oldest and best guarded in all Rhadaz; he could keep the child inside his walls and no one would ever find him, if Vuhlem didn't want him found. And—well, there's the sea at his back door. I'm sorry, Jen, this is just the kind of thing Shesseran does nothing about best: no proof except Wudron's word the boy went north, no sign of the boy, Vuhlem claiming ignorance of the whole mess—"

"There has to be something we can do," Jennifer said flatly. "You think about it; I will, too. We're not going to let that old pig win, not this time." She drew another message from the stack, read it, sighed, and handed it to Dahven wordlessly.

DUKE'S FORT; ALETTO AWAKE, WEAK BUT GOING TO BE FINE, THANKS FOR HEALER. LIZELLE DEAD, SUICIDE, HAD CACHE OF THAT BRANDY, INCLUDING BOTTLE MEANT

FOR ME. GOD, IT'S MAD HERE, WHERE'S MY RUBY SLIP-
PERS? ROBYN.

Dahven crumbled the sheet, dropped the wad of paper.
"Wretched woman; I'll wager she suicided to make them
feel guilty. She would. And—poor Aletto, he will, too. But
I thought they took all the drug away from her!" He slid off
the table as the door to the kitchen swung open and one of
the new girls came into the room with a heavy tray. She set
it on the table, glanced at Jennifer curiously, curtseyed and
left quickly.

Jennifer stared at the table with dismay. The tray held
three kinds of fruit, a pile of bread, milk, even a dish of
scrambled eggs—the one thing she'd had success teaching
the kitchen to make. "I can't eat all that!" She eyed the
eggs, swallowed, and shoved them aside. "And in case no
one's noticed lately, I can't eat those just now, they make
me puke."

"Eat something," Dahven said mildly. "I'm supposed to
see that you do, and I'll get cross if your midwife nags me
because you don't." He snared a slice of apple and popped
it into his mouth. Jennifer spooned fruit butter onto bread
and bit into it, then tucked the bite into her cheek.

"Lizelle—I know Robyn, she probably did take everything away from the poor thing, but addicts like that have
hiding places, lots of them. It's too bad; Birdy doesn't need
the hassle, and I bet Aletto really *does* feel guilty. Birdy'd
never say, but I'll bet she's just pissed at Lizelle for doing
that to Aletto." She chewed bread, took another bite, and
reached for the next message. "Eat more of the apple; I
don't like the texture. We'd better get word down to Afronsan right away, about Wudron's boy."

"Already did." Dahven poured her more water. "Just,
'Vuhlem kidnapped Oloric, longer message to follow.'
Keep him from starting anything."

"As if he had the opportunity, with Shesseran breathing

down his neck," Jennifer retorted. "Let's see—Misarla's had more problems with the drug coming in; and her border guard says there are men camped on the Holmaddan side of the line."

"Men?"

"Small camp of soldiers. Couple of her Cornekkans went to check. The camp is Vuhlem's, captain says they're trying to find where drugs are coming into Holmaddan, grumbled about all that deserted shoreline. Misarla's man wonders if that was his real reason; says the Holmaddi guard usually send only a handful of men, and this was a full armed company. Also, the captain was awfully talkative for one of Vuhlem's."

"Mmm. Spreading the lie thick. Possible. She wire Afronsan?"

"Ahhh, yeah. Says here, same message, via Duke's Fort to Podhru; Robyn and Aletto will know by now, too. Old pig. Vuhlem's getting seriously above himself."

Dahven laughed shortly. "I'd love to be there when he's taken down. I do truly loathe that man. He's nastier than Father at his worst."

"Charming," Jennifer murmured. "Here—I think this settles it. Message from Lialla; there's a couple of Red Hawk caravaners waiting at the Cap and Feather in case we want to send word back to her. They—one of them, anyway— saw the boy being carried into Vuhlem's palace. *A* boy," Jennifer corrected herself. "Pale haired. Lialla thinks it must be young Oloric. Vuhlem has Lasanachi ships at his personal docks, boy came on one of them."

"All of which is illegal. Lialla's got no business up there, spying on Vuhlem, she'll get herself killed yet," Dahven said gloomily. "Stupid young woman."

Jennifer shook her head. "Not really stupid, just—like Chris. Thinks no one's going to get at her."

"I'd wager he doesn't feel *that* way anymore." Dahven snared the rest of her apple, spooned a little fruit butter onto one slice, and ate it. "Not with broken ribs to remind him every time he draws breath. More of the bread, you," he added sternly.

"You want me fat," Jennifer complained. She didn't sound too worried. She tore a piece in half. "Compromise, all right?" She ate with one hand, read the rest of the message. Sighed faintly and swallowed. "Lialla says she's probably going to return to Sikkre soon; things are too crazy around there right now for her to be any help to the women and—hmmm." She was quiet for a moment. "She doesn't say; I get the feeling that Triad scares her—the one Vuhlem's supposed to have."

"Probably has Jadek's old Triad," Dahven said gloomily.

"No—didn't I tell you about them, a while back?" He shook his head. "They start seriously bonding, changing from three individual people to one—well, one whatever—and they get religion, or something. Jadek's left him because he wanted to play rough, and they—it—wanted enlightenment."

"Sounds crazy enough to be true. Where'd you get that?"

"Talked to the Light Shaper your father used to keep."

"Oh." He eyed her sidelong. "You did? Brave you; doesn't sound exactly safe to me."

"Possibly why I didn't tell you. I'm still not sure Vuhlem *has* a Triad; where'd he get a young Triad these days?" Jennifer shoved the tray aside. "That's all I eat. I'm not hungry after a run, anyway; any more food and I'll be sick. Anything else in the messages, or can I go clean up?"

Dahven grinned, and held out a small folded square of blue market paper. "Just one—saved the best for last."

"Best? What—something good in all this?" She unfolded the paper, studied it in silence, finally whistled softly. "So, Audren Henry's decided to rat on his steel-mill employers."

"Keeping in mind, he says he doesn't know much," Dahven reminded her mildly.

"Well, yes. Still, he may know more than he realizes.

Give me a few hours to pick his brains, and we'll find out."
She smiled, folded the sheet, and dropped it onto the others.
"Hope Chris has some more input for us, and soon; this
may actually start turning things in our favor." She held out
her hands. "Here, make yourself useful, help me up, so I
can go get clean and get back to work."

THUKARA JENNIFER TO AFRONSAN: ENTIRE TEXT OF
MESSAGE FROM WUDRON OF DRO PENT FOLLOWS. SUG-
GEST CAUTION REGARDING INVASION OF SAME, FOR OBVI-
OUS REASONS. ALSO SUGGEST WE FIND A WAY TO GET
WRETCHED VUHLEM TO BEHAVE HIMSELF.

Afronsan reread the lower part of the message that contained Wudron's terrified plea. He sat very still for some
moments, staring vacantly toward the near wall; his lips
moved soundlessly. Finally, he dragged himself to his feet
and crossed the room, opened the door, and leaned into the
hall. "Messenger!" he called out. The sound echoed in the
long, high-ceilinged, cold hallway, followed by the echoing
clatter of rapid footsteps as one of the messenger boys
came at a dead run. "Go to the main floor, where the Emperor has his messenger chamber; if there is someone waiting, pass to him the message that Afronsan humbly begs
leave to meet with his brother. If not, return to me at once
for further instruction, or if there is anyone who might ride
to the Emperor, right away, send that one. It's quite urgent."

"Sir." The boy turned and sprinted back the way he'd
come.

An hour later, Afronsan shook rain from his waterproofed
cloak, dropped it and the broad-brimmed, oiled hat across
his saddle, and crossed the covered courtyard of the Emper-
or's city apartments. The servant had the main doors open
for him, bowed low as he passed. *Apparently, I am once*

more useful to my brother, Afronsan thought dryly. The first time he'd come to the city palace after Shesseran's birthday fete, the servants had averted their eyes and backed away from him, barely remembering sufficient protocol to bow. Even a handful of days ago, proper response to the presence of royalty was notably lacking here.

The hallway was colder than his own, sterile: bare of ornament, carpet, or window. Only two lights flickered at the far end, where another servant waited to bow him into the Emperor's bedroom. Shesseran's private room was overly warm, particularly after the chilly hall and the long ride across town in the driving rain and wind that marked an early winter storm.

The Emperor lay upon a thin-mattressed, narrow bed, a plain coverlet drawn to his waist, the half-dozen cushions at his back the only sign of wealth or rank in the entire chamber—aside from the well-tended fire. Afronsan bowed neatly, then held out the Thukara's message. Shesseran inclined his head a little in reply, coughed into the elbow of his rough-woven bedrobe, took the message, and read it in silence. It slid to the bedding, then to the floor. Afronsan let it fall and, after a long moment, took courage in his hands to ask, "Well?"

Shesseran coughed, grimaced. "I know Vuhlem." There wasn't much strength to his voice; Afronsan had to lean close to catch his words. "He would never dare—" The Emperor's voice faded; he gazed up at his much younger brother anxiously. Afronsan schooled himself to patience—*wants me to assure him Vuhlem indeed would not dare*—and took the Emperor's hand.

"He *has* done the thing Wudron says, unfortunately. I am sorry, brother; I know you are fond of Vuhlem. But—there is confirmation of the boy's appearance in Holmaddan by a caravaner who is heir to Red Hawk's grandmother. Also, a source known to and trusted by the Thukar of Sikkre says

there are men in Vuhlem's colors occupying Dro Pent city
and Wudron's palace."

Shesseran frowned; his hands shook. "All—all that?"

Afronsan nodded. He patted his brother's chill, trembling
fingers gently. "Red Hawk clan sent the message south
from Holmaddan City; the warning from Dro Pent is the
Duke's own word, his own writing, smuggled from the city
by a man loyal to young Thukar Dahven."

"Wudron fears—does he really fear we would attack Dro
Pent?" The Emperor's frown deepened. "But we would
never do such a thing! Warfare by the Emperor against a
Duke? It's mad!"

More patience. Afronsan managed a smile. "I know this,
sire. All Rhadaz knows it." *And upon that knowledge, Vuhlem has acted.* "I have sent Dro Pent's Duke a wire to that
effect already—"

"Wire." Shesseran shook his head. He was silent for
some moments. "That—that wire. Useful, my brother, I
admit it is of use. You have—a gift for such things which I
do not, which of the foreigners' innovations will serve the
land and its people, which might encourage ease and sloth.
But—the wire was not yet strung beyond Sikkre, or so you
told *me*!"

"It still is not strung beyond Sikkre, or you would have
known of it, my brother. Thukar Dahven will by now have
the message I sent by wire; he will forward a horse messenger to Wudron, a man who knows how best to circumvent
Vuhlem's soldiers, a man who carries a message that tells
Wudron you intend no action that might cause Vuhlem to
harm the boy."

"Harm. Ah, beloved gods! Who would dare harm a boy?
And this child of Wudron's—" Shesseran frowned. "I forget, Frons, how old is Wudron's heir?"

Silly, ancient nickname. Afronsan smiled. "Four or five
years, I fear I forget as well. He's very young. Of an age to

still be at his mother's side, and to weep for her if he was taken away."

"Taken—away . . . Oh, no; how dreadful. Vuhlem would surely not—" Shesseran shook his head again; this time, his mouth was set. Afronsan waited. "He would never—" He was silent again, finally sighed, very faintly. "Gods. I do not think he would harm a small child, anyone's son. Or take one. Then—he has none of his own, you know; such a curse would weigh upon a man like Vuhlem; he'd care for the sons of others." *Hah,* Afronsan thought sourly. Somehow, he kept the thought, and the anger, from his face. After a momentary silence, Shesseran went on. "But—but Vuhlem never cared for babes as you or I care, Frons. I remember that of him, when we were boys together: Vuhlem never understood why one might love a mere child, of whatever sex. Even—even a younger brother." The Emperor's fingers tightened on those of his Heir. "As I did, for all you might doubt it, Frons."

Afronsan smiled back and, greatly daring, addressed his brother in the nickname he'd given the much older brother when he was unable to pronounce the true heir's rightful name. "I never doubted your love, Sess." Shesseran laughed breathily.

"Sess." He sobered then. "A boy of such few years, how dreadful for the child. I—I remember being that small, Frons, how frightened I was when Mother was ill and they would not let me be with her. Poor—poor little babe. What does Wudron call him?"

Afronsan had to think about that, despite the recent messages; one of those minor details he so often forgot, the kind of thing Shesseran would remember. *Poor ill brother. Something I could well learn from him, if I had the time for it.* "Oloric? I think that's it."

"Good name." Shesseran drew a shaky breath, let it out on a very long sigh. For a moment, Afronsan thought he might have fallen asleep—all those powders his healers gave him, any more, his age, the pain he clearly suffered when the powders failed—but Shesseran opened his eyes and used his elbows to lever himself a little higher on the pillows. "If—*if,* mind you!—my friend Vuhlem has gone mad and done such a dreadful thing, he would never admit it. And with Holmaddan's palace so isolated, he might never be caught out." The Emperor frowned, thought for a long moment. He laughed then; Afronsan's eyebrows went up. "This wire of yours, Frons—where does it go? How many of the Duchies?"

"Directly? All save Dro Pent and Holmaddan, brother. Why?"

"And into Holmaddan—the caravaners still post their own messages to that dreadful slab of a building Vuhlem put them in still? The grandmothers' own form of swift message?"

"Why—yes, they do."

Shesseran laughed again, a deep boyish chuckle that erased years from his lean, pained visage. "Then send—*wire*—this message as soon as you can. I think the problem will be resolved for now." Afronsan inclined his head formally and pulled a small cube of paper from his deep pocket, an English reservoir pen from his sleeve. Shesseran dictated; Afronsan wrote. After a moment, though, the Heir's arm dropped from the cube, and he began to laugh. Shesseran gazed at him in sudden surprise, then began to laugh with him.

TO EACH OF OUR NINE DUCHIES, AND TO THE DUKES AND DUCHESSES THEREOF, THEIR EMPEROR SAYS UNTO THEM: A CHILD HAS BEEN TAKEN FROM ONE OF YOU BY ANOTHER OF YOU. WE ARE WELL AWARE WHICH CHILD AND BY WHICH DUCHY, THOUGH WE DO NOT *YET* KNOW WHERE THE CHILD IS PRESENTLY HELD. FOR THIS REASON, AND NO OTHER, SHOULD THE BABE BE RETURNED TO HIS MOTHER AT ONCE, THERE WILL BE NO ACTION TAKEN BY

THE EMPEROR—AT THIS TIME. SEE IT BE DONE, AT ONCE, LEST DIRE CONSEQUENCE FALL UPON THE ONE WHO HOLDS THE CHILD UNWILLING FROM HIS PARENTS.

IT HAS ALSO COME TO THE EMPEROR'S ATTENTION THAT CERTAIN OF THE DUCHIES MAINTAIN MORE ARMS-MEN THAN ARE PERMITTED BY OUR LAWS IN TIME OF PEACE. DESPITE PROBLEMS AMONG THE FOREIGN NATIONS AND ALONG OUR SEACOAST, THERE IS NO NEED FOR SUCH ARMED STRENGTH WITHIN OUR BORDERS, AND THERE-FORE, WE ORDER THAT ANY SUCH ARMSMEN, SOLDIERS, OR TROOPS OF ANY KIND HELD BY WHATEVER DUCHY WILL BE IMMEDIATELY REDUCED TO THEIR PROPER NUM-BERS AND LOCATIONS. IF THIS IS ACCOMPLISHED AT ONCE, THE EMPEROR WILL HAVE NO CAUSE TO CREATE AN INVESTIGATION FORCE—SUCH AS HIS MANY-TIMES GREAT-GRANDSIRE DID, WITH CONSEQUENCE AND COST REMEMBERED SURELY BY EACH OF THE DUKES AND DUCHESSES. RECALL WHEN HELL-LIGHT AND THE TRIADS POSED A THREAT TO THE LAND, AND HOW THAT MATTER WAS RESOLVED! BLESSINGS UPON YOU ALL, AND UPON THE LAND ITSELF: SHESSERAN XIV.

Vuhlem strode from the windowless chamber high in his north tower and yanked the door to behind him. The sound reverberated from chill stone, echoed down the winding flag stairway. He stood in the hallway for a long moment to catch his breath and gain control of a towering fury, but his color was still high when he turned back and shoved the door open once more, just enough to lean in and shout, "I want results! And I want them soon! I already know she is in the city *somewhere*! I want you to find her!" Silence; a flare of ruddy yellow-orange Light his only response. He swore furiously, drew back into the hall, pulled the door closed behind him with deceptive care, and clomped down the steep, narrow flight of steps to his personal apartments.

It was much warmer here, though not much brighter. The

servants had drawn curtains across the windows against the chill of yet another north storm, and retreated through the small plain door close to the fireplace as they heard his entry. Vuhlem caught the faint click of the door latch, nodded his approval to the spacious, empty room. He wished no paid help hovering over him in here! The curtains: he didn't particularly want them closed but it didn't matter. It would be as dark outside as an hour after sundown, anyway, thanks to early winter storms and thick cloud cover. "Bah." He scrubbed his hands together before the fire, then drew his favorite chair nearer the enormous stone fireplace, shoved his boots off with his toes and stretched heavily stockinged feet toward the blaze. "I must have been mad," he snarled under his breath. "Fetching in a Triad. Worthless creatures, always wanting things that cost too much, and not paying me back with decent results, either."

Actually, that wasn't *quite* true; he had to admit (to himself; never to the Triad) that even from their usual sanctuary in his distant hunting lodge, they had been able to use their particular skills to track pockets of discontent for him, often pinpointing the location so well the Duke's city guard didn't need to search very hard for traitors.

Forty-seven women and twelve men executed this past month, thanks to his Triad's work—and that not counting those stupid coastal villagers who'd stolen so many crates of treated southern brandies.

"But they—*it!*—cannot locate one miserable sin-Duchess! And I know she is here, somewhere in the city, I know it! She simply must be!" Because how else had Shesseran learned about Wudron's boy, *and* about his army?

But Shesseran! He'd done nothing direct, oh, no! No, he'd sent that revoltingly roundabout message to all the Dukes, how typical! "Anyone knowing of—whatever Duke or Duchess, bah!" He spat into the fire. "He knows damned well which of us has the wretched, whining brat! But who

warned him the boy wasn't in his own palace? It must be
her! Aletto's dratted sister! Because Wudron would never
have ignored my warnings—he's spineless, under the
thumb of that woman of his. He knew I'd gut the boy if he
even *thought* of begging aid." The mother wouldn't have
dared, either; she might have no sense for her own head,
but the heir— So, not Dro Pent. "Besides, none of the regular messengers left his palace, my men swore to that." Such
swearing was enough; Vuhlem knew the quality of the men
he based in Dro Pent. They wouldn't lie to him, any more
than they'd dare let something slip by them—loyalty, of
course, but bolstered by knowledge of his anger, and his
Triad. He bent down, stripped the foreign machine-knit
woolen socks from his feet, and held bare soles to the fire
again.

That girl, then—that caravaner the guard had told him
about, lurking about where she had no business to be.
"Filthy caravaners! They're behind this, somehow—in
league with the sin-Duchess!" His eyes narrowed. "Wait—
yes, it's just possible. If *she* is with them, here in the city,
encouraging them." Not that he'd dare search the building
for her; Shesseran would leap down his throat again, anything to protect his wretched nomads even against his good
friend.

The caravaners were moderately useful in the outlying
villages, but overall a pestilence: it didn't balance out. Just
the attitude of their women about men, obedience, all the
things women should pay heed to: The damned caravaners
gave Holmaddi women notions no sensible man would put
up with.

The more he thought about it, the more it made sense:
Only a fool would have remained in Holmaddan once she
escaped his prison. Lialla was such a fool, she had to be
here with the caravaners. *Should have broken her arrogant,
snotty neck when I had the opportunity. What could Aletto
have done to me?* Women like that showed what came of a

mother who used Thread, a spineless and physically weak
brother, an uncle more concerned with being called Duke
than with keeping his women in line.

How Lialla had escaped those dungeons—but he'd
know, eventually. Men talked out there in the city and the
market; his own men listened, and so did his Triad. Nothing
escaped the palace, and eventually the Duke.

"Dare to put yourself within my reach again, arrogant
bitch; you'll have more than a bruised cheekbone to remember *me* by. If you live long enough to remember anything!"

Women getting above themselves. His fingers drummed
against the hardwood armrest of his chair. There were signs
all over the southern Duchies, result as much as anything of
those outlanders coming into Rhadaz four years ago. Jadek
would spin in his grave, seeing how his adopted son let his
woman do as she chose, and it was just as well Dahmec
hadn't lived to see his son and That Woman in Sikkre.
Vuhlem's hands cramped, made claws. *One chance at her,
just one!* But it didn't seem likely Dahven would give him
the chance—or the woman, either. Vuhlem kicked a thin
branch into the fire, scowled as flames popped and
snapped.

Everything had gone wrong when those three outlanders
were pulled into Rhadaz; the boy was as bad as either of the
women. Not surprisingly, since one was said to be his
mother, the other his mother's sister. Whose fault? Jadek's,
of course, for letting that old Wielder run free in Zelharri,
letting her drag outlanders into Rhadaz. But the blame was
equally selfish old Dahmec's. He knew from the start what
he had in those women, that boy—and he'd let them escape
him alive.

*A sensible Duke would have put monkshood in their
soup. Dahmec was greedy, and paid for his greed. So, now
I have snotty women cropping up all over my own Duchy,
thanks to one doddering Wielder and all she inadvertently*

brought into our world, and a "brother" nobleman who hadn't sense enough to kill what was clearly a danger to all of us.

There were petitions piled high in Vuhlem's council chamber, women everywhere in Holmaddan seeking equality; seeking rights the gods never intended they have. In the villages, such things wouldn't get very far; village men wouldn't stand for such impudence, and neither would their Duke. In the city—*I have that matter under control; my Triad does. It had better.* And once he had sufficient women's names, and household names: The Emperor might have banned public whippings and dunkings to death years earlier, but Shesseran wouldn't live forever. Possibly not through the end of the year, if matters went according to plan. Afronsan wouldn't hold the throne any time at all—if *he* lived to assume it.

Vuhlem smiled unpleasantly and drew a large crockery jug and cup from warm ash where they'd been buried against one side of the fire. Mulled fruit; but it would make Shesseran blink. *Old fool; he thinks I'm as pure as he is.* It had initially been something of a bother, creating a facade the Emperor would accept. No worse than wearing a mask all through those years of school together. *My good fortune I saw at once what kind of person he was, what would please him.* These days, there probably wasn't much weak, aging Shesseran wouldn't swallow, if it came from Vuhlem.

Well—except for the boy. *I should have seen it; Shesseran has no son of his own—like me. Weak women, obviously, his and mine. But to think he'd care for the sons of other Dukes. That's mad. Sanctimonious old pig.* He wouldn't blame himself for not following Shesseran's thought processes to arrive at such a conclusion. All those religions, nothing else could explain it—and Shesseran had always shown a·bent toward the kinds of gods that asked sacrifice and privation of their followers.

Too late to hope for change in the old man, Vuhlem would have to give in this time—or appear to. Bite on his blades, return the boy, pull his troops back from the borders of the three neighboring Duchies—apologize humbly to his Emperor for the "misunderstanding," even crawl, if he must. Though the very thought made his blood boil. But if it took that to appease Shesseran and to keep the old man's rein hand tight on his Heir—well, it wouldn't draw Vuhlem's blood, and in the long run would be only a small setback. Provided Afronsan's spies were kept in check by the Emperor, there would be ways around Shesseran's edict ordering that Vuhlem cut his army; plenty of places to hide the new companies and still have them ready to fight in short order. *Once Shesseran is dead.*

Afronsan claimed he maintained no spy network. *Ridiculous. Does he think I'm so naive as that?* All rulers had spies. Then, Afronsan was as blind in his own ways as Shesseran was in his. Weak blood in the ruling household; better to get a strongman on the throne, with such days ahead as Rhadaz would face. With such allies—and enemies—as she presently had. And who could say which of them would change sides, without warning? The Incan empire had already done so twice, according to old Casimaffi.

Allies like Casimaffi. Vuhlem wasn't about to trust *that* one, the way Dahmec's fool twin sons had. The aging Bezanti was too fond of coin and comfort, too smug over his large clutch of sons—too willing to sell himself and his ships to the highest bidder. *They don't learn from each other's mistakes. If that young outlander and his half-French wife had been in my hands, I would not have let them escape—they'd never have left Podhru alive. The man Dupret might have been angry at first, he'd eventually have seen the sense of killing them immediately. Surely he sees it now.*

At least, rumor from the south, via the Lasanachi, told Vuhlem that the two had been caught once again—well, surely this time, Dupret wouldn't let them go. Vuhlem

scowled at the fire. He could almost wish for the foreign
wire: still, he couldn't be certain the Emperor and his people had no way to overhear messages, or he might have allowed it into Holmaddan. Most of the other noble houses
knew what was going on much faster than he did.

Well, once matters were in his hands, he'd let the wire
spread all across the land—and those Mer Khani steam ma-
chines on metal tracks, too. Render the caravans obsolete.
Their new Emperor wouldn't have any use for them anyway; such a remnant of the first years in exile could go the
way of the Old Church and the Home Language. Only
faster.

Vuhlem poured, drank deeply; mulled fruit brandy—
fine, unzeroed French Jamaican fruit brandy—fired his
stomach and heated his blood. This time a year forward,
he'd have *all* of Dro Pent. And Cornekka and Sikkre, those
three for certain. All Rhadaz, with any good fortune. "To
fortune," he murmured; laughed softly in his throat—and
drank again.

Enardi came down the shallow steps from the civil service
building and looked cautiously both ways before edging
into the heavy late-afternoon foot traffic. A tall man in
plain brown leathers eased into the flow right behind him,
and fetched up at his left elbow. Enardi glanced at him,
scrubbed his hands on a fresh white handkerchief, and
shoved it into his vest pocket. He wasn't supposed to ac-
knowledge the man's presence; the city guard had told him
that. Nor talk to him. *Don't point him out to anyone watching you; don't distract him from his job, which is keeping
you alive.*

His palms were still damp; he thrust both hands deep into
his pants pockets. Too much had happened the past days,
almost none of it within his control. He hadn't slept in
days, couldn't remember the last time he'd eaten that it
hadn't hurt his stomach. The pants that had been too tight

mere days earlier needed a proper belt to keep them from sliding.

They'd been too tight the afternoon Choran had accosted him in that alley. Enardi swallowed, licked his lips, and shook his head a little. An older woman passing in the other direction, her hands full of melons, gave him a startled look, and edged as far from him as she could. The guard touched his shoulder and he jumped.

"Be easy, sir," the man murmured. Enardi nodded, swallowed dread, and tried to remember how to walk normally.

Afronsan had initially suggested he go back to Bezjeriad, when the Emperor was still so angry; maybe he should have. But Casimaffi's vast house wasn't that far from Fedthyr's; the man and his sons knew the city as well as Ernie did. *I'd be a prisoner in my father's walls—and likely not safe there.* Choran wouldn't care who he hurt, getting to anyone he thought an enemy. *If anything happened to my family because of me—*

But the Emperor had relented somewhat after those first few awful days; the wire stayed up, and Chris had gone south, taking the others with him. Things were coming back to normal, though *that* whole mess had cost him sleep for certain; to get word this afternoon that Chris and Ariadne were free and more or less of one piece was a serious weight from his shoulders.

The rest of Afronsan's news hadn't been so good: No sign of Choran anywhere, but word everywhere in the lower city had it that the man was still in Podhru and staying low, looking for someone. . . .

And so, the brute with a broadsword, as Chris would (laughingly) call him—one of Afronsan's off-duty guardsmen, with two more to watch the new house which was CEE-Tech's quarters, front and back, in shifts, until the Heir decided everything was safe. *Until someone drowns Choran in the harbor,* Enardi thought gloomily. *His mother's midwife should have done us all the favor.*

But that was a "Chris" thought, or an "Eddie" thought. Ariadne would make violence and never worry it, or so Chris said. Well—good for her. It made Enardi feel a little sick. It was said midwives did aid new mothers sometimes, if the child was misshapen or ill, or born blue and the midwife compassionate—or if the child were a girl or boy and the father desirous of the other sex, and the midwife unscrupulous. *That anyone could . . .* He couldn't even consider doing harm, even to someone like Choran, without wishing the thought hadn't happened.

Eddie pushing him to use that bo, or even a knife. *But I know how it feels to be hit by that stick; how could I hurt someone that way? Or—or worse!*

He blinked, came to an abrupt halt; the foot traffic around them was suddenly very heavy, going nowhere. The guard touched his shoulder, said, "Wait," and craned to see over heads. "Disturbance up there," he said finally, and took Enardi's elbow. "We'll go the other way instead." He gasped and fell, vanishing suddenly into the milling crowd. Enardi stared wildly, then turned to run. Choran had both his arms just above the elbow. Enardi opened his mouth to yell; the larger man exerted pressure, and shook his head.

"Don't shout. Say nothing." And as Enardi drew another deep breath, Choran squeezed the nerve at both elbows. It brought tears to his eyes. "Shout and you die here and now," Choran added, his voice deceptively soft. "Come with me. Listen—you might live." He kept his grip tight; barely loosened the murderous pressure on nerves. Enardi staggered, held up only by the other's hold on him. "I am waiting."

"Yes." Choran probably didn't hear him; he could surely tell the slight, soft merchant wouldn't give him away. Turning, he draped an arm over Enardi's shoulders and led him north, away from the center of Podhru and toward the old walls.

They walked in silence for some minutes. The foot traf-

fic became sparse; Choran turned into one of the many
dead ends created by centuries of building and rebuilding
around the old outer walls, and there was all at once no
other traffic at all. He turned into a narrow alley, began to
climb a flight of cracked steps, bringing his trembling companion with him. "You never sent word to my father,"
Choran began. He kept his voice low but it still echoed in
the high, enclosed space. "He is—disappointed, Enardi."
Silence. Enardi swallowed; he couldn't get any words out.
"All he has done, all he's offered you—" They came out
onto a broad walkway; unused for years. Grass greened the
cracks between stones and bricks, the protective wall had
crumbled away in places.

"No." It didn't sound like his voice. Choran halted, dragging him around so his back was to that awful drop, stared
at him blackly.

"He offered you more than your *friends* can offer you,
just now. He offered you your life."

Chris was right, Enardi realized suddenly. Get angry
enough, and things began to work again. Like his voice,
which rang off the surrounding walls. "I didn't need that
offered to me, until you and your father wanted to kill me!
And what about Chris and his lady? Edrith down on the
docks? That was your father's ship, Choran!"

Choran's black eyebrows went up. "So? Of course it was
his ship. And I'll tell you, if it had been *my* decision, all
five of you would have gone into that harbor right then,
properly weighted first. It's what Vuhlem—"

"Vuhlem?" Enardi demanded sharply. Choran went very
still; he closed his mouth with an audible snap. "So which
of them bought your father *this* time: Vuhlem or the man
Dupret? Or both at once?" he added, his voice going up as
Choran stared blankly. "He's good at taking money that
way, isn't he? Your father! When Afronsan hears this—"

"Oh?" Choran laughed flatly and leaped: Enardi found
himself spun halfway around, arms pinned painfully high

behind his back. "Well, he may hear something eventually, if he lives that long, but it won't be from *you*! Not on this plane!"

A red haze filmed his eyes, but he could clearly see the gap in the protective wall Choran steered him to; he dug in his heels but the larger man simply laughed and hauled him off his feet. "Help—please, help me!" Enardi's voice spiraled across deserted walls and roofs, echoing from the higher wall behind them. Choran laughed again.

"Not likely," he said, and shoved. Enardi flailed wildly, completely off balance, and fell. Lights exploded in his head as his cheekbone slammed into old, rough stone; his hands clawed frantically for hold. Somehow, he found one. His feet scrabbled against the ancient wall, but found only the faintest bit of outcropping, barely enough for one boot. Enough, maybe . . . He glanced down, shuddered, and looked away immediately. The wall sloped slightly here, a man might have enough good fortune to slide all the way down, or he might hit a projection, perhaps catch his foot in a niche formed by cracked and aged stone, then he'd fall all the way to . . . *No!*

Up: The view that way was worse. Choran loomed above him, not far enough away by half. Enardi set his hands one over the other, managed to clasp his fingers together over the projection, and began edging his free foot along the outwardly sloping wall in search of another hold. *That guard: He must know I was taken, and by whom!* But if the guardsman were dead, if he'd fallen because Choran killed him . . . What easier than to shove a knife between a man's ribs in such a crowd?

Choran's brows were drawn together, his face dark with fury, teeth bared. He clutched at the remnants of stone retaining wall and tried to reach Enardi's fingers with first one foot, then the other. He grinned, evilly, as one toe grazed the outcropping and then pressed hard on soft flesh. "Say hello to your outland friend, Chris, for me," Choran

said. "The Frenchman's caught him and his woman, and
killed them both. We just heard." The grin widened; his
boot exerted pressure on Enardi's knuckles. "I thought you
would want to know."

"Liar," Enardi gasped. "*I* heard, too; they escaped." He
hissed with pain as Choran's boot pressed down on his left
hand; the left fingers tore free of his right and rough stone;
his free foot slipped.

A loud, sharp voice came from along the wall. "What
chances here? You, seaman!" The pressure on Enardi's
other hand eased as Choran spun around to stare back the
way they'd just come. Enardi scrabbled madly for a new
hold; his free hand caught hold of the loop of chain on
Choran's boot. Choran flailed wildly for balance—no use.
He went over backward; his head hit the projection Enardi
had clung to, breaking his hold. He gasped, clawed for a
new one as Casimaffi's black son slammed suddenly and
painfully against him and was suddenly gone. Found nothing. Enardi slid down rough rock and mortar, stone tearing
at his skin; his feet slammed hard into another projection,
throwing him off balance and out. He found himself simply, sickeningly, falling.

Dear gods, your protection . . . There wasn't time for
anything else. He blacked out, his last vision the rapidly ap-
proaching alleyway, and Choran's sprawled, lifeless body
directly below him.

A familiar drone of voice greeted him; his own, he realized
after a long, black moment. He couldn't see. "I hate falling,
I hate it. Hate to fall. Hate heights."

Another voice, from somewhere just above his head, a
hand on his shoulder. He hissed with pain; the hand was
withdrawn at once. "Sir—Enardi. Don't move, sir." The
guard who'd left the civil service building with him—he
thought. Hard to think anything, just now. The guardsman
sounded worried. *I must look awful.* "The—the merchant's

son's dead, sir; he broke your fall, but you have injuries, we'll get a healer for you at once. Just—don't move, sir, please."

Enardi nearly nodded; decided it wouldn't be a good idea to move anything. His neck ached, all of him ached where it wasn't actually sharp pains. "Won't move," he assured the other man. His voice wasn't much above a whisper. Stone under his cheek; his legs were cushioned by something—*by dead Choran*, he realized bleakly. *I grabbed hold of his foot and pulled him down, and he's dead.* Fedthyr's family and Casimaffi's went back generations, into Zelharri, back to the first days out of the east, after the black men won and everyone else died or fled. "Ruined—oh, gods," he whispered.

"Sir?" Another man's voice.

"Killed—killed Choran. Father—never forgive."

The voice said something; he couldn't make out what, but it sounded angry. "Sir, he tried to kill you. We saw him, heard him! But everyone in Podhru knew about Choran and his father! They meant to turn things back—"

"Yes."

"It was an accident, what you did, anyone could see that! And you did the Emperor and his Heir a service, surely you know that?"

"Service." Enardi laughed breathily. It sent sharp pain through his ribs. *Me and Chris, broken ribs and who has the most? Gods of easy profit.* None of it was worth laughing about: Choran was dead, but Enardi was alive for the moment. Whatever else came of it, he'd killed a man. A dreadful man—that didn't matter. Someone who had been alive, and now was no longer alive. However long he lived, he'd regret it.

10

～

THE main street of Mondego was packed: carts headed to and from the portside fish market, men and women afoot everywhere, children carrying messages or simply running, all in a hurry. Half a dozen mounted Portuguese soldiers in their distinctive purple and gold, trying to direct traffic, so a compact square of pike-armed footmen could pass, only added to the confusion. The day was cool, fortunately, and a strong, dry wind from the low southern hills blew the usually thick harbor smells away from the narrow, smoothly cobbled way.

Ariadne's face showed nothing but mild interest in her surroundings, but she clung hard to Chris's arm and her fingers latched sharply onto his sleeve when a woman carrying three squawking, live chickens by the feet shoved past them, slamming into the slighter woman's shoulder and nearly taking Ariadne seaward with her. Chris drew her smoothly back, then set his hand over hers, securing her a little better to his arm. He was taller than most of the locals but even he couldn't see over horsemen, or purple-and-gold flags—or canvas or thatch-covered produce carts. Ariadne, most of the time, was completely unable to make out anything beyond the immediate ring of people around her.

Which spooks her. Fair enough: I don't like it, either, Chris thought. Hard enough to sense that anyone—any man or woman of Dupret's—could be in the crowd, blending in so they'd never be aware of enemy sneaking up on him and Ari. Worse still, just now—for him, anyway—breathing. He ached all over, and the ribs weren't healing very rapidly, for all the local healer'd promised. *Better than just letting them mend on their own—but not by much.*

The healer had shrugged aside his sunburn, clearly considering it nothing but a very minor discomfort. Pressed, she had given him ointment he suspected was the this-world equivalent of cocoa butter, and said the red and pain would go away in time—and then gone away herself. *Wonder how she'll be, healing skin cancer, if I have to look her up in a few years?* Well—no use borrowing more trouble than necessary.

Having to dress like an honest-to-goodness gentleman never helped in the best of times, and just now it was nearly physically beyond him: The vest and shirt together, when properly buttoned, put uncomfortable pressure on his lower chest; what he referred to as Eddie's Rich-Pig jacket was just a bit too small, and lined besides. Extra layer of cloth, over too many layers already. He couldn't button it.

But the look was what counted at the moment. Eddie's jacket took him out of the Errol Flynn class, put him into the gentleman category—by look, at least. Well, maybe Rhett Butler. Quasi-*hombre*.

All the same: The physical effect was very unpleasant, like being swaddled in mounds of cloth. A straw hat and a brand-new pair of gloves completed the sensation. *I don't think I ever in my life wore gloves before this. Mittens, once, when I was a little kid and Mom took me out to play in the snow—swear that was Arizona, when she was still in the commune near Flagstaff.*

All these clothes, clean and pressed, the whole bit, just to create an impression on the Mer Khani—on the Alliance of New States—ambassador. So the man would even bother to see them—and listen to them. And, most important, believe them, because they appeared to be solid citizens, not mere

troublemakers. *Not bleeding-heart liberals or countercul-
ture types, creating hassle for the Establishment. Thanks,
Mom; I needed that.* A faint grin pulled at Chris's mouth;
he tugged at his moustaches and put the smile aside. Still—
Robyn must be feeling some odd twinges at the moment,
and wondering why.

Only just something to do with her only son Going
Straight: doing the equivalent of wrapping a power tie—
burgundy and navy, if he recalled correctly, and diagonally
striped—around his neck and going to dinner at the White
House, making nice with good old Milhous or Ronnie. *Heh,
heh,* Chris thought irreverently. *Some people like Mom are
out front with the bloated-thumbs-to-the-lantern bit; others
of us, like me and Eddie, are a little more sneaky about it.*

Don't laugh, he hastily admonished himself. *Hurts the
ribs when you do.*

At least it wasn't midsummer hot, though it was, to his
mind, disgustingly warm for the season. And too humid.

Ariadne was used to the fancy-clothes thing and, fortunately, the behavior attached: He was counting on her to
help him over the rough spots. She wore the whole kit, including white gloves, and even carried a frilly parasol to
match her emerald green skirts and jacket—the brolly
closed because of the crowd, pinned firmly between upper
arm and her ribs at the moment.

Edrith had been a pace or so in front of them, in and out
of sight as he tried to watch everyone around them; he momentarily vanished, came edging back through the crowd
as Chris whistled sharply. Two old women on his right side
broke off a high-pitched, furious-sounding conversation to
stare at him; one of the horse soldiers swore and worked his
mount around them. Eddie looked entirely too comfortable
at the moment, Chris decided sourly as he contemplated the
picture his companion presented: sleeves rolled to his elbows, the shirt itself open at the neck, tails hanging over his
britches. Old boots, and that disreputable hat that changed

his appearance so much, depending on how he bent the brim. Edrith must have been able to read his mind; he grinned cheerfully from under a deeply creased brim and waved them on.

"Don't get so far ahead, you!" Chris had to raise his voice to be heard. Edrith merely nodded, turned to lead the way once more, indicating direction now and again by lofting one arm or the other and pointing. Two side streets further on, away from the ocean and toward the center of town, the street opened into a square; the crowd thinned out and there were suddenly fewer people, and most of these mounted on fine horses. *Locals. Rich ones; look at all the silver on the tack.* Chris glanced at Ariadne, smiled, and nodded; she smiled back, though her eyes remained anxious, and eased her grip on Chris's sleeve. Edrith slowed down so they could catch up, then pointed past the enormous stone fountain that took up the center of the square; the boulevard beyond was tree lined and nearly as broad as the square; a raised stone curb separated carriage and horse traffic from a narrow white, shell-covered walkway.

"Two doors down," Edrith said cheerfully. Chris scowled at him sidelong. How the man could stay so *cool*!

Well, obviously, he could. Of course, he wasn't about to walk into the Alliance embassy and check out how good his credentials were. Chris nodded. "See it." The embassy was a three-story slender house, much like its close neighbors, save for the Alliance of States—surprisingly nothing like *his* American—flag hanging above the door. He ran a nervous finger over his moustache, glanced down at Ariadne. Repressed an urge to laugh aloud that was probably half nerves but the rest a sudden image: "Jeez. We look like a remake of *Gone with the Wind*."

Ariadne scowled up at him. "This is—? What?"

He did laugh this time. "Hey. Past-life experience, maybe." Edrith laughed with him, and in chorus, the two men said, "Tell—you—later." Ariadne muttered something under her breath and caught hold of the bell pull; it jangled harshly inside somewhere. Moments later, the door opened and a tall, extremely pale man in red-and-gray livery bowed them into a cool, long hall.

Half an hour later, Chris wondered why he'd been so nervous. Charles Barton had them shown into his study—a spacious, high-ceilinged room with little furnishing save a low table and several comfortable chairs, and three walls lined with bookshelves—and immediately offered tea. Chris let Ariadne graciously accept for both of them, and allowed her to make most of the small conversation with the ambassador while they waited for what turned out to be tea and a tray of small cakes and fruit.

"Now, then, Mr. Cray"—Barton smoothed white hair back from his forehead, smiled at Ariadne, and set his cup aside—"your message said 'a minor favor.' "

"Yes, sir." Chris nodded. He put his own cup down and leaned forward. "I hope it's a minor favor, at least. You're aware of the situation in Rhadaz, of course—" He hesitated.

Barton nodded, took another sip of tea. "To a degree. Rumor everywhere, of course."

"The Emperor's closed the borders," Chris said.

"We knew *that*."

"Because of the outside traffic in drugs."

"Yes." Barton's face gave nothing away. He took an oblong cake from the tray, then proffered the tray to Ariadne; the corners of her mouth turned up, she took a cake in turn, and sipped at her tea.

Chris met her eyes, gravely winked when the ambassador's gaze was elsewhere. "Of course, sir, you're aware that the Emperor has no specific suspicions *where* the drug is coming from, or who's responsible."

"Yes." His voice was mildly inquiring, vaguely and to

Chris's mind unsettlingly English; it still gave nothing away.

"Whatever the Emperor suspects, sir, the Heir's feeling is the Mer—the Alliance itself isn't involved. Perhaps a few men acting on their own—but nothing else."

"Yes, well. Thank you," Barton replied dryly.

Chris managed a small smile, sipped tea, set his cup down. "I myself don't think the Alliance is involved. Not as an entity."

The Alliance ambassador frowned, finished his tea in silence. Chris waited him out. "You think someone inside the Alliance *is* involved, by the sound of it." Chris nodded. "I don't know how you think I can help. We—I can pass word to the government. Still—"

"Yes, sir. I understand there are factions, plenty of them, within the Alliance—really, within the Parliament—because of Zero. Sir, I—that isn't my business. I'm concerned with a particular facet of business within the Alliance borders, certain men who are trying to work things their way, whatever their own government or our own say. I thought—depending, of course, upon how politically touchy the matter is—I thought you might help with this."

"I—see." Nothing on Barton's face to give him away.

Chris swallowed behind his linen napkin, went on. "Thing is, because Shesseran closed all the ports, everyone's ready to say no, about nearly everything. You know, we're angry; we're going to make you even angrier." Barton chuckled appreciatively, gestured for his companion to go on. "Things aren't quite so simple, way I see it. Zero isn't just a threat against Rhadaz, even though we have such a high percentage of people with magic abilities, and therefore more people who might die of the stuff."

Barton considered this for some moments. He spread his hands, shrugged. "I understand. Consider, Mr. Cray, those who pay my salary won't necessarily do me any favors on your behalf." He got to his feet, walked over to the wall, and tugged at the heavy rope pull. "I'll have my secretary convey the message."

"Thank you, sir. I appreciate it—and I know the Emperor's Heir will as well."

"You've done us a favor or so in the past, Mr. Cray." The door opened, and a small, slender man in dark gray hurried into the room, a portable writing desk clutched to his chest. The ambassador spoke to him in a low, non-carrying voice for some moments. He waited until the secretary left, still clutching his desk, then came back to take his seat next to the tea table. "I told Andrews to bring word back here, I trust you won't mind?" He turned to smile at Ariadne. "More tea, Mrs. Cray?" Ariadne smiled politely, held out her cup. "I did think," Barton went on mildly, as he poured, "that we might use the time to discuss matters of, ah, current *regional* interest? Say, for example, why the captain of the Kamrun vessel *Maborre* should lodge a vigorous protest with the French branch office in New Lisbon?" He raised one eyebrow, drank tea. "And why the captain of the English ship *Hawk* found it to his interests to take two last-moment passengers from a French Jamaican beach?"

"Mmmm." Chris cleared his throat cautiously, drank a little tea himself. He'd fully expected the questions; had planned on an explanation whether the ambassador asked for one or not. In this formal setting, unfamiliar clothes making him at least outwardly a gentleman, it was suddenly difficult to get the words out. Dupret's violence seemed a world and a lifetime away.

He took a deep breath; sharp pain flared across his lower right side. *World away, until that reminds you, dude,* he told himself. He nodded. "Of course, sir, you're familiar with Henri Dupret?"

The skin around the ambassador's eyes tightened. "To my infinite sorrow, sir." He glanced at Ariadne. "Your pardon, ma'am."

Ariadne shook her head. "No. Not apology to me, for the man who *was* my father." She looked at Chris. "Tell him," she added flatly.

Two hours later, the tea and cakes were long gone and a small blue envelope from the French ambassador lay under Chris's fingers. He shrugged. "The *Hawk*'s captain put out fast, sent us below decks. I frankly don't remember much until we got into New Lisbon, and even that's patchy."

"But Dupret deals in this drug, this Zero. You're certain of it." Barton was pacing behind his chair, hands clasped behind his back.

"I am certain of it, M. Barton," Ariadne put in quietly. "I suspected as much, years ago; I heard him speaking about it in the hall, before we escaped the house. He and my *grandpère,* between them, they set it up to put the powder in brandies and ship them to France for use in the eastern war—and for other purposes."

"And elsewhere?" Barton asked sharply. "Because we've had an influx of the substance the past year or so in New Amsterdam; it's brought into the country somehow, winds up in cheap gin, down in the slums. There's been more death by Zero the past year than from fever, bad water, and the red pox all together."

Chris nodded. "Yes, sir. Unfortunately, I doubt Dupret's behind that; unfortunately, because I'd love to see you nab him for such a thing, but there are others dealing in the stuff. The Mer Khani—the Alliance men I suspect are involved in metals, like I already told you, in steel and iron. The new lightweight metal—aluminum? I can't say for certain they're also dealing in Zero, or that they're trying to use it to undermine Rhadaz. And I can't check on that myself."

"So, the French ambassador?" Chris nodded. The Alliance ambassador leaned against the back of his chair, made a steeple of his fingers, and stared over the top of it.

"And in case my government should have reasons of its own for not investigating the men, and the matter?"

Chris shrugged. "It occurred to me, sir, that the Alliance itself might be aware of the traffic. Some high in power in the French government appear to be, also. Basically, it was important to me that someone should know where we'd gone. The two of us. Though obviously that wasn't my main reason for coming to you."

"It would have done." Barton's mouth quirked suddenly. "Have you ever considered a career in diplomacy, Mr. Cray?" Chris laughed, shook his head. "After all, your Rhadazi will one day need representation, and you certainly think the right way—".

"Yes, sir, I know they will, and honestly, I appreciate the compliment." Chris tugged at Edrith's jacket sleeve. "In all honesty, I would *die* if I had to dress like this all the time." The ambassador chuckled. Chris picked up the little blue envelope and got to his feet. Barton deftly handed Ariadne up and kissed her fingers. "Sir, I definitely owe you a favor for this one."

"Repay it by staying alive, and cutting more deals like the one you made recently for milling machinery," Barton said as Chris hesitated. "I think our two countries can be good for each other. Mrs. Cray," he added gravely as he kissed her fingers, "it was a very great pleasure to finally meet you."

Ariadne smiled and gave him a graceful, low curtsey. "*Merci,* M. Barton—for an excellent tea, and for your aid to us both." She took Chris's arm, tucked the furled parasol under her other arm, and let him lead her back to the street.

Once they were past the fountain, Chris slowed. "Hey, lady," he said quietly. "Thanks. I think you turned things our way."

"You think? For what I said, or because the Alliance man likes to look at young women?"

"Ari! I swear!" Chris could feel his face turning red.

"This is me, all right? Would I use you like—I mean, like a—"

"Oh, hush." Ariadne laid one gloved hand across his mouth. She sounded irritated but didn't really look it, and her eyes were definitely amused. "This is like any battle, any duel—remember what I told the husband of your *tante*: you use what you have. If the stakes are high, like ours, and the matter turns upon whether I smile at a man who fancies himself a little as the terror of women—Chris, I have done this all my days since I became fourteen years, for that man who was my father."

"Oh, jeez, Ari—"

She tugged at his arm, hard. "No. Do not look at me so, I know the difference between what my father wanted of me, to smooth his business matters, and what I did there for *us*. The ambassador is an innocent compared to most and I think a kind man. Do you think *I* thought you would allow him to—to, what? Make a try upon my virtue if that was the price of his message to his masters and to the French?" Her own color was as high as his suddenly.

Chris gaped at her. "Ariadne! Hey, I swear!"

She shook her head. "No. Do not. I do not need the words. Not from you, beloved." She glanced skyward, opened her parasol, and added, "It grows late, the French ambassador will wonder what keeps us."

CHRISTOPHER CRAY TO HIS HIGHNESS AFRONSAN: HOPE DUKE ADREBAN CAN SOMEHOW FORWARD THIS TO YOU. MER KHANI AMBASSADOR IN NEW LISBON PASSED WORD TO HIS MAINLAND PEOPLE, INVESTIGATE NEW HOLLAND MINING COMPANY, ALSO OWNERS BELLINGHAM AND PERRY, FOR LINK TO ZERO. WAS PROMISED FULL COOPER-ATION, MAY EVEN GET IT. FRENCH LESS OPENLY COOPER-ATIVE BUT SENDING WORD TO VISCOUNT PHILIPPE REGARDING BROTHER HENRI'S TRAFFIC IN ZERO AND THIS LATEST ESCAPADE REGARDING SELF AND WIFE. STAYING

IN MONDEGO FULL 7 DAYS, HOPE TO RECUPERATE FROM
DUPRET'S HOSPITALITY. ALSO HERE IF YOU OR THUKARA
NEED TO REACH US.

AFRONSAN TO CRAY: THANKS FOR NEWS, THUKARA
SAYS MERCHANT HENRY COOPERATING, KNOWS VERY
LITTLE, THOUGH. MESSAGE FROM THUKARA TO FOLLOW.
CASIMAFFI SON CHORAN DEAD AFTER ATTEMPT ON
ENARDI FEDTHYRSON, MESSAGE FROM ENARDI APPENDED,
CASIMAFFI THOROUGHLY IMPLICATED IN ZERO TRADE
AND ARRESTED IN BEZ. EXPECT SEVERAL DAYS IN EMPER-
OR'S PRISON WILL PERSUADE THE MAN TO MAKE FULL
CONFESSION. AFRONSAN.

JENNIFER TO CHRIS: YOU WATCH YOURSELF, KIDDO,
DEAD'S PERMANENT, REMEMBER?

ENARDI TO CHRIS: DICTATING TO MERIYAS, BROKE
BOTH ARMS THANKS TO STUPID CHORAN, THOSE AND
HEAD HEALING SLOWER THAN LEG DID. TWO GOOD
THINGS OUT OF MESS: CHUFFLES INCARCERATED AND
SELF WED FIVE DAYS NOW, SINCE TWO AFTER FALL AND
OVER EVANY'S FURIOUS OBJECTION. MERIYAS SENDS
LOVE.

The caravaners' building was filled to capacity; Red
Hawk still spread its blankets around the east hearth—
crowded into half of the great hall since all of Silver Star
had come in just after what would have been sundown,
without the thick blanket of cloud. The west hearth and
most of the area around it reeked of wet wool and soaked
leather, both overcoming even the highly spiced meat two
of the women had trussed to a thick spit.

At the moment, Lialla could see a scattering of empty
blankets and mats, almost as many as were occupied by
women and toddlers, or the very old. No men sprawled

over the complex board games, laughing or squabbling as pieces were knocked down and money changed hands. Only a few older boys in sight, most bringing wood or fetching the last of family goods to the various blankets. A chill, dreary winter rain had been falling most of the day, turning the courtyard into a sea of icy mud and spilling water into the stables. Most of the men and older boys and a few of the stronger girls were down shifting crates and boxes to higher shelves and doing what they could to divert the rush of water that was rapidly making a stream of the aisle between stalls. Small relays of people came up to thaw by the fire; now and again men staggered into the main chamber with dripping boxes to stack against the back wall.

Small children played chasing games in the main chamber, darting up and down the room, using the individual family mats as touch or not-touch spots according to some elaborate set of rules Lialla couldn't begin to fathom. The shrieking and giggling echoed from the high ceiling; she had given up even trying to be heard, let alone to instruct. Ryselle had gone off somewhere with Sil not long after Silver Star arrived, but Kepron still sat by himself, close to the hearth, red string draped over his knee; he had been working on the seventh pattern until the new arrivals broke his concentration. At the moment, he was rubbing a thick wax into a small hide for Red Hawk's grandmother. Two boys threaded their way between blankets to drop tied bundles of wood on the hearth; the old woman stirring an enormous pot of soup murmured something that made one of them laugh.

Very homey, Lialla thought gloomily. At least, for caravaners. The noise—the sheer numbers—was beginning to get on her nerves. "Maybe I should go back to Zelharri," she mumbled. "I'm doing nothing worthwhile here, Aletto's probably driven Robyn half-mad, fussing over my absence, and Mother—" She swallowed. Closed her eyes briefly.

The Red Hawk grandmother had given her the message; had offered sympathy over the woman's suicide and an ear, if the sin-Duchess needed it. Lialla simply couldn't believe it. Hadn't been able to weep yet; it was all stuck deep in her chest. Lizelle deliberately giving Aletto drink—Zero-laced drink, *knowing* he couldn't handle drink or drug, either one. Then swallowing the rest of it herself, leaving that note to make Aletto feel dreadfull. . . . "I should go." Yes, go. Then, again, to know she'd failed these women twice; to go home and face Aletto, knowing that. Knowing he'd know. He'd never come out and say, "I could have told you." She'd see it in his eyes every time he looked at her.

He thinks I should marry; because marriage solved so much for him, he thinks I should do what he's done. She couldn't really blame him for feeling as he did; Robyn *was* good for Aletto. And he'd never had much imagination, never been able to see others as people different from himself. Having other wants, other goals. He'd been against her marrying fat old Carolan, of course, partly because Carolan was Jadek's cousin, more because he found the man as repulsive as Lialla did. She sighed, tired all over, all at once. *Forget that. As if thinking about it here would change Aletto one whit.*

She turned as someone shouted her name. Sil and Ryselle had come up the near stairs. Both women were dripping wet; Sil's teeth chattered. The woman stirring soup shook her spoon at them both, said something to Sil that Lialla couldn't catch, and stepped aside to let the women have the hearth. Sil caught Lialla's eye and gestured urgently; Lialla stopped long enough to scoop up two blankets from the nearest stack and shook them out.

"Here, put this around you, Ryselle, your lips are blue. What were you two *doing* out there?"

Sil drew her soaked cloak off and wrapped the blanket

around her shoulders. "Ahhh, thank you, my friend. Doing—I left a message for you, didn't you get it?" Lialla sighed, shook her head. "I should know better than to trust any of Red Hawk's boys, sorry."

"They're all down shifting boxes, stable's flooded," Lialla said.

"Bah. Everything is flooded—or going to be. Filthy storm, and it's getting worse by the moment. Fog right down to the paving stones, too, but the wind's starting to pick up. Well, I left you a message, honestly: Ibys sent word to me, Chiros—you know, denim breeks and—?"

"I remember Chiros," Lialla said. Hard to forget a man that large—or any Holmaddi male that improbably nice to caravaner women. Of course, he'd wanted denim to make breeks to sell in that large, old shop of his—but most of his brethren wouldn't have thought *that* out, they'd have been nasty to foreign women just because. "Here, sit, both of you, right now! Let me get you something hot to drink."

"I'll do that, sin-Duchess." The older woman set her spoon aside, picked up a long, hooked implement and used it to pull a slightly smaller, steaming pot from well back in the coals.

Sil eased herself down cautiously. "Chiros was ill all last night; Ibys wanted to send for the healer, but his eldest brother was there and wouldn't let her, said Chiros had merely drunk too much and needed rest. She knows he has no taste for alcohol and so she thought poison or drug, of course. And I told you Chiros's brothers have a lust for that shop, and she thinks they'd do most anything to get control of it. She managed to smuggle her daughter out about an hour ago, when her wedded brother was in the kitchen eating. When the girl discovered the healer wasn't home, she kept her head and came here instead."

"What a mess," Lialla said, as Sil paused to take a steaming mug. "How's Chiros?"

"Better, we think. The healer thinks he was poisoned,

and of course, the wedded brother's a pig, one of the worst. I can't stand him. Fortunately, he can't take caravaner women, either, so when Ryselle and I suddenly popped into the shop with an offer on denim cloth from Silver Star's grandmother, he stomped off; the healer was with Chiros when I left." Sil drank cautiously. "Mmmm, that's wonderful, spiced apple and just a little kick to warm the belly. I'm chilled all the way down." She eyed her wet companion critically, pulled the blanket high around Ryselle's throat, and held the cup to her mouth. "Here, Ryselle, my sweet, drink the rest of this, your lips really *are* blue. Not your best color." Ryselle closed her eyes, shook her head a little, but as Sil pressed the cup against her lip, she obediently sucked in a little liquid and swallowed. "We're going about this all wrong," Sil added crisply. "The city women aren't going to get anywhere until Vuhlem's gone. Let's murder him in his bed."

Lialla laughed sourly. "Or anywhere else! Except then Shesseran would hang us both; I may be a noblewoman and you one of his precious caravaners, but Vuhlem—"

Sil sighed, took back the empty mug, and let the older woman refill it. "I know. He and the Emperor, boyhood friends. As if old Vuhlem was ever friends with anyone except himself!"

"As if he was ever a boy," Lialla retorted. "I think he sprang from a spell gone wrong just as he is now: aging, set in his ways, large as a bull, and thoroughly nasty." Sil laughed, shook her head. Ryselle mumbled something; Lialla knelt next to her, laid a hand on the village woman's cheek; it was very cold. "Oh, Ryselle! We need to get your hair dry, you'll catch your death sitting like that."

"I'm fine." Ryselle looked at her; she looked far from fine. "There's—" She frowned, stared down at water-puckered hands. Sil swore good-naturedly, shoved a warm, nearly full cup into them, and dragged the blanket back around her villager friend. "Something's wrong out there."

"Something," Sil said blackly. "A wretched winter storm and Vuhlem—"

"No." Ryselle shook her head; the cup, forgotten, started to slip from her hands. Lialla caught it, handed it to Sil, bundled Ryselle back into the blanket. "Something in the air," Ryselle went on, mostly to herself. "Like when a summer storm approaches and the air's crackling and thick? Like—like that—" Her voice trailed off. "I don't feel it in here. Outside, though—"

Sil held the cup to her lips again, waited until Ryselle roused herself enough to drink deeply. "That's the fog and damp," she began cheerfully, but Ryselle pulled back from the cup and shook her head.

"No—any woman who grew up in Gray Haven wouldn't be afraid of mere fog and damp, we have it more days in a year than not. This: it's like something—some*one* watching, with more than eyes, aware of you." She caught her breath harshly; Lialla's hands were suddenly hard on her upper arms.

"You felt something watching you?" Ryselle stared at her wide-eyed, nodded.

Sil gripped the sin-Duchess's shoulder. "Don't! Don't frighten her, she's cold and tired—"

"No, let me," Lialla said flatly. "Ryselle. Like a thunderstorm? You—was the hair on your arms standing up?"

"It felt like—like the hair on my head was trying to," Ryselle replied. "Prickly. Why—that's why I thought of lightning."

"Your—no, Sil, honestly, it's *important*," Lialla snapped as Sil tried to object again. "Your stomach—how did that feel?"

"Mmmm." Ryselle's eyelids sagged shut. "Like—my father was waiting just outside the goat barn for me to come out, so he could—could hit me. Scared."

"Gods of the Warm Silences," Lialla whispered. She was vaguely aware of Sil watching her warily, the rough blanket they'd wrapped around Ryselle catching at roughened fingers. Kepron, who'd set the hide down and came across, wrapping the red string around his left fingers. "Wait, Sil, please," she added sharply. "Ryselle, please—trust me." Ryselle, her eyes closed, swallowed and nodded. Lialla closed her own eyes and *reached*. Ryselle's inner being shone a pale gold, as it always did, but there was something else there: dark, infinitely small—wrong. New, brilliant. And growing. "Triad," Lialla whispered. Ryselle twitched in her grasp; startled, the sin-Duchess nearly let go of her. Her fingers clamped around the village woman's elbows; her eyes flew open.

"Triad?" Sil had heard that much; Kepron echoed the word. "Vuhlem's Triad, do you mean? But what does— they were outside the city, you said they were!"

"No!" Lialla shook her head, scrambled to her feet. "They aren't now!" She spun around, listening intently. Sounds within the caravaners' compound were suddenly muted; she could hear rising wind outside. And *feel* it, questing for entry. "Dear gods," she whispered. The distant whine became a shrill sound, rising by the moment. That much audible to any with ears; underneath it: Lialla threw up a warding sign before her, clutched at Sil's arm, pointed at Ryselle, who was beginning to glow under the prosaic caravaner blanket. Lialla dragged at the multitude of charms hung about her neck, drew the tangle of cords over her head as one and said flatly, "Get her out of here, Sil— now, *fast*! Vuhlem's Triad is trying to use Ryselle, to destroy us all!" She draped the tangled strands over Ryselle's head, turned to catch hold of the cook's arm, and drew her to her feet. "Go, quickly, the building's about to fall!" The woman hauled her terrified gaze from the ceiling by sheer strength, turned, and ran.

To her credit, Sil didn't argue; she dragged Ryselle to her feet, threw an arm around her shoulders, and hauled her toward the near stairs. Lialla caught her breath; the pressure in the oversized barn of a chamber was suddenly oppressive. Kepron held out a hand; she touched the back of his fingers, swore as a spark arced betwen them. "Go, keep an eye on them!"

"No!" he shouted. "I do not leave you here to deal with that!"

"You will! I say so!" Lialla shouted back. The sound echoed; the vast room had gone suddenly quiet. Mothers rose to their feet, clutching small children; the tag players turned toward her. Lialla caught her breath sharply, stared across the chamber, eyes moving unwillingly up as something above her creaked, groaned, and began to separate with a shrill noise that set her teeth on edge. One of the Silver Star women shrieked, pointed up; the long beam running the length of the chamber had developed a sudden, dreadful crack. "Out!" Lialla's voice topped the sudden, terrified babble of voices. "Everyone, out! *Now!*"

She spun around; Sil and Ryselle had reached the doorway leading to the east stairs and were gone. Kepron cast her one black look and followed. A dozen, two dozen caravaners pelted after him; more ran toward the wide west stairs that dropped into the stable and storage below. The beam creaked and splintered with a vicious, rending sound, then began to tear itself apart. Lialla drew a deep breath, dropped cross-legged onto the hearth, and drew inner strength. *Net. Silver Thread, double woven, net filled with Light. Do it, do it now!* She closed her eyes, caught hold of rough stone two-handed, aware of the weight of that beam overhead, the stone and roofing it held in place, the storm beyond that—*and Vuhlem's Triad, beyond all else.* People were going to die here by the dozens unless she could hold the beam against Vuhlem's Triad.

She was aware of people running; women and small children shrieking; the floor shook beneath her and the fire was much too warm against her back. She ignored it; ignored the people and the noise. Concentrated her whole being on raising a dome of Silver Thread net and filling the holes with Light.

A chattering, terrified corner of her mind tried to argue with her: "A Triad! Vuhlem's Triad! A *young* Triad, no moral sense to it whatever! You think you can stop *that*?" She silenced it as best she could, continued to fill silver net with golden Light. Nothing else mattered.

A cold wind wrapped around her; she gasped, cried out as icy rain blew in from the northwest, suddenly drenching her clothes and burying the fire. The smell of spilled soup and wet ash twisted in her throat. A vast, gaping hole in the roof where the long beam had been; a faint sense of sky and fog and something *pale* and malevolent hovering just beyond the hole; the far end of the room nothing but cold, dark stone and rubble. Distant cries—nothing near. Directly above her, the roof trembled; broken beams jutted into the night, and fog draped down into the chamber. Just beyond her, two women were helping an old man limp toward the stairs. Half a dozen others, dark shadows, ran back the other way, where a child's shrill, terrified wail came from somewhere near the west stairs. She could hear equally shrill and terrified horses somewhere out or down there. Down in the stables—nothing for her to deal with, not now. The beam overhead creaked once again; small stones and several roofing slates struck the floor.

Voice reverberated through her bones, more chilling than the sudden rain had been: *You were warned. He warned you, and took you into his dungeons for safekeeping, and you did not heed the warning. Fool, female, and meddler all three at once, die here and now!*

Lialla gasped, blotted a sweating and too-warm brow with a rusty black sleeve. "What—let you win without contest?" she snarled. One of the few remaining caravaners turned to stare at her; she bared her teeth, gestured urgently toward the east stairs. The woman eyed the sin-Duchess nervously, cowered under the creaking ceiling, and fled.

"What?" she demanded of the sense of *something* beyond the broken roof. "Are you so weak and useless, even fear of Vuhlem's wrath can't help you break me?" Twenty—fifteen—a handful of caravaners left at this end of the building. Hold that beam where it was until they were out; maybe, who knew, she could even maintain the net long enough to find her own way from under certain destruction.

"Are you mad?" Kepron's voice cracked, the last word soared into falsetto. Shaking hands caught hold of hers where she gripped the stones of the hearth. "They're gone, all of them—there's nothing else for you to do here. Get out!"

Lialla glared up at him. "I told you to go! Follow Sil and Ryselle, get them to safety!"

"I did!" Kepron shouted back. "I came back for you!"

"Get *out* of here!" Lialla caught her breath on a sob; the side beam that ran across the hall just above the hearth creaked ominously; the sense of *presence* was growing by the moment. Kepron swore and dragged her up; her knees gave and she fell, pulling him down on top of her. "Go now! I can't hold this for much longer!"

"I *know* that! I can tell!" Kepron bellowed; he had to, to be heard above the sudden, shrill wind that swirled in the middle of the ruined chamber; small stones, then larger ones, began to rise from the floor, spinning up through the broken roof, falling back to the floor. Something at the far end crashed; a horse screamed horribly. "I'll get you out!"

Her vision was blurred; she couldn't see his face. The room faded; everything was dark, but the sense of Light grew by the moment. "No—can't," she said, gasping. "Can't—move. Go. Please."

"No. Do you—do you think I have any hope here or south of Holmaddan without you?" She sensed rather than saw the boy drop cross-legged before her; his hands caught hold of both hers. "Tell me—what to do. Anything. Tell me, I'll do it."

"Go. Go now! Vuhlem's Triad—"

"To the blackest of hells with Vuhlem, *and* his Triad," Kepron said flatly. "Tell me what to do, to get you from here in safety. I'll do it. Somehow."

"I—all right." Her fingers tightened on his. "The net. A—above us. See it?"

Silence; she'd almost begun to fear she'd lost him somehow when his grip tightened even more. "Silver Thread—something between."

"That's—that's Light. Between. Keeping the roof from flattening us. If—you can, wrap the highest part of the net—in silver."

"I can't!" He swore angrily. "I can't access silver!"

"You can! You have to—or you've killed yourself, coming back here!" Lialla forced her eyes open; two of Kepron swayed before her blurred eyes. She blinked furiously. "*I* can do it, and I'm a mere female!" she added nastily. "If I can do this—"

Kepron swore viciously, this time at her. "I can manage it," he added sharply. "This, here—"

"No! Not that, *that* one! Over—yes! Just so!" She forced herself to sit very still, to maintain what she'd already created, to leave the boy in peace while he fought with Thread that should have been years beyond a mere novice; while he drew it forth, wrapped it around her net, braiding it where he could, simply looping it around hers otherwise. Doing what he must—what most Wielders would never think to try. The ceiling still creaked, but more distantly; the sense of *presence* faded, a little.

Kepron's voice seemed to echo; her cheeks felt burned by the constant cold wind. "I—it's holding," he whispered. He slewed around, onto his knees, forced himself onto his feet, dragging Lialla up with him. "I think it's holding. We—we have to go."

"Go," Lialla said dully; the net was holding; her Light was beginning to slip from the net, to puddle on the wet floor. "You go. Please, go!" She tried to pull from Kepron's grasp, but he had her firmly tucked against him, one hand gripping her arm just below the elbow. Someone in the street was wailing nonstop; the sound set her teeth on edge. "Make them quit, please make them," she mumbled. Her legs didn't want to work; Kepron was dragging her across wet stone and someone's blanket had wrapped around her ankles.

A loud, hideous splintering directly above them: Kepron yelled in surprise; Lialla cried out in shock and pain as a large stone glanced off her back, numbing her whole right side. She fell, and Kepron went down with her.

"Ceiling is falling!" His voice assaulted her ear, breaking through the loud ringing that filled her head. "Come on!"

"No." She swallowed bile. She tried to move; nothing responded. "Can't—can't. You go."

"Not without—" Another startled yell; this one seemed to go on forever; another stone crashed into the floor, breaking into sharp little shards. Lialla threw her right arm, the only one that still responded, across her face. Nothing else moved. Something came down hard across her back, shielding her head, something warm. "Kepron—no!" She couldn't hear her own voice, couldn't breathe. Dust, wood, and stone came crashing down with a roar, taking everything with it.

11

JENNIFER came awake with a sharp cry, halfway to her feet before she realized. Her hair was sweaty, plastered to the back of her neck, the sleep shirt slick, soaked and chilly to the touch. She subsided bonelessly onto the bed. Dahven mumbled something, still half-asleep; in the faint blue light from her dressing chamber, she could see him blinking at her curiously, muzzily, as he sat up. But when he touched her arm, he came alert at once and bundled her back into the thick quilt. "You were dreaming," he said quietly. "I heard you. Bad dream. Everything's all right."

"No." She shuddered gratefully into the quilt and into his arms. "I—I mean, yes, a dream, but I—I don't think—"

He pulled her against his shoulder. "You were talking— almost shouting, something about Lialla, a Triad."

"I know. I saw it, Dahven." She could feel him eyeing her dubiously. "I did! Vuhlem's Triad, outlined in storm clouds and lightning, a—a ruin of some kind. I—didn't see Lialla, just, I know she was there because something with Light and netted Thread was holding it back, no one in all Rhadaz but Lialla—" She swallowed. After a moment, she swallowed again. "Something awful's happened, I know it has."

"Jen, no. I've had dreams that vivid, I know how real they seem at the time."

"Vivid—yes, I know. This was—it wasn't what I *saw* so

232

much as what I *felt*." She pulled away from him a little. "I'm awake now, Dahven, and I *still* feel it. And I've been confronted by Light before, by a Triad. You know that."

He nodded. "I remember."

"It's—I don't know how to explain it, but there's a nasty feeling in my gut that's not leftover nightmare, it's purest Triad." She sighed, let her head fall against his shoulder. "I could sense Jadek's Triad, you know, from halfway across the country, and that was when I was still a green outlander. Now—it's Vuhlem's, something it's done. Up there. There's no wire into Holmaddan—nothing even close, is there?"

"You know there isn't. But—let me think." He was quiet a moment, one hand absently stroking her cheek. "There's almost always a good-sized segment of one caravan or another in the market, especially just now. Surely there's a grandmother in residence up in that building Vuhlem had built for them, wouldn't you think?"

"I think so. The last I heard, Red Hawk's grandmother said they weren't leaving the building unoccupied because of Lialla and Sil—they were afraid Vuhlem might send men in to take both of them; if there weren't any other witnesses, he'd probably kill them. After all, who would know?"

"All right, then. In its own way, that's as quick as wire; we'll find out what we can for you, as early as possible." Dahven tugged the quilt higher around her throat, laid a hand against her face. "You're absolutely soaked, and it's awfully cold in here. I'm going to get a drying cloth for your hair. And—all right, I think my man slept in my dressing room last night; if he did, I'll wake him, ask him to take word down for one of the guard to go out at first light, find us a caravaner. With any luck, we'll know something by the time Siohan lets you out of bed." He slid off the bed, gasped as his feet hit the floor, but padded quickly, barefoot into his dressing. Jennifer clutched the quilt, listened to the murmur of low voices beyond the mostly closed door. Dahven came out a moment later, a thick fold of cloth in his hands, and shortly after, Widric, clad in a long sleep shirt and thick socks, went out into the hall, pulling the door quietly closed behind him.

"There. All settled." Dahven climbed back onto the bed, shook out the cloth, and vigorously toweled Jennifer's hair. "Better? Would you like a dry nightshirt?"

"Please." She managed a smile for him. *Don't let him think you're still spooked,* she decided. Her stomach felt like she'd swallowed a rock, and the sense of dread was almost worse than it had been when she first woke. Better if one of them could get back to sleep; he wouldn't, if he was worried about her. She waited until he came back from her dressing room, peeled wet fabric away from cold skin, and rubbed her chest and arms briskly with the drying cloth before he pulled the clean shirt over her head, then let him ease her back flat once she'd turned the top pillow dry side up. Dahven tucked the quilt high around her throat before he burrowed under it with her. "Really all right?" he murmured drowsily a moment or so later. He was asleep before she could answer him. Jennifer gasped; his feet were like ice.

AFRONSAN TO THUKAR AND THUKARA: UTTER SECRECY BINDS YOU REGARDING THE FOLLOWING MESSAGE, YOUR EYES, THE WIRE RECEIVER'S, AND NO OTHER. SWEAR YOUR RECEIVER TO SILENCE. RED HAWK GRANDMOTHER REPORTS STATE HOLMADDI CARAVANERS' BUILDING DESTROYED, LOSS OF LIFE INCLUDES MANY OF RED HAWK AND SILVER STAR, FOUR HOLMADDI WHO WERE ON STREET NEARBY, AND SIN-DUCHESS LIALLA. DESTRUCTION BLAMED UPON STORM AND HIGH WINDS BY DUKE VUHLEM; GRANDMOTHERS OF RED HAWK AND SILVER STAR REFUTE THIS, CLAIM ACTION ON PART OF TRIAD REPUTED KEPT BY VUHLEM. THUKAR ASKED TO GATHER

TROOPS REQUESTED BY MYSELF AND HOLD THEM READY.
REGRETS TO THUKARA, WHO I KNOW WAS CLOSE FRIEND
OF SIN-DUCHESS. MORE WORD TO FOLLOW AS I HAVE IT,
ALSO WILL˙HAVE CARAVANERS COMING SOUTH REPORT
TO THUKARA AS THEY PASS THROUGH SIKKRE. AFRONSAN

It was even colder than usual in the Emperor's town
house; much too warm in his personal chamber. Afronsan
peeled down to the light tunic he'd had the foresight to
wear under the padded, quilted rain cloak and came across
the room to kneel at his brother's side. Shesseran sat in the
room's only chair, a plain, high-backed seat close to the
fireplace; he was swathed in blankets from his waist down.
His face was drawn and his lips trembled; his hands were
cold despite the heat of the room and the blazing fire. Surprisingly, he wore the high, heavy bejeweled diadem with
which he had been crowned so many years before, though
ordinarily he didn't even bother with the everyday plain
gold circlet of ten interlocked rings that the Emperor was
supposed to set about his brow during all waking hours.
Afronsan pressed his lips against his brother's fingers.

"What—new word from the north?" Shesseran asked
breathily.

"Not good, sire. I'm—I'm sorry. The chief grandmother
of Red Hawk should arrive tomorrow, late, to tell you in
person what she saw and felt, but I've already received her
wire from Sikkre." He pulled it from the tunic pocket, held
it out; Shesseran shook his head.

"My eyes won't manage such—small writing. Tell me,
Frons."

Afronsan cleared his throat quietly, read the lengthy
message. "A hundred seventy injured in some degree or
other," he concluded. "Forty dead, including the sin-
Duchess of Zelharri, though the count of dead would have
been much higher, had that young woman and her apprentice not remained behind to front the Triad, shore the roof,

and let most escape before it fell upon them." Afronsan sighed, refolded the message. "Ten horses, seven camels, and forty mules as well, and nearly every wagon in the central portion of the stables. Another fifty people dreadfully ill from shock, injury, and exposure to the weather that night, before they could be got into what shelter could be found for them among the remaining wagons."

Silence. Shesseran sat very still, his eyes closed; his lips moved. "It is my fault,"he said finally.

"Brother, no."

"Yes," Shesseran said flatly. "I doubted you, and any other person who dared tell me straightly what that—that man was. Beginning with my tutor in Latinus, who said the boy Vuhlem had no conscience and cared only for himself." He sighed heavily. "Brosian was right, you were right. I was too—stubborn to believe—"

"Vuhlem put on a fair face for you, Sess; he knew what things to say to please you." Afronsan hesitated. "And he will continue to do so, even in the face of that disaster, you know he will! If he feels there is the least chance you will accept his word there was storm and high wind; that he has no Shaper, let alone a Triad, that he seeks only to serve you. . . ."

"I—I know it." Shesseran covered his eyes with a thin, trembling hand for a long moment. "Frons, I am too old for this seat and this crown. I understand so little of anything outside Rhadaz, or how best to serve our people—even simply whether to keep them from most of that outside world as I still think best, or to work with it as you do, taking certain of its goods while holding the rest at bay." He held up a hand as Afronsan would have spoken. "No—let me finish, please, I—haven't much strength, just now. I cannot deal with the English, the brash and arrogant Mer Khani; I cannot understand the French and the Gallic when they try to speak our language. I have no understanding of this wire, these—factories. The English music was rather nice," he added wistfully.

"And so it was. We'll have more, brother, if you like."

"If we do, it will be your decision, Frons. From tonight forward." He pointed toward the table. "Pull the wire, admit my council when they come."

Afronsan's hands suddenly felt as cold as his elder brother's had; he rose to his feet, moved to the table, pulled the bell wire, and then walked to the door, opening it for the twelve men who were already coming down the hall. Foreboding dried his mouth. The Council of Twelve passed him without a glance, but when Afronsan closed the door behind them and turned back, they were facing him and bowing, very deeply indeed. And Shesseran held the ancient crown in his hands. When he spoke, his voice was firm and steady, as it had not been in many long months. "Come," he said. "Afronsan, whom I have before this hour named as my Heir, who will succeed me within this hour as Shesseran XV, and who will be known assuredly as Shesseran the Foresighted. Come and take from him who was Emperor the ancient crown of Rhadaz."

Afronsan swallowed, then crossed the room and knelt before his brother's chair. Held out his hands. Shesseran placed the crown into them; it was surprisingly light but it weighed heavily upon his brow when the two chief councilors took it from his nerveless fingers and set it upon his head. "May I be worthy," he whispered, "of your trust, my brother, and of the land itself."

"I do not doubt you will," Shesseran said very quietly. He gestured; the scribe who had followed the Council of Twelve came forward with a message box and a quill, and sat cross-legged at his side. "Take this message, to all the Dukes and their households, to spread at once among the people: This day have I, Shesseran XIV, given unto my brother Afronsan the sacred ruling of our land. Obey him as you did me, and my blessing upon you all." The man scrib-

bled rapidly, ducked his head as he shoved the quill into its
holder, and as Shesseran nodded, he turned and sprinted for
the hall. The Council of Twelve bowed once more as
Afronsan got to his feet.

"Your bidding, sire?" one of them asked.

"Bidding—" Afronsan cleared his throat. "Yes. My
brother—do you wish to be part of all this, or would you
rather rest?"

"It is your plan now," Shesseran whispered. "I am—not
strong enough or prepared in any fashion to deal with
events, in Holmaddan or anywhere else, brother. And they
are no longer my difficulties. I have another—road for
which to prepare myself. Go, brother, take my council and
let them serve you until you are ready to appoint your own;
do what you can to reclaim control of Rhadaz and her
Dukes. My greetings to your lady; tell her—tell her
Shesseran gives her his love and wishes her strong sons for
you both. My—prayers will go with you, know that." He
licked his lips. "Send my servant to ready me for bed, if
you will be so kind."

Afronsan bent down and kissed both his brother's lean,
wrinkled cheeks. "Gladly, brother. Rest well. I swear to
you I will do my best, not to fail the land and her people."

"I—know you will." Shesseran closed his eyes; he
coughed harshly. "Go."

An hour later, Afronsan returned to the massive civil service building and his own apartments; where he had ridden
out with only one servant, he found himself accompanied
by seven, and an additional man to carry and guard the ancient crown. *I did not think it would ever come to this.
Never so soon. Not within—within my brother's lifetime,
for certain.* The speed at which events had moved during
the past two hours left him dazed; he had to concentrate on
keeping his seat. "A pity, such an end for such a great emperor," he whispered. The wind was rising; the men on ei-

ther side fortunately didn't hear him, or see him surreptitiously blot his eyes. A moment later he was grimly deep in plans for the next several days; there would be little sleep for him, particularly this night—and the telegraph wires would be hot indeed before the sun rose.

One other thing, he decided; he wrapped reins around his right arm, and with his left fumbled free the silver contraceptive bracelet, shoving it deep into his pocket. As events in Holmaddan showed, life was uncertain. Better that the new emperor—and the lady who would be named empress as soon as possible—do what they could to make certain the ancient line went on.

AFRONSAN WHO IS NOW SHESSERAN XV, TO THUKAR DAHVEN: YOU WILL HAVE RECEIVED ALREADY THE MESSAGE OF MY BROTHER, WHO WAS EMPEROR. TO YOU AND THE THUKARA JENNIFER AND ALL HEIRS OF YOUR BLOOD AND HERS, I RECONFIRM SIKKRE; FROM YOU I ASK THE FOLLOWING. DIVIDE YOUR TROOPS; KEEP THEM STILL SECRET SO LONG AS YOU CAN FROM THE NORTH, SEND HALF OF THEIR NUMBER TO THE DRO PENTI BORDER, WHERE THEY WILL REMAIN HIDDEN; THE REMAINING HALF TO THE NORTH VIA THE ROAD PAST HUSHAR OASIS. UPON MY COMMAND, THE WESTERN ARMY WILL SET UPON ANY HOLMADDI TROOPS OR MERCENARIES OF ANY BREED WHO WITHHOLD DRO PENT FROM ITS RIGHTFUL DUKE; BEZJERIAD WILL ATTACK SIMULTANEOUSLY FROM THE SEA. AT THAT SAME COMMAND, THE NORTHERN ARMY WILL MOVE QUICKLY INTO VUHLEM'S CITY AND MAKE ALL EFFORTS TO TAKE THE DUCAL PALACE AND THE MAN HIMSELF, IF THIS IS POSSIBLE. THERE WILL BE A FORCE OF SHIPS THERE AS WELL, AND SHOULD THEIR OWN BATTLES GO WELL, SUPPORT FROM LAND FORCES IN CORNEKKA AND THOSE COMING NORTH FROM DRO PENT—YOUR OWN MEN AND DUKE WUDRON'S (THE GODS WILLING). MY BLESSINGS UPON YOU, AND UPON THIS VENTURE, XV

TO LEHZIN OF BEZJERIAD, THE CONFIRMATION OF YOUR NEW EMPEROR, THAT THE DUCHY IS YOURS AND THE HOLDING LINEAR, TO THE HEIRS OF YOUR BODY. FROM YOU, I ASK THE TROOPS AND SHIPS YOU PLEDGED PREVIOUSLY TO DRO PENT AND ALSO ASK THAT YOU SEND TO SEA YOUR FASTEST SHIPS TO GARNER THE ATTENTION OF A LASANACHI, PREFERABLY ON ITS WAY SOUTH AND THEREFORE NOT EXPECTED IN HOLMADDAN BY THE TRAITOR VUHLEM. HAVE CONVEYED TO THE CAPTAIN OF THAT SHIP THAT A NEW EMPEROR SITS UPON THE RHADAZI THRONE, AND A NEW ORDER RULES. ALSO TO THAT CAPTAIN, THIS: WHATEVER PRICE VUHLEM, WHO WAS LEGITIMATE DUKE OF HOLMADDAN, OFFERS YOU FOR THE TRANSPORT OF THE DRUG ZERO AND OTHER GOODS—SUCH AS SMALL CHILDREN CARRIED IN SECRET FROM THE DRO PENTI PALACE TO THAT OF THE HOLMADDI DUKES—THE NEW EMPEROR WILL TREBLE THE PRICE, AND PAY IT IN GOLD IMMEDIATELY UPON SATISFACTORY RESULT. IN EXCHANGE HE ASKS LOYALTY FOR ONLY ONE MOON-SEASON, AND SHIPS AND MEN TO AID THE RHADAZI EMPEROR IN HIS CLAIM AGAINST THE HARBOR OF DRO PENT AND THE COASTLINE OF HOLMADDAN. ONCE DRO PENT IS IN THE RIGHTFUL HANDS, AND HOLMADDAN AGAIN LOYAL TO THE EMPEROR, THE LASANACHI MAY FEEL FREE TO WITHDRAW TO THEIR OWN LANDS, OR TO MAKE NEW BARGAIN WITH EMPEROR AFRONSAN, WHO IS ALSO SHESSERAN XV, AND WHO WILL NOT PROVE UNGRATEFUL.

SEND ALSO TO THE GALLIC STATES FOR BATTLESHIPS, IF THEY WILL PROVIDE THEM. WHETHER OR NO, ASK ON OUR BEHALF IF THEY WILL TRADE WITH US IN WIRE FROM THEIR LANDS TO OURS, AND IN STEAM TRAINS AND OTHER GOODS, ONCE THIS PRESENT CRISIS IS SET ASIDE. BLESSINGS UPON YOU; YOUR AID IN THIS DIFFICULT TIME WILL NOT GO UNREWARDED, XV

TO DUKE ALETTO AND DUCHESS ROBYN OF ZELHARRI,

AND TO DUKE JUBELO AND DUCHESS MISARLA OF
CORNEKKA, BLESSINGS OF THE NEW EMPEROR UPON YOU
AND YOUR LINE, READY THE MEN YOU PROMISED ME A
WHILE SINCE, AND AWAIT MY COMMAND, IT WILL NOT
PAY YOU FALSE COIN IN THE DAYS TO COME, XV

TO DUKE ALETTO, YOUR NEW EMPEROR'S SINCERE
SORROW AT THE DEATH OF YOUR SISTER, AFRONSAN

MERCHANT CHRISTOPHER CRAY, CEE-TECH, MONDEGO,
NEW LISBON: EVENTS MOVING QUICKLY NOW; ANY IN-
FORMATION YOU CAN SEND NORTH REGARDING ZERO AND
THOSE DEALING IN IT, PLEASE DO, AND AT ONCE. MY PER-
SONAL SORROW TO YOU; I KNOW YOU WERE FOND OF THE
SIN-DUCHESS. ALL THE MORE REASON FOR BOTH OF US TO
SEE VUHLEM PAYS FOR WHAT HE HAS CAUSED TO BE
DONE.
WEDDED BROTHER PREPARING TO EXTEND WIRE AT
ONCE FROM FAHLIA BORDER INTO PODHRU, ALSO GALLIC
RAIL WHICH YOU AND HE BOTH ASSURE ME WILL NOT
HOLD OR FIT MER KHANI ENGINES, SHOULD THEY BRING
THEIR OWN RAILS WEST OF GREAT MOUNTAINS. IF TIME,
CONCLUDE THAT DEAL AND SEAL THE BARGAIN WITH THE
GALLICS, A SMALL PERCENTAGE, PERHAPS, TO WEDDED
BROTHER FOR HIS AID IN THE MATTER.
SAFE TO RETURN HOME, IF YOU WISH, AFRONSAN

Chris set the wire aside and rubbed his eyes on his
sleeve. "Damn him!"
"What? Damn who?" Ariadne laid a hand on his arm.
Chris held out the telegram Edrith had just brought, let
her read it. "Hell," he said bitterly. "All those years with
her uncle and that old bat Merrida, she was—she was still
just a—a neat person. And now—oh, *damnit*. Vuhlem—"
He got up, paced the small room the Mondego inn had let
them have as a sitting room. Ariadne watched him anx-

iously; he still looked dreadful, and the ribs clearly hurt him. "Eddie. Mind going back out?"

Edrith shook his head. "What—more liquid from the healer?"

"God, no," Chris said feelingly. "Gotta send a wire." He crossed to the room's only table, turned over several sheets of paper, tore one in half, and began to print rapidly across what was left. "Here, this should do it. Get back here, fast as you can, though. The French should be sending for us any time now."

CEE-TECH TO EMPEROR AFRONSAN, SHESSERAN XV: DOING WHAT WE CAN HERE, BRING DOWN VUHLEM AND AVENGE LIALLA. MER KHANI VERY HELPFUL RE ZERO FOR NOW AND PHILIPPE DUPRET SENDING STEAMER FROM PARIS TO TAKE TESTIMONY RE DUPRET—WHO SOLD ZERO-TREATED BRANDY TO VUHLEM, VIA LASANACHI. SHOULD HAVE FULL PROOF OF THAT SOON, CHRIS

SHESSERAN XV TO THE ONE WHO WAS DUKE OF HOL-MADDAN, VUHLEM: WE ARE WELL AWARE WHY THE CAR-AVANER BUILDING YOU CHOSE FOR THEIR HOUSING WITHIN YOUR DUCHY FAILED; IT HAS NOTHING TO DO WITH STORM WINDS, AND ALL TO DO WITH A TRIAD WHICH IS EMPLOYED BY YOU. KNOW, VUHLEM, WE DO NOT ACCEPT YOUR LIES, NOR DO WE PERMIT SUCH ATROCITY AGAINST OUR PEOPLE; BE WARNED WE WILL EXACT PAYMENT FROM YOU FOR THE LIFE OF THE SIN-DUCHESS AND ALL OTHERS YOU HAVE SENSELESSLY MUR-DERED.

WE ARE NOT OUR BROTHER, VUHLEM; WE ARE WELL AWARE WHAT YOU ARE; WE DEMAND FROM YOU TRUE ADHERENCE TO YOUR OATH AS DUKE OF HOLMADDAN; YOU WILL OBEY US, THOUGH NOT AS YOU "OBEYED" OUR BROTHER. YOU KNOW THE PENALTY FOR DISOBEDIENCE.

GIVE OVER AT ONCE YOUR TRIAD, AND ALL DEALINGS

IN THE OUTLAND DRUG ZERO; SWEAR TO US IN HONESTY
AND WITH FULL TRUE INTENT—AND WE SHALL CONSIDER
WHETHER TO PERMIT YOU TO REMAIN IN POWER UNTIL
YOUR ELDEST CHILD IS OF AGE TO ASSUME THE DUCAL
THRONE.

REFUSE ANY OF THESE DEMANDS—AND DO NOT DOUBT
THEM TO BE EXACTLY THAT, VUHLEM—AND WE SHALL
TAKE YOUR THRONE AND YOUR LIFE. AFRONSAN,
SHESSERAN XV, EMPEROR OF RHADAZ

Vuhlem crumbled the message sent by wire to Sikkre
and forwarded to his palace by horse messenger, and swore
furiously. The servant who had delivered it somehow maintained an expressionless face as his master tossed the wad
of paper into his fire; he turned and fled as the Duke glared
at him and shouted, "Out. Out!"

Vuhlem paced the length of his floor, waited until the
discreet "click" told him the pasty-faced wretch was gone,
then swore again. "How *dare* that man? How dare
Shesseran? He's—he did this on purpose! To entrap me!"
Well, little did the onetime Emperor and would-have-been
friend know, Vuhlem had matters well in hand; Afronsan's
wire was all bluster. By the time the new would-be Emperor managed to gain control of his vast land and feeble
resources, Vuhlem would have long since taken his own
steps. He stopped pacing, tossed back his head, and
laughed. "Fool! Idiot and fool! Both together, both of you!
I said all along the line was weak, this merely proves it!"
He turned to stare into the fire; the coals had burned low
but there was still a small, bright spot that had been a
would-be command from the so-called Emperor. "Dare to
think you can best me, Afronsan. Dare to think it." He spun
away on one heel, began pacing again as he considered his
options.

Many of these: His to choose from. That message—ignore it, best policy all around. Shesseran would not know

how to deal with an ignored command; Afronsan had still to placate the old man's council, which was just as weak as the old man himself. It would take time for him to choose his own men, set his policy. . . . Yes, ignore the message. By the time the weakling Afronsan realized exactly what the northernmost of his dukes intended, it would be much too late.

For the rest, he'd better seal a new bargain between himself and the Lasanachi; they were useful, their longboats better than anything Rhadaz had, and faster—and several of those who plied the southern waters were also well armed with the foreign projectile weapons.

Unfortunate that fool Casimaffi had been arrested; well, it hadn't been unexpected, really, and there were others Vuhlem could contact, on his own or via the Lasanachi, who could supply him with the same liquors and the same weaponry. The French nobleman maintained his control over the trade in Zero and over his island; it would do, for now.

It could make him truly furious if he thought about the boy. But there was no point to it: Wudron's heir was no doubt already back in his mother's arms, and the gods only knew what Wudron intended. With any good fortune, the message that had accompanied the boy held his attention: "What was yours, and then mine, and is now yours once more—that could become mine again, at the least stirring of fortune. Be cautious, *brother,* where you bestow your loyalty and your confidences." Wudron would understand what he meant; he'd have a care for his only son, and dare speak no word against Vuhlem.

As for the sin-Duchess—well, only one such as Afronsan would create civil war over her! "He'd take my throne, give it to my eldest child? A daughter? He's madder than old Shesseran!" The sin-Duchess had an easier death than she'd deserved. Still . . .

Vuhlem cast a wary eye upward, licked his lips, and

went to feed the fire. The Triad—they had been too eager to please him—or perhaps simply too eager. "I wanted merely to frighten them, not so many deaths. *I* knew the old man wouldn't accept so many caravaners and that dratted female both; one, yes, a few of the other, yes, perhaps! All of them, though!"

But how did one rid oneself of a Triad? Jadek's—They had become it, according to his own Triad. His Triad claimed not to understand what that meant, really; Vuhlem didn't care, it was nothing to do with him, after all: the True Way, or some such nonsense only a truly ancient Triad could know and accept. His was far from that level; one of it had been Dahmec's father's Shaper, another the Shaper serving Jubelo's uncle, and the third—well, the creature had come from somewhere, who cared where? Still, together, it was strong and arrogant all at once. Since the hour it had torn through that building—it had changed, not for the better. When he'd ordered It to go away, or at least to return to his hunting lodge, it—they—had laughed at him, the three-part voice making his very bones ache.

Three-part. That means it's not yet truly bonded. He had that knowledge from somewhere, possibly Shesseran, who'd been so vehemently against Triads and Light. It meant nothing to him; except the Triad still needed a wealthy patron to keep it in the enclosed space it needed, to provide the things called for in its spells or in its rituals that—supposedly—permitted it to gain strength. For now, it would obey him, at least in the things that mattered most.

Still—

If Afronsan somehow became certain there was a Triad here. If he came himself, as he seemed to threaten, and discovered a Triad in Vuhlem's palace . . .

Well, a man that heedless of his own safety could die of Triad, Vuhlem told himself. He laughed grimly. "And serve him right."

DUCHESS ROBYN TO THUKARA: IS CHRIS HONESTLY
ALL RIGHT? WIRE FROM HIM SOUNDED A LITTLE PHONY,
MUCH TOO CHEERFUL, AND I KNOW HE'D TELL YOU WHEN
HE'D LIE TO ME, ROBYN

CHRIS TO JEN: ASK AUDREN HENRY ABOUT BAUXITE
MINES IN FRENCH JAMAICA. MAY BE FINAL ZERO LINK, IN-
CANS TO DUPRET TO MER KHANI. NOW HAVE TWO ENG-
LISH SAILORS WHO HELPED TRANSFER CRATES OF
DUPRET'S BRANDY TO LASANACHI GALLEY, YEAR AGO.
GALLEY LEFT GALLIC LAKE BOUND NORTH. WILL GET
PROPER SWORN DOCUMENTS, SEND VIA SHIP IF NEW EM-
PEROR REOPENS PORTS SOON, OTHERWISE BY GALLIC
TRAIN. GOING BROKE SENDING WIRES, CHRIS

Jennifer sat cross-legged on her bed, bare feet tucked under
the thick coverlet, all her pillows and Dahven's at her back
and a red silk quilted robe warmly and discreetly covering
her from throat to wrists to ankles. Sil and the Red Hawk
grandmother had both the room's comfortable chairs; Ryselle stood behind Sil's chair. She looked, Jennifer thought,
as if she felt very much out of place. *Village woman, after
all. And used to Vuhlem as what nobles are like.* Her eyes
stung and her throat was much too tight. She blotted her
face with her fingertips. "I apologize for receiving you so
informally. The midwife won't let me out of bed at all this
morning."

Sil nodded. "I'm sorry you aren't well—"

"Just—precaution on her part. I haven't slept well the
past few days, and because of the Zero the Thukar's brothers gave me not long after I started this baby, she's cautious." She shook her head. "That's not so important, just
now. I feel fine, honestly; I'm tired, but not too tired to talk
with you." She looked at the grandmother. "I know you
have a long way to go to reach Podhru, and you're eager to
get going. So I won't keep you long. But there's a docu-

ment case I'd like you to carry to the new Emperor, I asked them to bring it here when the last letter is readied. If you wouldn't mind . . . I'd feel better having it in your hands, rather than a rider's. There are some sensitive documents, and once or twice something has happened to a sole rider, between us and Podhru."

Red Hawk's grandmother nodded at once. "It's no difficulty. We're protected—well, so far south, we are," she added bleakly. "By my gifts and sheer numbers." Red Hawk's grandmother laid a hand on Sil's arm. "They weren't any use the other night, of course. Such a swift, deadly attack—" Her voice trailed off; she looked and sounded old, all at once. Sil took her near hand; *she* looked worried. "It's all right, Sil. I frankly saw very little: The beam began to creak in a nasty fashion and the sin-Duchess shouted. Two of the men simply scooped me up like a bag of flour and ran. Before I could so much as protest, they had me into my cart and the cart itself well away from the building." She sighed heavily.

"You lead Red Hawk," Sil said. It sounded like an ongoing argument. "Of course they got you out quickly—you and Silver Star's grandmother both." She shrugged, spread her hands wide. "You couldn't have done anything in there but counted as another of the dead."

"I know."

"There isn't much I can tell you myself," Sil went on. "What everyone saw, of course: The main beam was splintering, stones and wood shifting, and utter panic. We were both wet and half-frozen, and then, to be back in the storm, outside—watching the top of the building just—just drop. Everything." She shivered. "Stones and slates fell into the courtyard and then into the street; we made a line, passing the babes and what few goods anyone had brought out, as far from the building as we could. Some of the city people were helping. And then no one else came out, and the wind blew so hard I couldn't catch my breath. The—someone

grabbed me and Ryselle, helped us around to the front side
of the building, got us into one of the whole carts. I didn't
think—I'd ever be warm again." She was quiet for a long
moment. "All—those people. They—some of the men had
to go back into the stables, kill three of the horses; they
were hurt bad, there wasn't any way to get them out.
And—and we kept waiting and waiting. It was—almost
dark again, the next day, before they came out with word,
they'd found her—and—and the boy." Ryselle closed her
eyes, bit her lip. "I never did sense anything odd, but then I
don't see magic."

"You will," Red Hawk assured her. "Once you've borne
a child, it will come to you." Sil cast her eyes up slightly.
"She didn't suffer much, remember that. The boy—my son
said he surely never knew what struck him."

"It's no help," Sil replied sharply. She swallowed. "I'm
sorry, Grandmother."

"It's all right. I am angry, too. Such—waste."

Silence. Jennifer looked at Ryselle. The village woman
was twisting her hands together. "He used me, honored
one," she said; her voice was husky.

"It's Jen, please," Jennifer said. "Or Thukara, if you'd
rather. Who used you?"

"Vuhlem, of course. His—Triad used me, to enter the
building, to attack her, all of them but her because he hated
her so. I—was there, when his soldiers came to our village
and took her prisoner; they would have killed her. She—
when I asked her about it later, about the Duke, she said"—
Ryselle swallowed, shook her head angrily—"he hated her.
And it's my fault she's dead, because I asked her—I could
see Light, she used it and I was so surprised by it, it didn't
feel evil like they all say, and I thought that—" She swallowed again. "So I asked—if she would teach me." Sil got
to her feet, wrapped both arms around her friend's shoulders, and drew her close. "It's—I'm all right," Ryselle
whispered after a moment.

"No, you aren't," Sil replied softly. "No one expects that of you, Ryselle. But you aren't to blame, Lialla *wanted* to teach you. How was anyone to know *that* would happen?"

Jennifer shook her head. "You aren't at fault, Ryselle. Vuhlem is. He's the one who acted—I think he hoped the shock of what he did would kill Shesseran, or at least cause such chaos he could profit from it. He has men in Dro Pent, and he's poised to take Cornekka. Probably Sikkre, too, though if he has troops on our border, no one's found them yet." Ryselle simply looked at her. "Lialla was my friend, too. We—we went through a lot together, getting her brother's throne away from their uncle. Vuhlem's actions are—unconscionable, and you aren't responsible, Ryselle, because he'd have found a way. You were convenient, that's all." Silence. "He won't get away with it."

"No." The grandmother touched the silver-and-moonstone pendant she wore. "The Holmaddi think it the end of the world, a disaster like this. And every caravaner pulled back from the city—from the entire Duchy." She shook her head. "I had originally thought to suggest Green Arrow or another of the smaller households, remain north to learn what they might of Vuhlem's movements for the Emperor, but it isn't safe, of course. He's already proven he'll kill."

"What kills a Triad?" Ryselle demanded suddenly. Sil pulled back to stare at her. "What—how is it done?"

"If any of us knew," Jennifer replied gloomily, "we'd have found and broken Vuhlem's as soon as Lialla sent word out he had one. It stood to reason he wouldn't want it for any good cause—any more than Jadek did. And this one's young; it has no conscience."

"And neither has Vuhlem," Sil added crisply. "We know all that. Ryselle, I don't like that look in your eye. If Lialla couldn't destroy—"

"She—wasn't trying to destroy it!" Ryselle snapped. "She was trying to keep it from using *me* and then to hold the roof against it so everyone else could get out!"

Sil gripped her shoulders, shook her gently. "Ryselle, you're not thinking! If Lialla had known how to destroy a Triad, she'd have done it the first time there was an opportunity! *You've* heard all the arguments, you were part of most of them; she didn't know!" Sil shook her again. "You can't blame yourself, I won't have it." Silence. Ryselle wouldn't meet her eyes. "We'll go back to Hushar Oasis, wait for her brother's guard, and ride with them to Duke's Fort, to see her properly—properly buried. Her and the boy both."

"You should come with me to Podhru," the grandmother said mildly. "There isn't enough distance between the Duke's palace and Sikkre *or* Zelharri; not for someone whose inner being has been touched by a Triad."

She isn't planning on going anywhere, Jennifer realized, *except back north.* No point arguing that now; she'd get Sil aside, warn her. She probably would have felt the same as Ryselle did, but there wasn't any use in her throwing herself at Vuhlem. *Keep her here, perhaps.* Dangerous, the grandmother said . . . Still, if it was dangerous here for Ryselle, it might be dangerous for a certain Thukara, too. *Jadek's Triad invaded me; I'm stronger than I was back then, and I know more, but that doesn't mean I know enough.* And if Ryselle could actually Shape—something Jennifer had never been able to do—it might be possible for the two of them to work out a way to at least neutralize that Triad. *Long enough for someone else to fry it,* she thought grimly.

Sil resumed her chair; Ryselle sat on the floor next to her, her head resting against Sil's leg. Her eyelashes were starred with tears; one ran down her cheek.

Jennifer's throat tightened: Lialla dead. It didn't seem possible. *All the warnings we gave her, all the times we said she was asking for just—oh, Hell, just what she got.* But Dahven wasn't going to let her go as far as Hushar to say good-bye, let alone to Duke's Fort for the funeral; he was right, of course, it wasn't safe. Vuhlem would love for another hostage to take young Oloric's place. But even if Dahven had let her go, the midwife would never permit her to travel. *She's probably figuring on how to get hold of my sneakers and cancel my runs.* She swallowed hard, ran a discreet finger under her nose, then looked up as Siohan tapped at the partly open door. She came in with a pot of coffee, warmed cider, and fresh rolls on a tray.

Not long after, one of Jennifer's clerks eased into the room, the heavy dispatch case in her arms. Red Hawk's grandmother held out her hands to let Sil aid her to her feet. "I'll see the Heir—I forget, the Emperor—gets this at once." She glanced at Sil, then at Ryselle. "You're still determined to accompany the sin-Duchess, I suppose?" Silence. "Yes. Well, you take care, both of you. I'll be quite put out if I have to begin training a new Heir at this point in my life, mind that!" Sil nodded. The corners of her lips twitched briefly.

"Yes, Grandmother. We'll take the south road as soon as we can, after—after. Go straight to the civil service. You'll be—where?"   .

"Usual hostel, if there's room. With the port closed for so long, there should be." The older woman crossed to the bed and held out both hands. Jennifer took them. "Take good care of yourself, Thukara."

"Oh, yes." Jennifer sighed faintly. "I'll certainly do that."

"Good. Ryselle, carry the case for me, will you? And you've riding boots in my cart still, you'd better retrieve them now, we're leaving at once." The clerk handed the case to Ryselle, who bowed deeply, then followed the older woman into the hallway.

Sil hesitated. "Thukara—Jen. If there's any message you'd like me to pass to Duke's Fort—"

Jennifer held up a hand. "You watch that red-haired child," she said quickly, one eye on the open door. "She means to get away from you and go after Vuhlem."

Sil nodded, glanced over her shoulder. "I—I know what she wants. She utterly refuses to go south to Podhru, we've argued it until my head aches. I—don't know what to do with her."

"Go south via Sikkre," Jennifer said. "Even with the extra jog from Zelharri, it won't cost you much extra time because the road's so new and flat. Leave her with me."

"Why? I mean," Sil turned red. "I didn't mean that the way it sounded. But—"

"She was Lialla's friend and she's yours. I personally don't think we should sacrifice anyone else to Vuhlem. More than that, though, if she's actually begun to Shape Light, if she's willing to help me—"

"Help you—against Vuhlem." Sil freed a strand of hair, twisted it around her finger. "She'd be more than willing, couldn't you tell? But I—frankly, I would rather she didn't; he'll kill her simply because she's dared rise what little she has above a village woman's lot. Or he'd give her back to her father, who'd drag her out onto the sand, make her dig her own hole at low tide—"

Jennifer shuddered. "Yes, I know about that. I don't intend to let harm come to her through me. Obviously, I can't guarantee that won't happen. But don't you think she's more likely to stay put somewhere at least halfway safe if she feels she's doing *something* against the man?"

"Gods. Yes, of course. I just—" Sil's cheekbones were still very red. "She's my good friend and she's a villager, an innocent. I—we're nearly of an age, but I sometimes feel I'm years beyond her, and a wealth of experience wiser. It's not—I don't want to see her hurt. If I can somehow keep her safe—it's not what you think, either," she added sharply.

Jennifer shook her head. "I didn't particularly think—what, that she's your lover?" Sil went red right to the hairline; Jennifer's face felt hot, too. She kept her voice level and expressionless. "Frankly, it wouldn't matter to me, either way. It's beside the point, too. If you'll talk to her, convince her I mean well, that I want to find a way to at least slow that Triad. If—you know Afronsan means to invade Holmaddan, if Vuhlem doesn't give over—and Vuhlem never will. Imagine how much luck a green army would have taking that palace."

"Gods. With Vuhlem and his Triad free to—gods," Sil said, very softly. She glanced toward the door. "They'll wonder where I am, I'd better go. I'm—sorry, Thukara."

"For what? That was a personal question, you had every right to snarl at me. And it's Jen, remember?"

"Well—I *am* sorry. I'll—bring Ryselle back here."

"Good. We'll find a way, Sil." Jennifer tucked her feet back under the covers. The caravaner managed a faint smile, turned, and went. Jennifer thumped pillows flat and lay down. "She doesn't believe it any more than I do, right now," she mumbled. A tear ran down her face, slid down her throat. She blotted it angrily. "Oh—damn you anyway, Lialla."

"*I* said that all along." Jennifer started, rubbed her eyes hastily. Dahven came into the room, sat on the side of the bed, and drew her close. "Siohan thought you might like company, and I was tired of arguing with Grelt anyway." She sighed, leaned into him. "Learn anything useful?"

"Doubt it. Messy details."

"Mmmm. I'm sorry. She exasperated me, but I know you liked her. And the rest of it—you feel all right?" he asked after a moment. She nodded. "Eat something?"

"Ate. Drank cider, ate a roll, had some coffee. Is it midday yet?"

"Close enough, I suspect."

"I'm getting up." She shoved hair out of her face, looked up at him. "You aren't arguing with me."

"No, ma'am," he said evenly. "Argued enough with Grelt."

"Still not letting you go to Dro Pent, is he?" Dahven hesitated; shook his head. "That's not a real answer."

"Um—" He eyed her sidelong. "No, I'm not going to Dro Pent." He reached for one of the remaining rolls on the small tray, tore it in half. "They're good; want to share?"

"You're stalling," Jennifer said flatly. She pushed away from him. "And trying to divert my attention, it won't work."

He chewed and swallowed. Set the rest of the roll back on the tray. His shoulders were tense. "I'm not going to Dro Pent." He turned to eye her sidelong. Jennifer folded her arms and waited. "Grelt doesn't like it, but there aren't any other choices."

"I don't like it, either," Jennifer said mildly, "and I don't even know what it is I don't like, yet."

"I'm leading the other half of our men north, into Holmaddan."

12

꽃

CHRIS didn't care much for the French ambassador to New Lisbon: Frenault had the pinched-nostrils look of someone who detected a bad smell; he was polite toward Ariadne in an extremely chilly fashion, barely civil to himself, and as for Edrith—well, Eddie always claimed he didn't notice such things. Dija was too obviously awed by the outrageously ornate room and by the legal proceedings to pay attention to the ambassador, except as another overly decorated item in the chamber, so far as he could tell.

Frenault: *I thought an ambassador was supposed to promote goodwill, or something! This guy doesn't look like he'd know goodwill if it bit him.* He didn't speak English, of course—Chris doubted he spoke Portuguese, either. *So I'm not noble, but Frenault isn't, either. He's not as far above me on the ladder as he'd like to think he is.* It would be a pleasure to haul the man down a rung or so, but hardly sensible. *Make nice, Cray. Ignore the look; after all, he's helping us pack Dupret in ice.*

Maybe. Frenault might be in Dupret's pocket. Ariadne didn't know, and Chris still couldn't decide, even after several hours of the man's chill company—especially that first extremely unpleasant meeting: just Frenault, himself, and Ari—which the ambassador had clearly only reluctantly agreed after he'd received the introduction letter from the Alliance man, Barton. All the same, to Chris's surprise, at

the end of their talk, Frenault had immediately drafted a
message to Philippe Dupret in Paris, and another to the
King's Council for Foreign Affairs. All right, he *was* cooperating, where it counted. Probably not Dupret's man, after
all. Just a snob. The down-the-nose look had *better* not
have anything to do with any facet of Ariadne's parentage,
Chris thought flatly, or Frenault would have more problems
than he could count on both overly clean, be-ringed hands.

It had been—what? How many days after Frenault's
message went overseas? Too many, he decided gloomily.
Dupret had had enough time to—Well, whatever he'd done,
there hadn't been any reverberations up in Mondego; nothing at all, word or rumor, from French Jamaica. It seemed
forever; hadn't been that long, and his ribs still protested
sharply whenever he took too deep a breath or rolled over
the wrong way in his sleep.

He couldn't *do* anything; that was a large part of the
problem, of course. He still hurt and his energy level was
near rock bottom. But neither Ariadne nor Eddie would let
him try anything more strenuous than a slow walk down to
the nearest beach and back to their inn, once a day. There
was nothing to do except send and receive letters and wires.
He was going to break the bank, all those wires back to
Afronsan and Jen. *A guy gets spoiled back up there, all that
free wire time. Something better come of all this, get that
crap out of Rhadaz before it takes out more than people
like Lizelle. Rotten woman, getting hooked, trying to get
Aletto hooked, and then offing herself before anyone could
call her on it.*

Well, it was starting to look like something would come
of all those wires and all the hard work so far—the Alliance
was actually cooperating, Jen and Afronsan were still wad-
ing through stacks of contracts and letters, and even the
local French were helping—grudgingly in some cases, but
still. *Well, who can blame 'em? Dupret's noble, after all.*

Bet they'd rather wash the dirty laundry back home, quietly and out of sight.

Fortunately, his second meeting with Frenault had been extremely brief—the man could as well have sent him a message that the investigation team would expect all four of them this morning. Even more good luck, he didn't have to handle Frenault alone this time—though the two younger sons of high French noblemen who'd come on the steamship *Auguste Lyonne* spoke scarcely more English than Frenault; they were barely aware where Rhadaz might be located and of course understood none of its language. Chris's French was just passable, but they had brought their own translator—along with three secretaries, two of whom were presently busy copying down everything anyone in the room said—and an aged King's Notary who sat by the window, his hands resting on the long case that would carry the sworn testimony back to the Council, once it had been stamped, sealed, and done to in whatever other fashion that would make it official. The questions themselves—picky, Chris thought tiredly. They wanted to know everything, minute by minute. *Jen used to do this kinda thing for a living? Pass!* His own testimony had taken well over two hours, with first dark, chubby little Joulon and then the even darker, neatly bearded Giraut asking the questions. They'd spent next to no time on Dija, but of course, she'd seen and heard almost nothing. Eddie had seen Albione, Albione's men, overheard the talk when they boarded the *Maborre*. But both of them had been questioned briefly and early on, had signed where told to sign, repeated the oath in French, and left together. Hours earlier.

Ariadne—he didn't think they'd *ever* finish with Ariadne. Frenault paced the room, occasionally muttering something under his breath: repeating a question or an answer to himself, or simply mumbling. Mostly staring down his long, thin nose or playing with his shiny, rose-colored cuffs or his rings. Chris couldn't make out most of what he

said, and didn't really care. The others ignored him, too,
unless one or another of them wanted something—like tea.

"But you do definitely know, madame, that he was engaged in the production of drug-tainted brandies, and for
certain with the aid of the man Sorionne?" Joulon asked—
for perhaps the fifth time. Ariadne sipped pale amber tea,
set the thin cup back on its ornate legged tray, and nodded.
Her eyes were dark with irritation, though it didn't show in
her voice; she even managed a faint smile for the man as
she patiently reiterated the pertinent conversations she'd
overheard at various times. Including the one between
Dupret and Maurice outside her locked bedroom door, that
last night in Philippe-sur-Mer.

Chris sipped his own tea. *Really dislike this stuff. One of
those herby things Mom would drink. I'd still kill for a cold
Coke. Or even coffee.* Probably lucky the ambassador had
offered as much as he had.

It was done, finally; late-afternoon sun came through tall
windows to lay across the long, handwritten sheets of thick,
laid paper. The Notary sealed both in blue-and-gold wax;
Chris signed, Ariadne signed; the two noblemen countersigned across the bottoms and Chris watched as the Notary
rolled everything together and fitted it into the narrow case,
then sealed the case itself and prepared wax for each of the
other two men to complete the outer seal. Ariadne let Chris
pull her to her feet; the two noblemen rose with her.

Giraut bowed over her fingers. "Madame, our regrets and
those of your uncle the Duc for these unpleasantries."

"*Merci.*" She inclined her head. Joulon opened his
square leather folder and drew out a thick envelope, which
he handed to her.

"From your uncle. We shall remain in Mondego until tomorrow evening, if you wish to send a reply to him with
us."

Ariadne handed Chris the envelope; he slid it into the

deep pocket of his jacket. "You go where—first to Philippe-sur-Mer?"

"No, madame. First the city New Lisbon; we have word Lord Albione was seen there, two days ago. Better to take both men back to France at once; by your words and yours, M. Cray, Lord Albione is deep in M. Dupret's confidences." Giraut rubbed a neat little blue-black beard with one small hand, kissed the air just above Ariadne's fingers. "Madame—"

Ariadne brought her chin up. "We go with you." The two men exchanged startled looks; Frenault mumbled something. "It is our right, mine and Chris's, by French law, to confront the man as he is arrested and say to him the paper you have is my own word, and is sworn truth, is that not so?"

"Well, yes—" Giraut began doubtfully.

"And if this is done, there is no cause he or I must appear at that man's trial?"

"That's so—"

Chris touched Ariadne's wrist, gestured with his head. "Just a moment—excuse us, if you don't mind?" He drew her several paces away, then whispered, "Are you nuts?"

"I?" She spread her arms in a broad shrug; her eyes were black. "You think I let matters go so simply? To sit here and talk and talk—and then we walk away and let *these* men do the filth—do the dirty work, you call it? I see him taken, Chris, this is important to me. And those men who are his agents around the island—there, at least, I know every man who is Henri Dupret's. They take all such men, not simply Henri Dupret and Albione." She glared up at him; he glared back, shook his head. "I must see this thing finished, Chris. I must!"

"Both of us swore we'd stay away from the man after this last little fiasco." She folded her arms, and simply looked at him; his temper went. "Ariadne, damnit! Remember how pissed—how mad you got up in Sikkre, when you thought I was coming back down here to get your old man?"

"Because that was alone, you and Eddie, and without *me*," she snapped back. "This—they have a steamship, with men and guns, and even my father and all his hired men will count for nothing against them!"

"Yeah. And what if Dupret decides he wants to take us out and doesn't care if they kill him for it?"

"You," she whispered icily, "do not have to go with me!"

"Oh, yeah?" He scowled at her. "What about, 'I do not leave you, ever again in this life?' I *thought* you meant that!"

She glanced beyond him. "Hush," she said in a low, sharp voice. "They come."

"Oh, hell," Chris muttered, then bit his lip.

Ariadne put on a smile for them that somehow managed to take the heat out of her eyes. "You will take me to Philippe-sur-Mer?" she asked in crisp French.

Joulon eyed Giraut, who nodded. "Madame, of course, if you insist upon it, but—"

"Good."

Chris sighed heavily. "All right, lady, you win! Both of us," he told Giraut.

Joulon spread his hands in a broad shrug. "It is reasonably safe, M. Cray—given the man himself, I make no guarantees, but you understand this, of course."

"Don't I, though," Chris mumbled.

"And," Giraut put in neatly, "of course, it saves you the journey to Paris, when the man is brought to trial."

Chris glanced at the elaborately sealed tube in the Notary's hands. "All that—and we'd *still* have to be there?"

"Well—because of his rank, you understand. A man of the Duc's blood can challenge the authenticity of such papers and testimony, and then—"

"Yeah. And like he wouldn't," Chris mumbled in English. "Yeah, okay. Fine. We'll do it your way, Ariadne. I swear, though, if something happens to you—"

"Nothing bad happens," she said firmly. "Only to Henri Dupret and those men on French Jamaica who deal with him in Zero." Chris sighed resignedly, then squared his shoulders and shook hands with Joulon and Giraut.

Ariadne stepped back to draw on gloves. *Your face,* she ordered herself. *That it shows nothing, except possibly satisfaction for winning the argument against three stubborn males.* If they suspected what she planned—or even worse, if Chris did! *Nothing must interfere, whatever else happens, from here to there, or afterward. I see him, to his face. One—last—time. And then—* Chris turned to take her arm; he still looked very put out; and he only knew, as he himself would say, the half of it. Ariadne set the thought firmly aside, laid her hand atop Chris's, and let him walk her from the room.

He was quiet all the way back to the inn; Ariadne glanced at him now and again, but his eyes were on the people around them, moving constantly. *Leave him be,* she decided. He clearly still didn't feel safe here; it was fair, she didn't herself. She wouldn't distract him with talk. She glanced at his face again as they entered the inn; it was drawn, his lips clamped firmly together, but he didn't look angry. Once they were inside the main room, she caught hold of his wrist, drawing him to a halt. "How long since you took the healer's powders?" she asked quietly.

Chris shrugged; a frown quirked his forehead. "Don't know. Eddie gave them to me."

"Those?" She shook her head. "But that was—it has been hours, before breakfast! Have you more, in the box up there?"

"Maybe one," he began. Ariadne swore under her breath and strode over to the high counter, where a young woman leaned on her elbows. She was talking to one of the messengers; both looked very bored.

"Boy," she said as she drew the small embroidered coin bag from her pocket. "Two *sous* extra for you if you go to Marie Elorra, in the Street of Tall Cane and bring back at once for M. Cray a new box of powders. She will know what to send." The boy caught the coins deftly and sprinted for the door, nearly colliding with Chris as he ran out. Ariadne went quickly up the stairs; Chris, mumbling under his breath and holding on to the wall with one hand, came right behind her.

Dija pulled the door open and sighed with relief. "Ah, madame! I thought I heard your footsteps. So many hours—but you are here, all is well." Her French was even better than his own, Chris thought tiredly, and she'd been at it only a few short weeks. *Ari's right; I don't have that kind of gift for languages.* Then again, Dija and Ariadne spoke nothing else between them. And he could manage basic communication in most of the European tongues, as well as Incan and Cantonese. *Not so bad. Depends on what you need.* He drew a deep breath, winced, and set his hand against his side.

Ariadne began unpinning her hat as soon as she passed the doorway, and tossed it onto the bed. Dija made a vexed little noise, scooped up the hat, and settled her mistress on the upright chair by the window so she could shove dislodged pins into the elaborate coil of braids beginning to slip down the base of her neck. "All those words," Ariadne droned. "His and then mine, and then all the meaningless pleasantries. Nothing more." She wasn't telling Dija about the trip back via French Jamaica, Chris noticed. Just as well; Dija's nightmares had brought them all awake, the first two nights in this inn. What the girl didn't know couldn't hurt *anyone,* just now.

"So long you were gone, though! You must be hungry."

"We were given cakes and tea—sweet things only, and

not enough of either, actually," Ariadne admitted. Dija stopped pinning, leaned forward to eye her anxiously. "It is fine, I am fine—we both are. They wish to make certain of my uncle, to skewer him with words. I wanted to be sure they could do this."

"Only with words, huh?" Chris asked. Ariadne laid a hand on Dija's to restrain the hairpins, turned to face him.

"I left the knife between his feet outside Philippe-sur-Mer, if you remember," she said flatly. "I have had no time to purchase another such knife."

"I know you haven't. And let's keep it that way for now. You know you're gonna get pissed when you see the dude, and I bet your uncle Philippe's men won't be thrilled if you gut the guy before they can interrogate him. And there's the small matter of a trial?"

"Perhaps—or perhaps not. Uncle Philippe might like for all this dirt with Henri and his papa does not come public."

"Well, let's not find out, all right?" Chris put in sourly. Ariadne shrugged. Chris subsided on the bed, cautiously, one hand against his side. "In any case, I'll bet Henri will hate being back in Paris because he's on trial for dealing drugs more than anything anyone could do to him." He laid back flat with a faint sigh. "Dija, Eddie didn't really leave you alone, did he?"

"I am all right in these rooms. And there was a wire—he went somewhere to get it," Dija said. She tucked two more long hairpins between her lips and went back to fussing with Ariadne's hair.

Chris closed his eyes. "Oh. You opened the door before we could knock or say anything, though. That's dangerous, remember?" Silence. "Keep it in mind, please. Vey'll kill me and Eddie both if you get mangled by someone looking for any of the rest of us." He let out his breath in a gust. "Ariadne, I am *not* taking more of those powders, they make me dizzy."

"They make the ribs heal faster, she said so, remember?"

"It's my *ribs* that're messed up, not my brain, all right?"

"And it will remain your ribs unless you take the powders," Ariadne replied sharply. She set Dija's hand aside when the maid would have shoved another pin into her hair, got to her feet, and went over to sit at the edge of Chris's bed. Chris opened his eyes, closed them again as she laid the back of one small, cool hand against his brow. "You are still too warm, and I hear you at night when you try to move, and you think we are all asleep. The powders—a little of dizzy is nothing, compared to days and more days like this."

"You're trying to distract me," Chris mumbled. Ariadne shook her head, laid the hand across his lips when he tried to say more.

"I try to make you better. *I* cannot myself; my mother's craft is not in me, you know this. I do what else I can, so you do not hurt an hour longer than you must."

Chris sighed and captured her hand. "Look—I'm sorry, I'm just a lousy patient, all right? It—I don't do sick well at all, never did, you can ask Jen. Honestly, Ari, I'm not yelling at you—"

"As you did in M. Frenault's *chambre*?" she asked dryly.

He sighed, very heavily. "Ariadne, come on, be reasonable, what you asked them for is too much, all right? You don't want to see that man again! I sure as hell don't want to see him again! And I—all right, I didn't know about the thing where he could make us show up in Paris for his trial." He considered this, sighed again, very faintly. "And he'd probably have arranged for someone like Albione to pull us off whatever ship we took there, and dump us in the middle of the ocean."

"No. As you say, we do not do things that way," Ariadne said. She stared at the wall over his head, eyes black and her mouth tight. She sat like that for a moment, finally shook her head; Chris wondered what she'd been thinking about. "We—if we are upon the *Auguste Lyonne*, in the

company of all those who sail her and serve as soldier upon
her, we are safe. He is brought, we speak the oath before
him and in the presence of the sworn King's Notary—why,
it is over, *fini,* and we go our own way and create a real life
between us—while *he* goes into the bowels of that ship on
his way to a dungeon cell in Paris." She scowled at her
hands. "And his spies. And serve every one of them properly, too."

"Right. Me, too." His voice was sharp with sarcasm, but
when she looked at him, his eyes were closed once more;
lips compressed. *Maurice died much too quickly,* she
thought in a sudden fury and got up from the bed. The bedroom, unlike the tiny sitting adjoining it, was fairly large—
of course, it had to be, to hold three big beds, two heavy
cabinets for garments, and linen chests at the end of each
bed. There were two many-paned windows, one facing the
main street, the other overhanging the tile-roofed portico.

No one she knew, out in either direction—no Eddie,
coming back from the telegraph office, no boy returning
with the healer's powders. But a moment later, she heard
steps outside the door, and Edrith came in, a thick wad of
paper clutched in one hand, a bundle in the other. "One of
the messengers was on his way with this for the lady." He
held it out; Ariadne took it and broke the package open,
shook one of the small black folds of paper free, and
dumped it in Chris's cup.

Behind her, Chris caught his breath sharply as he tried to
sit up. She set her teeth together hard, concentrated on
readying the cup, and brought it across as Edrith sat on the
far side of Chris's bed and held out the thick bundle. Chris
eyed him warily. Edrith's eyes were dancing and he was
having a hard time not laughing aloud. "What's so funny?"
He shook his head as Ariadne held out the cup. "Ariadne, I
am not drinking that!"

She glared down at Edrith. "He drinks, or you tell him
nothing."

Edrith chuckled. "Hey, you know?" He spread his hands wide; the bundle remained just outside Chris's reach.

"He is hurting, look at him," Ariadne said flatly.

The laughter was gone. Edrith set the packet on the far edge of the bedside table, took the cup from her. "She is right, I looked like that and you would think me dying. And badger me into taking wretched powders. Nasty goo first, you." Chris rolled his eyes.

"It's a conspiracy. I should have known better than to *ever* leave you two alone together. Ari, this stuff is—"

"Drink," she said flatly. "We go back to Philippe-sur-Mer, I get some decent from Oncle Frère."

Edrith turned his head and stared at her; he had an arm behind Chris's shoulder, the cup at his lips. "Uncle—Uncle Brother?"

A smile pulled at the corner of Ariadne's mouth; she shook her head, waved a hand toward the cup. "Give him that first. *He* can tell—you—later."

Chris giggled faintly; he winced and set a hand between his mouth and the cup. "That's not fair, making me laugh. And will you at least let me have some of the flat bread in that tin, to wash this stuff down? You would not believe how *bad* it tastes."

A short while later, he was sitting up, reading the voluminous message, eating dark triangles of flat bread, and shaking his head. "I still don't see what's so funny, Eddie," he said finally. He let the last sheet slip to the counterpane, looked at the remaining half-piece of flat bread, shrugged, and popped it in his mouth.

Edrith gathered up the pages, stacked them neatly together, and dropped them back on the small bedside table. "Not in the message, just the fuss we all had, leading up to it, you know?" His voice dropped to a dramatic whisper. " 'Do we dare go to the Mer Khani over this matter? How do they react? Do they murder the messenger? Make as though there could be nothing wrong with these two men? Are they part of it all?' And then, after so much hair pulling, a message like this?"

Ariadne turned from the far window. "If you even begin to think I read all that length of message in English," she said, but fell silent as Chris shook his head.

"You don't have to, I'll—yeah, it would take too long to 'splain, so I'll som op." He shook his head again, broke into spluttering laughter. "God. Humiliations galore, all right—for your old man and a couple Mer Khani." Ariadne simply stared at him. "Never mind, old data. Even if I told you later, you wouldn't begin to figure it.

"Some committee in the Alliance Parliament decided we had at least the basis for an inquiry, so someone dropped a formal notice on New Holland Mining Consortium, told 'em, 'We hear you're dealing drugs to our Third World neighbors across the mountains, and we'd like to hear your explanation of events. And we want the explanation three days from now, when we come to your headquarters to look through all your paperwork, your smelting plants, and your personal effects.' " He paused.

Ariadne shook her head. "But wasn't that what M. Barton said he would ask?"

"It's the money aspect," Chris said. "Like your old man—like Dupret. Those who have the big money don't play by the rules the rest of us have to play by; New Holland probably never expected anything like that."

"But this inspector investigates on what we told him?" Ariadne gestured toward the voluminous message.

"Barton said the Alliance government *really* doesn't like the drug traffic, remember? I guess they don't, if they're willing to investigate based on less than hard evidence. You know, if one of us had actually *seen* your old man and this John Perry shaking hands over a crate of Zero."

"Oh." She considered this.

"They went in, turned everything upside down. Didn't

find any Zero, but they took piles of contracts and letters
away with them, said they'd come back in a day or so. John
Perry and Geoffrey Bellingham were both there, protesting
madly, Bellingham on about his family honor, Perry about
the disgrace, raising the roof. Perry followed them out,
though, and told them he put family money into the company but didn't have anything to do with the day-to-day
business. And when they went back two days later, the man
was gone. Just flat disappeared."

"Oh," Ariadne said again. "And the other—Geof—I cannot say it, that man? Has he also vanish?"

"Geoffrey Bellingham. No—they *found* him," Chris said
flatly. "He left a long note, they *think* it's his writing but
they aren't certain. Bellingham's note said John Perry kept
a large part of the company business to himself. He doesn't
know, but suspects the Parliament should check Perry's
family finances and his links to southern French and French
Jamaican bauxite mines—and to a French nobleman named
Henri Dupret, down in French Jamaica. A long bit about
the Bellingham family honor, then a lot of other stuff I
don't really understand, about Perry, his family, his connections—" Chris sighed. "Whatever it all meant, I hope
the Inspector Whoosit has it figured out, because he can't
ask Bellingham. Guy hung himself, right before they
showed up."

CHRIS TO THUKARA: INFORMATION TO FOLLOW VIA
SHIP RE ALLIANCE INVESTIGATION, COPY GOING SEPA-
RATELY TO NEW EMPEROR; APPEARS THEY AND FRENCH
BETWEEN THEM CLOSING DOWN LARGE PORTION OF DRUG
TRADE, THIS SIDE OF THE CONTINENT. PLENTY OF SHIPS
AND FINISHED ZERO STILL OUT THERE, THOUGH, DON'T
GET COMPLACENT.

FOUR OF US GOING WITH FRENCH TO PHILIPPE-SUR-
MER, GOTTA SWEAR BEFORE DUPRET THE STUFF WE
SIGNED IS TRUE; TELLING YOU NOW SO YOU KNOW

WHERE THE BODIES ARE, IF SOMETHING GOES WRONG.
CHRIS

First trains, now a ship that actually moved at a decent speed. Chris leaned against the high, polished wood rail of *Auguste Lyonne*'s bow and sighed happily. The air temperature wasn't nearly what it had been the last trip he'd taken to Philippe-sur-Mer, the humidity was reasonable—he could almost forget where they were going and why, and about the cargo down in the hold. *They should haul Albione's aristocratic backside up here, him and all his lousy crew, make them sit on the deck in full sun, see how they like it.*

Then again, the hold of a ship wasn't the nicest place to be. For a snotty nobleman like Albione—yeah, he was better off where he was. *Besides, he's not up here to spoil my view.* He pulled the hat cautiously over his brow; the sun was bright and would burn him, no matter how cool the air felt. "Burn me worse than I already am," he mumbled. His face still felt too tight. One of the French crewmen slowed; Chris shook his head, waved the man on. *Talking to myself out loud again. To think I used to pick on Mom for that.*

He stretched cautiously; the original powders that healer gave him must've been old or something. The new ones were doing a much better job; only an occasional twinge when he pushed too hard to let him know he had cracked ribs, and he felt alive again for the first time in way too many days. He leaned against the rail once more, this time with his back to the sea, gazed from the long, graceful bow of the ship to her low, smoking stack, to the two small decks above this main deck. *Auguste Lyonne* had three masts, but the sails were furled and covered in dark green cloth. Backup, in case something went wrong with the steam engine, which had only recently become reliable. According to the steward, nothing had in her initial ten swift voyages across the Atlantic and back.

So, Chris thought idly; his eyes fastened absently on the
broad wake behind the ship and the very blue water to either side. *So how do I find the right lever to persuade the
French to build some of these for Rhadaz?*

Nothing came to him at the moment; there'd be something they'd like in trade, though. He'd work on it. And
Ariadne had a good in with her uncle, that could only help.

Poor Ariadne; she'd been closeted most of the morning
with Giraut and a massive, impressively uniformed French
navy captain, compiling a list of Dupret's men in French
Jamaica and those she knew of around the Caribbean; what
addresses she could recall. She must be about ready to
throw something. He grinned faintly. Like maybe Dupret
into the harbor.

He turned back to look in the direction they were heading. At this rate, they'd reach Philippe-sur-Mer in a couple
of hours; he should be able to see it before midday. Behind
him, two soldiers clomped by, heavy boots making the
wood beneath his feet vibrate as they took the regular
hourly turn around the whole deck. Soldiers everywhere—
Ariadne'd had that right, they'd brought a full company,
and every one of them armed to the teeth—seasoned veter-
ans of the eastern wars, all ready for action. *Nothing to
worry about. Maybe she was right about that, too.*

He still didn't feel totally safe—he definitely wasn't
looking forward to seeing Dupret again, even with the odds
tipped so heavily in their favor this time around. But that
wasn't the situation, that was Dupret; the man made him
nervous. *You got cause. But there isn't a thing the man can
do to you this time; get this done, behind us. Maybe Ariadne even meant it, about starting a real life together after
it's over.*

Hard to even conceive of such a thing: they'd had so little normal, ordinary time together since Dupret'd brought
them together. Maybe—if her uncle Philippe was serious
about deeding her Dupret's properties in French Jamaica,

like he'd suggested in that fat letter, and if Chris could work out a deal with him on those steam cars—*Yeah. We could have—not Dupret's old town house, but maybe something else, in Philippe-sur-Mer or better yet, out in the country for part of the year. And then, the place in the mountains I picked out that very first trip north of Podhru for part of the time. Maybe after this, it really will be time for me to start setting up branch offices, letting someone else do the traveling except when there's a touchy deal or a major one like the cars. . . .* He settled his chin on crossed arms, began considering possible sites for branch offices, men he could trust to run them. It was with considerable surprise he heard the bell announcing the approach of land, what seemed only minutes later.

Another hour; the *Auguste Lyonne* lay hard against the wharf and Giraut had gone ashore moments earlier with all but five men of his full military company, leaving two to guard the locked entry to the hold, the other three on deck. Ariadne stood near the ramp, hands clutching her skirts as she watched the last of the bright uniforms disappear between two of Dupret's warehouses. She looked pale and very tense, and when Chris cleared his throat, she jumped convulsively.

"Hey," he said quietly. "Sorry. Didn't mean to startle you."

"I know. It is—" She glanced up at him, then back at once toward the docks. No one moved out there; there wasn't anyone in sight and not another ship in the entire harbor, except for a long, ramshackle fishing boat tied to a step some distance away. "The waiting," she managed finally.

"Yeah. It's tough. We could go back to the cabin—"

She was already shaking her head. "No. I stay here, get it—get everything over with, as quickly as may be."

"I understand." Her hands were creasing the dark green silk skirt. "Um—you decide yet what to do, once that's taken care of? I mean, if you want them to leave us here, if you think it'll be safe—"

"I—I haven't thought."

"Sure. All right." He wasn't wild about staying here, waiting for the next available ship to take them back to the mainland, so they could catch the train north. Even with Dupret gone, with most if not all his hired help taken away. Even with a dozen or so of the French soldiers staying behind to maintain order. The alternative wasn't wildly appealing, either; going back to New Lisbon on the same ship with Dupret and Albione, even if they *were* separated by several decks and a couple of large locks. If something went wrong—

Too late to worry about it, though. *Hell. Should've found a way around this. Look at her.* She looked as tense as he felt.

The soldiers left on deck walked around the ship, watching the shore, watching for incoming ships, for any sign of trouble. It was extremely quiet; a gull shrieked as it swooped low over the stack, and Ariadne caught her breath in a shrill little squawk.

The soldiers had made three complete circuits of the ship and were well into the fourth when Chris touched Ariadne's arm. "Listen," he said. She was already nodding.

"I hear—they return. I—if they—" She bit her lip, caught hold of the railing, and leaned across it to stare into shadow. Half a dozen soldiers emerged from the gloomy street, at least that many men, heavily fettered, in their midst. Ariadne held her breath, finally shook her head. "No. Not—not there."

Dupret's men—a few of them. Not Dupret himself. One of the fettered men glared at Chris, another said something under his breath as he passed Ariadne; the soldiers shoved them across the deck and toward the stern. He vaguely recognized one or two; didn't actually know any of them. Several minutes passed; the soldiers went back down the ramp, back into the streets. More came a short while later, five bound men with them; another ten right on their heels. A long break; shadow had moved considerably before the first soldiers came back, two dust-covered men in their midst. Ariadne watched them cross the deck, disappear toward the stern and the hatch leading down to the hold. "From the sugar plantation," she murmured. She glanced upward, drew the small watch from around her throat, shook her head. "If he somehow—"

"They might be holding him out of sight," Chris said. "Make sure they've got all his men so there isn't any trouble when they do bring him in." Ariadne bit her lip again, dropped the watch back into the open throat of her white shirtwaist, and leaned against the rail once more as three men came into sight: the captain and one of his junior officers flanking a slight dark man. Ariadne's shoulders slumped. "Merely the eldest son of Sorionne," she murmured. She counted on her fingers, lips moving silently. "Thirty—there are only a few not yet here, and some of those may have left the island." She brought her chin up as Sorionne's heir and his guards passed; the man glared at her and clearly wanted to say something nasty, but the two men flanking him hauled him off his feet and down the deck.

Another long, silent hour. There was more sound from the streets now: people shouting in the distance and the echoing clatter of men running close by, a horse going the other direction. Edrith came up next to Chris. "What goes?"

"Not much at the moment," Chris said. He took off his hat, blotted his forehead against his shirtsleeve. "I wonder if—"

"Wait," Ariadne said tensely. She pointed back along the docks, where late-afternoon shadow lay heavy. "Listen—"

Chris listened; horse or horses, and the creak of carriage wheels. "I—yeah, wait, I see it now." He pointed. Ariadne caught her breath; her hands gripped the rail so hard the knuckles stood out white. Henri Dupret's matched horses and his carriage came slowly along the wharf.

"Peronne," Ariadne whispered. "Driving the team, you see?"

Chris did, but next to Peronne, easily half again his size, the navy captain sat, his sword upraised and glinting red in a stray sunbeam. "Oh, *jeez,*" he whispered, and touched Ariadne's hand. "They—they really did it, they got him. I—" Blood thudded against his temples. *They actually nailed the bastard!* He could have cheered. Ariadne, though: "Are you up for this?"

She glanced at him; her hand closed over his fingers in a painfully tight grip. "I am ready. Oh yes," she whispered, "I am ready indeed."

Chris eyed her sidelong, but her attention was for the carriage that had just drawn up next to the ramp, and her face, like her voice, was frozen into a complete lack of expression. The captain jumped down, opened the near door, and stood with his sword at the ready; one of the junior officers emerged first, followed by one of the bottom-ranked, followed by Dupret—bare headed, in rolled-up shirtsleeves, his wrists manacled. Giraut came out behind him, a pistol in his hand; he gave it to the common soldier, turned to take a gentleman's travel case from Peronne. Dupret staggered; the captain caught hold of his arm, steadied him, indicated the ramp with his chin. Dupret spat, freed his arm, and started up the ramp, his eyes searching the rail. They touched on Ariadne, froze; he hesitated, then came onto the deck and stopped. The captain muttered something; Dupret ignored him as Ariadne took two quick steps sideways to bar their way. She held up an imperious hand for silence when the captain would have protested.

"*Canaille,*" she hissed. "I laugh at you and at your dishonor! Return to France and your brother, and know that *I* did all I could to see you shamed!"

"Unnatural child!" Dupret brought up his hands and

doubtless would have struck her down but Chris stepped between them, shoving her out of the way. His face was hot and he was as angry as he'd ever been in his life.

"Hey, you dumb jerk, pick on someone closer to your own size. You're getting everything you deserve." Dupret hesitated only briefly, then delivered a sharp, open-handed slap. Chris laughed and hit him back, hard enough to send him staggering into the men guarding him. "Eat that, Dupret!"

The soldiers would have led him away; Dupret dug in his heels and shouted, "My honor! You saw, all of you!"

"Your *honor*?" Chris laughed again. "You wouldn't know honor if it bit your nose off!"

"Whatever accusation is brought against me, I am still noble, still a Dupret, and *still* son of the Duc D'Orlean!" Dupret topped him; his voice echoed from the nearest buildings and bounced off the water. "That—that outland commoner *struck* me, you saw, all of you! I demand—I have the right to demand satisfaction, here and now!"

Chris stared at him; the laughter was gone. Before he could say anything, Ariadne came from behind him and caught Giraut's attention. "You *dare* not let such a farce occur!" she said flatly.

"Shut up!" Dupret snapped at her. He turned his head. "You! You are second son of the Comte d'Arles, you *know* what the law of France is. I am accused, not convicted, and a Duc's son! You *saw* that man—"

"I saw it all," Giraut said; he sounded and looked unhappy and very worried both. Dupret waited him out. "He—unfortunately, M. Cray, he has the right of it."

"He hit me first, what'd you expect me to do?" Chris said flatly.

"Yes, but he is noble, and—"

"You dare not!" Ariadne began. Dupret growled something extremely obscene at her in gutter French and she went red to the hairline. Giraut protested weakly.

"No, Giraut, whatever he and this misgotten child of mine say of me, I have yet rights!" Dupret drew a deep breath, expelled it in a gust, and smiled unpleasantly. "I challenge you, M. Cray. And you, Giraut, you tell me my *cher ami* Albione is aboard this ship: I name him my impartial witness." And, very softly, "You will pay for that, M. Cray."

"Good luck," Chris snarled. "You don't have Maurice to soften me up this time." Farce, he thought sourly. He'd give this snotty nobleman farce. "Eddie," he said; not quite a question.

"Of course," Edrith replied at once.

Dupret drew himself up. The smile broadened. "My choice of weaponry, of course." He turned, touched the point of the captain's sword. "Nothing quite so heavy and *common* as this, if there is better aboard. As for time and place—why, what better than here, and now?"

"That is not yours to choose," Ariadne snapped. "Aboard this ship, *oui,* because only a fool would permit you to leave it alive! But we wait an hour, when the sun is below the hill so *you* do not use that against him!" Dupret's lip lifted slightly.

"Um—ah—first touch," Giraut stuttered anxiously. "First touch only!"

"If you say." Dupret's mouth quirked; his eyes remained dangerously expressionless.

"I do say!"

"First touch," Chris snapped. Dupret clearly intended first touch to go right through him; well, things weren't going to go Dupret's way this time around.

Ariadne brought her chin up, gazed at Dupret furiously for a very long moment. "First touch," she said. "Giraut, upon you if things go beyond control." Dupret flashed her a nasty, teeth-only grin. She turned away and strode off.

13

CHRIS turned on his heel and stalked down the deck; Edrith was right behind him. Ahead of them, Ariadne's back was stiff with displeasure, her head high; her skirts swished crisply. Chris caught up with her just out of sight of the main deck, under the sheltered entry to the first-class cabins, and gripped her shoulders, spinning her around to face him. She met his eyes squarely. "Ari! What were you trying to do out there, collect one last bruise to remember him by?"

She was still very red, practically trembling with fury. "It was not necessary that you—*non*. Never mind." She averted her face and fixed her eyes on her fingers.

"More to the point," Edrith put in mildly, "what do *you* plan on doing, to keep from being killed? You're worse with a sword than I am, Chris."

"Thanks for the reminder," Chris said. He licked suddenly dry lips. "Thanks a lot." Ariadne caught hold of his hands and shook her head.

"You do not get killed. Not today, not by him."

"I do, and I'll haunt you forever, I swear," Chris replied sourly. He looked up as heavy footsteps came along the deck, from the direction of the hatch. A bare-headed, grubbily shirtsleeved Albione went by, escorted by two armed junior officers. The reek of hold wafted over them.

"Pay heed," Ariadne said, tapping his shoulder with one

hard little finger to get his attention. "You are not good
with sword but you know how to use one, I have seen you
and Eddie."

"Yeah. Fooling around, handful of lessons from Dahven,
four years ago," Chris retorted. "Real useful. But I—" Ariadne held up a hand.

"I finish, please. *He* has a trick he will try upon you at
once, he uses it in every duel, to win with a quick flourish
and before any time at all passes. He leans so, with his left
shoulder toward you, then turns on his heel very swiftly, to
bring the blade down overhand, and at the last moment
across, backhand." Chris shook his head; she showed him.
"It is easy to counter; you ignore the overhand, cut like so
before he can shift the direction. It slices a line across his
ribs and you are done."

"Yeah. Then he guts me because he's pissed." Chris bit
his lip. "Uh, look, if we can find something to talk about
besides cutting people and bleeding, you mind?"

"You must touch him, to stop the fight, and then you
jump back from his reach; it need be no more than touch, a
drop of blood—even a scratch—for proof. If Giraut is slow
to remind the soldiers and *he* attempts more fight, if he is
yet able, I shout and remind them myself." She gazed out
across the deck, at the long shadows lying there. "You need
a good sword, you and Eddie both—I have those you
bought me in Sikkre. And you," she added as she leveled a
finger at Chris's nose, "need one of the new powders."

Chris sighed heavily. "Forget it. Absolutely not."

"You already tell me they ease the pain, and they do not
make dizzy of you." She turned away, eased her arm from
his grasp, and walked toward their cabin.

He came right on her heels. "They don't make me *as*
dizzy. Any dizzy at all is a little too much if I'm playing
duel with Dupret, all right?" She merely shook her head,
went on.

Edrith touched his shoulder. "She's right, you know. Be-

sides, I would like to see you practice that maneuver she
suggests once or twice, if you're really gonna do this. You
know?"

"Oh—I'm gonna go through with it. I owe the jerk, even
if this wasn't quite the payback I had in mind." Chris
waited until Dija closed the cabin door behind them, then
went over to the chest, where his single clothes bag was
stored, and undid the clips, rummaged in it for some moments. "Ah-hah!"

Ariadne stared, visibly horrified, at the three-foot length
of dark, smooth wood. "You—oh, no! You do *not* fight a
skilled swordsman with that!"

"Hey, lady," Chris said flatly as he spun the stick. "This
is how I fight. The only way. I've used nothing else since I
got hauled into this world four years ago. I was good
enough to stop practiced, grudge-holding swordsmen back
then. Now—well, now I'm four years better at it. Dupret's
a trained duelist, he fights by certain rules and he's used to
certain kinds of response to what he does. He'll never know
what hit him."

"You—" She'd gone very pale, couldn't get any additional words out. Chris waited; she licked her lips, shook
her head.

"Trust me. Better yet, ask Eddie. This is what I know,
and it will work." Silence. "Think about this, too: He's
twice my age. Oh," he added as she opened her mouth to
protest. "I know, he's good at this stuff; he's killed a lot of
men. He's damn near fifty. His legs are old, so's his heart.
Even if he did this a lot, he'd never be as young or as fit as
I am—and he spends most of his time behind a desk. I'll
play him out until he starts staggering, then cold-cock him.
Piece of cake."

"He—he will never fight that," Ariadne protested faintly.

"He started this. He'll fight. I can make him." Chris
laughed; there wasn't any humor in the sound.

Ariadne sat on the cabin's only padded chair, hard. "He will—"

"He won't." Chris tossed the stick deftly from hand to hand. "Show me that trick of his again, how he does it."

She got to her feet, crossed to the dry sink that held the water pitcher and a tray with several enameled cups. "Powders first," she said. Her voice trembled.

"No powders." She turned, brought her chin up. "No way, Ariadne. Some plain water—yeah, I could use that, it's hot out there, it'll still be too warm for real people after the sun goes down." He leveled the bo at her. "Water only, you got it?"

Ariadne glared at him for a very long moment. She was still so furious she could hardly contain herself. She didn't dare let them know; wouldn't let him, any of them, see how very angry she was. *All I planned, everything I did, to make certain of that man, to see to it he did not leave this ship or this port alive, and Chris—to save me a slap, he ruins all!* Well, he didn't realize what he'd done—but he wasn't going to fight Dupret, either. *Thanks to my beloved papa, that I know always to have a plan behind the first plan should the first fail. But Chris must suspect nothing.* She did have such a plan—and he wouldn't suspect. She gave him a nasty look and slammed his cup down on the edge of the dry sink, poured water into it, set the cup to her lips, tipped it up a little and swallowed. *That he believes I sipped some of this stuff first, and trusts, and drinks it down unsuspecting . . .* Emilie swore this particular liquid mixed immediately with water and tasted not at all. She had better be right about that—and about how well and quickly it worked. "There. I test it first. Have you—are you satisfied?" She made a show of turning the cup so the opposite rim was toward him, waited until he drank, and carried it back to the dry sink, stood there with her back to him. *Get away from him, he will see it in your face, he will suspect . . .* "Keep in mind," she announced suddenly, sharply, "that I wish even less, now, to become a widow at not yet twenty. You die at his hand, and I will haunt *you* forever!" She slammed the cup down once more and stormed out of the cabin, hauling the door closed behind her with a teeth-rattling slam. Dija made a vexed, unhappy little sound and went after her.

Edrith waited until the door closed behind Dija, then turned to Chris. "For once I agree with the lady, if not with her particular style of diplomacy, or her logic. You are mad to even think of using that against Dupret."

"I'd be nuttier to use one of those nasty sharp-edged things; I haven't even touched one in over a year, remember? That would be even more dumb than if I let you take him."

"Which, being a sensible man, I would not," Edrith said flatly. "Not with sword, and certainly not with a short staff. You tell me all the time it's the law-and-order thing, let the guard do its job, let them handle the Casimaffis, the Chorans, the Duprets—and then you let him provoke this?"

"What?" Chris spread his hands. "I shoulda just said no?"

"I would have!"

"Hey, Eddie, damnit, don't you start on me, too!"

"That kind of macho pride is stupid; you always say so. I agree with that."

"This isn't—well," Chris said thoughtfully, and much more quietly. "Guess maybe it is, some. Not entirely, though. It's—not just what he did to me, what she went through, waiting for him to—hell," he growled. "If I didn't think I could take him, I'd've told him to stuff his noble rights."

"And if you can't?"

Chris sighed. "Eddie, it's me, remember? Besides, think about it—he's hauled out of his house and onto this ship, everyone in Philippe-sur-Mer knows where he's going and why, and then, he gets decked by me? Humiliations galore, remember?" Edrith started to shake his head; Chris gripped his shoulder. "I owe the guy," he said flatly. "I've always said that, too."

Silence. Edrith got to his feet. "If I were you, I would think of what else you owe him for."

"I'm thinking of her. I probably saved her a—hey." Chris was quiet for some moments; his brow furrowed. "You know what?"

"After all this, a trick question?"

"No trick, Ariadne. The way she looked out there waiting for Dupret to show, the way she went for him—" His voice trailed off.

"You don't think she was trying to provoke a fight? Herself to duel him?" Edrith laughed shortly. "You think she tried to make him smack her in the face so *she* could challenge *him*?" He laughed again.

"Well? He almost did, didn't he? Until I got between them. But you didn't see her take on Dahven; she's—she's pretty good. She knows it, too."

"That's dangerous knowledge. But it sounds a fantastic plot, even for her," Edrith said.

"Yeah—I guess. Like Giraut would let her pick up a sword and go to first blood with her old man; in his book that would be unnatural, and besides, he thinks she's spun sugar." He got to his feet, frowned uncertainly. "You don't think she went out to jump him?"

"Jump—who, Dupret? With all those soldiers around? And a straight attack?" Edrith laughed; the sound was rather forced. "Walk past all those men and run him through? I thought you said she preferred the sodden drunk, black night and back alleys."

"Yeah—I guess." Chris said slowly. He shook himself. "Sure, with Dija right in the middle of things; she might not care for her own hide but Dija—"

Edrith gestured toward the room's sole window, the shadows across the deck beyond it. "It's nearly sundown."

"Oh, thanks, guy."

"I mean to say," Edrith overrode him sarcastically, "that if you really mean to use that short bo, do you want to work out a little first?"

Chris shook his head. "Save my energy, what strength I got." Edrith frowned at him; he shook his head again. "I'm not hurting or anything, don't look at me like that. Just not a hundred percent, you know?"

"Not dizzy, not sick?"

"Hey. I'm not doing any of that stuff anymore, remember?"

"You had better not be. What's my job, out there?"

"Not totally sure; you don't have to step in for me if he does me, or anything—not like my world, where a second could fight if the first guy chickened out or got killed or like that. Think it worked that way, anyhow; I know duels only from old movies. Far's I know, an impartial witness only has to stay close and make sure everything's done the right way."

"Oh, wonderful," Edrith replied gloomily. "I get to say he ran you through properly."

Chris sighed and said with heavy patience, "Nobody's running me through. Not today, anyhow." He gave the bo a final spin, ran his hands down it both ways to make sure the wood was still smooth. "Let's go; I'll go nuts in here and I wanna make absolutely sure Ariadne hasn't snagged a knife and gone Dupret stalking."

She was standing under the canopy, arms folded, scowling along the main deck toward the bow. Chris looked that direction; he couldn't see anything except soldiers. Just then, three more ordinary soldiers came up the gangplank, a very tall black man in their midst. Ariadne swore and darted toward the plank. Chris snatched at her arm, too late. "Damn. Wait here," he told Dija. "Eddie, you stay with her, okay?"

"Dija is fine, you may not be," Edrith said mildly. Ariadne was already at the head of the ramp, fists jammed into her waist, arguing vehemently with one of the soldiers; he spread his hands and shook his head. The three went on across the deck toward the short stairs that led to the officer's cabin; the tall man stayed with her. "Not one of Dupret's, apparently," he added as he caught up with Chris. "But he looks familiar."

"Works on the docks. That's Uncle Brother," Chris said tersely. Ariadne had his near hand in both of hers, she was listening as he spoke in a rapid, low voice. Patrice looked up, gave Chris a brief glance; his face was very grave.

"You look better, M. Cray," he said. "I am glad. We saw the soldiers, heard all that has passed in the city this afternoon. I came to see if you and she were about, or if the soldiers could give us some word of you." He planted a loud kiss on Ariadne's fingers. "I cannot stay, child; I go with some of these French to the plantation, see if there are more of your disgraced papa's men there, and help them find where the bad brandies are mixed."

"Have care," Ariadne urged, her voice low and worried. "And—and if you can, if there is time, bring from my *tante* a box of her bone-mend powder, for Chris."

"I do it." He gripped Chris's hand, turned, and strode down the ramp; half a dozen soldiers followed him.

A cool breeze slid across Chris's back; he turned to look down the deck. "The sun," Ariadne said; her voice was suddenly husky; she caught her lower lip between her teeth.

"Yeah." Chris watched it slide behind the mountain, then turned back as light footsteps came from the bow. Giraut looked even more nervous than he had earlier and was all but wringing his hands; Joulon appeared merely harassed. "I'm ready if he is," Chris said. Giraut dabbed at his throat with a damp-looking handkerchief and nodded sharply. "Fine. Cool. Let's get it done."

The soldiers still on deck had moved back, along the rail and across the foredeck, enclosing a space maybe ten feet on a side. Chris swallowed, stepped into the open, bo dangling from his fingers. Not much room; no room for mistake, definitely. Dupret—he couldn't see the man yet, but there was Albione, staring impartially down his thin, rather smudged nose. Ragged beard covered his cheeks and throat, ruining the line of the neat little imperial he ordinarily sported. *Ship's hold is a far cry from your fancy cabin, huh, dude?* He shifted; Dupret came from somewhere behind Albione, visibly confident and certain of himself despite the stance of the guards, the metal bands on his wrists. He stopped short of the captain, raised his chin in a disturbingly Ariadne-like gesture, and held out his hands. One of the soldiers removed the fetters; one of the junior officers came forward with a short rack of swords. Dupret gazed at this thoughtfully, hands rubbing his wrists; he finally drew one partway from its niche, then another; he took out a third, hefted it judiciously, and sliced the air with it. It was slender, like the rapier Ariadne had used to fence Dahven. He smiled at his opponent then; that glittering, mad-eyed smile that was Dupret at his most unnerving.

Chris bared his teeth in reply but his mouth had gone very dry, and as he took another step forward, the ship's deck seemed to move under his feet. His stomach twisted sharply; nerves, he told himself. Not fighting; not even fighting Dupret, who'd probably been at it more years than Chris had been alive: it was more the formality of the whole thing, the deliberateness of it, as opposed to the kind of surprise-attack, kill-or-be-killed fight he'd faced so many times in Rhadaz those first few months. *So what, and also big deal,* he ordered himself. *It's no worse, no different than if the dude dropped on you like the Sikkreni guard did, way back when. Take him out like you did those guys.* Everything fell into place all at once. This was *right*. Dupret: *Yeah. Last fencing lesson, you jerk. Watch out for your head.* The junior officer turned toward him and held out the rack.

Chris waved him aside, smiled unpleasantly, held up the
bo. "I don't use those."

"You have no choice!" Dupret snarled. He crossed the
deck, tapped at the bo with the tip of his blade. "I named
swords! What is this, a jest?"

"Hey, you afraid of a stick?" Chris sneered. "It's a plain
piece of ash, no bells or whistles, no tricks. Let Giraut examine it if you're spooked. Oh, hell," he added in disgust as
Dupret began to protest once more, "let Albione examine it,
if you're that scared."

"Scared," Dupret hissed. "I take you, whatever you have
in hand!"

"You *wish*!" Chris laughed, spun the stick, and stepped
back. Dupret brought up his blade, hesitated as Giraut
protested sharply, and darted forward to step between them.

"You remember what was decided, what you both swore;
it is first touch only!" he said loudly; his voice cracked on
the final word.

"First touch," Dupret said; his eyes were glittering dangerously.

"Hey," Chris replied as Giraut turned to him. "I got no
problem with that." But he couldn't breathe all of a sudden;
a wave of dizziness hit him, hard. Giraut exclaimed sharply;
two of Dupret took a step back. "Let's do it—" He flailed
for balance, took one sudden sideways step in a desperate
attempt to keep himself upright, two more the other way,
then simply folded.

He didn't go completely out; he could hear Dupret cursing in a full fury, Ariadne's anxious-sounding voice over
everything else. One of her small, slightly damp hands suddenly trembled on his jaw. He forced his eyes open and
wished he hadn't: there were at least two of everything, and
he was almost as light-headed as he'd been on her balcony
after Maurice—

"A trick!" Dupret shouted. "He tricks you all, playing he
is ill. I knew he would attempt a way from this! That stick,

instead of a blade, can you doubt he never intended to duel?"

"Be silent!" Ariadne leaped to her feet; the board under Chris's head jolted. "How dare you say these things?"

"Giraut," Dupret warned, "I am as yet an accused man only, and a noble one! It is not permitted that a common man toy with a Dupret so!"

"Less common than *you*!" Ariadne snarled, and Dupret swore at her.

"Giraut, get this demon of a child away from me, before I—"

"Before you what?" Ariadne demanded flatly.

"Chris!" Edrith's voice, low and worried against his ear. Edrith hauled him partway upright, so his head rested against the other man's shoulder.

He panted for air; almost impossible to remember how to talk at the moment. "God, I—I feel awful, like I'm gonna pass out if I move. Damn. Like, back at the Parrot—oh, hell, Eddie, this was *not* what I had in mind."

"Not your fault. You aren't well yet, we knew it if you did not. I will move you a little, out of the way."

"No, don't, if I can't fight him, then it's over—" Edrith probably hadn't heard him; he was back on his feet, hands hooked under Chris's arms, scooting him down the deck on his backside. Sudden, total silence; Chris bit his lip, forced his eyes open once more. Ariadne was right in Dupret's face.

"He either plays at coward or you have done this, some-how," Dupret said sharply. "To keep him from my blade."

"Oh, jeez," Chris whispered. Edrith had to bend down to hear what he was saying. "She did! She dosed my water!"

"*Again* from your blade!" Ariadne hissed. "But that is what your man Maurice did, beating him senseless. You know his condition when you saw him last; let the ship's healer look at him, if you dare! Let *all* of them see what you and Maurice did to cause him such harm, and such

pain! For him to return here despite broken ribs and to face
you, stick against sword—*he* has courage enough!" She
laughed, snapped her fingers under his nose. "That for your
so-high honor, man who was my father! I see it in your
eyes, that first touch would have been through his heart!"

"Madame," Giraut began nervously. Ariadne chopped a
hand at him for silence, and he backed hastily away.

"Chris," Edrith whispered. "Where's your—wait, got it."
Chris caught his breath as his companion slid the short bo
from his lax hand and got to his feet.

"Eddie, damnit! Don't you dare!" He sagged, fell heavily
onto his side. Dija caught him before his face could hit the
deck, eased him up against her knee. "No one *listens* to
me," Chris mumbled in an aggrieved voice. "Dija, go back,
you aren't safe here—"

"I go nowhere. She is my responsibility, and for her
sake, I watch you."

Dupret glanced across his daughter's shoulder as Edrith
started toward him; his eyes widened. Ariadne turned and
caught her breath, then shook her head furiously. She
strode across the deck to intercept him, one hand deftly
slipping into the waist of her dark green silk skirt. Edrith
stopped short: She held a knife at waist level, small but narrow bladed and visibly very sharp. The tip brushed his
shirt. "This is not your quarrel," she said; her voice was
low and hard. "You are impartial witness, responsible for
Chris, nothing else."

"You did that to him, didn't you?" Edrith said quietly;
his words were clipped, his mouth tight and white at the
corners. "You planned it. All of this, everything." She
shrugged. "Chris will murder me if I let you do this. I can't
just—"

"I can," she hissed. "It is you who does not just anything!" Edrith swallowed hard as the knife pressed against
his shirt, cast his eyes up, and slammed the bo down with a

particularly obscene curse; it hit the deck, clattered, and rolled away. He turned on his heel, went back to Chris.

"You cannot believe how glad I am that she is yours," he growled. "And you are welcome to whatever he leaves of her!" Ariadne had already turned away to level her hand— and the knife—at Dupret. Her voice was pitched to include the whole—unnaturally still and silent—main deck.

"That man dares speak of honor—what of *my* honor? I am also of noble blood!"

"Half only!" Dupret snapped. Giraut and the men around him looked suddenly exquisitely uncomfortable. Ariadne closed the distance between herself and Dupret with a cat-like bound, knocked the sword aside with her dagger, and slapped him, hard.

"That for my mother," she said softly. Dupret's face had gone the color of parchment, save for one brilliantly red cheek.

"That I did not strangle Marie before she ever bore you," he said evenly, and loudly enough for the men around them to hear. He brought up the sword; Ariadne gave him a cold little smile, spun away from him, and pulled a rapier at random from the rack, then knelt at Chris's side.

"Chris," she whispered. He shook his head.

"Ari—look, don't do this. For me, all right?"

"You would have, and I must." She set the sword on the deck, hesitated, then wrapped her hands around the back of his neck and kissed him full on the mouth, very hard. "You said it first: I know what I do," she whispered. "Trust me." Before he could even catch his breath, she had scooped up the sword and was back on small bare feet, moving swiftly across the deck to confront Dupret. His lower lip was numb.

Giraut was still arguing with Dupret, now with Ariadne; Chris couldn't hear what any of them were saying. It didn't matter, anyway: Giraut finally threw up his hands in disgust and let Joulon pull him away. Ariadne spun the back hem of her skirt around her left arm and brought the sword up. Dupret laughed unpleasantly; he touched her blade with his, slapped it skyward. "Oh, God," Chris whispered. "He'll kill her."

Ariadne skipped back, got control over her blade at once, nimbly dodged a slashing overhand cut aimed straight at her face. If he didn't kill her, he clearly intended to mark her for life. "I can't watch." Chris closed his eyes, but after a moment opened them again.

Ariadne laughed. "But you were so fond of Marie, why would you cut a face so like hers?" she whispered. "Man who was my *beloved* father?" She dodged half a dozen furious blows, ignored Dupret's mutterings. *Remember what Chris said; his age, he is not the young papa you remember, striding across French Jamaica and dealing death where he would, by his own blade; he is a man of years and one who spends his days at a desk. He is angry and proud, but that is not the same thing.*

The man who smiled while Maurice—she dared not think of that, nothing of Maurice, not now. It would weaken her to recall what Maurice had done to Chris. *I gutted Maurice for what he did; this man who was father will not survive him for long.*

Dupret dropped his left shoulder and tried to take her with his fancy, swift maneuver; she countered it sharply and he pulled back to begin stalking to his right. "How did you—I knew it," he whispered. "Peronne!"

"Peronne?" She lunged twice in swift succession; he stepped back, almost into the surrounding watchers. Half off balance, he lunged in turn, seeking any touch at all this time; she was already two sword-lengths away from him. "But I am *femme,* daughter of an unwed servant, who teaches a nobleman's sport to a doubly marked one?" Ariadne leaped forward, catlike; five sharp, swift clashes rang across the deck, and then she was away from him, circling, laughing once more. She was still unwinded. Dupret's forehead shone with sweat, but he didn't seem to have slowed yet.

"*Garce!* You and that—that man—"

"Yes. You gave me to him over cards and you planned murder upon us both. See how well you have succeeded!" She whipped the blade in a blurring backhand; Dupret jumped aside, off balance, but before she could pursue his mistake, he'd recovered, aimed two nasty short jabs at her ribs, and backed away. "We shall outlive you—he and I and our children!" Ariadne bared her teeth at him. Dupret snarled and lunged, faster than she'd expected; she parried the blow so near the hilt that Chris cried out somewhere behind her. She used the momentum of the blow to spin away and off side, parried again, nearly fell when the tip of his blade caught in her skirt. Dupret bared his own teeth in a mirthless grin.

"Touch," he announced, and then, loudly, imperiously, "touch!"

Ariadne laughed somehow; the blade had gone through silk and underskirts alike, missing flesh by no distance at all. "You cannot tell skirt from skin?" Giraut came forward, clasping his hands anxiously. She laughed again, then drew the skirt to her knee, extended her bare foot and lower leg; the little nobleman went red to his hairline. "No touch," she said evenly, and released green silk.

"No touch," Giraut echoed unhappily. He withdrew a pace, a second; Dupret made as if to lunge, drew sharply back and came at her off side; his point came away with a small bit of lace from the throat of her shirtwaist. Her smile wavered.

"Whatever Peronne taught you, it will not be enough," he hissed. "You'll pay for this, Ariadne." She brought her chin up and went after him again.

Chris strove to sit up; sagged into Edrith. "Trust me, she says," he mumbled. "Trust *me;* I'll strangle her if I ever get my hands back." Edrith's hands tightened on his arms and he fell silent. Dupret was on the offensive; hair plastered to his forehead, chest heaving, he was still unnervingly quick, and if he'd repeated anything yet, Chris hadn't seen it. Ariadne wasn't smiling at all now, and her face was flushed.

He is stronger than Chris thought; I did right to keep him from this. Not that Chris would ever believe it. Dupret's blade described a swift, tight circle and sliced the air; she ducked sideways, assuredly saving her neck or her ear. A long, dark curl slid down her shirtwaist and slithered to the deck.

"I can't watch," Chris whispered, but he couldn't look away, either. Behind him, Edrith swore flatly and kept him upright.

Ariadne backed away from her father; he laughed breathily and pressed the advantage. A step, a second—she took two wild slashes at him, backed away again. "One touch, eh? I will mark you so *he* does not look on you with pleasure ever again." Giraut tried to say something; Dupret snarled at him and he went abruptly silent.

"No," Ariadne whispered. She hesitated; Dupret lunged at her, his blade a down-slashing blur; she caught her breath, turned sideways, and slammed the side of her blade against the tip of his. Clearly nothing he'd expected: his blade rebounded hard and high, pulling him off balance. Ariadne spun neatly on one heel and came up beside him. "First touch, beloved Papa," she said flatly, and lunged.

The rapier caught him low in the side, angled sharply up and in. Dupret shouted, a wordless cry of pain. His sword hit the deck with a loud clang. Ariadne stepped back, using both hands to bring the blade with her. She staggered, then braced the point against the deck. Her eyes were fixed on Dupret, her face expressionless. Dupret's lips worked, but no words came. Blood dribbled from the corner of his mouth and he fell.

Momentary, deathly silence; someone near the ramp began shouting, someone else ran down the deck, and suddenly everyone seemed to be talking much too loudly. Ariadne stood immobile, her eyes still fixed on Dupret; she appeared unaware of anything else. The ship's physician knelt beside the fallen man, laid a hand against his throat. He looked up as Giraut came over, shook his head. Giraut brought his head up, stared dumbfounded at Ariadne, who sighed very faintly, shook herself, and held out the sword. Half its length was red; Giraut shuddered, caught hold of the hilt gingerly, and handed it immediately to one of the soldiers. "M-Madame—" he stuttered.

"M. Giraut?" Ariadne's voice was distant; she blotted her forehead with the back of one hand. "M. Cray is—is unwell. Allow me to return with him to our cabin, see him settled. After that, whatever you demand of me for that man's death—"

"Ariadne, no." Chris tried to get to his feet; Edrith mumbled something under his breath and helped him up, held him as the ship swayed alarmingly and everything went momentarily black. Giraut turned a worried face toward him.

"M. Cray, you do indeed look not at all well, and you must be extremely anxious, all—all this. Madame—"

Joulon held up a hand. "Madame, this is all exceedingly unfortunate. Go rest and see to your husband."

"You—"

"Madame Cray," Joulon broke in. "Unfortunate, I say and mean and for you *and* he. Clearly Dupret intended more than a simple touch to whichever of you he fought, he meant disfiguration or death. Fortune was yours instead of his. It may be your uncle Philippe will wish to further question you once we have reported to him, but for now—" He shrugged broadly. "We have yet much to accomplish here, and you and M. Cray need be no further part of it. Go and rest."

She inclined her head. "I—we shall. Thank you."

* * *

It was wearing off as quickly as it had taken him—whatever it was. His legs were almost working by the time they reached the cabin, though he still needed to lean on Edrith and the dizziness—fainter but still unnervingly *there*—caught him every few breaths. Edrith eased him down onto the nearest bed. "What do I get you, Chris?"

"Nothing." Chris gazed at Ariadne, who stood statuelike by the small window, her back to them all. Dija hovered a few paces behind her, visibly uncertain what to do. Chris sighed very quietly, waited until Edrith had his boots off, then jerked his head toward the window. "Take Dija; she and I need to talk." Edrith gave him a sidelong, rather worried look. Chris nodded. "Talk. You know?"

"I—all right." Edrith turned to Dija, spoke softly against her ear. It took him a few minutes; the girl finally nodded, cast Ariadne's back one final, unhappy look, and went with him.

"Ariadne." Chris's voice came out too high; he cleared his throat. Her shoulders tensed, she didn't move otherwise. "Ariadne, please. Don't—don't try to cut me out completely. Not after everything else. Please."

"Please," she whispered. She turned to face him, one hand braced against the windowsill; her lashes were beaded with tears. "Chris—"

"*Shhh.* No. Please come here. This is me, remember? Chris—not your old man, not any other man like him. Besides, I'm too limp to pound on you right now, even if I wanted to."

"I—" She managed a very watery smile, swallowed hard, rubbed her eyes angrily with the side of one fist, finally came over to sit on the edge of the bed. "I never—that was not to harm you; what I gave you—" She fetched a shuddering breath. "You—are furious with me."

"No. Not furious. Okay, maybe a little bit pissed off, but mostly disappointed. I thought we were starting to trust each other."

"Trust—I—" She shook her head; her shoulders sagged. "I should never have told you, the Anlu. But you will not believe anything I say."

He kept his voice casual. "Well—you could try me."

"What I meant, only to protect you—"

Chris caught hold of her hand. "I know, you were trying to keep me from getting killed out there. Right?" After a moment, she nodded. "But you did it wrong; the way Dupret or that old woman would have, the one who lumped me with your dad, and Sorionne and all the rest of those 'all men.'"

"I—I did not mean to—"

"No." He gripped her fingers; she fell silent. "Ari, listen to me, hear me all the way out, will you?" A long silence; she finally nodded, but she wouldn't meet his eyes. "I know you had it real hard, growing up with Dupret. And I'm sorry about that. I understand it, too: You know about my mom—my having to put up with her stupid, or drunk, or downright mean men. Seeing her drunk or stoned—life with her wasn't a picnic, either. Thing is, I saw what that way of living was like, and I didn't let myself fall into it. I don't drink like that, I don't get stoned. I can't imagine ever hitting someone I cared about, even though when I was a kid, that was about all I ever knew." Silence. "Once I saw something better, I changed. You've done that, too: remember the first thing you ever said to me?" She nodded. "Ariadne, we had everything in the world against us from the start, you and me, but even with all the stuff going wrong, we were starting to matter to each other—"

She fetched a little breath. "And—and now, we do not. I understand—"

"That's not it. Please just—listen to me, let me get it all out. I could be pissed off, if I let myself. Maybe even angry enough to think, 'Hey, she tells me about this bunch of assassins she belongs to, then instead of talking to me, she sneaks crud in my water and knocks me silly. How's a guy

supposed to ever trust someone like that?' But that's not
right, or fair; I'm not dead, and I—I really do care about
you, and how are you supposed to know how I feel unless *I*
talk to *you*? We don't know each other well enough yet,
we've got to *tell* each other things. Not just—just do something and let the other person try to guess what you meant."
He paused. "Ariadne," he said very quietly, "look at me,
please. God knows I don't do this kind of thing well, remember I had to have Jen talk to you up in Sikkre because I
couldn't? I was scared to death I'd say the wrong thing, or
even say the right thing and you'd take it the wrong way.
Scared you'd hate me forever."

His face felt flushed; her color was high as her eyes
flicked toward his face, quickly back to her fingers. When
she finally spoke, her voice was very husky. "All right, this
is fair. I could not tell you what I meant, what I thought. I
dared not chance the French King somehow might be—be
involved with my *grand-père* in the drug, and then what?
He turns Dupret free and again he comes for us both, with
even more cause to kill." She laid her hand on his shoulder
and shook her head, hard, as he cleared his throat. "No, let
me talk now, all at once. My uncle Philippe has spent so
much of his life running the estates, he has few connections
at the court, unlike my *grand-père* and so, even though
Philippe is now called Duc, and Orlean is of great power,
he is still not of great stature among his kind. *He* does not
wish the drug, or any part of it; he may not have the final
say. I—I knew after the French embassy in Mondego, if I
say to you, 'We go back here, not just to confront Henri
and to swear against him, but so I can force him to defend
his honor and kill him dead,' then you say even more flatly
no than you did. I—I did what I thought best." She shook
her head again, blotted her eyes with the back of one hand,
fell silent.

"I understand that. All right, in pure honesty, I'm trying.
But I'm not your old man, not anyone like him. I'm not—I

won't just flat *tell* you things, order you around like you were a kid or something. Tell me what you think, what you want; I may disagree with you, I may say you're totally nuts—but even that afternoon in Mondego, I still let you persuade me, didn't I? We talked it out, you had good reasons, I listened." Silence. He captured her hand once more. "Right?"

"Yes. Yes, all right. A—man of my father's class would have—"

"Never mind; that's behind you now, for good. But it works both ways. I made a mistake back in Sikkre, trying to sneak out of Rhadaz without saying anything to you. I'm sorry I did that, even though I'd have spared you the trip on that steam yacht and those hours in your room. You were right, you've been helpful, useful, and I'm—just glad you were with me. I can't swear I won't goof like that again, but I can promise I'll try not to. Just—I'm just asking honesty. It would have been better all around if you'd just told me, out there on the deck—"

"What, tell you to step aside so I can challenge that man to a duel?" She still wouldn't look at him, except in darting, sidelong glances. "And then, after all has chanced and you take that—that bit of stick to go against a sword, do you blame me that I—?"

"Hey. That *is* my fault, it's a new thing to you and I should be used to that reaction. One of these days soon, Eddie and I'll show you just how good it is. Yeah, I'd probably have thought you were completely nuts and tried to argue you out of it. Or maybe I'd have had a better idea, or maybe we could've come up with something together that—well, it's possible. Putting something in my water, though—put the shoe on your foot, if I'd pulled a stunt like that on you." Another silence, this one very long. Ariadne's lips tightened; she nodded.

He couldn't begin to decide what she was thinking. *God. I don't know what to do. If I just let it ride—but I couldn't, not something like this. Not after*— He couldn't think of anything to add, any way to make things a little less stiffly, embarrassingly tense. He sighed, very faintly, let go of her hand. "Um. If you wouldn't mind, I'd like some more water."

She stared at him, clearly astonished. "You—after the last water I gave you?"

"That's in the past, all right? We don't live back there."

She crossed the cabin, filled her own enameled mug, brought it back to him. Chris forced himself onto his elbows, rolled so he could sit up properly, and took it. "Thanks."

"Of—of course." She had gone even more distant, wary, he thought; she watched him drink, wordlessly took the cup when he'd finished, carried it back to the dry sink, and stayed there, her eyes fixed on the narrow window, her hands moving along the carved rail that held the pitcher and cups in place.

Chris could almost hear Jennifer saying sharply against his ear, *Don't leave it at that, you idiot. Talk to her. Do something.* He got to his feet, one hand braced against the wall for balance—not so bad, this time. He crossed the cabin; Ariadne started as he came up behind her; she didn't look. But when he took her shoulders and drew her back against him, she didn't resist; her head lay against his throat. After a moment, her hands came up to cover his.

Chris let his cheek rest against her hair: wonderfully soft, fragrant with whatever Dija used to wash it. "What I said, that afternoon, in—in Dupret's house—how I felt—"

"I remember." So low, he scarcely caught the words.

"I meant it. Still do."

She turned to face him. "Despite—?"

"No matter what." He drew her close once more. Ariadne wrapped her arms around him, rather gingerly, and leaned into him. "Tell you what, though, that's no way to kiss a guy—even if you think it might be your last. One of us'll bust a tooth." He drew a deep breath, set a hand under her chin to tilt it up. "Here. Let me show you." Ariadne's eyes were very wide as he bent his head and gently touched his lips to hers.

14

❧

DUKE LEHZIN TO EMPEROR: SHIPS READIED IN BEZ HARBOR, TEN BEZANTI, TWO ENGLISH WITH CANNON, FOUR LASANACHI, ALL WHO WOULD OPPOSE VUHLEM. WILL SEND NORTH TO DRO PENT TO ATTACK PORT AT EXACTLY MIDDAY, THREE DAYS HENCE.

DUKE JUBELO, DUKE ALETTO TO EMPEROR: JOINT COMPANY UNDER DUKE ALETTO'S CAPTAIN GYRDAN MASSED JUST SOUTH OF CORNEKKAN-HOLMADDI BORDER READY TO TAKE VUHLEM'S COMPANIES AT EXACTLY MIDDAY, THREE DAYS HENCE.

A N hour before full dark, the courtyard of Duke's Fort teemed with men: a full company with Gyrdan at its head had just ridden out to let people give them a send-off. Robyn stood above the gate with Aletto; her feet were blocks of ice and her thoughts exceedingly grim. *It looks like I approve of this; like I was for fighting Vuhlem.* Most of the people in the Fort and in Sikkre surely knew her better than that by now; the realization didn't particularly help. Her eyes moved along the neat double line of armed riders; back over the little clutches of people on the far side of the road. Mostly women and children; most with drawn faces. Families of the guardsmen, she knew; that did nothing to ease her own inner conflicts.

Aletto held up a heavily gloved hand as the last of the men rode out, then turned Robyn toward the stairs. He paused, gestured with his chin toward the west market. "Listen."

"I hear them." Loud, excited cheers cut through the chill air. "There must be a fair-sized crowd."

"Loud, too, for the noise to carry this far. Gyrdan was right, letting at least some of the company parade openly through the streets. People need to feel proud of their men." He gripped the heavy rail and started down the steep steps cautiously, his other hand on Robyn's arm, to help her balance—partly, she knew, for his own.

"Easy," she warned. "And slow. You know I hate this place, it's like a ladder, and I swear it's cold enough for ice."

"Not quite cold enough." He slowed down, though; Robyn clutched his arm and let him help her down the last of the steps, onto packed dirt. "There's time; let's go in, get you properly warm. You don't need to come out when the rest go—" Robyn bit her lip, merely nodded.

It was warmer in the family corridor; quiet for the moment. The children had gone off somewhere across the Fort with Frisa. The Christmaslike scent of baking spices teased Robyn's nostrils; the tip of her nose itched with returning circulation. She rubbed it on her gloved hand and let them into the Ducal suite, closed the door behind her. Aletto drew the cloak from her shoulders and walked her over to the fire. "Here, sit," she said. "I asked them to send a spiced cider, I'll pour us both some." She stripped off the gloves, tugged Aletto's favorite chair nearer to the fire, and knelt to drag the black clay pot from the ashes. Aletto took his cup and waited for her to fill her own, until she'd settled on one of the fat cushions close to his legs, then touched the rim of his cup to hers.

"To quick success," he said.

"All right. And to *you* coming home in one piece." She drank quickly, set the cup aside. He was watching her, eyes troubled. "I know, don't look at me like that. I'm not trying to talk you out of going. I know you have to."

"If it was only the Zero, even Mother—but—" He bit his lip, closed his eyes, and drank.

Robyn laid a hand on his leg; his own fingers covered it. *How many days now—fifteen since she died, seven since we buried her, and he still can't even say Lialla's name.* She'd always known he'd take it very hard, if anything did happen to Lialla. If she went before he did. Particularly if something went wrong up north.

She still felt the same about fighting and killing: it was wrong, no matter who did it, or what their excuse. Her mind and her stomach had been in turmoil for days now, that strong ideal coming up hard against a reality like Vuhlem. Let the man get away with this most recent outrage, and what would he do next? Shesseran's way had proven he couldn't be persuaded or coerced, some people didn't understand anything short of force. *Look what he did, the night of the Emperor's fete: not only the drugged wine but Wudron's boy, Chris—*

Aletto had always respected her feelings on the subject, even if he'd never really understood; she could do no less for him and what he believed. And he had every right to be there when Vuhlem was defeated; he'd already sworn he'd take no part in the general fighting, and hard as it was to keep her mouth shut, she wasn't going to coddle him like a child, or demand he reassure her on that point yet again. *Marsh fever weakened his body; it didn't hurt his mind, or his common sense.* She finished her cider, tightened her fingers on his knee. "Drink that; it's not nearly as good cold. Swear you'll ride in the grandmother's cart at least through Cornekka, save your strength for where it counts."

He sighed faintly but managed a smile for her. "I will; I spend so little time on a horse these days, I'd probably fall off after an hour. Quite frankly, I'm glad of the cart. I'm—

honestly, I'm not as bad these days as I was when you first came."

"You needed that macho pride back then," Robyn reminded him tartly. "Just like you need this now, against Vuhlem." She looked up; a tap at the door, and Zepiko stood there, one of the guardsmen behind him. "Just—" She bit her lip. Aletto got to his feet, set the cup aside, and pulled her up. Robyn wrapped her arms around him, let herself be hugged fiercely in return. "Just come back, all right?" Her voice was husky, and Aletto seemed unable to say anything. He kissed her forehead, both cheeks, turned, and was gone. Robyn clapped her hands across her mouth and turned away as the door closed behind him.

THUKAR TO EMPEROR: TWO COMPANIES READIED; FIRST UNDER HOUSEHOLD GUARD CAPTAIN GRELT ALREADY MOVING TOWARD DRO PENT AND WILL HOLD READY IN RIVER SWALE OUTSIDE CITY UNTIL HEAR CANNON FIRE FROM PORT. SECOND COMPANY UNDER SELF LEAVING TONIGHT VIA HUSHAR OASIS, WILL ENTER HOLMADDAN AND SECURE BORDER EXACTLY MIDDAY, THREE DAYS HENCE.

Jennifer sat cross-legged on the bed she and Dahven shared—*Every single night for nearly four years, until now*—and glared at the piles of fabric squares around her feet. A colorful variety—her aunt Bets would probably have said, "a passle"—of thumb-to-index-finger-tip-sized squares of fabric for a baby quilt. A basket of brightly colored threads, with several needles stuck along the edge. "Swell," she mumbled. "He goes off to play soldier, tin sword and all, I get to sit home and knit. Or quilt. Either of which I do particularly well. Because Siohan and the midwife won't let me off this bed until midday. As Chris would say, I am *so* sure!" She drew a large amount of air through her nose, let it out through her mouth. Cast up her eyes, grabbed the nearest pile, and flung it across the room. Pink, red, and Zelharri blue squares fluttered to the floor.

A faint noise from the direction of the door caught her attention: Vey stood there, looking slightly embarrassed, fist upraised to tap on the slightly open door. Jennifer laughed shortly, indicated a chair with a sharp wave of her hand. "Come on in. I won't bite you."

"No, Thukara," Vey replied formally. "I never thought that."

"Oh—cut it out." Humor won over anger—she'd asked one of the palace seamstresses for the quilting materials, after all. And none of this was Vey's fault. He glanced at her from under his brows, managed a faint, abashed grin, shook his head. "You know me," she said. "I'm upset with Dahven just now and I'm about half-willing to take it out on anyone or anything that thwarts me." A smile tugged at the corners of her mouth. "Not you. Come on in and sit down."

"They're expecting me—"

"Grelt knows you're here, it's all right." She waited until he was perched on the edge of his chair, shoved quilt patches aside, and picked up an egg-sized, nearly flat, un-faceted stone, held it out. Vey leaned forward to take it; he turned it over in his hand, ran his fingers across the smoothed milky blue surface. Finally looked up at her, his eyes questioning. "You're staying close to Dahven, up in Holmaddan." It wasn't quite a question. Vey nodded at once.

"Of course—Jen." He still had to work at it, not calling her Thukara in private.

"Look, I know you'd stay right with him without *my* asking, I'm just—call it a little unsettled at the moment, having to stand back and let him go play war with the big boys. People get killed doing that, and Thukars bleed just as easily as anyone else. I need reassurance."

"I would be worried in your position. I won't let him far

enough from me to get hurt." Vey considered this, shook his head. "I'll stay close to him."

Jennifer sighed faintly, managed something of a smile for him. "I know you can't guarantee, Vey. We both know what he's like, I'd never put that kind of responsibility on you. That thing you're holding—"

"A protective charm?"

"No." God knew Dahven was weighted down by enough of those, mostly to make her feel better about the whole mess. Quite likely he'd already taken half of them off. She'd debated ever since getting this thing, whether to tell Vey what she wanted; better to let him know. "It's a focus stone; I had Dahmec's old Shaper in yesterday—"

"Yes, I heard."

"Oh." She frowned. "Dahven doesn't know, does he?"

"I doubt it." Vey turned the stone over once more—he didn't seem particularly worried by it, or its source—and laughed shortly. "Busy as he's been these past days, I very much doubt it."

"Good. Don't let him know about the stone if you can help it. Just—keep it on you. You're both part of the group that's supposed to take Vuhlem's palace."

"Yes, if we can. What does this do?"

"I know Eddie told you about our trip south, when Jadek used a focus to speak to me—"

"The night Chris disappeared; I remember."

"This is a little like that one; it won't suck the life from the carrier, though—"

"I wouldn't have thought so," Vey said. He continued to turn the stone, studying it thoughtfully.

"I'm the one attuned to it, rather than a Triad or someone like Jadek. Once it's inside the palace—or close to the walls—it should allow a magic user proximity to that Triad in order to weaken, or possibly neutralize, it entirely."

Vey snorted inelegantly. " 'A' magic user," he scoffed. "Perhaps, a certain Thread Wielder?"

She shifted her weight so she could swing her legs off the edge of the bed, and leveled a finger at his nose. "If you dare even think of telling him—"

"I won't. But—" Vey hesitated. "Maybe you should tell me exactly what you plan. In case—if something goes wrong."

"It won't," Jennifer replied shortly.

"Of course it won't," Vey said. "But *if* it should, don't you think Dahven should know you didn't just—just set yourself against—" He frowned at the stone, shoved it into a pocket. "I'm not expressing myself very well."

"You're doing fine." Jennifer studied her hands a moment. "I'm not just going blindly after a Triad; you know me, Vey."

"Yes. You're the woman who ran hotheaded into a trap and got herself taken by Dahven's brothers."

"So did you, if I recall right. Besides, that was for Dahven—"

"And so is this, isn't it?"

"Partly. But I've planned this, it's no hotheaded jump into danger. I've had a fair amount to do with Light, one way or another, and I know something about Triads; I know they aren't safe and I've worked it out carefully. No, don't say it, I know. Things do happen." He nodded. "All right. The English and the Lasanachi ships are going to attack the palace from the sea, distract Vuhlem and his men. The English will train most of their cannon on areas of the outer walls that have no visible openings."

"I'd heard that—not why, though."

"An immature Triad needs complete enclosure; good seals on the door—even Jadek's had a windowless chamber. And even a fully bonded Triad has to remain above ground to hold that bond and to Shape. Vuhlem's will be high up, probably in one of his towers. A breach in the right spot would weaken the Triad, possibly even kill it." She drew a deep breath, expelled it in a gust. "No guarantees, of course: In which case that Triad—well, we know what it's already done."

"Yes." If Vey was worried about any of that, it didn't show on his face; he'd always been fairly good at concealing what he thought, though. "Why Grelt and Dahven handpicked his personal company, of course."

That and the fact Vuhlem's men might well have foreign guns. "And why Dahven put himself right out in the middle of things," Jennifer said tiredly.

"It won't be like that," Vey reminded her. "He's commander; he has to be able to see what's happening and direct the company."

"You yourself said it first," Jennifer shot back. "Things happen, and we know what Dahven can be like. Good against Eprian doesn't guarantee good against half an army."

"Or guns. He's aware of that. And he has a powerful set of reasons to stay where he belongs: Seventy-five of us, not to mention everyone else in the Central Army."

"I—thanks," Jennifer said. "All right. That stone goes with you. I'll be waiting in Hushar Oasis, with that northern village woman. Don't look at me like that, there's a caravan there, Green Arrow and its grandmother. I'll have enough people to guard my back."

"They're not armed guards," Vey protested faintly.

"No. They have a stake in seeing Vuhlem brought low, and they're more useful against magic than brutes with broadswords."

"They weren't—" Vey hesitated.

"Didn't do much last time? No. But that was a surprise attack, there were old and children to evacuate, and a roof coming down on them. This is different—planned. Once the stone is near enough for me to use, you'll know; it'll become warm, and when it does, you drop it. I'll give you time for that, and anyway, I'll be able to tell when it's safe for me to access it. I'll find the Triad, destroy it if possible, neutralize it otherwise." *And if I can't do that, I'll distract it long enough for someone to break the door down.* Vey didn't need to know that; he'd be horrified and probably give her away. "There, see? It's reasonably safe."

"I suppose," Vey replied dubiously.

"It's not graven in stone, no. There are some ifs, some holes, but there are in what Dahven's doing, too. And this: Someone *has* to, Vey. Do you actually *want* to attack that palace, knowing there's a Triad?"

"Of course not. Well." He considered this, shrugged. "Hushar Oasis, though. You'd be safer here, truly."

"Perhaps. Two things, though: Most important, it's a matter of distances. I *might* be able to work that focus from here, but from Hushar, it's certain. And the Triad will be occupied; it won't have time to search for trouble beyond Holmaddan—or even beyond the palace once those ships are in place." Vey still hesitated. "I know something about big guns: they're loud, highly destructive; unnerving and distracting when men expect them. This will be new and therefore doubly terrifying." Silence again. "That's the other thing, of course: this palace during the day—there's enough noise around here, anywhere, to be a possible dangerous distraction for *me,* and Ryselle's much less capable of dealing with noise than I am."

"Well—" Vey got to his feet. Jennifer watched him. "I'll do what you ask. I won't say anything to Dahven. I hope," he added mildly from the doorway, "you mean that, about being careful. He'll cut off my remaining fingers."

Jennifer patted her stomach. "I have a very good reason to be careful, remember?" He merely nodded and went.

Nearly an hour later, she was scowling once more at the fabric squares; she'd talked herself into laying out patterns. Nothing looked right. "I never was good at the color thing," she mumbled, swept the bits up, crammed them into the basket under the thread, and set it aside. Check the watch—

not much longer till midday. No pending crises in the office at the moment; Afronsan had sent her nothing in days.

You're still too busy to play seamstress, and you don't want a tatty homemade quilt for this baby. Pack that stuff up, send it to Lizelle's twins; didn't Robyn say she was bringing them back to the Fort? It had been a nice thought, the quilt; it wasn't going to be a practical one, unfortunately.

Once the current crisis was past, Afronsan would be burning the wires and his messenger-riders would be eating up the road, keeping her entire office piled halfway to the ceiling; crazier than things had been before, now he was fully in charge and poised to open Rhadaz to greatly expanded trade. At the moment, she couldn't recall the last time she'd had vast tracts of cleared desk, and most of her staff was just pottering along, cleaning up loose bits of paperwork.

She slid her feet off the bed. Several of the standard contract paragraphs needed minor revisions, there were other tasks that kept getting put off, it would be nice to have an hour or so to just get better at that typewriter—it was nearly time anyway. But she scooted back against the pillows at once, tucked her feet under her. Voices out there—Siohan, talking to someone. A moment later, Siohan's familiar tap at the door. "The grandmother of Gray Fishers, her heir—"

"Fine," Jennifer said. "Something to do," she mumbled. Siohan heard, of course—her ears were nearly as good as Robyn's. She smiled cheerfully, let the women into the room and stepped back.

"I'll have tea brought."

"And coffee," Jennifer reminded her. She indicated chairs; the grandmother took one and Ryselle stepped back to give Sil the other, taking up a place behind her. "Frankly," she added to the grandmother, "I didn't expect you to return, certainly not right away." Not quite a question. The grandmother nodded and tugged at Ryselle's skirt.

"I could tell this child intended something; it seemed likely Sil was involved somehow, and on reflection, I thought it more proper the sin-Duchess be accompanied home by at least one ranking caravaner. I sent messages on to Podhru with the main wagons, and went instead to Zelharri." She glanced sidelong at Sil, who was quietly plaiting her fingers. "I got the entire matter from them last night."

"Oh," Jennifer said. She considered this; the grandmother sat quietly, hands folded in her lap, and waited. "And—you rule Sil, of course. I hope you don't intend to stop *me*?"

"Oh, no," the grandmother replied calmly. "I'm going with you."

Jennifer stared, then held up a hand for silence as one of the kitchen girls came in with a tray. She waited until the girl was gone, edged over to hand out mugs, and set the basket of muffins where the older woman could easily reach them. "You—madame, you're Gray Fishers' leader, I can't let you—"

The grandmother shook her head, silencing the other; she sipped tea, set the mug aside. "You cannot stop me, you know. Caravaners and particularly the grandmothers do largely as they wish. I suggest it, though; I don't demand. But I think you'd be glad of my aid."

"A Triad—" Jennifer began. The grandmother shook her head again.

"We haven't been tested against them since the civil wars." She set the cup aside, held a hand over it when Jennifer lifted the tall, thin clay pot. "But what I offer is practical assistance: the physical protection and support of several wagons and myself, as well as the grandmother of the subclan of Green Arrow—the four wagons that traveled largely within Holmaddan. They're in Hushar at present; she's one of the strongest of our kind."

"I know Green Arrow is there; I was hoping they'd—strongest?"

Sil set her elbows against the chair arms and levered herself upright. "Twelve children," she said gloomily.

"Oh. But, if we don't know that you or she can help—"

"Practical aid," the grandmother said once more. "If messages come here for you—particularly from the Thukar? Silver Star can pass them north to me, I can send your reply to her."

"Oh." Jennifer stared at her hands. "I hadn't considered that possibility. I'll leave a message here, for Siohan—my maid—and for the midwife, telling them where I am, warning them to keep that quiet. I'd prefer Dahven not ever know, really, but if he—thank you." The grandmother nodded. Jennifer turned to Ryselle. "Are you still willing to help me?"

"If there's a way," Ryselle replied flatly. "Any chance at all. I owe her that much."

"All right. Now, how much did Lialla have time to teach you? How good are you?"

For a moment, she thought Ryselle wasn't going to answer. *Afraid I'll turn her down.* The woman's shoulders sagged then. "Not very," she mumbled. "We only had fifteen days altogether. I can Shape," she added defiantly. "But—I can't do very much with it, and I—I can't Shape at all when I'm upset or angry."

"I can dampen emotion for you," Jennifer said. *Old Neri's soothing thread worked just fine on Lialla, it should work for Ryselle.* "You do feel Light, though. You see it?" Ryselle nodded. "Good. I can see it myself; I've dealt with it once or twice in dire need but only within actual reach." She turned to the grandmother. "You're comfortable where you are? I can arrange rooms in the palace, if you'd prefer."

"We have my wagon, and our usual place at the Crown

and Pitcher," the older woman said. Sil handed her to her
feet. "When you are ready, send. We'll come at once."

"Two days from now—and it'll be well after dark," Jennifer warned.

Sil shook her head; her eyes were amused. "So you can
sneak out of the palace without raising an alarm? Better to
go at an hour nearer this, don't you think? So many people
everywhere—who'll miss you until too late?" Her eyebrows went up; Jennifer was laughing.

"I'm years out of practice, this kind of thing. You're absolutely right. Thank you, all of you. I'll—I'll send."

COMMANDER, WESTERN LAND FORCE TO EMPEROR:
TOOK DRO PENT CITY WITHOUT MUCH FIGHTING. ONLY
TWO SHIPS IN HARBOR, ONE CASIMAFFI'S, OTHER VUH-
LEM'S, BOTH SURRENDERED AT ONCE. HARDLY ANY HOL-
MADDI ANYWHERE. WUDRON IN CONTROL OF DUCHY AS
OF THIS HOUR; CONFIRMS VUHLEM OVERWHELMED DRO
PENT, THEN TOOK HIS SON AS SURETY. SMALL COMPANY
LEFT BEHIND WITH WUDRON, SENDING SHIPS AHEAD AND
GOING NORTH AT FULL SPEED

COMMANDER, CORNEKKAN/ZELHARRI FORCE TO EM-
PEROR: MUCH LESS RESISTANCE THAN ORIGINALLY EX-
PECTED, FOUR COMPANIES KNOWN TO BE IN AREA LAST
MOON-SEASON. ATTACK YIELDED ONLY SPORADIC RESIS-
TANCE, LARGE NUMBER OF GREEN VILLAGE BOYS THROW-
ING DOWN SPEARS AND SURRENDERING. MANY CLAIM
VUHLEM HOLDS SONS OR ENTIRE FAMILIES HOSTAGE,
WILL KILL IF THEY DO NOT FIGHT FOR HIM. HAVE LEFT
ONE COMPANY TO GUARD PRISONERS; REST GOING NORTH
AND EAST AS AGREED

THUKAR TO EMPEROR: ONLY A FEW SEASONED FIGHT-
ERS AT BORDER; MOST OF FORCE RANGED THERE UN-
TRAINED, POORLY ARMED AND FRIGHTENED. SENT HALF

COMPANY TO MAKE CIRCUIT OF NEAREST VILLAGES,
MAKE CERTAIN VUHLEM DOES NOT HOLD CLAIMED
HOSTAGES, ALSO ASSURE NO SEASONED TROOPS BETWEEN
US AND BORDER. REST RIDING NORTH TO CITY, DAHVEN

DAHVEN TO JEN: EVERYTHING ALL RIGHT?

JEN TO DAHVEN: HORRIBLY BORED BUT FINE. WATCH
YOUR BACK.

Dahven's very teeth felt gritty at the moment; he couldn't
remember the last time he'd gone so long without bathing,
without warm, clean water. *Playing Thukar's spoiled you,*
he told himself flatly. None of the men around him seemed
to feel anything but a heady excitement over the way things
had gone so far; the predawn air was electric with anticipa-
tion.

The air in his tent was cold, mist laden, and the damp
and dirt were getting into everything.

But they *had* done well, thus far—no loss of life among
his own men, only one or two minor injuries. He'd lost
count of the number of Holmaddi who'd dropped visibly
unfamiliar pikes and spears and quickly rigged-up colors at
the sight of his small company to throw themselves flat and
beg to be taken away. Most of them wanted nothing more
of life than what their fathers before them had had, and
their grandfathers two hundred years back: a little land, a
share of a fishing boat. Probably very few of them had ever
considered another option. As for all those reports of companies of well-trained mercenaries, Vuhlem must be holding them—and any guns he possessed—close.

Uncomfortable thought this far from the planning tables
back in Sikkre; back there, it had simply been one more
thing to prepare against. But one way or another, it should
all be over by nightfall. They couldn't be more than two
hours from the city at this point, and therefore, only an

hour's easy ride to the low ridge where they were to wait
for the East and West armies. At that point, he'd relinquish
control of his Central army to Grelt and Gyrdan, retain
command only of his small, handpicked company. *And
gladly. I'm even less comfortable playing commander than
I am at playing Thukar.*

He glanced up from the low-burning fire and his bowl of
hot oats—inevitable bowl, Jennifer would have called it,
and laughed at him for it—as Vey brushed past the flap and
let it fall behind him. "They're ready out there."

"Good. Almost light?"

"Just barely. It's—" Vey's nose wrinkled. "It's all they
say of Holmaddan: no sun, thick cloud, but it *is* growing
lighter in the east. Drizzling, of course."

"Of course." Dahven laughed quietly.

"No wonder Vuhlem has such a bear of a temper," Vey
grumbled. "I'd go mad myself living in such a climate."

Dahven laughed again. "Yes. *You* wouldn't take in a
Triad, ally with a crazed Frenchman, send deadly liquors to
your fellow Dukes, and murder an admittedly irritating sin-
Duchess." He finished the hot oats, set the bowl aside, got
to his feet. "Still—even I never meant her physical harm
beyond a good shaking. Vuhlem's twice over a fool." He
sighed very faintly. "I suppose I have to give the usual talk
at this point? All for your Emperor and honor above all?"

Vey grinned, shoved hair from his forehead. He looked
odd, Dahven thought, in the reinforced leather breastplate
and crossed sword-belts of a soldier. *No doubt I look as odd
to him, all that as well as the Sikkreni colors on my sleeve.*
Something out of his grandfather's books; that far, at least
from Sikkre's lower markets for both of them. "Well—it's
you, after all, Dahven," Vey said mildly. "They expect
some rallying cry."

"And you had nothing to do with that, of course. Go
ahead, I'll follow in a moment." Dahven waited until Vey
was gone; he picked up the bowl again, turned it in long-

fingered hands. Duchy against Duchy. It was madness; nothing like it since the Hell-Light Wars. No one but a Vuhlem would be at the root of the affair, either: arrogant, self-centered, and ambitious. Everyone knew that— Shesseran aside, of course. *Still, who would have thought he wanted all Rhadaz? And that he'd go to such lengths to obtain it?*

Dahven set his bowl aside. If things went the way they were supposed to, Vuhlem would no longer be a threat to anyone, after today. He squared his shoulders, got to his feet, and went out to talk to his army.

Two hours later, the sky was a smooth, dark gray bowl overhead; rain fell steadily, a fine mist that looked like no rain at all from any distance but still got under the best waterproofing, made ruddy rivers of the ditches on both sides of the main Holmaddi road—and turned the road itself to a mire. Dahven's hair was plastered to his brow; his britches stuck to the saddle. Ahead of him, half a dozen men, Vey at his left, and two more of the household guard on his right side; the rest rode behind. Those he could see looked as uncomfortable as he felt. *Aletto will be truly miserable, all this chill and damp.* He ran a soggy glove across his eyes once more, drew his horse to a halt as one of the lead men stood in his stirrups, and held up a hand. "City," the man called back, and pointed.

The hills were deceptive; they looked low but they'd hidden all sight of Holmaddan City until now. The rain became a fine mist, then stopped altogether; Dahven shook out his hat. From this point, the road was covered in a rubble of small stone, and dropped down swiftly toward the city, which lay below them, perhaps a league ahead and a little to the west. Just within its boundaries, they could see the blackened, twisted wreck of the caravaners' building, which stood out starkly against low houses and brightly colored awnings.

Vey came up beside him. "There's the palace," he said. "Off side—to the east. See it?"

Dahven shifted his eyes. "Mmmm." He did, all at once; treeless, bright green land lay flat, perhaps a half-league between the far edge of the city and steel gray water, the brace of dull, dark towers blending into both sky and water. No movement out there—not on the straight, broad road that ran from city to palace, none near the palace walls, either. The city might have been deserted; people were lying low, no doubt. His eyes came back to the Duke's palace and the sea beyond it. "Vey—look. Out there. Ships."

Vey shielded his eyes with his hand as enormous raindrops pelted all around them very briefly. "English; isn't that their banner?"

"Think so. Four—five—"

"Lasanachi," someone behind him muttered; it sounded like a curse. Dahven's eyes touched the long, sleek ship, the distinctive black-and-red-striped flag, then winced away from the water entirely. Movement to the west, where Vuhlem's port and public docks lay: as he stared, a bright flash of fire shot skyward, brilliant against gray sky and water; a sooty, smudgy billow of smoke followed.

Dahven gripped Vey's arm. "Look—that's Grelt, firing the ships! We've got him!'

"That much of him," Vey replied cautiously, but he was grinning broadly. He turned the other direction. "There—there's the last of us, the missing part to the puzzle!"

A cheer went up as wet and chilled Sikkreni saw the long, triple line of riders coming at an easy trot from the east, the banners of Cornekka and Zelharri snapping in a rising wind, several wagons in their midst to hold spare weaponry and the cooks' supplies—and two of the bright caravaners' carts. The other way: Along the narrow road that led from the public docks and skirted the northern edge of the city, banners casting bright colors against a plume of black smoke, the East army.

*   *   *

Vuhlem's hands were bunched into tight fists, his face an unhealthy deep red under the thick, straight line of heavy brows. Beyond the low balcony, two companies of city guard and half his household guard sat already mounted or stood, reins in hand, their faces one and all carefully without expression. "They dare attack your Duke, your city, your very way of life!" the Duke thundered; his voice echoed from the surrounding walls. "You will not permit them to succeed! You will kill whatever commons you can among that army, find the commanders, and bring them personally to me!" Silence; he drew a harsh, loud breath, spat, and after a moment went on, his voice low and all the more frightening for its sudden lack of fury. "You will do these things," he said softly. "I have told you already what atrocity they committed on our borders, executing every man of those who were fool enough to surrender. You will fight, every one of you; you will give them no least square of ground but they must earn it in blood. If I hear otherwise regarding any man of you, you will answer to *me*—and I will be less gentle with you, and with your sons, than will the southern Dukes!" Dead, chill silence. "Go!" Vuhlem roared suddenly. Men already mounted turned their horses and spurred for the road; the remainder moved toward the gates to wait.

Vuhlem watched the first men through the gate and out of sight. "Fools and idiots; I am served by cowards, fools, and idiots," he snarled, and drove both hands through his beard. He'd seen the smoke from the city ports, and knew what it meant: Most of his ships sunk at anchor; what few ships he still possessed were well out to sea, on their way back in to cut off the foreign vessels. What army he had left—it would be enough, even without the promised new shipment of guns. It had been a mistake to send so many of them south on the Emperor's fete—most of those had wound up in Sikkreni and Bezanti hands.

Well, *he* knew the guns weren't accurate enough to be of much practical use in a pitched fight; if the southerners had brought the captured weapons, they'd have little ammunition and less training. He dismissed the guns; what few he still had were in trained hands, inside the city's north walls, where men afoot and in hiding waited. Men unfamiliar with Holmaddi streets, uncertain where the next shot would come from—there'd be slaughter.

Afronsan's force had overall superiority of numbers but no real experience in fighting. His own green men were gone; the southerners had bested them and would be over-confident when they came against his personal guard, and his city guard.

Who would have thought that sniveling paper-pusher could move so quickly? Vuhlem snagged his hair between gloved hands. "It was not what I planned!"

Afronsan had no proper training in weapons, tactics, and strategy, though: no actual experience in fighting. Some of those invaders probably fought the Lasanachi at Dro Pent years before, but that was one long skirmish, not a full-scale assault. Somehow, despite all that, the man had set up a tight, three-point invasion and carried it off: so far, quite well. But such a plan needed to be crafted in advance, and it would only continue to work when the enemy responded according to the plan. Afronsan's army moved according to a pattern set in stone; any move which was not one they expected might well turn their neat program into chaos. "We'll defeat them. Every last father's son of them," he concluded grimly.

He gazed after the departing company with narrowed eyes; once outside the gates, they'd slowed to a walk, so as not to tire the horses too soon: good. But these were his most seasoned fighters, the men who had made the rounds of the villages, who had recently helped him take Dro Pent. They had the most to lose, as the Duke's willing allies, if Afronsan won here. They knew that and would fight for their own miserable hides, if not for his. He turned on his heel, strode across his throne room and through the narrow, curtained entry behind his high-backed chair; it led to the servants' spiraling inner stair, which he took by twos. He scarcely slowed at their entry to his own chambers, hesitated, then went on to the uppermost level, hard against the long-slated roof.

But when he emerged on the enclosed, very faintly blue-lit landing before the massive wooden door, he stopped short. Stroked his beard thoughtfully. No, best not to interfere with the Triad just now; It would claim he had broken the seal They enforced on the chamber and thereby Its concentration, and use that for excuse if It—*still They!* he reminded himself angrily—could not Shape against the invaders. The words had sounded like so many poor excuses to him, the previous morning: the need to find one particular weak vessel among the foreigners, utilize that one to create a pool of Hell-Light—*Preparing the ground with yet another excuse if they fail me, that they could not find the right person.* He should have given them a choice among his *own* people. Too late now; he turned away, found the main staircase by feel, and went back down to his apartments. From here, he could watch the oncoming southern force, observe the fighting, and to an extent direct his own companies, if need be. *Four men outside my door, should I need them to carry messages to the fighters.* Better, if none at all were needed because everything went smoothly, as it had in Dro Pent. He stalked across the room, shoved aside the heavy drape, and settled one hip on the deep sill.

Beyond the city, all along the low ridge, were banners and horsemen. He unhooked the long, thin magnifying glass from his belt, moving the adjusting band back and forth until he could see clearly: Zelharri's banner next to that of Cornekka; Sikkre's beyond them. Two others, one wrapped around the pole by wind, the other plastered wetly

against its pole, both unreadable, but he knew them anyway: *My enemies.* Several poles without banners, only a
different brightly colored sphere atop each. No readily discernible purpose to those; possibly hastily made company
markers.

It didn't matter whose those men were, of course: they
were all against him. Including—yes, his eyes and the foreign glass hadn't lied to him; there were caravaners out
there as well. "Learned nothing from your last encounter
with my Triad, did you?" Vuhlem laughed mirthlessly,
lowered the glass and set it on the sill by his knee, settled
his shoulders against cool stone, and prepared for a long
wait.

Aletto gripped Dahven's hand. "Any difficulties so far?"

There was no strength to the man's fingers, Dahven realized with a shock, and he was bone thin. But Aletto's smile
was genuine; Dahven managed one in return. "None. I'm
wet to the bone and unused to the climate. How've you
stayed dry?"

"Cheated, of course; I've ridden with the caravaners the
whole way—until now."

He had no business on a horse, Dahven thought. No business away from the Fort, even if he had good cause to be
here.

"Thukar, you look good." Gyrdan came up to grip
Dahven's shoulder. "We took down a small company just
beyond the hills out there; a large camp, but only a few
men—probably meant to hit our flank once we engaged the
palace. No trouble to speak of; experienced fighters but not
enough of them to stop us. No word from our ships?"

"Nothing we've heard; we've only just arrived, though."

Someone in the fore with the banners turned to call back,
"Men coming from the Duke's palace!"

"How many?" Gyrdan shouted.

"Fifty or so!"

"Not enough," Gyrdan mumbled. "Where's the rest of his old guard?"

Dahven shrugged. "Maybe at the docks, the West army just came from there." He gestured toward the smoke, now very thick and so flattened out by the wet morning air the harbor itself couldn't be seen.

Gyrdan stood in his stirrups, looked that direction. "You saw West out there? I can't—"

"City's between us."

"Oh. No—the old guard will be waiting between us and the palace. Vuhlem's no fool when it comes to tactics, they taught *his* generation. Some probably posted just inside the city, ready to come behind us when we engage the men we can see."

Dahven chewed his lip. "I don't want any of us getting drawn into the city; it's even worse than the maps suggested. All those narrow streets—"

"I don't want that, either; that's why the West army is where it is, remember? *You* and Duke Aletto will certainly go nowhere near those walls, remember you have obligations the rest of us don't." Gyrdan stood once more, this time to look out over the city. Dahven's wordless shout of surprise brought him around. Just west of Vuhlem's palace, a stand of trees exploded, sending fragments high.

"Cannon," Vey said flatly. He held up a hand, thumb counting against fingers. "Four—five—" A muted roar washed over the ridge. Men cheered; Gyrdan spurred his horse forward, waved a long arm for attention.

"English cannon, that's our signal!" he shouted.

Dahven rode up next to him, stood in his stirrups, and slammed the soaked hat flat on his head. "Well? They know we're here, don't they? Let's take them now!" A cheer greeted this: Dahven dropped into the saddle, kneed his horse back around, and rode down the hill. Gyrdan swore furiously as the Thukar passed him, turned his horse to follow. Aletto drew down a tight rein on his own mount and remained where he was.

Vuhlem lifted his glass once more as the southerners poured off the ridge, shifted his gaze. The company that had come from the docks was ranged across the road, at least half of them facing the city; his first string of riders had drawn to a halt a short distance away; most of his archers were already off their horses, firing into the packed enemy company. Several men fell. He smiled, jumped as another explosion rattled windows and shook everything. Annoying. His own ships should be just coming into sight, though. Another cluster of trees just beyond the palace blew into splinters; some of his first string were having problems with their horses. Vuhlem swore, set the glass down, and jumped to his feet: The first section of army from the ridge had swept around the east wall; his men were surrounded.

"What are they doing?" There was sporadic fighting; not as much as he'd expected, or ordered. Even with the badly tipped odds and the surprise factor, something was very wrong out there. He strode to the door, slammed it open, and shouted, "Messenger!" One of the boys leaped to his feet. "To the courtyard, second company to move out at once and keep in mind my warnings!"

"Honor." The boy's voice wabbled; he bowed low, turned, and sprinted down the stairs. Vuhlem pulled the door closed with a slam that rattled the windows. Another cannonball hit somewhere beyond the palace; thick smoke rose above the wall, flattened, and was blown south, momentarily smothering his view. He stared out the window, fists hard on his hips. When he could see once more, the second company, a full hundred of his best-trained standard guard, was already partway up the road. More movement up by the city; one of the guard companies had broken out—or gone around—the invaders and were attacking its west flank furiously; he didn't need the glass to make out the occasional flash of fire and smoke that marked the guns. "That's right," Vuhlem muttered. "Keep them occupied." He smiled unpleasantly, resumed his seat on the window ledge, and picked up his glass once more.

15

An hour, maybe less: fine, misty rain was falling once more, making footing hazardous; the sky so dark it was impossible to track the sun. The southern army pushed slowly, steadily up the road toward the sea; the English cannon sliced off the tip of a tower roof but otherwise did little damage, save to create havoc. At one point, Dahven thought, he could just make out some kind of action where the English ship sat, more smoke at sea than there had been. But the land was too flat, too many men all around him to be certain of anything. And it was dangerous to take his eyes or his attention away from his immediate surroundings. *Battle's confusing—and exhausting.* He wondered how Aletto was holding up, waiting on that ridge, then forgot about him as yet another small company of swordsmen slammed into their flank. He'd killed or disabled three men, he could recall; he had a long slice in one sleeve and a hole, left by a Holmaddi arrow, in his saddle. Vey'd run the archer through; he didn't know what had happened to the swordsman.

They'd heard some of the foreign guns—behind them, mostly—back in the city. Some kind of shot had ripped a hole in the Cornekkan banner early on.

He wiped rain out of his eyes with a soggy glove. Vuhlem's palace was a little closer, but so were Holmaddi soldiers—coming at them from both sides. Dahven sighed, brought up his sword as one of the riders evaded the outer guard and headed straight for him. He ducked to avoid a slashing overhand blow, thrust hard. Blood everywhere, on his sword, soaking his glove; the man slid silently from his horse, vanished underfoot. *Ugh.* Dahven fought his suddenly skittish mount.

"You're all right?" Vey came up beside him once again; he had to shout to be heard. Dahven nodded; the horse danced sideways, suddenly stood still.

"Untouched."

"Good! Stay that way!" Vey's eyes moved constantly, watching the melee all around them. Dahven stood in his stirrups. Half a dozen of Vuhlem's men anywhere nearby, but every one of them was engaged some distance from him. He settled in the saddle once more, drew a deep breath. *Wait,* he reminded himself. *Catch your breath, give your sword arm a little rest.* Grelt's orders, back in Sikkre—good sense, too. He shifted the sword to his left hand, flattened the fingers of his right against his leg; they ached, didn't want to unclutch. This was nothing like a one-on-one duel.

All at once, sounds of fighting ceased. Near silence, broken by the occasional flat crack of gunfire from the city, men shouting back that way; another shot from the English. Smoke rose from the direction of the Duke's private docks. Gyrdan shouted, "We're clear!" The red poles carried at the head of the line dipped once, sharply. The company moved as a pack, slowly at first, picking up speed as the horses spaced out, and two of the Cornekkan border companies split off to either side of the road. "Banners high!" Gyrdan bellowed. "Let the English see who we are!" Dahven was near enough to his horse's heels to see the man, but for all the noise around him, he'd barely been able to make out the words.

Wild pandemonium at the palace gates; horses milling and men shouting; the cannon and sounds of fighting much

louder here, echoing from thick stone walls. Vuhlem's
guard held its own just inside the grounds, but not for long
against a force three times its size and equally determined.
The blue poles dipped twice; Dahven looked around, found
his own pole-bearers. "Lead group's in the palace; signal
we got that." Yellow poles dipped twice. "And look, there's
Gyrdan, on the steps." Blue dipped once more. "Our signal—come on!" He slid from his horse, drew his second
sword, and started forward. Vey swore, dropped to the
ground, and edged in front of him. A full dozen men right
behind then, and half a dozen more surged forward to sur-
round him.

Unnecessary, Dahven thought impatiently; some of the
Holmaddi had apparently run for the dungeons, but most
left standing had surrendered. He could hear someone a
short distance away: "He's lost and he lied about the border
armies. Why should we kill ourselves for a lost cause?"
Someone else snarling at him to shut up.

The distant boom and high-pitched scree of a cannonball;
sudden silence in the courtyard as men cringed and looked
warily all around themselves, then up. An explosion rocked
one of the high towers, sending small, sharp fragments of
roofing slate pattering all around them. The tower itself
leaned precariously, and as they watched, the topmost part
of it toppled toward the water.

The whole palace shook; the window where he'd been sitting only moments earlier shattered. Vuhlem threw up an
arm to protect his eyes, then stared at falling rubble. He
shook himself finally, sent his eyes unwillingly back toward the city. No fighting out there at all, just now—in
fact, no movement of any kind. High on the ridge, horsemen and wagons still waited, though a fresh double line of
riders was on its way down the main road from the city, the
Zelharri colors in their midst. The southerners still maintained an immobile line of horsemen just beyond the city

walls, spread three deep across the road. Dead or wounded men littered the road this side of them, and the ground on either side. He couldn't see the gates or the courtyard from here, but through the shattered window he could hear men's voices: too many men, all shouting at once, a babble of sound with no discernible words in it. No sound of fighting there, either.

"They've taken the road, blocked the city, sunk my ships—invaded my courtyard." Sudden dread left his mouth dry. The upper ranges of this tower were lying in the narrow west courtyard. "My Triad," he whispered.

The servant's door wouldn't open; jammed somehow. The main one—he had to tug hard to get it to move, and it scraped against the floor. He edged out—the messengers were nowhere in sight. *Bolted, no doubt. They'll pay for that, I'll have the hide from them.* His inner circle of household guards still waited down the hall, blocking the main staircase, just as he'd ordered—no matter what happened elsewhere. The long, narrow flight of stairs up was clear; perhaps the damage wasn't as bad as he feared. He took them as quickly as he dared.

"You know where to go, all of you!" Gyrdan shouted. "Move, and watch your backs!" Companies of ten or twenty scattered; to the stables, down into the cellars, through various doors along the inner wall. Dahven skirted four dead Holmaddi, took the low steps two at a time; Gyrdan nodded sharply as the twenty-five men he'd hand-picked assembled on the outer steps. "Second floor, Duke's apartments," he said tersely. "Out there!" he shouted. "More of you, at least twenty, to turn out the main floor and pay special heed to the throne room! All of you"—he turned back to his immediate group—"we go straight up, ignore distractions, engage no one if it can be helped. Find Vuhlem!" He raised his voice as more men came up the steps. "Remember that! Clear the main floor, then move

elsewhere as quickly as you can. We take Vuhlem now!"
He stopped short, stared over their heads. Dahven's neck
prickled; he turned. Aletto had just ridden through the gate;
he came up to the foot of the steps, pulled the long bo from
its strap, and dismounted stiffly.

"I am going with you, Gyrdan," he said flatly. Somewhat
to Dahven's surprise, Gyrdan merely nodded, turned, and
strode into the building.

It was dark, exceedingly gloomy, and eerily still in here,
Dahven thought. Their footsteps echoed in the damp, chill
hallway. Gyrdan slowed at the entry to the throne room,
picked up speed again. A sudden clacking noise brought
him around. "What was that?"

"Nothing, sir," Vey replied. "I—dropped something. Not
important." Dahven eyed him sidelong as they moved on.
Vey's cheekbones were red; odd. He dismissed the whole
matter as they started up the main staircase. Odd little
noises everywhere—the building creaked and wind whistled through cracks somewhere above them. Somewhere
behind and below them, someone was fighting, a swift
clash of blades and a shrill cry. Men clattering up the stone
floor and into the throne room. A shrill wail echoed across
the courtyard—woman or child. Probably the whole wom-
en's wing was terrified half to death. Vey touched his arm,
pointed. Above them, at the top of the long, broad flight, a
clutch of Vuhlem's men waited, swords drawn and their
faces exceedingly grim.

"It's inside," Jennifer announced. Sil jumped at the sound
of her voice; it was the first thing any of them had said in
hours. "The focus." Sil's hands tightened on Ryselle's
shoulders; Jennifer leaned forward, took the village woman's hands in hers. "Are you ready?" Ryselle nodded once;
her face was pale, her mouth set. Jennifer glanced at the
grandmother. "I wish you wouldn't stay in here with us,
just in case. You and your heir both—"

"Yes," the older woman retorted. "And you and yours. Don't waste time." Jennifer sighed faintly, closed her eyes, and shifted into Thread.

The one she wanted came to her grasp immediately; deep purple, nearly black, its only sound a high-pitched scree that set her teeth on edge. Not one she had ever needed before now but she'd accessed it days earlier, worked hard since then at instantly recognizing and catching hold of it—at putting the unpleasant noise aside.

Sense of the caravan, the warm cinnamon scent of it, the lemon rinse the grandmother used on her skirts—it faded slowly. *Not as frightening as old Neri's black travel-Thread; still nothing to fiddle with lightly.* She bit her lip, brought her full concentration back to Thread, and to searching its length for the stone Vey had carried: attuned to that particular Thread by a Light-Shaper. Not so different, after all, Thread and Light: Lialla had known it gut-deep; Jennifer was learning.

The focus stone was a warm, blue blur that softened the colors of surrounding Thread. Stone and purple, and now the orangy red that sparkled just a little, and reminded her of wind chimes. Between one breath and another, Vision: "We're in a cold, dark place," she whispered. Voice inside Thread still felt awful and left her stomach roiled, but Ryselle was something less than proper novice, even: She would need vocal directions to guide her. "Triad—" She was quiet for some moments, then nodded sharply. The unpleasant sense of three as almost one was unmistakable, the presence easily marked by the ruddy glow that dampened sound on all surrounding Thread. Still—she'd done this before, she was ready for that. *By feel, not by music—as you practiced these past few days and as Lialla learned it and practiced it all her days.* "Up, above us, a little forward." Men everywhere—she ignored them. It was harder than she'd thought it would be, shifting Vision away from the stone, moving it toward the sense of Light, high above the ground.

"It's—I sense it now!" Ryselle murmured suddenly. "Light—so much of it! It's—it's not the right color, too dark!"

"Weakened."

Who dares invade this place with Night-Thread? Thread shifted like oil on a puddle; tri-part, chill laughter tried to freeze her very bones. Jennifer bit down on her lip and fought to hold on to what she must. Ryselle shivered.

I dare. You committed mass murder and killed a noble-woman. Did you hope to get away with that? "Ryselle. Now." She sensed the woman's nod; Ryselle's fingers tightened on hers.

We had the orders of our master—

"Arrow of Light—" Ryselle's hands were wet, slippery, but Jennifer could feel her drawing down Light and slowly, awkwardly beginning to Shape it. Keep them occupied, she told herself. Don't let them see. If they did—she wasn't certain what they could do. Bad to find out if there was anything at all.

She flung the thought at them, let outrage flood it. *Orders mean nothing, if it's so wrong as what you did! Jadek ordered, and his Triad left him, rather than obey!* Silver Thread, another corner of her mind ordered; wrap it around herself, and wrap it once again—more length to it, that won't ever be enough, especially if somehow Ryselle must . . .

The tri-part voice was not quite so arrogant, she thought; merely fainter, perhaps. Weakened somehow. *Jadek's were old, much older; less apt to expanding the craft, less willing to learn. Afraid! You do not hold us to their standards!*

"Ready," Ryselle whispered; her voice trembled.

"Hold it, just—hold." Thread echoed with sound; Triad, her voice, Ryselle's—it was going to make her sick. She swallowed; there was no time for that. She had to search;

distract the Triad, she ordered herself angrily, you have to find the one thing. *You're a young Triad!* She let the thought fill with her anger, her scorn. *So what? Everyone knows that, Vuhlem's Triad is young, it's unstable, it isn't accountable! That's a lie! Everyone is accountable, anyone who acts deliberately as you did, or with malice—as you also did. You were once all three plain Rhadazi, like any-one else, but you deliberately chose to Shape Light and then to become Triad.* Sense of destruction here, a lot of it. They/it must be weakened; she could suddenly, if faintly, detect the water-Thread; the bland, New Age sound left a bad taste in her mouth. She swallowed it. *You have no ex-cuse for murder.* She saw it all at once: a ball of Light that so oddly resembled Thread, ultrafine, wrapped incredibly tight, noose of silver Thread . . . "Now," she whispered. Ryselle's Light-spear spun awkwardly across her inner vi-sion, jerked back and forth as the girl fought to control it, then flew in a shining arc and dropped. Jennifer looped sil-ver toward the ball of Light; she made two tries, she barely had strength for the third. It caught; she gingerly tugged, then snapped the ball toward her. It flared for one blinding instant, then went dark; flame roared up all around her.

"Focus . . . " Hard to concentrate; this was probably a more dangerous moment than actually fronting that Triad. *Find the focus, use it to get free of this horrid place.* Ry-selle's hands were limp, clammy in hers; she gripped them hard. "Focus!" she snapped. "Focus." The woman's voice was faint, but she was still there. Nothing else counted at the moment; Ryselle to steady both of them, draw her back through Light to Thread she could again properly *hear.* The water-Thread receded sharply; the sense of dark, dank walls all around them and then the reassuring blue glow of the focus stone. Jennifer drew a deep breath, whispered the word Lialla had taught her on the road four years before, and regained the real world.

* * *

"They'll pay," Vuhlem mumbled; there was small stone litter on the steps near the landing and he could see daylight;
rain had made the steps dangerously slick already, and plastered his hair to his brow. He hesitated. What were they
doing in there? Had they deserted him, too? He shoved hair
aside, swore under his breath, came onto the landing and
into a patch of pale daylight. He stared at the closed doorway and the ruin of wall above it. For a moment, he couldn't
remember why he was here. He shook his head angrily,
gripped the door latch in his free hand, and pulled. Locked,
or more likely jammed. He stepped back, looked up. The
whole roof must be gone in there; he could see Light puls-
ing, turning the raindrops red. They were still there, doing
something—he shook himself, sheathed his sword. "It isn't
enough, whatever they are doing! They'll listen to *me*, by
all the gods at once!" He took hold of the latch two-handed
and yanked at the door with all his strength. It still wouldn't
move for him, but as he stepped back to consider what to
try next, it burst open suddenly; he reeled back from heat
and flame that roared out the door, up through a massive
hole in the roof.

The fire was as brief as it had been intense, the smell of
wet ash and smoke thick despite the destroyed roof. Blade
once again in his hand, he warily edged into the room.
Fallen stone everywhere, and fire still licked at the heavy
draperies hung to alleviate the dampness of stone walls.
Shattered bottles and vials; the air was pungent with nasty,
reeking liquids. Vuhlem eyed the destruction in a rising
fury, stopped short as his foot came down on something
brittle. He rocked back on his heels to stare in shock at the
three blackened, twisted bodies.

Gods. What could do that, and so quickly, too? This was
no place to be. *Go. They'll come for me; they must not find
me here. Go, escape the palace, come against them later.
At least choose the time and place for yourself when you*

front them. His mind felt frozen; he couldn't think, and there was a thin, high whine in his ears, matching the rapid beat of his pulse. His own apartments—yes, there first! After—he could decide about after when it came, there were ways out of the palace the outsiders wouldn't know, places in Holmaddan where he could lay low for the time being; if the passages were blocked, well— He shoved the door as closed as he could, shuddered, and turned to go back down. A handful of armed men blocked his way.

Vuhlem stared. He'd heard nothing. Seen nothing. *Once, no one would have come nearer me than the landing below, but I heard him!* These—most of them were boys, half his age, slender— Was this what the south bred for men?

A slight man in black leathers, a soggy hat, the colors of Sikkre on his sleeve, took one step forward. Two blades in his hands, held with the casual ease of a trained swordsman. "Vuhlem of Holmaddan?"

"Who asks?" Vuhlem shifted his grip on the sword, took a step back. *Draw him on, gut him; he's no match for a man of my size and skills. Take the back stairs before the rest can recover—it isn't over yet.* But the younger man wasn't drawn; he stayed where he was, though the swords moved to a position that would counter Vuhlem's.

"I am Dahven, Thukar of Sikkre. We have the Emperor's orders and his warrant to take you prisoner."

"Choke on them, Lasanachi rower!" Vuhlem hissed, and brought up his blade. Dahven's color was suddenly very high; dead silence. To Vuhlem's surprise, the Thukar shook his head and stepped back a pace; he kept his eyes on the man two stairs above him, gestured. Four large men came around him, backing the Holmaddi against the half-closed door; one of them ripped the sword from his hand, another brought out heavy steel manacles.

Silence. "You'd have liked that, wouldn't you?" Dahven asked; his voice held nothing but mild interest. "Fight to the death here and now, go out in a blaze of glory." He shook his head. "However things are in the north, we're more civilized in the rest of Rhadaz. And you've done nothing to earn such an easy end. The Emperor will prosecute you according to law." He watched without expression; it took all four of the guards to subdue Vuhlem. When the man looked up once more, Aletto had come forward to stand next to Dahven. Vuhlem's lip curled.

"Even the cripple," he said flatly. "I am surprised your outland wife *permitted* you to leave the fort! If you had kept that unnatural female at home, as any true man would, she might still be alive!"

Aletto was very pale; his hands tight on his bo, as though, Vuhlem thought sourly, to keep them from visibly trembling. "No." Aletto's voice was low, soft; his eyes murderous. "Will you blame the traffic in Zero on my mother next? You brought all this upon yourself, Vuhlem, and I am here on my sister's account, to tell you *she* was responsible for much of the Emperor's evidence against you." Cold silence; it stretched. "I hope the Emperor finds a truly unpleasant way for you to die." He turned and went back down the stairs. Dahven went after him.

Aletto stood in the middle of the carpeted hall, staring blankly toward the main stairs; his hands clutched the tall wooden staff. Dahven touched his arm. "Does—did it help? Being there? Telling him all that?"

"A little, I think." Aletto cleared his throat, swallowed hard. "Enough to justify coming, yes. For the rest, no, it's not enough. After Afronsan—deals with him. Maybe." He sighed. "I'm sorry, Dahven. I don't think I can walk much farther just now; I'm—tired."

Dahven eased a hand under his elbow. "Don't be sorry, you've had a bad time of it lately. It was difficult enough for me standing that close to the man."

"And not attacking him; he wanted that."

"I know. So did I. Here—they're coming down, let's get

you out of the way, no need for you to confront him twice. In here." He drew Aletto through the open door and into Vuhlem's apartments. Bare moments later, they could hear scuffling on the stairs, Vuhlem cursing furiously. The sounds passed the door, receded down the hall. "The man's own room; chair and fire. Sit here, thaw a little." Cool, damp air flowed through the broken window; Dahven turned the high-backed chair to block the wind and shoved Aletto into it. He tried the other door. "Locked or jammed; you'll be as safe in here as anywhere. I'll find someone to get one of the carts." Aletto nodded, let his eyes close. Dahven cast him a worried look and went.

He almost collided with Vey, who was coming back up the hall at a near run, several of the handpicked guard behind him. His face was so pale Dahven could see freckles across the bridge of his nose. "Gyrdan said to remind you we've *nearly* secured this part of the palace. And to keep us with you. Where's—?"

"Aletto's in there." He lowered his voice. "He's exhausted; he shouldn't ride from here. One of you go, see if you can get word back to the ridge for him." One of his guard went back down the hall, clattered down the stairs. "Vey, are you all right?"

Vey nodded; he didn't look it. "That—you didn't see what was—on the other side of that door."

"Oh. It *was* Vuhlem's Triad in there, wasn't it?"

"What was left of it."

Dahven's nose wrinkled. "I thought I smelled—well, never mind. The English did a good job."

"Um—yes. Of course." Vey turned to look back down the hall. Dahven frowned. Something wrong—he'd worry about that later; too much still going on here.

"Where's Gyrdan?"

"With Vuhlem. The English ship is sending a boat in as soon as the tide's right, another hour or so, someone said."

It was better than the north company escorting him to

Podhru, Dahven thought. A man like that—he wouldn't give up because he'd lost everything, including his freedom. Dangerous. "I hope they know what they're getting. And that they aren't wrong about how secure their brig is." *Or that Afronsan hadn't been wrong, letting the Lasanachi out there to aid them.*

"Gyrdan's sending ten of his own border guards to make certain the man reaches Podhru."

"Good." Aletto came up beside him. He was still too pale, but a little more steady on his feet.

"I couldn't stay in there. And—I really do feel better now."

"Good," Dahven said. "We'll still get you that cart; it's unpleasant enough out there, I'd ride with you if I could." That brought up a faint smile. Dahven smiled back. "Don't laugh at me; you know I've got a soft side. Especially now I'm older, wed, and nearly a father." Aletto waved a dismissive hand; the smile was very briefly in his eyes. "Vey, did Gyrdan want anything else of our crew, or did he say—other than to stay out of trouble?"

Vey laughed shortly. "Stay out of dark corners, was what he suggested. Remember what the Thukara will do to me, personally, if you get mangled; but Gyr doesn't think everyone's accounted for. No, nothing else until the women's wing is secured. He still wants to send a full guard along when you present the Emperor's papers to sin-Duchess Veria."

"That's fine; no drawn blades in the women's wing, though. Not if it's been secured. The girl's almost a Duchess, remember; we don't want her thinking we're *her* enemy, do we?"

Cold wind blew in Vuhlem's shattered window; Aletto shivered. "This is no place to stay, it's frigid. Dahven, I'd like to go with you; it can't hurt to have another Duke in that party, can it?"

"Can't hurt at all," Dahven said. "And you're right; let's go down, I'd like to see for myself what's going on."

Jennifer groaned as someone's soft little hand patted her face. "Don't—I have the worst headache," she mumbled. It was all she could think for the moment, too much effort to open her eyes.

"You're both all right." Gray Fishers' grandmother. "I have tea for you and a willow bark sachet, if you need it."

"Aspirin—oh, Lord, lead me to it."

"Wait, Grandmother, let me help you." Sil's voice. Jennifer's temples throbbed viciously as the younger woman helped her sit up; the grandmother wrapped her hands around a thick, warm pottery mug, guided it to her lips, and held on to it for her while she drank. Her nose wrinkled. *Honey in my tea.* But under that, mingling with the hot, fruity herb, the unmistakable tang of willow.

"Mmmm." She took another deep swallow, nodded cautiously. "Think I need to—go flat again."

"You're all right?" Sil asked.

"Seem to be. Just—bad headache. Fix it with Thread—in a bit." There was a soft, low pillow under her head, another under her knees, something fluffy draped over her. "Ryselle?"

"Sleeping," the grandmother replied. Sil made a wordless little noise; Jennifer could feel her moving away. She wasn't about to open her eyes while her head was pounding this bad. "I doubt she'll waken any time soon. You were worn when you broke free but she was utterly exhausted."

"You're certain—" She hesitated. The grandmother patted her hand, shifted the fluffy thing.

"I know healing; it's truly sleep."

"Good." Jennifer drew a cautious breath. "How long has it been?"

"Three hours. No, don't try to move, there's nothing urgent you need to do, nothing but rest. Green Arrow came a little while ago with a message from the north. They've taken the palace, and the Duke."

"Oh. Anything else?"

"No, not yet. Maybe there will be when you awaken again."

"You're bullying me," Jennifer murmured.

"Of course. Rest now." She got to her feet, moved away. Jennifer heard her talking to Sil but couldn't make out the words. The willow was helping just a little, she thought, and fell asleep.

THUKAR TO EMPEROR: PALACE SECURED, VUHLEM TAKEN, ENGLISH SHIP SORCERER WILL DELIVER HIM TO YOU. OUR CASUALTIES UNDER FIFTY, WITH ANOTHER HUNDRED WOUNDED, THEIRS HIGH, NUMBER OF DESERTERS ALSO QUITE HIGH. LEAVING WEST ARMY OUTSIDE CITY TO MAINTAIN ORDER WHILE DUCHESS VERIA NEEDS, ALSO FIND ANY STRAY HOLMADDI SOLDIERS. SELF, DUKE ALETTO, AND REST OF FORCE RETURNING SOUTH AT ONCE.

Afronsan crumpled the wire. After a moment, he smoothed it out against the small table where he and Aleyza still took their meals, reread it. The messenger who'd brought it was waiting. "No answer just now," he said. "I'll send later, perhaps."

"Sire." The boy bobbed his head and went out. The Emperor's fingers drummed the tabletop. Tell Shesseran—yes, he'd have to, unfortunately. His brother would be terribly unhappy, probably over the loss of life as much as the Duke. *No way to make that right.*

Wires to all the Duchies, of course: Sikkre would already know, because of the caravaners, and so would Cornekka and Zelharri. Wire anyway.

He set the message to one side, read the one under it that had come only a short while earlier—this one via Fahlia.

CRAY TO EMPEROR: DUPRET DEAD. HAVE SWORN STATEMENTS BY TWO MORE WITNESSES, LINKING HIM TO INCAN EMPIRE AND SOURCE OF ZERO. MER KHANI CLAIM TO HAVE PROOF AGAINST NEW HOLLAND, SPECIFICALLY PERRY, WHO'S DISAPPEARED. STILL TOO MUCH ZERO LOOSE IN THIS END OF THE WORLD; SUGGEST PERMANENT WATCH ON RHADAZI COASTLINES.

MESSAGES SENT TO GALLIC STATES, INITIATING TALKS ON TRAINS, SAME TO NEW DUC D'ORLEAN ABOUT STEAMSHIPS. WILL BRING PAPERWORK, ARRIVE PODHRU APPROXIMATELY TWO WEEKS.

Final link, Afronsan smiled grimly, folded the message. With the two Mer Khani and their steel firm effectively out of business, with the man Dupret finished and now Vuhlem no longer in a position to deal the substance to his own countrymen—it might not be the end of Zero in Rhadaz, but it would certainly cut the traffic sharply. The boy was right, though: this was no time to think the drug vanished because a few of its main traffickers were dead or taken. A permanent watch on the coastline—yes; as much for the drug as for other smuggled goods. There would surely be outsiders—and some Rhadazi—who sought to make easy profits by going around the Emperor and his trade laws.

Use of the drug had surged in Bezjeriad earlier in the year; there was little sign of it now, and his household guard had brought him local market rumor about the stuff: par-Duchess Lizelle dead of it, Duke Aletto nearly killed by it; others made dreadfully ill by a mere taste. More to the point: commoners down by the docks, one left a little giddy by his experience, his friend dead. Eight boys partying at one of the cheap inns—of all of them, three were horribly ill, one was as unconscious as the Duke had been but less likely to ever awaken again, one was dead.

It kills those who can use magic. Perhaps in the islands where it was so prevalent, fewer worked magic, or it might be that the stuff reacted differently on those who did. Here, where the gift had been inbred over five hundred years, where it ran strong in so many, and was present to some degree in nearly everyone—here, his guards said, there were fewer and fewer willing to risk dying.

Get word out, now Shesseran no longer controls things. He was wrong; everyone surely knows by now what Zero is. Tell them it is dangerous, even deadly, and why. There will be hardly anyone foolish enough to tempt fate. There was no keeping the stuff secret; that being so, there was no point to keeping anything about it secret. Wire the Dukes, have bulletins placed in all the villages and cities; have criers out in the smaller hamlets to tell what it is, what it does.

He got to his feet, smothered a yawn with the back of his hand. Long, hard days—too many of them with too little sleep, since the ships had gone north and the armies north and west. On balance, worth the time spent in planning and executing. But he'd need to catch up on some of that lost sleep the next few days. There was not much of a pressing nature on his desk just now; he had plenty of men and women around him, he could delegate, the way a sensible Emperor must. "A sensible Emperor would want to be properly awake and fully aware when Vuhlem is brought to trial." *If* he was brought to trial.

That would make Shesseran terribly unhappy. "Not something to factor into the equation if all Rhadaz is at stake and there is no alternative, of course." Still, it could not hurt to spare his brother that particular sorrow. Especially if—Afronsan smiled, then chuckled softly. "Yes. That might answer all. We'll have to examine the question of law." There would be time for that, however. Four days at least, likely more, considering the season and that the English *Sorcerer* was one of the older, heavier, and therefore slower vessels.

Complex issues of law—Afronsan strode to the door, leaned into the hall. "Messenger!" One of the boys came running up—a street boy until very recently, this one, Afronsan remembered. Until he had become Emperor, and Aleyza had gone from their apartments to find boys like— *like Berdyas, I remembered a name, this once*—had them instructed in what etiquette the civil service utilized, and turned them into court runners. He smiled; the boy colored, smiled back. "Berdyas, go down to the main clerks' room, ask that Emilid come at once to see me."

"Mmm—sire." The boy bobbed his head, carefully holding to what he'd been taught. "Emilid, main clerks, at once, here."

"Good. Go." The boy turned and sped off down the hall. Afronsan watched him until he was out of sight, then went back into his apartments. This one last thing for the evening; he'd keep his promise to Aleyza then, and spend a quiet, pleasant hour or so with her before retiring.

Jennifer sat on the edge of her desk, feet on the thin chair cushion where she usually sat, a pile of telegraph paper on either side, within easy reach. The curtains were drawn aside, her pseudo-Japanese garden brilliant with white, raked gravel and dark erratics under a pale blue sky and early-morning sun; she had the room all to herself at this hour, the usual cork-stoppered pot of coffee at her back, a steaming mug of it on the corner of the desk, where it wouldn't ruin half a dozen documents if it somehow spilled.

Blessed quiet; she didn't usually get this. *Separate office, for the times you need it, girlfriend. There's room here, you find it.*

She eyed the garden wistfully, returned her gaze sternly to the handmade, pressed gray paper she held. "The midwife promised you could walk tomorrow and run again in another day or so," she reminded herself—not too resentfully. "She's let you out of bed as soon as you wanted to get up today, isn't that something?" Better than all that, the messages from the north were all good: Vuhlem taken, Triad somehow destroyed, and according to this one, Dahven on his way south. Probably, she thought judiciously, he'd arrive just after noon. Order something he likes for midday.

She set the Gray Fishers' note aside, atop the other messages from Dro Pent and Hushar; picked up the first of the telegrams. Chris, on his way north and reasonably intact. She'd have to pump him, hard, once he got here, find out what she had to keep from Robyn *this* time. "More than I care to hide, I'll bet," she grumbled. Trains, though: and track the Mer Khani couldn't use. "Clever of Afronsan; I wouldn't have thought of that, but he and Chris both did, bet you."

Another: wire begun between Podhru and Fahlia, and between the Gallic States and Fahlia. "Now, *that's* practical. Especially if Chris plans on spending half his life down there, waltzing around with the rough boys." Maybe he wouldn't; something about that last wire from him, short as it was . . . Keeping things hidden, as usual. "Still, sounds like he's growing up." She considered this, set the Emperor's message aside, and shuddered, elaborately. "*Brrr,* what a thought, Chris a grown-up!" She laughed aloud. "Give him a hard time about *that*."

"About what?" Dahven's voice, just behind her; she caught her breath, whirled around, and the mug went flying to shatter on the tile floor. She ignored it; Dahven leaned against the edge of her desk, his hands and clothing mud splattered, his hat a ruin, and his face sagging with exhaustion—still, Dahven, here and in one piece.

"I—nothing important. You look like you rode straight from the north."

He laughed faintly. "Well—as nearly as the horses would permit. Once we crossed the border, Vey and I came on ahead, changed horses at the mail points and Hushar."

Hushar. "Oh? Well." Jennifer shook herself mentally,

gripped his hands. "Which do you want first, hot water or food? Because—"

"Mmmm—I've dreamed more of hot water than of you, the past two nights."

"More than your wretched bowl of hot oats?" He didn't know what she'd done; he couldn't, and keep it from her. *Thank you, Vey; and all Dahven's little brown sand gods, too.*

He sighed. "Inevitable bowl, isn't it? We ate—bread and something, forget what—just out of Hushar. I think I ache everywhere, I see now what you mean about horses."

"It isn't the animal, it's the smell," Jennifer replied tartly. She slid off the desk, came around, and leaned against the front of it; he turned, settled one hip on the cleaned-off wooden surface, rested his head against her shoulder. She ruffled his hair. "Speak of which, sir, hot water first for you; you reek."

"Yes, ma'am," Dahven said.

"Yah. You sound as meek as you did the first time I seduced you."

"You—seduced *me*?" He sat up. "I will have you know—"

Jennifer chuckled, low in her throat, silencing him. "Yes, and didn't you do it well? 'They're going to cut off my head at sunrise, grant me one final wish!'" She touched her finger to her lips, then to his. "You can't think how much I look forward to a long, boring life with you."

"Boring?" Dahven laughed suddenly, wrapped an arm around her shoulder and drew her into the hall. "Is this dull, like your 'safe sex,' or another trick question?"

Jennifer laughed. "Is *that* a trick question? How dull has it been so far?"

Five days after the fall of Holmaddan and the arrest of its Duke: rumor was wild in the Podhru markets, and a fair number of people had gathered along the main docks when the English *Sorcerer* came into port. To their disappointment, there was little to be seen: The grand English vessel with its two-tiered gun ports, the massive sails on four impressive masts—but of the Holmaddi Duke, only a glimpse of a bear of a man in prisoners' fetters being escorted by armed guards into a longboat, the boat lowered to the water and rowed the short distance from ship to dock. An enclosed carriage waited at the end of the dock; the prisoner was hustled into it and the horses moving almost before the doors were closed.

The streets leading to the clerical offices had been kept clear; the carriage drew up before the main steps within minutes, and red-and-gold-clad guards were there to lead the prisoner into the building and up to the second floor.

Vuhlem's eyes held the same smoldering anger they had when he was taken; after so many days in a ship's hold, he was less willing to push the guard over minor details, and when one of them took his elbow to guide him left, he let the hand be, and went quietly. *Not tamely,* he reminded himself. *Never tamely.* A man could await his moment, and be ready for it.

A closed double door blocked their passage; one of the guards went forward to tap on polished wood and after a moment, one door opened. Red carpeting here, fine draperies above and along the windows, sun and too much heat everywhere. Another closed doorway near the end of the corridor; the guard pulled the door open, followed Vuhlem and the other guard inside, and closed it after them.

After so much light in the hallway, he couldn't see much in here: the room was faintly illuminated, two blue lights, one glassed taper on a small, square table set beside a high-backed chair. A low-burning lamp on the wall, near another door. Silence. The second door opened and a man in black robes came in, pulled the door closed behind him, set two thick books and a stack of paper on the table, then settled on the low bench behind it. Plain, ordinary, common-looking man, but for the robes, Vuhlem thought dismissively; he caught his breath sharply as one of the guards turned up the lamp; light glinted on gold linked rings crossing a pale brow. Emperor's crown. Which meant this—

Afronsan smiled coldly. "Yes. The paper-pusher."

Vuhlem found his voice with an effort. "What—will you try me here, and in secret? You don't dare!"

"I? Dare?" Afronsan replied. His voice remained mild. "But this is no trial; this is a meeting. I have something to tell you, and then something to offer. You will listen to all of this without presuming to interrupt your Emperor." Vuhlem's eyes were furious; Afronsan folded his hands and waited. After a moment, the once-Duke nodded. "Good. I have here"—one hand lay on the pile of paper—"a variety of sworn documents." He lifted one, then another. "The statement of sin-Duchess Lialla, who overheard men under your command ordered to ascertain a shipment of Zero was the correct amount, and then to turn it over to those who would transport it. Another, from a messenger in that company, that he took a bottle of liquor from crates bearing your name—" He paused as Vuhlem made a remark under his breath. Silence. Afronsan set the sheet aside, picked up another. "Your name. From an apothecary in Sikkre, confirming the seal untouched, the bottle filled with brandy and heavily tainted with Zero. From a woman of your coastal village, Gray Haven, that such bottles in such marked crates were brought ashore from a wrecked Lasanachi ship, and that your guard later retrieved those crates and executed two of the headman's sons in reprisal." He set this sheet aside, folded his hands over the top of them. "I have traced the drug from the Incan Empire to French Jamaica, to the Mer Khani firm New Holland Mining, to the Lasanachi who loaded boxes of yellow rope rings and an English sailor who helped load crates of brandies distilled by one Henri Dupret. The proof against you for the import of Zero and for using it against your people, the Dro Penti and your fellow—your *once*-fellow nobles—is that deep, and very complete. This does not even touch the matter of Dro Pent, or your alliance with the prior Thukar's twin sons, and your complicity in their attempted coup."

"I was never—" Vuhlem shut his mouth with an audible click of teeth. Afronsan smiled very briefly.

"All the rest, but not that? But I have custody of two men who say otherwise: The once merchant Casimaffi, and the present Thukar's remaining brother, Deehar. He's come more to his senses, the past few days; he's said things—but you'll see what he says." He paused; Vuhlem appeared beyond words. "You will be given copies of each of these statements; that is your right. If you insist upon it, there will be a trial, three judges, an open chamber, an impartial panel of nobles, ten days from now—everything exactly according to law. But I warn you, Vuhlem: If you have that trial, you'll be named traitor, and you'll face public execution."

"You wouldn't dare!" He didn't sound so certain, this time.

"I would, though for my brother's sake, I'd greatly prefer not to. But you doubted me before this, Vuhlem. Don't make that mistake now, it will see you in a head-foreshortened coffin. You might bluster to my brother; I am not he. We both know who and what you are, and what you've done. There is an alternative for you. Swear here and now you'll claim guilt for all crimes you've committed, and you'll face only exile."

"Exile!"

"You'll be given a full purse, passage to the Gallic Lake. What you do, where you go from there—that is your concern, no longer mine."

Vuhlem's teeth flashed, briefly. "It's death at a safe remove from you. I've made enough enemies these past years; I won't last a full moon-season out there!"

"No? Possibly not." Afronsan squared the corners of his stack of papers. "Understand, I make this offer only to spare my brother. Personally—it would cause me no grief at all to hear you'd gone missing from your ship halfway to that lake." He looked at one of the guards, nodded, then got to his feet and picked up his documents. "Your copies of these are in your cell; you have nine days to decide. If the ninth goes by and I haven't heard, I'll have the trial room prepared—and also the ax." He turned and left the room. The guards pulled a dazed-looking Vuhlem to his feet and led him out the other way.

Epilogue

❦

I T had rained overnight in Sikkre; a spring shower, just enough to dampen the roads and streets, and deal with the dust, though by second hour from sunrise the sky was a deep blue, the sun warm and the air dry. Trees bloomed, lining both sides of the main boulevard that ran to the Thukar's palace. Sikkreni stood several deep, cheering as their new Emperor and his Empress rode by in the shining royal carriage, followed by the honor guard in their bright red and gold, and the Sikkreni household guard. Their own Thukar, who rode side by side with the Duke of Zelharri. Others followed: the blonde outlander Duchess Robyn in an open coach, a small, excited child on either side of her; the Ducal family and an honor guard from Bezjeriad. The procession passed under the arch, into the palace grounds; some people stayed where they were, to see the last horse disappear, but more scattered at once. There were celebrations throughout the market, music, food, good drink—a gift of the Emperor and the Thukar.

Jennifer sat at one end of the formal ballroom, several pillows at her back, a cushion under her feet. Siohan ran the long-toothed comb through her hair one last time, adjusted the pale blue silk around her feet. She stepped back, nodded. "You look—"

"I'm not the center of attention, you know." She smiled,

let one hand drift into the basket at her side; tiny fingers gripped her thumb. "Either of us."

Siohan shook a finger at her. "Well, madam, *you* remember why the Emperor chose Sikkre for the royal reception. Because you couldn't ride, and why."

"Yes. It's also central, remember." She looked up as the door opened; Siohan took a step back, behind her chair.

"Hey, lady!" Chris's jubilant voice. He came across the room, Ariadne's hand clasped firmly in his. "They said you were down here, waiting for the big fuss." He bent down, planted a loud smack on her cheek. "Everything all right with you? Oh—hey." He went to one knee, extended a tentative finger. "Just neat. Did that all yourself, did you?"

"Dahven helped a little," Jennifer replied dryly. Chris laughed. "And I'm fine, just a little tired. It's—not the most fun I ever had—but she's probably worth it."

"What Mom says." He touched a small, pink cheek. Ariadne let go his hand and hugged Jennifer cautiously. Chris brushed baby-fine, dark hair with his finger. "Amazing. You a mother, yet. Thought you'd like to know, Jen: First track's just been laid out of Fahlia to Podhru."

Ariadne tugged at his hair. "Chris, no business at this hour! Remember we are not dressed for reception. At least, I am not. You tell—told me before, you need a clean shirt to meet with the Heir. Now that he is Emperor—"

Chris sighed but he was grinning as he got back to his feet and recaptured Ariadne's fingers. "She picks on me all the time, you know? C'mon, lady, let's see if we can't make you pretty for the party."

"Easier me for pretty than you," Ariadne retorted; she tipped Jennifer a grave wink and went with him.

Jennifer waited until the door closed, then laughed. "Those two! Hard to believe, isn't it?"

Siohan made an odd little noise. "They're giddier than last time, at midwinter." The door flew open again; this time it was Dahven.

"Well, that's done. I think poor Aletto felt even sillier out there being cheered at than I did."

"It's good for you both." Jennifer blew him a kiss.

"Of course. Every Duke needs a swelled head. They'll be here in short order; do you need anything?"

"Water—oh, thank you, Siohan," she added as the woman handed her a cup.

"You should have a small table, a jug. I'll see to it."

Dahven touched her finger, the tiny fist clutching it. "You really think she'll be all right here?"

"Siohan or one of the other women will take her back to the nursery if she fusses. Here"—she patted the opposite chair arm—"sit and talk to me; I always get the preparty jitters, and the way they've got me decked out and settled in, I feel like there's a spotlight on me."

Late afternoon: Jennifer had lost track long since of people she'd been introduced to: Leyzin and his red-haired lady, early on; Jubelo and Misarla she knew, but none of their nearly grown children or his brothers; Wudron and his lady had left their enormous brood home, fortunately. Dozens of others: minor nobles, wealthy merchants like Fedthyr, who was visibly and vocally delighted to see her once again— somewhere in all that, a very complacently happy Enardi and his new wife, Meriyas, absolutely stunning in costly pale pink brocade, her flame-colored hair partly up and mostly loose to her knees.

Everyone so—so radiant, she thought. Happy. Well, why not? A new Emperor, new trade, new wealth and—well, anything good seemed possible, just now.

Chris and Ariadne out there somewhere, inseparable and so visibly happy: she'd caught a glimpse of them whispering together in a corner, later talking to one of the French who'd arrived some days earlier—trains or hot-air balloons, no doubt. *Good for him—and her, too. Bet he'll have that summer house in the mountains before much longer.*

She looked up as someone came toward her; Robyn held her close, kissed the air just above her cheek. "How do you do that?" she demanded. "After I had Iana, I looked like—"

"Not my doing, I looked like purest Hell before Siohan took me in charge. What's this I hear, you're bullying Aletto into building a winter palace?"

Robyn laughed. "You've been in that Fort in summer; you don't want to *know* how bad it gets, rest of the year. Yeah; it's never been a good place for kids but we can't just up stakes and move the residence altogether; too hard on the town. So—Fort for the summer; down off the mountains, just into the flatlands for the rain and snow season. He needs dry—you know. And the building and all—it'll be something to take his mind off—things."

"Is he any better?"

"Lialla?" Robyn shrugged. "I think so. He isn't ready to talk about it yet, but—can I?" She bent over the basket.

"Sure." Jennifer eased her finger from the baby's near hand as Robyn scooped her up.

"Looks like you, at that age. Cute. Everything—you're really all right?"

Jennifer gravely crossed her heart. "Honestly. Tired and a bit sore."

"You look it. Name her yet?"

"Working on it." Amazing how complex naming could get.

"Come up with something before she starts talking, okay? My big kid—he sure does look good, doesn't he? Turning into someone, who'd've thought? Speak of kids—" She kissed small fingers and settled the baby back in her basket. "Better go check on my small fry, make sure they aren't pulling your house down."

"Bring them up after dinner, meet their new cousin."

"All right."

Jennifer watched her go; Robyn had turned into someone, too: capable, practical, very much a Duchess.

She was growing tired, but the party was going strong as ever. Siohan carried the baby off late in the afternoon; Dahven was suddenly at her side. "You all right?"

She dredged up a smile for him. Thread had never been as exhausting as a baby. "Sure."

"Emperor wants to talk to us both, just a few minutes. Since they'll all be leaving early tomorrow morning, I thought—"

"Help me sit up a little straighter. Ought to look less like a new mommy, more like a Thukara."

To her relief, but not to her surprise, Afronsan hadn't changed at all, though the high, glittering diadem and the formal white trousers and jacket with their thin edge of red certainly were a far cry from what he'd worn the first time she'd seen him. He looked very much like an Emperor at the moment, but she wagered he still dressed for comfort in his offices or his apartments—same as she did. Pleasantries exchanged, he took the bench Dahven had brought for him and planted his elbows on his knees; Dahven settled on the arm of Jennifer's chair.

"We completed the list of evidence against New Holland just before I came north, I thought you'd want to know it's being printed now and it'll go to their Parliament as soon as I get back to sign it. Also, the English government sent me a formal statement; any future influx of the drug from that source, they'll stand ready to aid us. They and the Alliance are supposedly bringing pressure against the French and the Incans."

"Good—if anything actually comes of it," Jennifer said.

"Another message from the English; they're sending a small orchestra this summer," Afronsan went on. "They've agreed already to a limited tour, which will include Sikkre." He hesitated. "Word from the south, three days ago; Casimaffi's gone missing from his ship."

"I'm only surprised it took someone so long," Dahven said. "What about Vuhlem?"

"Still no word, not since he was seen along the Incan coast. Rumor, though: Chris brought me all of *that* he could this last trip, and he says the Lasanachi have put a price on the man's head." He paused. "Enough of all that. His daughter's doing well up north—surprising, considering how she was raised."

"Well," Jennifer said, "she was clever enough to realize she wasn't ready for the job, and to pick good advisers. Gray Fishers' grandmother tells me she can see the change in the city already—not much of one so soon. A start."

Afronsan nodded. "I'd heard; of course, the decree I sent gave little room for misinterpretation. Holmaddi women aren't a class apart from other Rhadazi women. Period. There'll be problems among the more hidebound men, and the outlying villages of course—or, more correctly, they think they'll be able to evade the decree." Men like Ryselle's father, Jennifer thought sourly. He'd met his match in Afronsan, though. He was speaking once more; she focused her wandering attention. "The caravaners' building should be completely demolished by midsummer."

"They're not rebuilding—"

"No. That was never an option; Duchess Veria flatly said no, but held out several alternatives for the site and let the city people choose: It'll be a small park and memorial, a large open market."

"I'm glad." Sil and Ryselle were back up there, aiding the network of Holmaddi women; this time, they had a good chance of success.

"Ah—I knew there was a last thing, though they may already have told you. Chris and his lady have accepted his father's estates in French Jamaica, and the French have given him permission to establish a CEE-Tech base there."

"I had heard," Jennifer said. "The economy's not good and the sudden loss of Dupret and his refineries didn't help." Chris wasn't any better at economics than she was but he understood poor and hopeless; so did Ariadne—all those poor kin of her mother. Jennifer hadn't been pleased about the project at first—the island was still under the control of men of Dupret's class, after all. Chris and Ariadne would probably be shunned at best. Robyn had been frankly horrified. But with the Duc himself keeping an eye on them, or at least marking them as favored and not to be messed with—

The Emperor's voice pulled her from her thoughts once more. "Well—the Thukara looks tired, I won't keep you." He kissed her fingers, got back to his feet, and went back across the room where he was drawn into conversation with Enardi and Edrith. Dahven stood, held out his hands to help her up.

"He's right, lady; you've had enough fun."

Jennifer sighed. "God, I'm killed. No more fun. Like some more water—"

"After we get your feet up."

"I was about to say." It took them a while to reach the door; people wanting one last word, offering congratulations. Somehow they were outside at last. "Quiet out here," she murmured. "Nice."

"Very."

Their apartments were warm and sunny. She let Dahven settle her with two extra pillows at her back, drank a little water—it was warmer than she liked ordinarily. Not worth the trouble sending for fresh; most of the household was out celebrating anyway—Emperor *and* Thukar's Heir. Dahven sat next to her, then swung his feet up.

She took his hand. "Aren't you supposed to be back downstairs, playing Thukar?"

"Done for the moment; playing adoring husband and proud papa instead. I'll go back down in an hour or so and probably find no one's even missed me." He went flat, his eyes closed; she slid over so she could settle her chin on his shoulder. Silence for a long time. She thought he might be drifting toward sleep; his deep chuckle surprised her.

"What?"

"Just thinking. How much I owe Lialla, of all people. If she hadn't bullied Aletto into leaving the Fort with her, that old Weilder would never have—Lialla. Little brown sand gods."

Jennifer laughed, and set a kiss on his forehead. "I owe her more than you do." He opened his eyes, quirked one eyebrow. "*She* had enough sense to refuse you, left you for me. Speak of proud papas, or lack of them: Did you notice, down there earlier? Chris has a silver bracelet."

"I know; my man got it for him. Chris says they talked it out, they're both much too young for more than married—"

"God. Not only grown up, but sensible. Her, too. Spooky."

"They both should be; Chris, in particular, after this past year. Mmmm—tired. Sure you're all right?"

"Fine," she assured him; it always amazed her, how quickly he could fall asleep. She was warm, tired, pleasantly comfortable, nothing more. He still didn't know about the Triad—after so many months, it was unlikely he'd learn. *I don't want that, ever again.* She'd said as much the night she confronted Jadek, when he'd tried to force a physical fight. "I don't need that to feel alive. We don't." No warfare, no drugs, no Hell-Light—she could live quite happily without any of it. There were improvements to be made in the market; her own help, financial or otherwise, for Sil and Ryselle; paperwork that would bring railroads and perhaps even steam cars into Rhadaz—not dramatic but important for all that. Even hot-tempered Chris and his volatile lady seemed glad to be done with violence.

Boring, she'd told Dahven; poor choice of words. Say, rather, normal. Ordinary. All the small, pleasant day-to-day possibilities—little in her first few months in Rhadaz could compare. Except—

Dahven stirred, mumbled sleepily, wrapped an arm across her. She smiled, closed her eyes. The future stretched before them, bright with possibilities. For all of them.